STRING ME ALONG

STRING ME ALONG

LILIAN T. JAMES

Crystal Pages Publishing
is an imprint of Aleron Books LLC

First printing edition 2023

Cover Design : Murphy Rae
Editor : Allusion Publishing
Floorplan Designs : Sarah Crisp
Chapter Header Designs : Etheric Tales & Edits
Original Music/Lyrics : Whitnie Means

ISBN-13: 978-1-958763-10-0

To my best friend who has always believed in me, sacrificed for me, and been there for me, even when I didn't deserve it. I love you, ya asshole.

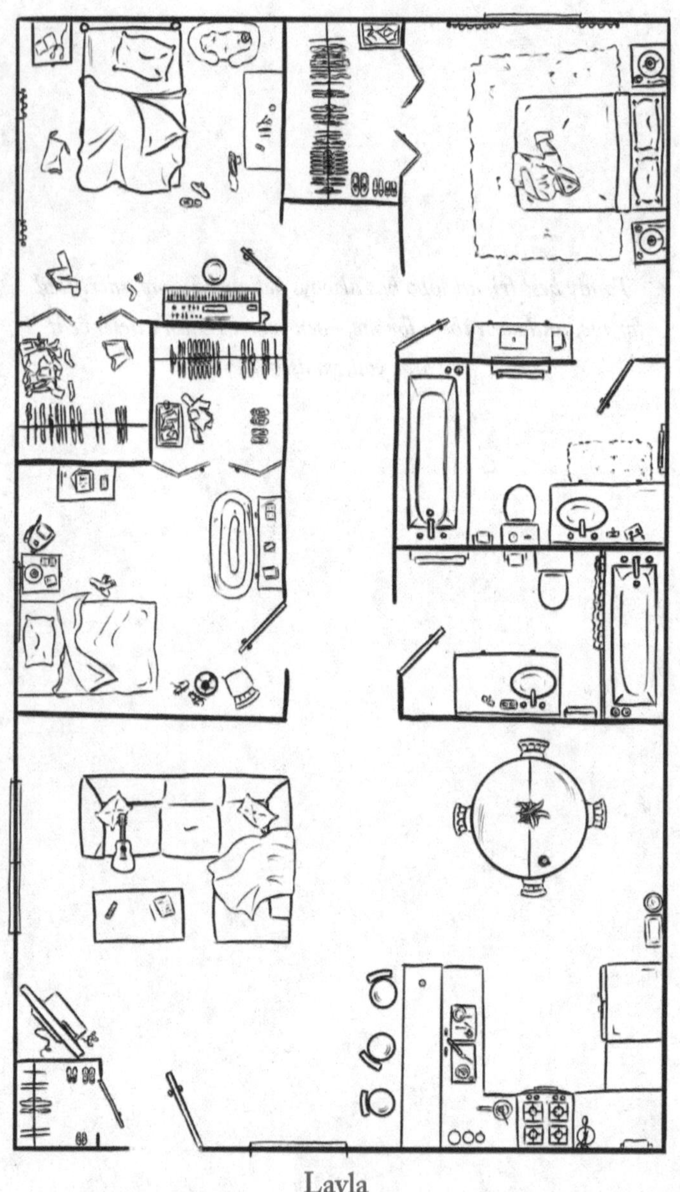

Layla

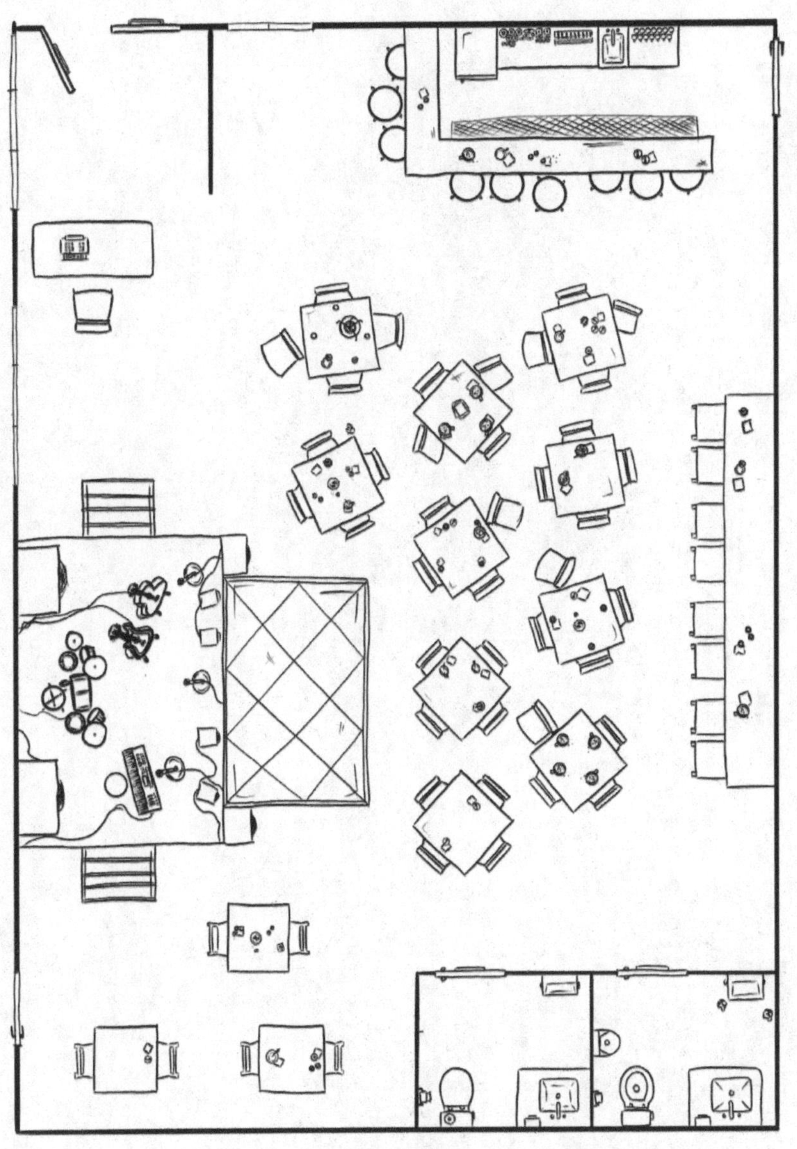

Jemmy's

Scan the QR code below to hear the song Layla writes throughout **STRING ME ALONG** :

Also available on all streaming platforms, including:
Spotify ♪ Apple Music ♪ Amazon Music

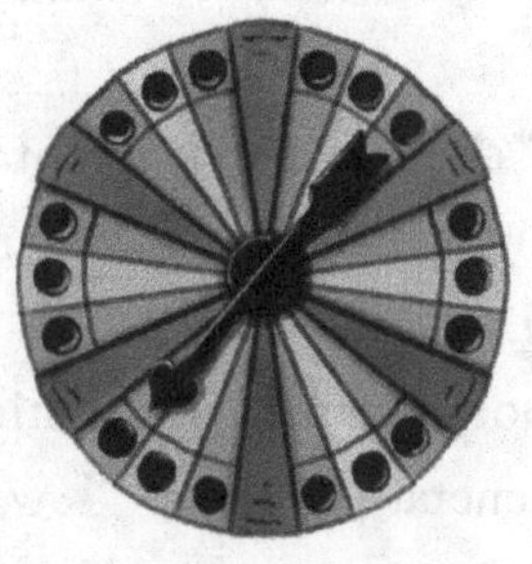

Chapter
1

HER CROTCH RESTED over my torso, the warm skin of her thighs on either side of me as her pale arms caged my head in. I shifted, adjusting my weight to my other arm as I crawled my fingers across the floor.

Although I couldn't see past her arm, I felt the moment my hand brushed against the third participant, and I grunted, attempting to stretch my limb past its capabilities and slide my hand beneath him.

"That's my butt."

I smacked it with the back of my hand. "Well, move it. It's in my way."

"*You* move. It's your turn."

"Mads, did your child just sass me?" I asked, turning my

head to look up at my best friend of over a decade, still straddling my torso.

"Sounds like it," she said, barely maintaining a straight face. She shifted, her thighs shaking against my sides, unused to squatting for so long.

A small head shot up next to us, twisting at an odd angle to glare over in our general direction. "I wasn't sass-mouthing. You're just trying to cheat so you win. You guys are taking up all the space anyway!"

Tipping my head and giving Madison a loaded look that only friends who knew each other inside and out could pull off, I lurched upright as she dove to the side and log-rolled off the plastic mat.

The short—yet quickly growing taller than I'd like— second-grade child barely had time to squeal before I tackled him, smooshing his cheek against a bright red circle, and called for reinforcement.

"Get him, Sadie!"

He squealed again, squeezing his blue eyes shut and trying to turn his face down into the mat to avoid a wet, lolling tongue to the nose. He failed.

I sat back, cackling as I watched my best friend's almost nine-year-old son wrestle my giant pit-bull golden retriever pup, desperately trying to get out from under her as her tail wagged a hundred miles an hour.

"That's such a good girl," I cooed, still laughing at Jamie's flailing limbs as he finally succeeded in pushing up to a sitting position. He wiped his shirt sleeves over his face, his cheeks pink and lips twitching at the hint of a smile.

Catching me looking at him, he stuck his tongue out. "Cheater. I would've won."

Considering all three of us had tangled ourselves up to the point that no one could reach the spinner anymore, I highly doubted any of us would've won.

I smiled. "You're just lucky Rugpants was too lazy to join, or you'd have been done for."

All three of us glanced over to the lump hiding beneath a bright, crocheted blanket on the couch. She hadn't even twitched at Jamie's squeals, let alone poked a nose out to see if he was in danger.

As if sensing we were talking about her friend, Sadie left Jamie's side, whacking her tail in his face in the process, to nose the curled-up hotdog.

Madison's miniature dachshund, whom Jamie had named Rugpants when he was two, wasn't much older than Sadie, but you'd never know it with how she acted. Rugsy was more of an old lady than an actual old lady.

Madison chuckled, pushing off her thighs to stand and wincing when her knees cracked. I rolled my lips in, swallowing back the urge to remark on her age. She was only a few months older than me, but that didn't change the fact that when she turned thirty, I'd still be a sweet twenty-nine.

However, my efforts to take the high road were in vain because she saw the unspoken words on my face anyway.

"Oh, shove it, Layla. Twister isn't nice on anyone's joints."

I stood as well, brushing dog hair off my sweatshirt. In

truth, Madison was only twenty-five, but she was closer to forty-five at heart. Working seven days a week and being a single mother could do that to you.

"You say that, yet only one of us sounded like exploding popcorn kernels standing up."

She flipped me off behind Jamie's back, quickly hiding her insulting fingers behind her head when he turned around. Then, re-twisting her thick, brown curls back into a clip, she grabbed the box and began to fold the game mat into it.

After Christmas, Madison had put a new rule into effect that once a week, Jamie had to pick a board game or puzzle rather than a video game to play together.

I think she was feeling guilty about the screen time. But by the look on her face when Jamie brought out Twister, I had a feeling she was regretting her choices.

Handing Jamie the boxed-up game, she ruffled his dirty blonde hair and tipped her head toward his room, which was just off our tiny living room. "Go put this away and then hop in the shower while I clean up. A quick one, please."

You'd have thought the room was on fire with how fast the kid snatched the game and ran into his room, Sadie at his heels. Madison usually required that he win their evening game to get out of clean-up duty, and he apparently had zero intention of giving her a chance to change her mind or remember her rules.

I put my hands on my hips, surveying the room. "Do I have to clean up, too, or can I pretend to be Garrett and admire your butt with my manly sex eyes while you do it?"

She twisted her head toward me, brown eyes as wide as an

owl as they darted to Jamie's still-open door and back to me, her hands splayed out.

"What?" I asked, grabbing a handful of cheese crackers from the coffee table we'd shoved out of the way for our game and cramming them in my mouth. "He's heard me say worse."

Madison just shook her head, fluffing the couch pillows and putting them perfectly in the corners as if we wouldn't mess them up in ten minutes.

"For the record," she whispered, "Garrett may give me sex eyes, but at least he helps clean while he does it."

I scrunched my lips and tipped my head to the side. "Touché."

If there was anyone I couldn't talk shit on, it was Madison's boyfriend, Garrett. He was technically our next-door neighbor—or wall neighbor as Madison called him—and I swore the man would gladly lay on hot coals before he made her clean a living room alone.

However, if she was trying to compare him to *me*... "But has he held your hand for fourteen hours through childbirth? Because I'm pretty sure that still makes me the best baby daddy."

She chuckled, grabbing the edge of a crocheted blanket and lifting it, shooing the black sausage roll of a dog off the couch toward the slider door.

Wanting to avoid the blast of winter night air, I shuffled down the hall toward my room, shucking off my bra beneath my shirt as I went. We lived in a cute, three-bedroom duplex, and my room was nestled right between Jamie's and Madison's.

At first, I thought sharing a wall with an eight-year-old boy would be an issue, but honestly, besides a few random romps with a boyfriend I was no longer with, I never had company. Ever.

It was the wall I shared with Madison that I needed to worry about. She and Garrett weren't as silent as they liked to think they were.

I shouldered open the door, tossing my bra to the floor and massaging my wire-abused boobs as it landed on the quickly growing pile of dirty clothing.

It'd been several months since I'd moved to North Carolina to live with my best friend and her son, and I still wasn't used to not having my own washer and dryer. It wasn't the end of the world, of course. I knew that. But it made keeping up with it a little harder than I was used to.

Overall, I liked the duplex I shared with Madison, especially since her boyfriend had recently gone around fixing all the issues it'd had when I first moved in. But damn, I hated sitting at the laundromat. Because neither she nor I had the time. Not when we worked over a hundred hours a week between the two of us.

Sighing and mentally reminding myself I'd be working naked if I didn't suck it up and go soon, I trudged over the hills of sweats and t-shirts. I paused in front of my flimsy body mirror and yanked my hair-tie out, moaning as the tension left my head.

I finger-brushed the bright blue strands, glaring at the half-inch of blonde growth at my roots and adding *color my hair* onto my silent list of things to do as well.

In truth, I didn't have the time or money to keep up with it anymore, but the idea of letting it grow out hurt my heart. The vibrant hue made the blue flecks in my gray eyes pop and accentuated the freckles dusting across my nose and cheeks. It just…felt like *me*.

Reaching down, I grabbed the worn, black case propped up next to the mirror and heaved it onto my bed, unlatching it and popping it open.

"Hello, gorgeous."

I pulled out the rosewood guitar before reaching into the inner compartment to grab my capo. I hadn't touched my guitar since my previous Saturday night show, and it felt like a sin. I never went more than a day.

I wanted to kick myself for wasting several perfectly good evenings, but I just hadn't had the motivation to create anything. My day job had been putting me in a funk lately, and it was hard to find my muse when I spent the day miserable.

But since I had another show at the same bar I played at every Friday, I could really use a new song to change things up.

Grabbing a random purple pick—because I'd lost yet another one—I shut my case and headed back out into the living room, nearly crashing into Jamie as he dashed to the bathroom.

"Sorry," he mumbled, smashing his clothes into his chest and crossing his arms over the pile to hide them, as if I didn't already know he wore underwear.

I patted his head and stepped around him, heading toward my favorite spot on the floor. I plopped down criss-cross applesauce and leaned back against the couch, hearing the shower start up behind me.

Gently shoving Sadie's nose out of my face, I patted the

floor, scratching behind her ears when she curled up beside me.

I sang quietly, my mind automatically pulling up the last song I'd written. Lyrics that had come to me a few weeks ago. A sweet, gentle love song that fit Madison and Garrett perfectly.

"*You took my black and white, and you colorized the things I couldn't see,*" I sang, keeping my voice low as I warmed up. "*'Cause you make me dream, and you make me feel like the world ain't so bad.*"

I could hear Madison faintly humming from where she'd wandered into the kitchen.

"*I don't want to leave, no, our little blanket fort,*" I trailed off, noticing one of my strings was sounding a little out of tune.

"God, I love that one."

I removed my capo, setting it on my knee so I could adjust the string, and looked up at her. "I'd hope so, considering I wrote it for you and your sugar daddy," I said, enunciating the last two words.

She rolled her eyes and then looked down at the coffee pot she was currently prepping for her late-night study session. "Speaking of baby daddies and sugar daddies…"

I frowned before remembering what we'd been talking about before I'd disappeared to free the boobs and grab my guitar. "Yeeees?" I drew out, pretty sure I knew where she was going with this.

"Have you heard from Rick lately?"

I groaned, pretending to whack the neck of my guitar against my head. Good ol' Rick. I'd met the guy at a random coffee shop in town a few months ago, and we'd initially hit it off.

He was a nice guy and a musician with love for the same music as me, and the sex had been fairly decent, but there just hadn't been any real connection apart from that.

He could be funny when he wanted to, but I'd often found myself waiting for him to leave not long after he'd arrived. I'd tried to be gentle about it, which wasn't typically in my personality when it came to men, but he'd only panicked and professed his undying love for me.

"No, not since our last conversation," I said, watching Madison hold out a mug and raise her brows at me. I shook my head. I had no idea how the woman drank as much coffee as she did without having to spend hours in the bathroom.

"You broke his heart, didn't you?"

I pursed my lips, pretending to ponder it even though we both knew the answer. "Some things might have been said in the heat of the moment that may, or may not, have made it very clear where I stood."

Madison pressed her lips together, trying not to laugh. I just shrugged and focused back on my guitar, testing the strings and adjusting them as needed to get the sound I wanted.

I didn't feel the least bit guilty over how things ended. Rick and I had only dated a few months, and it wasn't in me to hold a grown man's hand just because he couldn't take a hint.

And by hint, I mean a woman looking him directly in the eyes and saying, "I absolutely do not, in any way, want to be with you."

Turns out, even supposed nice guys walked around the Earth believing women were all playing hard-to-get when we

♪ 9 ♪

said "no." God forbid we really just wanted them to go the fuck away.

We were both quiet for a moment, the only sounds the mixture of Jamie's shower, the gurgle of the coffee pot, and the random plinks of my strings. I leaned my head back against the couch again, closing my eyes and enjoying the comfort of a relaxing evening.

I had every Monday night through Thursday night off, but lately, the daytime hours I worked during the week at the shipping company and the evening hours during the weekend were starting to wear down on me. I tried not to complain, knowing Madison had it harder, but I'd just felt tired lately.

A deep, lingering tired I couldn't shake off.

But on nights like this, when it was still just the three of us playing games and hanging out, I felt better. More put together.

Part of me knew where my growing exhaustion stemmed from, but I held on to the belief that if I didn't give the thought space in my head, it wouldn't come to pass.

What could I say? I was a Pisces.

"So, I'm off on Saturday," Madison suddenly said, startling me out of my musings and pulling my gaze her way.

She was adding creamer to her cup and frowning at the now more white-than-brown, beverage. "Every Saturday for the foreseeable future, to be exact. Well, daytime, I mean. I still work at night."

I raised my brows, wondering if she'd somehow known what I was thinking, and watched her walk out of the kitchen. "You're not going to take guard shifts anymore?"

She'd never liked the job, hating that it took time away from Jamie, but she'd done it for the extra cash it put in her pocket for bills.

She shook her head, yelling over her shoulder as she darted past me down the hall toward her room at the end. "Garrett said he'd rather buy the entire duplex than ever see me take another unarmed guard shift just to pay rent."

Her voice grew louder as she returned to the main area, laptop and textbooks crammed in her arms. "I told him he was being ridiculous."

"Yeah? And how'd that go?"

Her face softened, a smile teasing her lips as she grabbed her coffee from the kitchen and headed toward the far side of the couch. "My uniform magically went missing the next day."

I cackled, imagining her tall as shit boyfriend sneaking out of the house and hiding her uniform in the trash like a teenager hiding a cigarette butt. "I bet it did."

She dropped onto the cushion closest to the slider door, somehow doing so with a highlighter, two textbooks, a laptop, and her coffee, all without spilling a drop. "I'm actually no longer working Friday nights at the restaurant either, so I thought I'd come to your show this Friday."

My heart swelled, and I couldn't stop a grin from taking over my face. "Really?"

Besides a few random daytime events, Madison had rarely been able to make it to any of my shows because of her schedule. And since she was the only person I knew in the state besides her family, it meant that I never had anyone come who wasn't a stranger. Or Rick.

She grinned back. "Yep. Sunday is the only day I'm working a double now, so I can come any Friday night I don't have school stuff."

I stuck my pick between my teeth while I clamped my capo back on. "How'd Garrett convince you to do that?" I asked, talking around the thin plastic.

There was a slight pull in my chest at the thought that she'd listened to him over something I'd been nagging her about for months, but I pushed it down. He and I were a team, helping out the woman we both loved in different ways. It wasn't a competition. What mattered was that she'd finally felt safe enough to pull back.

Since before I'd moved in, Madison had been working over sixty hours a week *while* taking online courses. It was literally why I'd moved to North Carolina from Kansas, even though I knew no one and had to start my music career all over again.

To try to ease her burden of being a single mom with a deadbeat sperm donor and a shitty ex.

I raised my brows, waiting for her to settle in and answer, but she stayed suspiciously silent. "Did he refuse you an orgasm unless you agreed or something?"

She opened her laptop, taking a sip of coffee and wincing before setting it down on the coffee table. "Something like that."

My fingers froze over my strings, and I gaped at her. "Wait, seriously?"

She refused to look at me, her ears flushing a deep red. "Something like that," she repeated.

I whistled. "Go, Garrett."

"So, anyway," she went on loudly, "he offered to hang out with Jamie so I can go with you Friday. I thought maybe we could head out early and grab a bite and a drink before you go on stage."

I started a popular cover song, tossing my pick to the ground and letting my calluses flick across the strings and push the melody out into the air.

"Jemmy's doesn't really have food unless you count their heavily fried appetizers, and I can't say I recommend eating them if you want to keep your liquor down. But we can definitely grab a drink, or three."

She glanced up from flipping through her textbook—statistics, from the look of it—and narrowed her brown eyes. "One drink. I won't be able to drive otherwise."

I blew a raspberry, waving a hand in dismissal. "You'd be good by the time we left, but fine. *You* can have one drink. I, for one, plan on having three and then going home with an attractive stranger to have hot, dominating sex."

That caught her attention. "I thought you weren't interested in dating so soon after Rick?"

"Who said anything about dating? My nethers are starting to frost over. I just need some warmth before they start to look like yours did."

I ducked, dodging the highlighter she threw at me, and laughed. "Did Garrett have to take an ice pick—" I stopped, snapping my lips together when the bathroom door opened behind me.

Madison glanced over her shoulder and smiled before meeting my eyes again, and I silently mouthed the rest of my question, earning me a death glare that would've lit a lesser woman on fire.

"Did you brush your teeth while you were in there?" she asked.

Feet shuffled over the carpet behind me, followed by an annoyed, "Yes."

"You sure?"

"Yes, *Mom*."

I snorted. Madison was in so much trouble when he got older.

They chatted back and forth about bedtime and what book they would read, and I tuned them out, humming quietly.

I really did need to write something new soon. Something different than all my others. But it was like the harder I thought about it, the more any ideas seemed to drift away. I was in a slump, and I hated it.

"Do you really plan on going home with someone Friday?"

The hushed question caught me off guard, and I looked up to see Madison standing next to the couch, Jamie nowhere in sight, probably climbing into bed to wait for her.

Her brow was drawn, concern etched into her features. Even with all the healing Garrett had helped her find, her trust in men would forever be ruined, and it crushed me.

"Maybe. That's how meeting people works, Mads. You have to take a leap sometimes. You know I'd send you a photo of his house and license plate if I did."

Her face didn't soften. "Try online dating so you can at least get to know them first. You were all about it when you were trying to get me to do it."

I flattened my hand against my strings, halting their thrumming and gave her my full attention. "Your situation was different. I don't need to list all my baggage or know a guy's middle name to ride him like a rodeo bull."

"I guess so," she said, edging around the couch, mouth tight. "But you could state you're not looking for anything serious. Weed out the Ricks."

True. I just wanted something casual, but I didn't want to bring home another guy who wouldn't want to leave. I hadn't lied when I'd told her I was done trying to date for a while. Hot sex? Yes, please. Everything else just seemed like too much right now.

"Will you still be out here when I come back?" she asked.

I picked up my phone from where I'd left it on the coffee table an hour ago and checked the time. "Probably not. Unlike you, we mortals need more than four hours of sleep to function."

She nodded, looking down at her school stuff and sighing. Then she bid me goodnight and headed toward Jamie's room, Sadie nearly tripping her as she raced her there.

My dog had abandoned me long ago to start sleeping with Jamie, but not a bit of me cared. According to Madison, between Sadie's snuggles and the therapist she'd finally been able to get Jamie into, he'd been sleeping better than he ever had, with fewer nightmares. The thought alone made my eyes burn.

I may not have been his mom, but I'd held her hand when

she'd given birth to him and had been around ever since. I loved him like my own and would give anything to see him happy.

I'd buy him ten dogs if that's what he needed. But considering my financial situation, I was going to need to write a new goddamn song and get famous before I could do that.

Chapter
2

GOD, I LOVED heels. There was something about dressing down with a simple cream blouse and jeans, and then slipping on a pair of strappy heels that immediately made you look runway ready.

Typically, I went all out for my shows. Full face, curled hair, off-the-shoulder top, and a mini skirt that made my ass the star of the show, but since I still hadn't gone to the laundromat, jeans it was. Luckily, all I had to do was add some blood-red lipstick and three-inch heels, and I was good to go.

My bare, ivory skin would thank me for covering it with jeans when I stepped out into the January wind anyway.

"You ready?" A voice asked from the doorway, a hiccup to it that told me the person asking was halfway hoping I'd say no.

I turned to look at my friend, standing in my doorway wearing a form-fitting, maroon top and black jeans that fit her like a glove. She fidgeted, yanking at the scoop-neck collar.

"Stop pulling on it, your boobs look fantastic."

Madison's nose curled. "That's exactly why I'm yanking on it. I don't need my boobs to look fantastic. This is not something a mother wears."

I waggled my finger at her. "No. Nope. Absolutely not. We've talked about this for two days. Mothers are allowed to be sexy too. Besides, you're not just a mother, and you know it. Now let's go before you try to find another reason to stay home."

Grabbing a lint roller, I ran it over my top while shoving Madison out of my room and down the hall. We were going out and having fun if I had to carry her there myself.

Still staring at my blouse, looking for rogue dog hairs, I wasn't prepared for Madison to slam to a stop at the mouth of the hall, successfully planting my downturned face into her back.

I cursed under my breath, aware there was a child hiding somewhere, and pulled back, eyeing the lip print on her upper shoulder blade. I pushed the roller back and forth over it, hoping to dull the mark. At least her shirt was red.

Glancing over her shoulder to see what had stopped her in the first place, I barely had time to shuffle to the side before Garrett came barreling toward us, snatching Madison by the arm and leading her straight back to her room. His hazel eyes undressing her before they'd even shut the door.

So much for grabbing a bite on the way there. I shook my head, continuing into the living room to wait out their quickie. Jamie was seated on the couch with the dogs, some superhero movie paused, and remote in hand, blinking at the empty hall.

"Is Garrett mad at my mom?"

"Nope," I said, popping the 'p' and throwing myself on the couch next to him to steal a handful of his popcorn. "He's just helping her fix her makeup so she'll look all pretty."

His brows furrowed. "She already looked pretty."

Jesus, I loved this kid. "Yeah, you're right. They're probably doing something else." A knock came from the back of the house, followed by several rhythmic thuds. "So, what movie are you guys about to watch?" I asked, raising my voice a few octaves in the hopes of drowning out the muffled performance behind us.

He darted one last look toward the hall before snatching his bowl away from me and launching into a full explanation of some connected superhero universe. I smiled and asked a few questions even as his answers went in one ear and right out the other. Distraction at its finest.

The soft thuds picked up speed before suddenly cutting off. Ugh. I *really* needed to find a man to climb like a tree tonight.

Jemmy's Bar was packed when we got there, just as it was every Friday night. Between the surprisingly clean bathrooms, one-dollar drinks, and live music every Friday, it was no guess as to why.

It was an extremely popular bar in town, and I still wasn't sure how I'd been lucky enough to grab the most coveted night as the Friday regular, especially since the owner didn't seem to be my biggest fan.

My resting bitch face did that sometimes.

But fan or not, he consistently booked me to play from six o'clock to nine every week before they turned to the DJ to finish the night up for the late drinkers.

No complaints here. I made more in three hours at Jemmy's than I did working thirty hours a week at my day job, which I tried hard not to think about. The truth of it was painfully depressing.

Madison and I worked our way through the crowd, slipping past full tables of rowdy college-aged guys, silent drunk old men, and high-pitched women all knocking back shots.

I stole a look over my shoulder as we approached the bar to catch Madison desperately trying to keep the panic from her eyes at the number of people around her. The restaurant she worked at never got this busy, so this was new terrain for her, and I couldn't help but feel guilty, wondering how long she'd last before she wished she hadn't come.

"Hey, Fran," I shouted over the noise to the bartender, a stunning individual with warm beige skin and dark hair, who didn't look a day over thirty even though they were knocking on fifty. They also happened to be the spouse of the thirty-five-year-old owner who didn't like me.

Their smokey eyes lit up as they saw me. "Layla, girl! What are you doing here so early?"

I hiked my thumb back at Madison. "Girls' night. We're here for your cheap ass drinks before I play, so feel free to be generous. This is the friend I told you about. Madison, Fran.

Fran, Madison."

They said their shouted hellos, and Fran got our drink order, vodka with cranberry for Madison, and vodka with a handful of limes for me. I'd just handed Fran my card to put on our tab when I spotted a familiar face in my peripheral, a few heads down.

Odd. What in the world was Larry doing here?

As my booking agent, the short, potbellied man had his fingers in a lot of places, including Jemmy's, but he never actually came to my shows. Ever. Although I couldn't tell who the guy was that he was talking to, since his back was to me, there was no denying it was definitely Larry.

I shrugged, brushing it off. He was probably off the clock and meeting with a friend. People had lives. But just as I was about to turn back to Madison and recommend we scout for a table to snipe, Larry's eyes caught mine from over his companion's shoulder.

His mouth snapped shut, and his head reared back slightly as he blinked at me. He recovered quickly, leaning in and murmuring something to his friend, who nodded, before grabbing his beer and beelining for our end of the bar.

"Layla! What a pleasant surprise!"

I raised a brow, sharing a look with Madison. Surprise? The man was the one who put me in contact with Jemmy for the Friday gigs. When I didn't immediately respond, he must've caught on to the stupidity of his comment because he cleared his throat, fidgeting awkwardly behind us.

Larry Bosenet was a booking agent whom I'd met right after

moving to town, thanks to Rick. The goatee-sporting, balding man wasn't the easiest to work with—his personality was cringey on his best days—but he had a way of weaseling me into all kinds of gigs I wouldn't have found on my own, so week after week, I suffered through it.

Starving artists couldn't be picky and all.

I swirled my drink, sipping it and feeling it burn the entire way down, warming my insides. "Guess that answers my question of whether you're here to support me, huh, Larry?"

A forced chortle exited his lips, and he leaned past Madison to set his empty bottle down, running his eyes over her in a way I didn't like before rising back up. "You know I think you're amazing, Layla-Bayla—"

"Don't call me that."

"—but my nights are always so booked. I'm just meeting up with a friend to talk business and then heading out of town. Gotta drive out to Raleigh and see if I can't get you into some new places, yes?"

He clapped his hands together, and although I knew he aimed to distract me, it worked. I desperately wanted to get shows in the larger cities.

"Really?"

He nodded enthusiastically, the few hairs combed over the top of his head bobbing as he did. "Absolutely. I'll be there all weekend, actually. With a voice like yours, it'll be no problem getting their interest, but with your schedule…" he trailed off, tipping his head and giving me a "disappointed father" look.

I took a sip of my drink and stepped away from the bar,

wrapping a hand around Madison's wrist to tug her literally anywhere else. She'd visibly stiffened when he'd brushed past her, and this conversation would only increase her stress level.

"My schedule is firm. That's non-negotiable, Larry."

"I take a percentage of your earnings for a reason, Layla-Bayla," he stumbled at my glare and coughed. "I'm just saying, I know this business, and if you want—"

I yanked on Madison's arm, yelling "Non-negotiable, Lair-Bear," over my shoulder as I pulled her through the crowd, trying not to twist my ankle as I dodged the elbows of dancing patrons.

Scanning the surrounding area like a hawk, I zeroed in on a couple at a back table, the guy tucking his wallet into his pocket, and the woman grabbing her purse strap. Bingo.

Their asses had barely lifted from their chairs before I gave them my best smile and swooped in behind them, tossing Madison to the other side. The guy side-eyed me a little harder than necessary but said nothing as he took his lady's hand and led her out.

I watched them go, pretending I couldn't feel the tension pouring off of my friend. Five, four, three, two, one—

"What did he mean when he mentioned other shows?"

There it was. Goddamnit, Larry.

"I thought there weren't any weekday gigs?" she asked, brow creased. "Isn't that why you took the office job?"

"There are a few," I hedged, looking around the bar in hopes of finding a hot guy I could point out and distract her with.

But her mom senses were tingling, sensing the lie I'd given her on more than one occasion. "Then why don't you take them?

You hate that job, and you'd make twice as much money doing what you actually *want* to do."

May Larry's pillows give him pink eye and his coffee always be two degrees below lukewarm.

"It's just a few small ones right now. They wouldn't be steady or worth it," I said smoothly, spinning my glass in a circle. "Anyway, enough about me. I want to hear what Garrett said to you when he hauled you to your room like a starving man who'd just found a steak."

She rolled her eyes but laughed, dropping the conversation and jumping into the story with enough detail, I found myself searching the room again.

After the second sweep, I was about to call it quits, taking the lack of single, attractive guys within all these people as my sign from the universe that it wasn't meant to be, when movement caught my eye. It shouldn't have, given the number of bodies all doing their own thing, but it was the way he moved that drew my attention and kept it.

Where Madison and I had been forced to squeeze and shove past people, he seemed to glide through, cutting through the crowd like a knife in softened butter. Like everyone around him all subconsciously parted to give him space.

I straightened my spine, trying to keep an eye on him as he approached the bar and signaled to Fran to order something. I wasn't one-hundred percent certain, but I was at least ninety-nine percent that it was the guy Larry had been talking to.

He was dressed casually, like most other guys in the room, with a dark—maybe navy—long-sleeve shirt and a jacket thrown over his forearm.

His shoulder-length hair appeared to be either dark blonde or light brown, and it was tousled like he'd either just had the quickie I was wishing for, or he'd recently run his hands through it.

Grabbing the cold bottle Fran handed him, he raised it to his lips before pausing, hand frozen in the air. His body seemed to tense for a moment, and he glanced over his shoulder, eyes darting around like he could sense the weight of my stare.

I squinted, staring even harder as more of his face became clear. Why did he look familiar?

Madison leaned in, tapping my arm and yelling something across the table. I nodded absently, unable to tear my eyes away from the man's side profile. I recognized him from somewhere. I'd bet my entire night's check on it.

She yelled again, and I leaned over the table, trying to make out what she was saying without looking away from the stranger. "What?"

"I said, I need to go to the bathroom, but there's a line. Are you okay to sit here by yourself for a few minutes?"

That drew my full attention, and I focused in on her concerned face, glancing down at her now-empty drink, and giving her an exaggerated eyebrow lift.

"I'm here alone every Friday night, Mads."

She ran her eyes over me and back to the bathroom, biting her lip and bouncing her foot so hard beneath the table that it vibrated.

"Are *you* going to be okay being by yourself?"

That earned me a glare. "Yes."

I finished my drink as well, biting back the burn of the vodka. "I'll be fine, Mads. But just know, if you take too long, I'll abandon our table to get another drink, so scurry along."

She stalled for one more second before her bladder won out, and she jumped from her chair and disappeared into the crowd. I watched her go, making sure she made it to the bathroom line before twisting my head to find my mystery guy again.

My eyes found him in an instant, only to discover him now facing outward, leaning back against the bar, and staring out into the crowd with a lazy expression.

His hair, definitely a dirty blonde, looked unruly yet soft, finger combed back out of his face with a few pieces dangling across his forehead. I couldn't tell the color of his eyes from where I was, but his nose was straight, and his jaw squared and scruffy. But not overly thick. It was that perfect amount that scraped across your skin just right and had goosebumps erupting down your arms.

He didn't look to be rippling with muscles like Madison's boyfriend, but he was clearly in shape, his biceps pushing against his snug, long-sleeve like arm porn.

Oh God. Wait. I *did* know him.

I gaped, blinking rapidly to make sure I wasn't imagining it. But no, it was definitely him. I'd seen his face more times than I could count on ads, announcements, and social media pages, usually marketing for huge venues and events.

The face of Adrian Waters.

From what I could recall, he was a solo musician in his early thirties with no spouse or kids. He wasn't rich and famous by any means, but he could be if found by the right people. He was already one of the biggest names in music in all the neighboring cities.

Why he was here, in our much smaller town, I had no idea, but I was already standing, eager to walk over and speak to him. A man that talented and drop-dead gorgeous was likely to be romantically spoken for, but that didn't mean I couldn't pick his brain, right?

I hadn't personally heard him sing yet, but Adrian Waters had connections and knew how to market himself really fucking well. One conversation with him could change the entire game for me, especially if I could get him to either drop the name of his agent or pass my name along.

I'd toss sleazy Larry in the dirt to get whoever worked with this man on my team.

By the time Madison came back to the table, I was practically vibrating with excitement. Enough so, she paused before taking a seat.

"I know that look. What'd I miss?"

"Nothing. Yet," I said, sliding off my seat and readjusting my top where it'd started to migrate over my stomach. I grabbed my empty glass and phone, giving myself an internal pep talk.

"Should I be worried?"

"Not this time," I laughed. I hadn't been this excited in a while.

The thought of bigger, higher-paying gigs made me feel like a firecracker was nestling inside my chest. I could quit my day job while also keeping my evening schedule open during the week. If I could make friends with Adrian, I could make everything work.

"See that guy over there? The one with the sexy smolder and the perfectly messy hair?" I asked, walking around to stand behind her and pointing in his direction.

"The one who looks like he'd rather be anywhere else?"

"That's the one," I said, nodding. "Adrian Waters."

She arched her neck, resting the back of her head on my shoulder to look up at me, eyebrows raised. "I thought the entire point of taking a guy home from the bar was to *not* know who he was."

I smacked her arm, earning me a chuckle. "He's a musician. A good one. I'm going to go talk to him real quick. Do you mind holding our table? I promise I won't be long."

She leaned up, eyeing him more critically like she was an FBI agent roaming through his internet search history. "All right. At least bring me a drink back."

"Same one?"

She shook her head, pulling her phone out of her purse and clicking on a new notification from *Sugar Daddy*. "Just water."

Agreeing to bring one back, I shoved my way toward the bar, again wondering how the hell Adrian had done it with such ease. I doubted anyone else recognized him since no one was trying to talk to him. It was more likely that his overall miserable demeanor just made people naturally shy away.

It almost made me change my mind as I stepped up beside him at the bar, waving my empty glass at Fran. They waved back, grabbing a bottle of vodka and heading my way.

Maybe Adrian was here to drink his sorrows away and didn't want to be disturbed. It was possible. But then again, Madison's boyfriend had a brooding look that made you think he was plotting your death even when he was happy, so maybe Adrian suffered from the same.

Thanking Fran and asking for a water as well, I took a sip of my new drink and leaned my elbows on the bar, turning my head toward him and trying not to drool over his impeccable jaw line. I did, however, confirm he wore no wedding ring.

Come on, Layla, grow a clit and just fucking go for it. Men approached women all the time. I could do this.

Plastering the same brave face I wore when I talked to a crowd while performing, I smiled at him. Or, at the side of his face, at least.

"Hey, it's Adrian, right?" I asked, liking the way his name rolled off my tongue way more than I should.

He held up a long finger, nodding his head at Fran, who was sliding a water toward me. I waited, but he didn't turn or acknowledge that I'd spoken at all. All right. Maybe he was just zoned out. Not to mention, the music over the speakers was loud as hell.

"Hey, you're Adrian Waters, right?" I asked again, louder this time. His head tipped my way ever so slightly, but that was it. No reply or acknowledgment. Nothing.

My hackles immediately rose, my inner bitch rising to the surface to defend me. But I pushed her down, deciding to go a different route.

"I'm Layla. I saw you earlier when you were talking with Larry Bosenet. Do you work with him?"

I really did want to know the answer to that one. I found it odd that Larry had never mentioned knowing freaking Adrian Waters. He wasn't a celebrity by any means, but he was well-known in the local music world, and good as hell from what people said. Larry would've boasted the hell out of that.

Then again, it could also be that Adrian didn't know him at all, and Larry had just been his usual annoying self and bugged him. Honestly, anything was possible with that man.

Adrian cleared his throat. "No." The word was low and clipped like it'd taken everything in him to pull it from his throat. Like he hadn't talked in a week and had to remember how it was done.

I was no stranger to signals. He might not have said it, but this man clearly didn't want to be disturbed. My excitement fizzled, acceptance settling in that tonight wasn't the night. I knocked back my drink, tried not to burst into a coughing fit, and took the failure for what it was.

The universe was telling me to stay in my lane. Noted.

I'd put one last olive branch out, and then I'd leave him alone. I worked again tomorrow night, and who knew, maybe he'd be out tomorrow as well. I doubted it, but hopes and dreams were all I had these days.

"All right, I can take a hint. But if you feel up to it later, I'll buy you a drink. I'll be here until nine." *Just let me pick your brain, please.*

He sighed heavily, like I'd just asked him to work a double

shift on his day off. It grated my nerves and hurt my feelings more than I wanted to admit. I knew my abrasive personality wasn't everyone's cup of tea, but damn, I thought I was being pretty damn friendly.

"Look," he finally said, *still not looking at me*, "you seem nice, but I don't sleep with fans." He took a sip of his drink and glanced down at the phone in my hand, adding, "Nor do I particularly like pictures."

Zero to one hundred. That's how fast it took my inner bitch to break out, ready to bite into this motherfucker. He thought I was trying to *sleep* with him? I'd mentioned goddamn Larry of all people. Who in their right mind would mention that man if they were trying to get laid?

"My name is Layla Davis, and I'm not a fan," I snapped. I was only partly lying. I hadn't heard the guy play yet, so I couldn't claim to be a true fan of his music, but I was definitely a fan of his face and general knack for marketing himself.

"But even if I was," I continued, getting more pissed off with every second, "is this how you treat your fans? Pretend they don't exist and then assume they want in your pants? You wouldn't even have a platform if it wasn't for the people who support you. Maybe keep that in mind the next time one of them dares to speak to you."

The air between us seemed to thicken as he finally turned his head, his blue eyes sharp as they landed on me and widened imperceptibly. They were mesmerizing, so light around his pupil they were almost white, yet vibrant blue around the edges, and cold as ice.

He looked like he was about to apologize before he seemed to think better of it, and he blinked, looking away again. He cleared his throat. "Well, fan or not, whatever it is you're hoping to gain from me, I'm afraid you'll leave here empty-handed and disappointed."

I set my glass down harder than necessary, drawing a glance from Fran down the bar, and probably a few people around us. But I was pissed. This was exactly the kind of shit that infuriated me to the point of fire blasting out of my throat.

Why was a man allowed to buy a woman a drink, touch her back or arm without permission, and toss cheesy lines her way, and he was just "being friendly." But if a woman approached a man to buy him a drink, it could only mean she wanted to exploit him in some way? Fuck him.

"I don't need anything from you, Waters. I think I've learned enough tonight already." I tapped my knuckles against the bar twice before snatching up the water and making my way back toward our table, thanking God when I made it without tripping.

Taking care to drop into my seat casually, in case he was watching, I crossed my legs and leaned back, draping my hair over my shoulder to block his presence.

Madison's eyes were huge, roaming over me to check for internal stab wounds only she could detect. She didn't need to have heard our conversation to know I was raging. But I was grateful for it because my anger hid the small hurt that made itself a home inside my chest.

The kind I didn't want anyone to see. Especially her.

"What's wrong?" she asked, setting her phone on the table and taking the water from me. "What'd he say to you?"

"Nothing worth repeating. Just another asshole in the sea full of them."

Her lips thinned, and she nodded, not needing more of an explanation than that. She'd had her fair share of experiences with asshole men. "Want me to go over there and accidentally pour my water in his lap?"

"Honestly, that's extremely tempting."

She glanced sideways, trying to nonchalantly look his way, but looking all the more obvious for it. "Looks like he's leaving."

"Good." Of course, he wasn't going to stay for my show. I'd expect nothing less from someone with his kind of attitude.

"He's really attractive."

Don't look at him. Don't look at him.

"Hard pass," I said, checking the clock on my phone. I still had some time before I needed to get my equipment out of my car. "I'd rather marry Rick and have his babies than give that man another second of my time."

She sat back, a knowing look on her face. "Does that mean I can make an online dating profile for you while you're up there playing tonight?"

I huffed and flipped her off.

But I didn't tell her no.

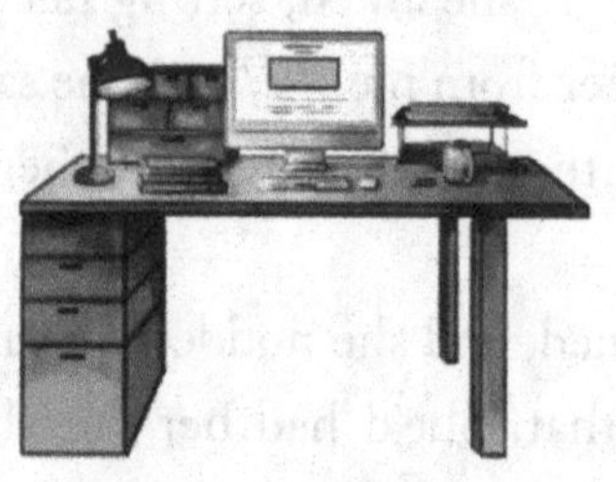

Chapter

3

I WASN'T A morning person. Never had been. Other than drinking a cup of coffee and spooning cereal into my mouth, the thought of doing anything directly after opening my eyes made me physically ill. Especially after a show night.

I hadn't worked late, playing until my usual nine o'clock, but by the time I'd gotten my check, packed everything up, and walked into our duplex, it'd felt like 3:00 AM. Singing for three hours straight was a hell of a lot more exhausting than people thought.

This, mixed with my hatred for waking up, was why, at almost twenty-five, I still wasn't sure if I ever wanted my own kids. I loved them—Jamie was practically mine in all the ways that mattered—but surviving off a few nonconsecutive hours of sleep or waking up at the crack of dawn to get a mini human ready for school every day sounded awful.

I could barely get myself ready on time.

Which was only further proven when I ran through our living room with one shoe on, mascara in one hand, my second shoe in the other, ushering Jamie toward the door like a maniac.

He ignored me, shuffling his feet across the carpet while his nose was buried in his newest book. Something about portals and fairy tale characters.

"Let's go, let's go!" I half-yelled, waving my mascara tube over the page and snatching my purse from the counter, all while somehow slipping on my second shoe and narrowly avoiding crashing into Sadie.

The last thing I wanted was to get him to school late, especially with how much of a bitch his principal and teacher were, even on Jamie's best days. I'd just sworn to Madison last night that I could take him.

She'd shuffled into the house long after midnight from her closing shift at the restaurant, after already having worked her day shift at her other job before that. Garrett had slipped in right behind her, squatting down to help her out of her shoes.

It'd been pure luck that I'd happened to be in the kitchen getting a drink of water and meds for a small headache when they'd walked in.

I'd peeked around the bar to make a joke, but it'd quickly died on my tongue at the look on her face. The circles under her eyes, the drawn slope of her mouth, and the weary drag of her feet as Garrett led her to her room.

And instead of the inappropriate comment I'd been about

to make, I'd found myself offering to get up early with Jamie and take him to school on my way to work so she could steal a few extra minutes of sleep.

"Come on," I said, pushing on the back of said child's backpack, "before your mom comes out and tries to take you."

Giving Sadie one last pat, I shut the door, and we jogged down the drive, squeezing between Madison's Jeep and my tiny Miata.

"Buckle up," I said, tossing my purse onto the tiny console between us and yanking my mirror down to apply a few quick swipes of mascara.

"Working on it," he mumbled. I glanced over, rolling my lips in as I watched the kid struggle to strap himself in with one hand while the other held his book to his face.

"Seriously, Jamie? You can't pause for five seconds? You're as bad as your mom."

Finally clicking the seatbelt in, he sat back and glanced up, looking at me like I'd just asked him what two plus two was. "I don't like stopping in the middle of a chapter. I only have three pages left."

I held my hands up in surrender, smacking my mirror shut and dropping my mascara tube into the cupholder. "All right, my bad. Your three pages are more important than hanging out with me. I get it."

"That's not what I—"

"It's *fine*," I said, drawing the word out as I backed out of the drive.

There was a pause, and then I heard him sigh. "You're

messing with me, aren't you?"

"Absolutely, dude. Finish your chapter."

I glanced at his furrowed brow as he dipped his head back over his book without another word, and my heart squeezed.

It wasn't that long ago he would've talked my ear off the entire way to school, excited to have one-on-one time with me. But lately, things had started to change. Madison had been noticing the same. It was like, with each inch he grew, he pulled away from us a little more.

We all still hung out, played board games and video games, and fought for the last pack of gummies, but it just wasn't happening as often. It was a hard pill to swallow that he wouldn't do any of that one day. And the worst part was we wouldn't even realize it until it had already happened.

Before I'd moved in, Madison had once told me that the hardest part about parenting was having to come to terms with the fact that one day you would pick up your child for the last time without even knowing it. I didn't understand it then, but I was starting to now.

Before I knew it, I was going to watch him drive his car to prom and wonder when he stopped wanting to marry me and watch cartoons inside a blanket fort.

Watching kids grow up was fucking hard.

Holding my key card up until the pad turned green, I readjusted my skirt and yanked the handle, stepping into the entry hall of my job.

I was earlier than usual, and it was dead quiet, a distinct difference from the loud, overbearing voices of all the men who usually hung around the offices. One of the few perks to being up this early, I supposed.

I made my way into my office, grabbing the stack of timesheets that the night drivers had left outside my door, and settled in behind my desk.

All in all, the job wasn't awful. The men could be crass, and several had no respect for personal space, but I liked my boss, Ken, and the freedom he gave me to come and go as I pleased as long as I got my work done.

The work was simple and straightforward. I made schedules and input time and pallet counts for a crap ton of truck drivers delivering cakes and muffins all across the state. Literally. Our offices were even tucked into a tiny corner of said baking company.

It was the position Madison had been doing prior to taking her job at the security company she was currently at during the week. Ken had hired someone to take over when she left, but the replacement had been caught having sex with a driver in one of the cabs and was quickly dismissed.

And since I'd started looking to make extra cash to pay my part of the rent and bills, and Madison still came in every Sunday to do payroll, she'd convinced him to hire me spot unseen.

I appreciated the opportunity and the trust they both had in me, but damn, this was not what I wanted to be doing with my life. Hidden away behind a desk, wearing a pencil skirt that caused the inside of my thighs to sweat and chafe, and a button-up blouse that made me feel like a can of biscuits about to explode.

Every day I came in, I felt my muse hide deeper and deeper within me, the motivation to write dying with the fear that I'd still be here in ten years.

It just wasn't me. But quitting wasn't an option. Neither was taking evening gigs during the week. So, day after day, I came in, willing myself to make it work out.

Twirling in my seat, I logged in, pulling up the programs I'd need to use, and watched as the emails flooded in. I sighed, resting my chin in my palms. I could do this.

For them, I could do it.

Thirty minutes later, I'd finished checking all my emails, organizing my to-do list for the day, and was doing my cursory look over the day's schedule when the door to the hall opened.

The jangling of keys told me who it was.

"Good morning, Ken!" I called out, welcoming my boss, whose office was next door to mine. My own wall neighbor. Except, unlike Madison, mine was not a hunky aircraft mechanic.

Ken was around the same age as most of the drivers and had a son just a year or so younger than me. He had the definition of a beer-bellied dad bod and kept his hair shaved close to his head to hide the receding hairline he didn't want to admit to yet.

He wasn't always the most ethical of bosses, such as the time he paid Madison even though she didn't come in on the promise that she would babysit his grandchild for him for free. But he was supportive in the ways that mattered, and was laid back and funny, so he was a winner in my book.

He poked his balding head around the corner of my office, his belt buckle smacking against my doorframe as he did. "Am I seeing things? What're you doing here so early?"

I fluttered my eyelashes, spinning a pen in my hand. "Oh, you know, I just love it here so much, I couldn't wait to come back."

His brows lowered, and he shot me an unimpressed look that made me chuckle. "I took Jamie to school, so I was already out and about and came straight here."

"Ah," he said, having met Jamie a few times while Madison had still worked for him full time. "Well, give me fifteen minutes to get settled, and then pop on over to go over today's schedule."

"You got it."

He walked away, and I listened to him shuffle around his office, his chair groaning beneath him. And before I knew it, I was up and poking my head around the corner, just as he'd done to me.

"Actually, Ken, can I talk to you about something real quick? Before we get started today?" The words flew out of my mouth before I'd even known they were sitting on my tongue. But I'd been thinking about something all morning—well, all night, really. Ever since Madison walked in the door.

He looked up at me over the large foam cup he kept on his

desk to spit in, the sides tainted brown from his daily tobacco use.

"Depends on what you want to talk about."

He gestured at the chair in front of him, and I ambled in, plopping down and doing my best to cross my legs in the goddamn skintight skirt without flashing my boss my goods.

"Is the topic of a raise up for discussion?"

"Not since the last time you asked."

"Then that's not what it's about," I said, plastering a cheeky smile on my face that had him shaking his head.

When an awkward silence fell, and I didn't say anything else, he raised a brow, poking his tongue at where the chunk of tobacco sat behind his lip. "Well, don't leave me waiting. But be aware, if you're about to give your notice, the answer is no."

I rolled my eyes, pretending to find him funny even though I'd give anything to tell him that. "The opposite, actually. I wanted to talk to you about Sundays."

"What about them?"

"Working them."

He tipped his head to the side, brow creasing. "Madison hasn't mentioned anything to me about being unable to come in anymore."

I shifted in my seat, intertwining my fingers in my lap. "She's still working a double on Sundays, and she doesn't need to be. She only does it to earn money for rent, but me earning it will cover it all the same."

He pursed his lips, looking down his nose at me like a dad trying to pull a lie from a wayward teen. "Wouldn't that put *you* working a double?"

I shook my head. "It's not the same. Madison's Sunday night shift is a minimum of eight hours, plus she still has homework and a child to get to school on Mondays. I have neither and only work a few hours."

Technically, I was the one who took Jamie to school today, but that was only because I'd offered, and was beside the point. "This is my job now, not hers. It's not fair for her to continue doing the payroll when I can take it over."

He considered me for another moment and then shrugged, picking up his cup to spit into. "I'm not against it, but she has to be okay with it and put her notice in just like any other employee."

My heart beat faster, excitement and dread mixing into an almost nauseating sensation in the pit of my stomach. "That's fine," I said, running my palms down my thighs. "I'll come with her next Sunday and take notes."

I knew the gist of it since I was the one who input the drivers' timesheets into the computer. I just needed to learn the program that entered it all for their checks. Plus, the account balance for the bakery side of things.

Swell.

Like clockwork, the second I left Ken's office and settled back into my own, the early morning drivers began making their way in. Unlike Ken, who had a small, private office, mine doubled as a waiting room, with a row of metal chairs along one side.

Which meant that anytime a truck wasn't loaded up on time—which happened almost daily—the drivers would park their asses in my office until it was.

Many of them ignored me after the required *Hello, how are you* small talk, but there were a few whom I would've been willing to help load their trucks rather than have them in my damn space.

The one currently passing by my window and opening the main door was one of them. His voice hit me before his face did.

"Hello, sunshine."

I set my pen down and folded my hands over my half-completed stack, looking up at the man now standing just on the other side of my desk. Skinny as a rail with long, brown hair and a beard, he might as well have been a replica of the supposed rendering of Jesus.

Which was only further supported by the fact that he was always trying to feed me.

"Wayne, we both know I am the furthest thing from a ray of sunshine. If anything, I'm a giant chunk of hail, so feel free to use my given name."

He blinked at me, but then covered it with a forced laugh, handing his timesheet over. "A good meal would probably melt that ice away, you know."

I shook my head, snatching the piece of paper and shooing him out of my office. The dude was double my age and had asked me out to lunch more times than I could count by my fourth week there.

In general, I hated the term *harmless* when it came to men, because it was usually used in a way that gave a creep a free ride to be…well, creepy. But in Wayne's case, it was true.

I had no doubt he'd jump at the chance to sleep with any woman who'd give him a chance, but I also trusted that he'd never try it without explicit permission. He just liked to shoot his shot when given the chance.

"Nah, if you melted the ice around Layla's heart, you'd just find solid stone beneath it. That, or poison."

And then there was Ames. A retired Army vet who doubled as a sexist on his best days. Misogyny? It was tattooed on his forehead and seeped from his pores. I fucking hated him.

Shaved head, somewhat in-shape body, and an inch or two shorter than my five foot, eight inches, he wasn't exactly the terrifying presence he wanted to be. But a chihuahua was often louder than a pit bull.

He slipped into my office, passing Wayne on his way out, and came right up to my desk, holding his sheet in front of my face rather than handing it to me or setting it in the tray on my desk.

I didn't take it.

"Always a pleasure to see you, Ames," I said, grabbing my stack and rolling my chair to the other side of my L-shaped desk to give him my back.

"So, you can take Wayne's but can't take mine? Someone's playing favorites."

I didn't bother looking up. He baited me every day, and

every day he failed to get a rise out of me only made him try harder. It was honestly pathetic.

"Just set it in the tray. I'll get it in a second."

"I don't want to put it in the tray. I want you to take it. You're literally working on them right now, Layla," he snapped, my name on his lips grating more than the sound of someone vomiting.

Why did men have to…men? "I understand that's what you want, but I'm guessing you want to get paid even more. So, again, set it in the tray, and I'll get to it."

The room went silent, the only sound being my pen moving across the timesheet I was counting pallets on. He was delusional if he thought he could outlast me in a game of stubbornness. I lived with an eight-year-old boy, stubbornness and patience were required traits.

"Ames," Ken's voice called from next door, irritation lacing his tone, "your load is ready. Go hitch up."

I barely withheld a sigh of relief when I heard the rustle of a page and then the angry steps as he left my office, slamming the main door out as he went.

I rolled my chair back over, taking his timesheet from the tray and adding it to my stack. Layla-101, Ames-0.

"One of these days, I'm going to punch him in the face with his timesheet," I muttered, but the chuckle I heard from next door told me it'd come out louder than I'd planned.

"Just make sure I have my door closed first so I can claim ignorance when it goes to HR," Ken said, making me snort.

Inputting my time, I clocked out, finishing earlier than usual due to my crack-of-dawn start to the day. I grabbed my phone, shooting a text to Madison.

Me: Headed home. Need me to pick anything up on my way?
Mads: No, but pull out some beef to thaw for spaghetti, please.
Mads: It's therapy day, so we'll be late.
Me: Will do.

With the change to my morning routine, I'd forgotten Jamie had it today. He only went every other week as it was, so it was hard to keep up. I grinned. That meant only the dogs would be home when I got there.

Oh yeah, I was absolutely going to curl up and take a nap.

I'd just finished replying to a text from my mom asking me how my weekend shows went when my phone rang in my hand, startling me.

Caller ID: Larry Bosenet

Weird. Larry rarely called, usually opting to shoot me a text if he had something new lined up or wanted to confirm my schedule. Maybe his Raleigh trip had gone well. I slid my thumb across the screen to answer, my heart picking up.

"Hello, Larry."

"Hey, Layla-Bayla."

I bit the insides of my cheeks, refusing to respond. The silence dragged on for three awkward seconds before he cleared his throat. "Sorry. Old habits die hard. Anyway, I'll make this quick. I know you're a busy, working woman."

I sighed, pressing my thumb and forefinger against my eyelids. "What's up?"

He cleared his throat again, something I was beginning to notice he did when he was uncomfortable. So, it wasn't good news for me. Figures.

"Well…the thing is, I'm actually calling to let you know that you won't be playing at Jemmy's this Friday. I just got off the phone with them, and it looks like they accidentally double-booked."

That caught my attention, and I sat up, holding the phone closer to my ear as if that would help me process what he was saying. I played at Jemmy's *every* Friday. "Who else did they book?"

"Well, as you know, you're not under contract with them, so technically, they can cancel your shows at any time and book someone else."

"I don't need you to mansplain what double-booking means, Larry," I snapped. "I'm just not understanding *why* they suddenly booked someone else."

I hadn't been aware of any issues during my last show. I'd even made good tips that night, which, at the time, I'd wished I could rub in stupid Adrian Waters's face.

"They still love you, Layla, as do I," he quickly added. "They just wanted to change their Friday night entertainment up and forgot to let me know about it, that's all."

I nodded even though he couldn't see me. I didn't like it, but it made sense. I'd been playing every Friday for weeks now, and it was inevitable that my music wouldn't be everyone's favorite genre.

Booking a band or a different style of musician every so often to change things up was expected. It didn't mean they wouldn't book me again in the future. Right?

"What about next Friday?" I asked, suddenly panicking.

"Still on, from what I know. It's just this week that's a little mixed up."

I relaxed my posture, forcing myself to take a deep breath. "All right."

"I'll shoot you a text later if I find you anywhere else to play, instead."

"All right," I repeated, already done with the phone call. Just because I understood Jemmy's decision from a business standpoint didn't make me like it any less, nor did it improve my mood.

I hung up without saying goodbye, my mind going a mile a minute. It was fine. It's not like I was the only musician in town. I couldn't hog every gig. Although, Larry's deliberate dance around the name had me questioning who my replacement was.

Shoving my phone in my purse, I left, tossing a wave at Ken, and began the long walk past the parked semis to get to the employee parking lot.

I had no plans this Friday now, and Madison was going to be busy doing something with Garrett, so maybe I'd swing by and support whoever was playing. Who knew, maybe it was someone I could collaborate or share a drink with.

I just hoped it didn't turn out to be Rick.

Chapter
4

I TOOK IT back. I'd have rather it been Rick.

Of course, it was fucking Adrian who had taken my spot. *Of course, it was.* Honestly, I should've seen that one coming.

I threw back my one-dollar drink, tempted to down three more and raise my middle fingers in the air. Screw you, too, universe.

Tucked against the wall, I sat in the corner and stared at him, at a loss for words for how shitty my karma was. Why did he have to be good? No, he wasn't even good, he was fucking phenomenal, and it made me want to clobber him over the head with his guitar.

I was good at the guitar. It wasn't a flex, just the truth, and I owned that shit. But Adrian? His fingers flew over the strings like he'd come out of the womb playing them.

His left hand slid up and down the neck, his long fingers

reaching each string with an ease I'd never match with my much smaller hands. His right hand hovered over the gorgeous jet-black body, holding a white pick between his thumb and forefinger, his other fingers splayed out in a way that was almost pornographic.

What would those long, calloused fingers feel like… No. Nope. Not going there. Asshole central, Layla. Asshole fucking central.

I brushed blue strands out of my face, still staticky from the scarf I'd had wrapped around my neck. The weather had plummeted tonight, enough so that I wouldn't be surprised if it started snowing.

My love for spiked heels made me naturally hate the snow. Because where there was snow, there was often ice. And my ass couldn't walk over ice in heels if my life depended on it.

I knocked back the second drink Fran had silently handed me, my guardian angel sensing I'd need it. Meanwhile, Adrian's deep, smooth voice sank into my skin until I wasn't sure I'd ever get it out.

When his song ended, he let his guitar hang from its strap and wrapped his fingers around the mic, pulling it close to his mouth. "I'm going to take a short break, so make sure you see Fran for some drinks. Thanks, guys."

A short burst of applause broke out, and then he leaned his guitar against a speaker and hopped off the stage. Oh, so he did know how to treat his fans decently. It'd just been me he was a jerk to then. Lovely.

I gripped my empty glass and watched him grab a water bottle from the small, square table to the side reserved for the musicians. His throat bobbed as he chugged it, but he immediately dropped it as people edged his way, wiping his stupidly perfect lips and thanking them as they tucked bills into his tip jar.

Doubt crept into my chest. Adrian didn't look like an asshole right now. With his cheeks flushed, a sheen across his forehead from the overhead lights, and a spark of adrenaline in his eyes, he looked sexy and…normal. Nothing like the man I'd met here the other night.

Maybe there really was a chance he'd just been having a rough go of it the first time we met. It didn't make how he'd treated me okay, but I could understand a bad night. Lord knew, I'd had plenty myself. I could give him one more chance and compliment his set.

That's something a casual, I'm-not-trying-to-sleep-with-you, fellow musician would do. Right?

Squaring my shoulders, I worked my way through the crowd, forcing my face to relax so I wouldn't ruin everything by accidentally glaring at him. But I froze a few feet away when I belatedly realized he wasn't alone.

Someone else had beaten me to him and was already at his table, raving about his performance with a familiar string of fake ass compliments I knew all too well.

Larry fucking Bosenet.

"See? What'd I tell you, Adrian? With a voice like yours, I told you they'd eat it up. I've never seen a tip jar fill so fast by the first break. You're by far the best musician they've seen here."

Adrian, currently checking something on his phone and frowning, didn't so much as look up to acknowledge him, but

Larry's words stuck in my head like super glue.

With a voice like yours…

You know I think you're the best musician in town…

He'd lied to me. Jemmy's had never double-booked. *He'd* double-booked. Purposefully, so he could squeeze me out and his new golden ticket in.

I wasn't sure why it surprised me, why it hurt so much, but it did. I wasn't Larry's biggest fan, mostly because he annoyed me, but I never thought he'd just…replace me.

You had to have a thick skin in this profession, I knew that. I also knew that you could be replaced in an instant if you weren't what people wanted any longer, but that hadn't been the case at all.

My shows were always filled with fans, and my tip jar was never barren. Larry had simply found someone he thought would garner even *more* and lied about it.

And the truth of that fucking stung.

Besides Madison and Jamie, Larry was the only person I knew in this state. Hell, the entire eastern coast. I didn't count Ken or the drivers at work since they knew nothing about my life outside of the office.

And I guess, I'd just thought, weaselly though he was, that Larry would at least have my back when it came to music.

The longer I stood there, staring at him gush over Adrian, the more the hurt sank away somewhere deep in my chest, and my anger rose to the surface.

And for a reason I couldn't explain, it zeroed in on the back of Adrian's head—not Larry's. Because, in the end, it all boiled down to *him*. It was his fault Larry had booked him over me.

Had he taken my spot on purpose because I'd pissed him off, or had they already been talking about it that night before I'd approached him?

It was one thing for an agent to book whoever would make them the most money—business was business—but for a musician, especially a seasoned one, to knowingly steal a gig from another? It was shady as hell. But I guess professionalism was another thing this jackass lacked.

As I continued to glare at the back of his unruly blonde head, Adrian's back tensed, and he straightened, spinning to look over his shoulder. And like he'd known I was there, his icy blue eyes locked with mine, not so much as blinking, even as patrons walked between us.

I don't know what he saw in mine, but something flickered across his gaze as we stared at one another. I didn't want to see it. I didn't so much as want to say two words to him. Not even the insulting kind.

So instead, as he took a step toward me, I raised my hand straight out in front of me and flipped him off. He paused, surprise coating his expression before he blinked it away. He tipped his head, his eyes running down my form and back up, sparking when they landed on my face again.

But he said nothing, nor did he come closer before he twisted away from me. He hopped back on stage, animatedly talking to the crowd and meeting my gaze again as he picked up his guitar and slung the strap over his body.

I narrowed my eyes at his challenge, and I could've sworn the corner of his lips tipped into a smirk as he began playing. "All right, let's get back at it, guys. I got a few good ones lined up for you, but this first one goes out to all the sore losers in the world…"

Then he opened his mouth and belted out a string of lyrics that had me seeing goddamn red.

I spun away, aiming for the bar and yanking out my phone. I'd settle my tab, schedule a car to come pick me up, and go straight home to bed.

Then tomorrow, after I'd rested and made Madison bring me back to pick up my car, I'd figure out what I wanted to do about Adrian jackass Waters.

Because what I *wanted* to do was bury him alive.

"He didn't."

"He did."

"He looked right at you when he said it?"

I nodded.

Madison growled, her crochet hook going in and out of the green baby blanket she was working on with violent intensity. "I wish I'd been there. I'd have thrown a tomato at his arrogant face."

I shot her a look over my glasses, resting my pen against my chin. "And just where would you have gotten the tomato, Mads?"

Her hands paused, and she huffed, yanking more yarn from the skein tucked next to her thigh. "I'm a mom. You'd be surprised what I carry in my purse."

A low chuckle came from the floor, where Garrett leaned

against the couch, rubbing her feet. I just shook my head and stared at the words I'd written in my notebook.

It was Saturday morning—well, early afternoon—and the only reason the three of us had shuffled out of our rooms when we did was to hold off the inevitable headaches we'd have had if we didn't consume caffeine.

Me, because I had, in fact, not gone straight to bed, and had instead laid there picturing a multitude of scenarios that involved Adrian falling off the stage and breaking his perfectly straight nose. And Madison and Garrett because it'd been date night. Enough said.

Jamie had stayed the night at his grandparents and wouldn't be home for another hour, so we'd all made our way into the living room to consume the holiness that was a first cup of coffee.

I'd snuggled next to Sadie with the intent of writing music, but I'd only gotten a few lines down before Madison asked me how the night had gone, and I'd let loose about the entire ordeal.

"Well, Adrian seems like a jerk," she continued, setting her blanket down to comb her fingers through Garrett's brown hair. "But maybe Larry really was just trying to give Jemmy's whatever they wanted to keep them happy."

I shot my head up, but she held up her free hand. "I'm not saying it was right. He should've been honest with you about it. My point is, maybe it was just a random chance. Jemmy's wanted to offer a different voice, and Adrian happened to be in town."

She shrugged, picking the blanket back up. Garrett stood smoothly from the floor and sat on the couch next to her, gathering up Rugsy and plopping her in his lap.

I ran my hand down Sadie's back, giving her a few scratches

behind her ears. "What I want to know is *why* he's in town. It's not like there's anything special here. And if he was just visiting family or something, why would he want to work?"

It didn't make sense. Considering what I made in a single night here, he had to be making extremely good money at the large venues he played at. So, unless he was extremely bad at budgeting his money, or had a drug addiction, I couldn't imagine he needed the extra cash a random, small gig would bring in.

"Maybe he's running from a crazy ex," I mused, noticing Garrett's arm tighten around Madison's shoulder as I said it.

"Or from a city gang he owes money to," she said. "I'd be an ass, too, if I was fearing for my life. That would certainly be your go-to," she added, laughing.

"Whatever," I mumbled, rolling my eyes and burying my face into my coffee. I didn't want to talk about his reasons. I didn't want him to have one. I just wanted to hate his stupid, attractive guts. "Larry still lied, and Adrian still ignored me to my face and then said that shit on stage."

"Yeah, well, men are cavemen—ow!"

I glanced up at her shriek to see Garrett's hand pulling away from where he must've pinched her side.

She smacked his arm and said something about pinching his nipples just before he leaned in and whispered something in her ear. I shook my head, ignoring them, and set my coffee down, squinting at the lyrics I'd been playing around with.

They were good, something the crowd would like, but there was something about them I didn't love. They just seemed so similar to every other sappy love song I played.

I wanted something different, something with more *oomph*

to it. I just didn't know what. Irritated, I tossed my notebook and pen onto the coffee table and leaned over my lap, rubbing my temples. It wasn't a good sign that I already wanted to go back to bed.

My phone gave a quick staccato vibration on the cushion next to me, startling Sadie. I laughed, patting her side as I picked it up to check the text.

Larry: How do you feel about playing at Meg's downtown martini and cigar bar next Friday?

My nostrils flared, and my fingers clasped my phone so hard I accidentally took a screenshot of the snake in the grass that was Larry's text.

"What's wrong?" Madison asked, tossing her bundle into Garrett's arms, and scooting toward me to read over my shoulder.

I didn't reply, my thumbs too busy flying across the screen.

Me: Can't. I'm scheduled at Jemmy's.
Larry: Not anymore. Jemmy's liked changing things up last night and wants to do it again next weekend.
Me: Jemmy's or you?
Larry: You know I love you.
Larry: Sorry, honey.
Larry: Let me know about the martini bar, though.
Larry: And don't forget about the party on Sunday.

I watched each text pop up in our thread, Madison reading

them along with me.

What. The. Actual. Fuck.

Adrian apparently hadn't bothered telling Larry that I'd seen them last night. So, like an idiot, the lies just kept coming. It had nothing to do with Jemmy's. Larry was the booking agent. He was the one working with Adrian, not them.

"What party is he talking about? A private event or something?" Madison asked, still looking at my phone.

I shook my head, speaking between gritted teeth. "No, it's like a get-together for a bunch of musicians and agents. It happens every few months, usually around holidays. This one's theme is Valentine's Day."

"Oh, yeah. I vaguely remember you mentioning something about that. Are you going to go or tell Larry to shove it?"

I continued glaring at my phone, willing his messages to go away. "Both." Free food and drinks and the possibility of finding a new agent? No way I'd turn down that opportunity.

Madison rested her chin on my shoulder, leaning her temple against mine. "Carrying an emergency tomato in my purse doesn't sound like such a bad idea now after all, does it?"

"Better make it two of them."

Chapter
5

THE PARTY WAS held downtown at a fancy, high-dollar venue with a red suit-clad gentleman offering valet parking to those who could afford it.

Since I was definitely *not* one of those who could afford it, I found the closest parking garage, parked my car in a crevice only motorcycles and tiny, red Miatas could fit into, and slipped on my Bad Bitch Shoes.

Tucking my parking ticket into my gold clutch, I buttoned up my favorite pale green, fur-cuffed coat that I'd snagged at a thrift shop and made my way to the event, the drone of traffic drowning out the sound of my heels on the sidewalk.

Besides the typical chill of the January breeze that made my breath puff out before me, it was a fairly nice night and still light enough out that I felt comfortable walking downtown alone.

Madison would've strangled me, but what she didn't know wouldn't kill her.

The outside of the building was nothing to write home about. A plain, gray rectangle hidden behind bushes and trees with no visible windows. It looked more like a storage facility for cardboard boxes than anything else.

But when I gave my name at the door and stepped over the threshold, the inside made up for it in every way.

It was a large, warehouse-like room with one wall—the back one I hadn't been able to see from the door—made of solid glass, while the others reflected an image of a sunset view from projectors on the ceiling.

A combination of couches and tables were sporadically situated throughout the room, with the bar tucked into the back, right corner, and the catering tables a few feet from there. Soft orchestra music played through the speakers, and the serving staff smoothly sailed past, prepping the tables for the incoming meal.

The event was funded by several agents, restaurants, and other businesses in the area, and was decorated as gag-worthy, lovey-dovey as I'd feared. Various shades of pink, roses, and heart cutouts were everywhere I looked. I wasn't sure who the actual coordinator was, but he or she needed to be replaced, pronto.

However, once I could swallow my disgust and see past the cupid barf, the venue was gorgeous. I could only imagine what the actual sunset would look like coming in through the large glass wall.

Sliding off my coat, I folded it in half and draped it over my arm while I made my way toward the bar, where they had rows of bubbly champagne flutes.

Tonight, I'd opted for showstopper and had chosen a midnight blue, fitted dress that hugged the wide flare of my hips and ass, paired with glittery, four-inch heels. My hair was piled on top of my head in a messy updo with rogue strands framing my face, and I was rocking my usual smokey eyes and red lipstick.

If Adrian and Larry thought they could dim my shine, make me hide in a corner, and accept anything less than what I deserved, they'd be sadly mistaken.

There were at least three other agents I'd recognized so far, and even a few well-dressed business owners I was determined to introduce myself to. Connections, connections, connections. That's what I was here for.

Well, that and the free booze. I didn't even care that it was dry champagne. Anything was a step up from the boxed wine I'd be drinking if I'd stayed home.

Grabbing two half-filled flutes, I topped one off with the other, so it was filled to the rim, and tucked the empty one back among the others. It wasn't my classiest moment, but I certainly wasn't going to hike across the room every time I wanted another *half-empty* glass.

I took a sip, grimacing at the flavor, and twisted toward the hors d'oeuvre spread to take a peek at what they had. As I meandered past tables and people, I nodded at two musicians I recognized, Keith and Shawnie, but didn't bother stopping to chat.

Keith was knocking on forty and was a full-time musician, and Shawnie was in her first year of teaching kindergarten, post-college. They were both nice—to my face, at least—but they weren't the ones I needed to buddy up to tonight. Both sang strictly country music and played at very different events than I did. And although Madison often said my voice was made for country, it just wasn't my thing.

Reaching my goal, I grabbed a white plate and loaded it with a handful of strawberries, eyeing the chocolate fountain next to them. Ninety-eight percent of my mind knew chocolate fountains were filled with the germs of a multitude of strangers, but the other two percent of me ignored that fact and shoved a berry into the waterfall of deliciousness anyway. The party had just started, and ignorance was bliss sometimes.

Trying not to moan over the chocolate strawberry explosion on my tongue, I caught sight of Larry a few yards away, running his mouth to a thin, older woman rocking a purple pantsuit.

He met my eyes over her shoulder and waved eagerly, only to falter when I did nothing but glare in return and turn my back to him. If he was too stupid to realize I was onto him, he was too stupid to represent me. Good riddance.

Drink in one hand, a plate of strawberries in the other, I wandered around, searching the nameplates for my spot. Besides the delectable berries, I hadn't eaten anything all day, and I was more than ready to drop into a chair, get a little tipsy, and stuff my face with fancy food.

The smells alone were making my stomach cave in on itself.

Some kind of baked chicken with a plethora of side dishes, from what I'd heard some people around me saying.

Finally finding my name scrawled in loopy cursive on a folded piece of cardstock, I hooked my coat over the back and slid into my seat. The table was tucked close to the back wall, and my designated seat put my back to the room, which was fine by me for the moment. I'd network after food when everyone was full and relaxed.

Setting my drink and clutch down, I shook my head at the center display. The table was covered in a pale pink tablecloth with an enormous pink and white flower display in the center. Little heart-shaped confetti littered every inch, and tiny bottles of cheap rosé adorned the plates.

Leaning back and raising my arms above my head to ensure I got the entire view of the table in a single shot, I snapped a photo and sent it to Madison.

Me: I feel like I'm in a romance novel.
Mads: What do you mean?
Me: You know, like I'm about to meet a sexy farmer who owns a failing flower business or something.
Mads: Somehow, I highly doubt that's his backstory.

What? I frowned and lowered my phone, wondering what she meant. The table literally screamed *Meet Cute*. It had a little plastic banner in the flower arrangement that read "Plant One on Me" for God's sake.

Reaching for my drink, I took a sip only to choke and spit

it back into my glass when my gaze finally noticed the folded name tent on the plate next to mine. The one Madison had immediately seen, but I'd been too busy thinking about strawberries and books to notice.

I stared at the name, imagining it catching on fire. The odds of him, not only being there, but being seated next to me were ridiculously high. I was torn between finding someone I could bribe to switch seats with me, and leaving to go buy a scratch-off ticket.

Raising my glass back up and taking an extra-long pull, I flicked the folded card off the table, satisfaction filling me when I heard the light *thunk* of it hitting the floor. Served him right. Why the hell would he have been invited anyway? He didn't freaking live here.

I leaned back and crossed my legs, proud of my personal win and simmering with the knowledge he'd show up, only to wander around aimlessly, looking for his chair.

But my joy died a quick death when an arm suddenly appeared at my side, making me nearly jump out of my skin.

I froze, watching it through my peripheral as it lowered to the floor. A shoulder and side profile appeared next for a split second before it paused and retreated out of sight. Then a throat cleared behind my chair.

Oh my God.

I was just about to turn around and profusely apologize to whichever event worker caught my immature action when a suit-clad, painfully familiar, male body stepped between my seat and the next, hovering uncomfortably close to me.

Embarrassment crept up the back of my neck, which only made me want to scream into a pillow. I shouldn't feel embarrassed for not wanting to sit next to him. If anything, I should only feel shame for getting caught.

Because, of course, out of every person who could have caught me, it was fucking Adrian.

You'd have thought with all the years Madison and I had snuck around as teens and gotten into mischief that I'd be a little better at checking to make sure no one was looking before I did something. But here we were.

Adrian slipped into his seat, his suit sleeve brushing against the bare skin of my arm as he did. I scooted to the far left of my chair, re-crossing my legs away from him until I was teetering on the edge.

What I really wanted to do was get up and leave, but the thought of his smug face at my retreat was enough to keep my ass planted in my seat. I refused to let him have the satisfaction of winning.

"Layla."

He practically purred my name, and I gritted my teeth so hard I felt my molars disintegrating. Why did his voice have to be so freaking smooth and melodic? I ignored him, staring at my plate like it was the most interesting thing in the world.

I may have also muttered "asshole" into my drink while pretending to sip it. But that was neither here nor there.

A low chuckle resounded beside me, and I hated that it made his voice sound even sexier. "What? No hello? I know you know my name. You said it no less than twice the night we met."

His fingers twirled the name card in his hand. Once. Twice. Then he leaned toward me just enough for me to feel the heat from his body and dropped it onto my plate.

His full, swirly name stared back at me, mocking me as much as his words had. *Asshole, asshole, asshole.* If I had a nickel for every time that word entered my head about him, I could buy Madison and myself a goddamn mansion.

He continued staring at the side of my face, arrogance seeping from his pores as he waited for me to concede. Still refusing to look at him, I set my drink down and tipped my head, sucking on my front teeth.

"Not sure what it says about you that I already forgot it then," I finally said, running the tip of my middle finger around the rim of my glass and smearing the residual lipstick on it.

"You sure? I could've sworn you even used my middle name at one point."

My finger froze, and my throat tickled with the sudden urge to laugh. I forcibly swallowed it down. *Absolutely fucking not.* Instead, I cleared my throat and picked up my phone to busy my hands.

"Are you going to ignore me the entire night?"

I sniffed, scrolling through social media but not actually seeing a thing. "Yep. Now we're even, so leave me alone."

He was silent for a moment, but I could still feel him looking at me. Part of me wondered if this was how he'd felt the night I'd approached him, but then I shoved the thought away. I had a good reason to be a jerk. He, however, had not.

"You know, besides Larry Bosenet, you're the only person I

know here."

Did he think that would sway me? Guilt me into not hating him for sliding into town, being an ass to my face, and then taking money from my pocket? *Twice?*

Setting my phone face down on my clutch, I picked up my glass and took a sip. "One might think that was your sign you shouldn't be here."

His hand went to his chest. "Ouch."

"And you don't know me," I continued, knocking back the rest of the champagne.

He crossed his arms and leaned back, balancing the chair on the back two legs. "We're on a full-name basis, Layla Davis. I feel like that means I do know you."

God, why had I ever approached this man? "Please go away."

I could practically hear the smile in his voice. I was going to have lockjaw by the time tonight was over.

"This is my chair. Didn't you see my name marking this spot?" he asked.

"Looked like it was on the floor to me."

He continued like I hadn't spoken, rocking his chair back and forth. "What were the odds they'd put us at the same table," he mused.

"Slim."

"Hm. I'd have to agree. Which makes one wonder if it was perhaps more than chance?"

Oh no, he didn't. I slammed my empty glass down, thanking God that it didn't shatter, and turned toward him for the first time, only to immediately regret it.

Adrian Waters cleaned up nice. Really fucking nice.

His shoulder-length, blonde hair was loose and brushed back from his face, but somehow still just as unruly as the first time I'd seen him. Long lashes framed his icy blue eyes, and his jaw was covered in a thin, trimmed beard that accentuated the stupid smirk on his face.

My traitorous eyes dipped down just long enough to take in his ensemble, a well-fitted, smokey-gray suit jacket over a solid black shirt and jeans. His fingers danced across both the tabletop and my sanity, making my eye twitch.

"Are you fucking kidding me? You think I *asked* to sit next to you?"

"Language," he chided, clicking his tongue. "You're at a high-end establishment, Layla Davis. Appearances are important." A wink. "Especially for someone who just lost her biggest gig and needs to network."

I masked my face—barely—but internally, I flinched, his words hitting home and burrowing into my chest. I fucking loathed this man.

"Presumptuous of you to assume you know my financial situation and quality of gigs."

He lowered his chair to all four legs and twisted toward me, resting his arm on the back of it. "Is it?"

I could hear Madison's voice in my head, telling me to breathe in and out. If I murdered him and went to prison, she'd be stuck paying the entire rent alone.

Exhaling, I put on my best bitch face, determined not to gift him with getting another heated rise out of me. "I'm truly curious, *Waters*," I said, refusing to utter his first name again and wishing it hadn't felt so good the first time I had.

"What's it like walking around with so much audacity? Is it heavy? Do you ever have to set it down and take breaks? Roll the shoulders out? Stretch your jaw?"

He blinked at me but recovered quickly, his lips curving in a way that was so sexy I immediately wanted to punch him in the face. "On the contrary, it's quite light. And I'd wager it feels a whole lot better than that stick you have up your ass."

And that was my cue to go, or I really was going to punch him. I'd rather miss out on the meal than spend another second sitting next to him. My time would be much better served mingling with literally anyone else.

I pushed away from the table and stood, adjusting my dress to make sure the underside of my rear wasn't showing. His eyes roamed down my body before quickly shooting up to my face. He swallowed hard, a grimace on his chiseled features as if the sight of me caused him pain.

Great. Fine. Not like I cared about his opinion anyway.

"I'd high-five you in congratulations for that sizzling, well-thought-out burn, but just the thought of touching you has ruined my appetite. Enjoy your night."

"Layla, wait."

"Kiss my ass, Waters.

His lips parted, but I didn't wait to hear what other insults he had to say. Lifting my glass in a mock toast, I spun on my heels and made haste toward the bar.

I would need at least three more drinks to get through the rest of the night with a smile on my face.

Chapter
6

I NIBBLED MY toast, watching Madison run around like a headless chicken. She'd accidentally slept in, which I'd bet my next paycheck was her boyfriend's fault.

"Jamie! We gotta go right now!" she hollered, hurriedly dumping some food into the dogs' bowls before grabbing her cold cup of coffee and chugging it.

She shuddered, setting it into the sink, and scurried toward the door to put her shoes on.

"Jamie!"

"I *know*," he yelled from his room, the sound of something—likely a book—flopping onto his nightstand.

A smile pulled at my lips as he stomped past my hunched position at the kitchen table. "Someone put on his sassy pants this morning."

He looked over his shoulder to stick his tongue out at me and promptly tripped over Sadie, who was attempting to merge into his skin and become one with him.

"Sadie, get your furry butt over here and leave him alone. You can't go with him."

She started trotting toward me until she noticed the fresh dog food and beelined for it, ignoring my existence completely. I shook my head and stuffed the remaining square of my toast in my mouth, washing it down with my own coffee.

Standing, I took my empty plate to the sink and listened to Garrett try to convince Madison he could take Jamie to school. I poked my head around the bar to see them staring at each other like stubborn bulls.

"I can take him," I said, uttering the words before I even realized I was.

I wasn't sure what made me offer, considering I definitely couldn't. Well, I *could*, as long as I didn't do my hair. Or put makeup on. Or brush my teeth.

Garrett shook his head. "No, it's okay, Layla. I can take him." He gripped Madison's shoulders and leaned down over her face. "Let me do this, Maddie."

My heart lurched at the look in his eyes. Love, determination, adoration, need. It was all burning and swirling as he looked at my best friend.

I enjoyed dating. I liked sex and hanging out with someone who shared my interests, but until I saw the look he gave her—and the look she gave him as she conceded—I didn't realize just how badly I wanted what she had.

Not Garrett, specifically. The man was hot, but he was far too whipped for my taste. I wanted someone who would look at me the way he looked at Madison, but who would also fight with me and tell me when an outfit made me look like a can of biscuits.

I wanted love. I just didn't want sweet and tender. I wanted something so hot and raw that it both singed me and made me crawl back for more.

Adrian's face flashed through my mind. His snappy comebacks and devilish smirks. But I shook my head, forcing the image of him out of my mind. I had no business thinking about him. Especially the ludicrous idea of that self-absorbed brat loving anyone other than himself.

"Layla?"

My head darted up from where I'd been staring, unseeing, at the bar to see Jamie standing on the other side. "Yeah?"

He raised his brow, scrunching his lips up toward his nose. "I said, I hope you have a good day."

"Oh, sorry, bud. You too. Behave at school, listen to your teacher, and all that good stuff."

He rolled his eyes as he followed his mom and Garrett out the door, but I caught the tiny grin he was trying to hide. He might outgrow me soon, but for now, at least one guy loved me. And I'd take it.

Yanking my eyelid to the side to apply some much-needed

eyeliner, I about stabbed myself with it when my phone went off. I cursed and glanced down to see my mother's face on the screen. Her time zone was an hour behind mine, so it was too early for her to call.

"Hello?" I said, fingers crossed that nothing was wrong.

"Good morning. Did I catch you at a bad time?" Her calm voice instantly soothed my nerves, and my shoulders loosened. My mother's voice could do that to anyone, not just because she was my mother. Something about it immediately put you at ease and made you feel welcomed and loved.

"I'm about to head to work, but I have a few minutes. What's up?"

I heard a familiar squeak, and then the sound of a quiet sigh. I could picture exactly what she was doing, laid out in her favorite recliner, thick white socks on, hair a feisty mane that suited her personality, and a cup of steaming tea in her hand.

God, I missed her.

"I just wanted to chat. You're always so busy with work on the weekends and usually spending time with Jamie and Madison on the weeknights, I thought morning might be the best time to get you all to myself."

Guilt gnawed at me. "You can call me whenever, Mom, you know that."

"I just don't want to be a bother," she said.

I rolled my eyes. "You and I both know you have no problem bothering me."

She laughed, and we continued chatting as I finished getting ready, mostly about my gigs and new songs—of which I didn't have any—and how she and my stepdad were doing. She asked about Madison and Jamie, and I couldn't help but tell her about a prank Jamie had orchestrated on Garrett the other day.

My mother was the queen of pranks and jump scares. But when her laughter died down, there was a slight pause. Not quite awkward, but somehow heavy.

"So, Madison seems pretty happy with her boyfriend, then?"

I nodded, and then remembering she couldn't see me, grunted my agreement as I applied the last swipe of my mascara and tossed it on the counter. I'd clean it all up later. Maybe.

She hummed. "I wonder how long they'll wait until they start a family."

I scoffed, clicking off the bathroom light and entering the living room to grab my purse and shoes. There was an embarrassing amount of dog hair on my slacks, but I'd used the last sheet of my lint roller yesterday, so it'd have to do.

"They've only been officially dating for a few months, Mom. I'm sure he wouldn't mind, but Mads is basically a sloth when it comes to commitment."

"Well, you never know. Accidents happen, and then there'll be a wedding, and a new house, and just a lot of changes."

Sensing the direction of the conversation, I sighed and snatched my coat out of the little closet by the door. "Stop with the passive comments; I know what you're getting at. I can literally see the bush you're prancing around," I said, moving my phone from one ear to the other as I slipped my arms through my coat.

A frustrated huff echoed through the phone. "I love Madison. You know I do. But I just want to make sure you're doing what's best for you too."

"I am. My boss is cool, and I actually have some amazing gigs here." *Minus one*, I thought. "I'm fine."

"I know, but you need to start thinking about what you want a year, or even five years, from now. Whether she's a sloth or a cheetah, Madison will want to live with her boyfriend one day."

An oily feeling swirled in my gut. One I was determined to ignore with every fiber of my being. "They practically do already. We all live in the same house. All that's missing is a doorway connecting his side to ours."

In truth, I often wondered how many times the idea of taking a hammer to the wall had crossed Garrett's mind. Knowing him, probably a few dozen.

There was a beat of silence. "He'll eventually propose to her, Layla. And they'll want to start a family."

"I know that," I said, harsher than I'd intended. I didn't need the reminder. The inevitable fact constantly dug into my head enough on its own.

She clicked her tongue. "Don't get snappy with me because you don't like the truth. Just because you hate green doesn't make the grass any other color."

"I didn't mean it that way, I'm sorry," I said, aware of the fact that my momma would gladly show up on my doorstep tomorrow just to whoop my ass if I needed it. Hell, the woman used to make me do pushups on the side of the road as a kid if I was misbehaving in the car.

She was terrifying when she wanted to be, but she was also a powerhouse, and I respected the ever-loving shit out of her.

She sighed again when I didn't say anything more. "The question is, how long do you truly want to live in North Carolina?"

"Madison still needs me." The words came without thought, but that niggling feeling remained. How much longer would she need me?

"She's settling down, Layla. And you need to decide if you want to stay there when it happens. Your family is here."

I chewed on my lip, not saying anything for a moment. I didn't have an answer. Not for her or myself. Because I didn't know what I wanted or what I'd do.

"Just something to start thinking about."

"I know."

We said our goodbyes, my mom sensing I didn't want to talk anymore. I needed to get to work anyway. Ken may be flexible with when I showed up, but he was only *so* flexible.

Giving Sadie one last goodbye scratch—Rugpants was already buried in a blanket somewhere—I slipped out the door, locking it behind me.

I headed down the porch and driveway, walking like a newborn giraffe to keep from slipping. Unlocking my car, I tossed my purse to the passenger seat and glared daggers at my icy windshield. It wasn't thick and could easily thaw in about ten minutes, but the idea of sitting in my car staring at ice melt always made me feel like I was straddling the line of "too lazy."

Grumbling out a curse and wishing I hadn't lost my only

pair of gloves, I snatched my ice scraper from behind my front seat and worked it across the windshield, one cold swipe at a time.

Yet another reason it'd be really fucking nice to have my own version of a Garrett. I was almost done, fingers pink and screaming at me, when I heard a slight shuffling behind me, followed by a throat clearing.

"Excuse me."

I whipped around, ready to shove my scraper into an eyeball if someone even thought to sneak up and rob me, only to find a pinched-faced woman standing a few feet behind me. Holding a soccer ball.

She smiled. Or what could almost be considered a smile. "You're Layla, right?"

She was dressed in a formless, brown dress that washed out her already chalky-white skin, with closed-toe, nude heels, and had her hair pulled back into a tight bun. I instantly recognized her sharp features and the slightly longer nose that always seemed to be in everyone's damn business all up and down the block.

Kathy Newman. Our bitchy neighbor who lived with her husband and two kids across the street from us. Madison had tried being friendly to her once only to discover the interaction hadn't been worth a second of her time.

Kathy had taken one look at Madison's sinfully unwed parenting status and instantly decided she was trash. That'd been months ago, and Kathy still refused to acknowledge Madison existed anytime they were both outside.

I fucking hated people like that. Which was probably why I felt zero guilt leveling an unimpressed look her way and crossing my arms. "Sorry, but I'm not interested in buying anything."

She blinked rapidly, her jaw jutting forward and her hands tightening around the ball she was clearly returning. "I'm not selling anything."

"Oh," I said, looking her up and down and crinkling my nose as if confused as to why she'd walk over. "Well, I'm not really interested in hearing about Jesus today either."

"I'm your neighbor," she snapped, before closing her eyes and gathering herself. She smoothed her palms down her dress, and it took everything in me not to burst out laughing at the disgust on her face.

I mastered my face just in time before her eyes popped back open. She held the soccer ball up an inch, a forced smile plastered across her face. "I found this in my yard."

I glanced down at it and back at her twice, clutching the scraper tighter in my hand. "Huh. Guess the wind must've blown it over last night. Sorry about that."

Lie. I wasn't. Jamie had a bad habit of not putting it away, but she easily could've dropped it in our yard at any point without saying a word.

But I tossed the scraper onto the floorboard of my car and walked toward her, taking the ball from her outstretched hands. "Thanks," I said, expecting her to immediately leave. But instead, she brushed her hands against each other and watched me.

"I thought you were just a visitor at first, which was why I never introduced myself," she said, like I gave a shit. "I'm Kathy Newman."

I just continued staring at her with the same unmoving, unimpressed expression.

Silence.

Keep it together, Layla. Don't you dare laugh. Poker face, poker face, poker face.

"Okay, well, it's been lovely meeting you, Katie Newport, but I'm…"

"Kathy Newman."

"What?"

She huffed out of her nose like a little angry bull. "Never mind." A pause. "So, your friend and Mr. Rowe are seeing each other?"

Yep, still nosey as shit. I nodded, inching toward my car and tossing the ball in to join my purse. I was definitely going to leave it in there for a while as punishment for Jamie leaving it outside again.

"Are they pretty serious?"

I mentally rolled my eyes. What did I look like, a fucking gossip pal? But I nodded again, allowing myself the tiniest of grins. "I honestly wouldn't be surprised if he bought the entire duplex," I said, knowing that was the opposite of the answer she wanted.

"Oh." She looked past me, her eyes darting from our side to Garrett's. "Should we be expecting a wedding sometime soon?" she asked, her words dripping with ill-concealed disapproval.

God, I seriously hoped that when the day came that we

moved out, someone far worse than us moved in. No one who would endanger her or her kids, of course, but a loud, obnoxious neighbor. One who mowed the lawn at five in the morning.

Or maybe an atheist who'd loudly challenge her on all the pettiness and judgments she hid behind her so-called religion. I'd cross my fingers for the latter.

But right now, I was done with the conversation, and definitely fucking late to work, so I decided to poke the bear one last time. For Madison.

"No wedding. Sadly, North Carolina hasn't legalized polyamory yet, so unless that day comes, we'll just continue on as we are. We're married in the ways that truly matter anyway."

"Oh…I—"

"In our hearts."

She took a quick step back. "I didn't realize—"

"And our beds," I tacked on before she could finish whatever rubbish she was about to spew, fluttering my eyelashes at her.

Her face turned a shade of reddish-purple I'd never seen on a human being before, and she whipped around, power walking to her house like her life depended on it.

I cackled, not even bothering to hide the sound, and wished I'd had the forethought to record the conversation. Madison was going to piss herself when I told her.

Chapter
→7←

I GLARED AT the phone in my hand, tempted to smash the ignore button. I had nothing good to say to Larry, and definitely nothing the drivers lingering around my office needed to hear.

My finger hovered over the red icon, but I chickened out at the last second and swiped my thumb across the screen. Just the thought of not answering when he might have a gig, and then him giving it to Adrian instead, was not something my pride could risk.

"I'm working. What do you need?" I snapped, making more than one head turn my direction. I shot a glare the drivers' way, letting them know to mind their own business and twisted my chair around so my back was to them.

"I know you're mad, Layla, but I promise you—"

"Your promises mean nothing, *Lair*."

"I didn't have a choice," he said in a rush. "They were asking for something new, and I'd just run into Adrian earlier in the day and had scheduled a meeting with him. It was pure coincidence."

I ran my free hand through my hair, shoving it angrily through a few knotted strands. Men were so fucking dense.

"I'm not mad about the gig, Larry." At least, not anymore. "I'm pissed because you lied to my face, and because you picked the worst person in the world to take my spot."

There was a pause on his end of the line, and then he sputtered out, "Worst person? Why do you say that? He's one of the highest-paid musicians in Raleigh."

"Because he's a selfish prick who thinks he's God's gift to music."

A chorus of low "Oh's" sounded behind me, and I rolled my eyes. People tended to think truck drivers were gruff, rough men, but in actuality, they were more like a bunch of gossiping old ladies.

"Let me make it up to you, Layla. I talked to Jemmy's, and I think you'll like what we came up with."

I sat back, tucking my legs beneath me in my chair and using the desk to twist back and forth. "Then tell me quick. I need to get back to work."

"Damn right you do," Ken hollered from his office. I snorted, knowing he didn't actually give a shit that I was on the phone.

"It's more than I want to lay out over the phone. Can you come out tonight so we can talk and plan out the schedule for the next few months? There's that new coffee shop not far from your place. I'll buy you the largest size with an extra shot."

I slouched, grumbling into the phone. I hated giving in to people who didn't deserve it. It made my skin crawl. But since no one from the holiday party had called me to talk about collaborating yet, I didn't exactly have a choice if I wanted to continue playing at new places. I needed Larry's connections.

"Fine. But you're buying me a brownie too."

My stomach had been growling for the last solid half hour. After driving straight home from work and taking the dogs for a walk, I'd fallen face-first onto my bed and passed out. If it hadn't been for Madison banging around the kitchen making dinner, I might've slept right on through the night.

I'd walked out with wrinkle lines down one side of my face to be bombarded by the comforting smell of spaghetti and garlic bread. Madison held out a plate for me, and I'd taken all of one step toward it before remembering I had to skip it and meet Larry for a measly pastry and coffee.

This man was number one on my hit list.

So now, here I was, hiding my face in a scarf, freezing my ass off, walking across a parking lot toward We Mean Beans-ness coffee shop.

Stepping in and shaking off the frigid air that had crawled into my soul in the sixty-second walk, I glanced around, expecting the typical—modern yet still smells like college textbooks—coffee shop vibe, only to do a double-take.

It was, indeed, a coffee shop, complete with dim lighting and small tables that barely fit a laptop. But behind the counter was also an entire shelf of liquor bottles and a menu listing every popular coffee and cocoa-flavored alcoholic beverage known to man.

Huh, guess they really did mean beans-ness. Noted.

Grabbing a to-go menu from the stand next to the door, I cut across the lobby, approaching Larry, who'd started waving his hands around like an idiot the moment I'd stepped in.

"You're actually on time," he joked, his voice carrying past me to every occupant in the room even though I stood a foot away from his high-top table. Apparently, my face wasn't enough of an indication that I didn't find him remotely funny because he continued, "I wasn't expecting you for another ten minutes."

I just stared at him, menu in one hand, phone in the other, contemplating my life choices. "And I wasn't expecting you to be annoying from the first sentence out of your mouth, yet here we are."

His lips snapped shut, and a tiny snippet of me felt a little bad when he looked legitimately insulted. I sighed, pulling out the seat across from him and plopping down, unceremoniously tossing all my shit onto the table.

"Sorry, Larry. It seems I'm a tad feisty today."

He shifted in his seat, fingering the pen and physical calendar on the table before him. He was one of the few people I knew who still preferred the paper one over a digital one.

"You're always feisty, Layla. It's a character trait at this point, and we both know that," he said, his eyes catching on something over my shoulder.

I shrugged and pulled my legs up to my chest, resting my feet on the edge of my chair and wrapping my coat around my knees. God, I hated winter.

"Anyway, I'm here. Now the real question is, where are the brownie and giant coffee you promised? Because I'm going to be honest, Larry, it better be a hot one. I'm a popsicle." My stomach let out an embarrassingly loud growl. "A hungry popsicle."

He only seemed to fidget more, shifting his pen back and forth across his paper and darting nervous looks over my shoulder. I raised a brow and sat up straighter, my spidey senses tingling when he still hadn't met my gaze.

"If you're about to tell me you left your wallet at home, I'm going to be pissed. I only came to hear you out because of the goodies you promised."

"I have them."

The reply was what I was looking for, but it didn't come from my agent. I froze. I knew that smooth, deep voice, just as sure as I recognized the barely contained smirk hidden within it.

Every muscle in my body tensed until I was certain I'd shatter if I fell. "Larry."

Finally finding his balls enough to look at me, he shrugged. "After what you said about him on the phone, I didn't think telling you ahead of time was a good idea."

So that's what his pause had been about. I dropped my feet back to the floor and laughed, shaking my head. Why was I surprised? Why did I still give this slimy bastard the power to disappoint me? I had no one to blame but my damn self.

"Goodbye, Larry."

An arm appeared at my side, sliding past in a way that was irritatingly similar to the night of the holiday party. Only this time, it was covered in a black coat rather than a suit. He set down the steaming cup, and then a second arm joined it, dropping a paper-wrapped muffin in front of me.

"I heard that earthquake from all the way over at the register. Eat. You'll be less hangry."

I reared back, twisting to glare at Adrian as he silently rounded my chair and sat beside me. He wore dark-wash jeans and a black coat that somehow made him appear both relaxed and put-together at the same time. His blonde hair was tied at his nape, drawing attention to his scruffy jawline, and his blue eyes sparked as he rested his ankle over a knee and met my gaze.

Fuck him for being so damn beautiful. Seriously. Only I would have someone who looked like a god walking among men as my self-proclaimed mortal enemy.

I crossed my arms. "I wanted a brownie."

"I'm aware."

I sucked on my front teeth and tipped my head, eyeing him. "Well, run along then. The deal was coffee and a brownie."

If it'd been anyone else, hell, even if it'd been Larry, I wouldn't have dared make such a spoiled comment—especially because the muffin smelled sinfully delicious—but it was Adrian. So my guilt stayed happily nestled in my chest, undisturbed.

He raised a brow, drumming his long fingers across the tabletop. "I said I was aware of your request. Didn't say I cared."

My mouth popped open. "Oh my God, I don't even know you, and I hate you."

He tipped his chair on the back two legs and laced his fingers behind his head, that stupid smirk plastered to his face. "Sure, you do."

Nostrils flaring, I shoved to my feet, stuffing my phone in my purse and looking at Larry, who'd wisely stayed silent. "Enjoy your meeting, or whatever the hell this was supposed to be. Let me know when you actually have work for me."

"He does."

I rounded on Adrian; surprised smoke wasn't coming from my ears. "I wasn't talking to you."

"Give us twenty minutes."

"No."

"Fine," he said, lowering his chair to the floor and resting his forearms on the table. "Enjoy all your quiet Friday nights at home."

My mouth snapped shut, and he grinned, knowing he had me.

"So, you're seriously going to continue taking my gigs? And admit to it? That's some real class you got there, Waters."

He shrugged. "I'm not going to feel sorry for someone who isn't trying very hard to get them back."

First, was he fucking kidding me? And second, why the hell was he right? I'd never met anyone who gave my shit back to me and made valid points while doing so. It was infuriating.

Because I *wasn't* trying very hard. I'd seen them working together and immediately gotten angry and given up. And knowing not only did I do that, but Adrian had noticed? Yeah, that stung.

He reached over, unbothered by my daggered expression that was meant more for myself than him, and tore off a chunk of the muffin. "Enjoy your night," he said, stuffing it into his mouth.

I watched him chew, stewing in my own insufferable pride. I'd been the one who wanted to leave, but now that he was telling me to? No, thanks. I stepped around my chair and paused next to his. "What? No 'Davis, wait' this time?"

He tore another chunk off the top, stealing most of the crunchy cinnamon morsels and making me immediately regret not eating it. "Nope. If you're set on continuing to be a raging bitch, then the door is right over there."

I fisted my hands at my sides, trying to keep my cool. "You're acting like I don't have a good fucking reason not to trust either of you."

"On the contrary," he said, dusting his fingers off on his jeans, "I acknowledge you have a reason. But now it's time to get over it. This is business. Either you want the business or not. I don't want to work with you either, but the fact is that Jemmy's wants both of us. And I can't afford to turn down anything I don't have to, especially a venue with such eager tippers."

"Why?"

"As you so clearly pointed out, we don't know each other, so I don't see how that's any of your business."

"Fine," I huffed. "But can you please explain what *your* reason is for not wanting to work with me? I haven't done a single thing to you."

He reached for my muffin again, and I smacked his hand away, grabbing the entire thing and taking a giant bite out of it. His eyes flashed to mine, heat flaring in them.

"No, you just bombarded me at a bar when I wasn't mentally capable of dealing with anyone, then verbally assaulted me at a holiday party instead of apologizing."

Verbally assault? *Apologize?* "Now, wait just a minute—"

"I feel like this will work out splendidly."

We both whipped our heads to glare at Larry, who'd piped in his unwanted opinion like we didn't both detest him as much as we did each other.

He withered slightly under the attention but swallowed and continued. "If you two put even half as much passion into your music as you do into each other, you'll be phenomenal together."

I snorted, unwrapping my scarf from around my neck and draping it over my forearm. "Not what I'd call it, but sure, Larry."

I didn't sit back down, feeling more equal with Adrian's tall ass while standing, but I also didn't leave. Keeping my focus on Larry, I asked, "So that's the deal then? Jemmy's wants not just us in general, but us performing together?" *Please say no. Please say no.*

Larry nodded.

"Every Friday?"

Another nod. Damnit.

I took an aggressive bite of the muffin, it was cinnamon apple, and it was ten times better than a thawed brownie. Not that I'd admit it. "And they're willing to pay for that? Because I'm not accepting half of what I usually earn."

Adrian's fingers resumed their eye-twitching tapping. "Already taken care of. I told them we weren't willing to split it, and they agreed to pay double, plus a little extra." He flicked some rogue crumbs off the table. "They certainly bring in enough revenue to afford it."

True. "All right," I said, stuffing the last piece of delectable goodness into my mouth to hide my reaction. "I'll think about it and get back to you." But the truth was he had me at *plus a little extra*. There would be no thinking unless I magically came up with another venue that paid as much.

Larry watched me pull my car keys out of my purse with a mild look of surprise. "Layla, we really need to know—" but Adrian cut him off, leaning forward in his chair until he was far too close to me.

"It's a simple yes or no, Davis."

"And I said I'll think about it," I said, hiking my purse higher on my shoulder and snatching the coffee from the table. I needed to leave and talk to Madison. Her level-headed-ness with shit like this was exactly what I needed right now.

But before I could twist away from the table and make haste out of there and away from those icy blue eyes that saw too much, Adrian's hand whipped out and grabbed mine, wrapping around both my fingers and the cup.

"The coffee stays."

I blinked at him. "Excuse me?"

"You heard me," he said, pulling the cup—and me—closer.

My nostrils flared, and I was seconds from stabbing my car key into his thigh. No one, and I mean no one, took my caffeine and got away with it.

"The only reason I even agreed to come out tonight was one, because I didn't know you would be here, and two, because Larry over there promised me this coffee." I yanked back, pulling his arm hard enough to make his chair screech across the floor like a snarling, unholy demon.

Adrian responded in kind until we were playing a fucked-up version of Tug of War right there in the middle of We Mean Beans-ness. It wasn't my most mature, sophisticated moment, but he'd started it.

"The coffee was a bribe to get you to work with me," he said after we'd begun to draw the attention of other customers, finally ripping the cup out of my hand.

In my perfect world, the lid would've ripped off and spilled scalding coffee all over his perfectly fitting jeans. But instead, the world laughed and gave me the finger, letting Adrian lift the intact cup to his lips.

"Don't you even think about it," I ground out. That was my only consolation prize. The only thing I had going for me that made this trip out in the cold worth it. Well, that and the muffin.

But he just raised a brow. "No agreement, no coffee." And he took a sip.

Chapter

I STEPPED INTO the house, keeping the doorknob twisted as I shut it so the latch wouldn't echo out and set off Rugpants's incessant barking. I'd barely turned the lock before Sadie's nose was ramming into my thigh in greeting, her tail thumping against the wall louder than Rugpants's barking would've been.

"Oh my God, yes, I see you. Give me a second," I said, pushing her bulk of a body away and directing her to the living room so I could remove my coat and shoes.

Madison watched me struggle, curled up on the couch with a giant mug in one hand, a chocolate chip cookie in the other, and a horrifyingly thick textbook in her lap. I waved, not surprised to see her sitting there, and aimed straight for the kitchen to grab my own drink.

She closed her book and took a huge drink before slouching

down and resting the mug on the side table. "I made a pot a little bit ago, but it should still be warm if you'd like some."

I opened the fridge and pilfered around, moving leftovers and condiments to the side until I found what I was looking for. "No, thanks, that sounds too heavy for my neglected stomach. I'll stick to a quarter pop."

"Soda."

Shutting the fridge, I set the dollar store, grape-flavored beverage on the counter and narrowed my eyes at Madison over the bar. "Soda…*pop*."

She grinned, shaking her head and looking down at Rugpants, who was slowly squeezing in between the textbook and her chest as if hoping Madison wouldn't notice if she moved slow enough.

Taking a sip of caffeine-free, carbonated sugar, I made my way into the living room, somehow both wide awake and ready for bed at the same time. If there was anything stress was exceptionally good at, it was confusing the hell out of my body.

I plopped down on the edge of the coffee table next to where Sadie had curled up on the floor, staring at Madison over my can as I took another sip.

"Well?" I asked, when she only picked up her own drink and lifted it to her face, not saying a word. "Are you going to ask me how awful it went?"

Smacking her lips, she tried to hide her smile. "No, I can already tell it went better than expected."

I huffed, setting the can down and leaning back on my hands. "Wrong. It was a fucking shit show."

She raised her brows, looking every bit like a mother listening to her kid's exaggerated story. Setting her textbook on the side table next to her mug, she adjusted Rugpants in her lap and gestured to my body.

"Really? Because you grabbed a soda instead of wine, and your bra is not only still on but clasped. I feel like it probably went better than your mind is telling you."

I narrowed my eyes but didn't argue. She was right. My bras didn't make it past the front door on my worst days.

She grinned at whatever look she saw on my face. "But yes, I do want to hear about all the excuses Larry laid at your feet."

"Fine," I said, "it wasn't a shit show, but someone did steal my coffee and piss me off." After buying me a muffin.

That got her attention. "Who? Larry?"

"I'll give you one more guess."

"No," she said, about as loud as she dared, with Jamie sleeping on the other side of the wall.

"Oh yeah. The one and only."

She sat up straighter, her brown eyes widening. "Spill."

"I mean, it's not the first time you've had to do something you don't want to do to get your foot in the door," she said, handing me a fourth cookie.

I received the first when I'd told her about Adrian's comment about my growling stomach, the second when I'd told her he'd called me a raging bitch, and the third when I'd explained how he stole back the coffee. This fourth one I was pretty sure was just an excuse to grab another, herself.

"What do you mean?" I said, shoving the entire thing in my mouth and speaking around it. "Like playing shitty gigs?"

She washed her bite down with what had to be cold coffee and eyed me under raised brows. "Do you not remember your Bluegrass days when you used to play the mandolin? And let's not even mention the fact that your mom had you performing that song about a whore house when you were like eight because it caught people's attention."

I burst out laughing, looking up from my phone—where I'd been in the process of stalking Adrian on social media. "God, I forgot about that."

Her smile faded as she glanced down to her lap and scratched Rugpants behind the ears. "In all seriousness, Layla, if you don't want to work with him, then don't. No man is worth your time if he makes you unhappy, work-related or not. But if he's someone you can tolerate and gets you where you want to be, I say do it."

I sighed and shoved the hair out of my face, looking back down at my phone and the icy blue eyes staring back at me from a three-year-old photo. "I just don't trust him not to screw me over somehow. He's already done it once."

"I get that," she said, resting her head on the couch. She looked exhausted. "But we didn't trust Garrett at first either, and he was a giant asshole too."

True. Still, even at his worst, Madison's boyfriend had never come close to screwing her over. There was a difference between having an asshole personality and *being* an asshole. But I didn't bother explaining that. If I decided to work with Adrian, which I both did and didn't want to do, she'd meet him soon enough and figure it out for herself.

"Where is Garrett, by the way?" I asked, going back to scrolling through tagged photos like it was an Olympic sport. It wasn't often we had a night at home by ourselves these days. It was nice.

Her smile widened. "He's having a guys' night with his brother and Michael." She glanced at her own phone. "Honestly, he's been gone longer than I'd thought he would be."

I looked up, frowning. "Michael?"

"Yeah, the single dad, remember? We met him at Jamie's soccer game a few months ago. His son, Ian, goes to school with him."

"That's right. Did Garrett go out by choice, or did you have to make him?"

"Both," she chuckled, moving Rugpants to the floor so she could flop face-first on the couch and snuggle into a pillow. Her dog's bug eyes stared at her for a moment in betrayal before she circled a few times and curled up next to Sadie.

"He's not the most social guy," she continued, "but he's working on it. Kind of like how you should be."

I glared at her over my phone and shoved off the coffee table, stepping over the dogs to plop on top of her, gratifying in her irritated *humph*.

"Says the woman who never leaves her house unless she's going to work or doing something with her kid."

I wiggled around until I got comfy and pulled my phone back up, continuing my online stalking of Adrian Waters. Besides photos other people had tagged him in, he didn't appear to use much social media. Which was admirable, but irritating, given I was actively trying to dig up dirt on him.

Like why he'd left Raleigh and all the bigger shows to come here.

"I didn't mean the social part," Madison continued beneath me. "I meant how you should be working on getting along with Adrian. Suck it up and figure out how to make it work."

My thumb froze in its scrolling, and I slowly lowered it to my lap, angling my face toward hers. "Be weary of traitorous words, Mads. They'll rot your pretty little teeth."

She sighed. "I'm just saying, sometimes you have a bad habit of molding nothing into something," she said, squishing the pillow down to make it easier to talk. "You find competition everywhere, and you make it a personal goal to win, even if the other player doesn't even know they're playing."

"I disagree. I don't *find* competition in everything; I just acknowledge that it's already there. Everything in life is a competition, Mads. Sometimes I can ignore it, and sometimes I can't. This is one of those moments I can't."

I spun, lying flat on my back on top of her so that our butts were smooshed together. Even that was a competition, with mine easily overtaking hers. I smirked, knowing she couldn't see it. "Why are you defending him anyway?"

She twisted her head to the side as far as she could to avoid suffocating with the additional weight of my head on top of hers.

"I'm not. My point is, it doesn't have to be you against him. Larry could be right, and you two could be amazing together. Not to mention, his name is bound to draw in more people. Isn't that the goal? To have a larger audience and entice more venues to book you?"

When a few seconds passed, and I still didn't have a comeback—because there wasn't one—she hummed. "That's what I thought."

"Shut up," I said, slapping the side of her thigh hard enough to have both dogs raising their heads. "I find you less attractive when you're right."

She snorted. "So, what are you going to do?"

"Go to his next show and watch him play, I suppose." I shrugged. "If I like what I see, I'll…agree." I said the last word slowly, pretending to gag.

"You're stalling. You've already seen him and know he's good."

I shook my head, earning me a growl when the motion rubbed against her curls. "It's not just about how smooth his voice is or how sexy he looks playing the guitar. I need to see him as a performer when he doesn't know I'm watching. Just because our voices are compatible doesn't mean *we* are."

"So, you think he's sexy, huh?"

That time, I pinched her. She squealed, bucking her hips and nearly tossing me off the couch onto the dogs.

"You know," she panted, rolling to her side and giving me an evil smirk, "you might be less of a raging bitch to poor Adrian if you got laid."

"True." No argument there. I squeezed my hand between cushions, searching for my phone that'd slid off me when Madison ass-checked me off her.

"Have you reconsidered online dating? I still think it's a good idea."

I poked my tongue into my cheek and gave her a look, still digging around for my phone. Where the hell had it slid to? Garrett's side of the damn duplex? "Why are you so pushy? You certainly had a different opinion when I tried to get you to do it."

"My situation was different, and you know it. You actually *like* meeting new people. You do it every night you work."

She got up and knelt on the floor to look under the couch, pulling my long-lost device out. I hadn't clicked the screen off, and Adrian's face still filled it. Her head rose slowly, and I snatched it from her hand, avoiding her eyes like she was Medusa.

"Just because I'm good at something doesn't mean I like it."

She pushed herself off the floor, wincing when her knees popped. "I'm sure that's what every man wants to hear."

I flipped her off, listening to her answering chuckle as she started picking up her stuff to head to her room. "I might. We'll see."

"You could always have hate sex with Adrian too. That's bound to release the tension." She headed toward the kitchen to drop her mug in the sink, her lips smashed together to keep herself from laughing.

I shook my head. "I'm down. As long as it ends with me sitting on his face and suffocating him."

Chapter

9

I WAS GOING to regret this. I wasn't even in the building yet, and I already knew it. But damnit, my bank account needed the money, and my pride refused to prove him right about me.

Not to mention that, whether I liked it or not, Adrian was the best way to get more attention to my name. More attention meant higher-paying gigs, and higher pay meant quitting my day job.

I'd get exactly what I wanted, but somehow it tasted a little less sweet than I'd thought it would when I approached him that first night.

Pulling open the door to the bar, I attempted to walk straight in past Tony, the bald, wide-chested brick wall who checked IDs at the door on heavier nights. Overall, at only thirty-five years old and with a primary job at some aircraft facility, he was a nice guy. But that didn't explain why he held up an arm to block me, his fingers splayed open for my ID.

I stared at his narrowed eyes, confused. Tony never checked my ID. It made no sense to. I was there every week and had been for a while now. Everyone, including him, knew how old I was.

Tipping up the ballcap I wore to narrow my eyes right back at him, he suddenly dropped his hand, smiling at me. "Shit, sorry, Layla. I didn't recognize you." He chuckled and took in my outfit. "To be honest, I still barely do. I'm not sure if I've ever seen you walk through here looking so…"

I quirked a brow, daring him to continue that thought.

"…short," he finished, his brown eyes falling to my dirty sneakers. We both knew that wasn't what he'd been thinking, but I let it slide. His quick cover wasn't wrong, either. I'd never walked through this bar without heels on before.

I pulled my hat back down, tucking a few loose strands of hair behind my ears. "Yeah, well, I'm not working anywhere tonight, so casual it is."

He smiled again, gesturing me by so he could move on to the next person behind me. "Go enjoy yourself then. Take an extra shot for me."

I nodded, having no intention of doing that, and stepped past him, making my way in the opposite direction of the bar. With Adrian nowhere to be seen yet, I weaved around the tables closest to the back wall, eyes peeled for an open seat.

Another band, a married couple who only did covers, had already been playing for the last few hours and were just wrapping up so, thankfully, there was already a decent crowd.

Which was only going to continue to increase as their show came to an end since Adrian was next as the headliner for the night.

Finding an open table in-between two small parties, I squeezed in and made myself comfortable, pretending like I didn't look like a complete stalker in my current getup. Oddly enough, it was hard to go incognito when you had a flowing mane of blue hair.

Along with my dirty sneaks, I was also sporting jeans, a brown hoodie that wasn't nearly warm enough for the unrelenting wind, and a random ballcap Garrett had lent me.

It wasn't my hottest look. But I wanted the freedom to stare and critique Adrian's performance without him knowing I was doing so. I didn't want him to change how he did anything just because I was there—which he would certainly do if he knew.

He was just as good, if not better, than the last time I'd seen him play. Maybe because I wasn't filled with unending fury this time. Either way, there was no denying that the man could play.

And he wasn't just good at guitar or vocals alone; he was also a natural performer. He didn't throw himself around the stage dramatically or toss his hair around, thinking he was a famous rockstar. He just shifted and moved with the music. Owning the entire stage with purpose while looking fluid and natural.

My fingers itched to play with him.

I wanted to stay mad about it, but regardless of how it came about, working with Adrian was exactly what I'd hoped for. And even if it backfired and ended with both of us throwing ourselves off a cliff in frustration, I'd at least make it worth it before I died.

I rested my chin on my hand, watching him work the crowd, his persona so much different than the first night I met him. But again, that's what you did when you were a performer. The face on stage was rarely the same face you wore off it.

His current song—a combination of two covers he'd brilliantly mixed—came to an end, and applause filled the air around me as the rowdier, tipsy patrons began shouting requests. He smiled and dipped his head, sweat glistening on his brow under the stage lights as he stepped up to the mic again.

"Thanks again for being here, everyone. I know it's more for Fran's dollar drinks than for me, but I appreciate your presence anyway."

The crowd chuckled, the majority of people, indeed, holding up glasses of cheap liquor.

"I'm going to go ahead and take a short break, and then we'll be right back at it, and I'll see if I can knock out some of those requests."

Pulling his strap over his head, he held his guitar by the neck in one hand and ran his other through his hair, shoving the sweaty strands away from his face. I was admiring the way the act highlighted the sharp planes of his jaw when his eyes suddenly sliced through the crowd with purpose and connected directly with mine.

There was no hint of shock or disbelief as he held my wide gaze and tipped his head sharply to the side. Silently directing me to meet him off stage.

My ass was frozen to my seat as I stared at the empty stage, several minutes after he'd hopped off. How in the fiery depths of hell had he known I was there? It's not like he'd surveyed the crowd and accidentally noticed me. No, he'd known exactly where I was sitting.

It made no sense. Tony saw me all the time and hadn't even recognized me standing two feet away. There was no way Adrian Waters noticed me in a crowd of unfamiliar faces. I glanced around, unsure what I wanted to do.

I hadn't planned on him even knowing I'd shown up, let alone actually talking to him. I'd planned on just sneaking out afterward and shooting a text to Larry.

In the end, my pride won out, refusing to tuck tail and run out. I was a strong, independent woman, damnit.

When I finally made my way over to the musician's table, Adrian was leaning against it, a half-empty bottle of water in one hand and his phone in the other. He shot his eyes up as if sensing me, and a flicker of surprise shot through me when he immediately put his phone down and gave me his full attention.

"Took you long enough."

"Sorry," I said, turning my arms around and pretending to check them out, "I had to make sure there wasn't a tracking chip somewhere in my body first."

"Cute," he said, coming around the table to stand a few feet away from me. "Well, sorry to disappoint you, but I don't need to implant tracking devices in someone to be aware of my surroundings."

I snorted, gesturing to my body. "I'm dressed like an unremarkable white man about to follow an innocent woman home from a bookstore. I didn't even order a drink."

Then again, maybe it was those exact two things that made me stand out. Damn.

But Adrian just shook his head, looking like he was restraining a smile. "Trust me, Davis, that wasn't it. You couldn't look unremarkable if you tried."

I blinked. "What?"

His mouth snapped shut, and he looked away, huffing out his nose. "Nothing."

I wasn't sure if he'd been trying to compliment me or insult my ability to be incognito, so I decided to do us both a favor and move on.

"Seriously, though, Waters, how'd you know I'd show up tonight?"

He crossed his arms and looked over at me, resting his elbow on the back of a chair. "Because as testy as you are, you love your fans and take your job seriously. I figured you'd come to make sure I fit your image."

My brows disappeared under the bill of my hat as a smile pulled at the corner of my lips. "Is that a compliment?"

He rolled his neck, clearly uncomfortable, which only made me smile wider. "It's not a compliment to say you take your job seriously. That's setting the bar a little low, don't you think?"

My smile fell. "Well, aren't you just a steady ray of sunshine?"

Ignoring me, he tilted his head toward the stage. "Come up

and do one song with me."

Um, say what? Did he not see what I was wearing? He wanted me to go up, sans instrument, in my hoodie and ballcap, and sing harmony to him on some random song we've never practiced?

"Absolutely not."

"Really? Figured you'd appreciate the opportunity to give me a test ride before agreeing."

An image of me test driving him flashed through my head, unbidden. An image that definitely didn't involve us on stage. I shuddered. God, Madison was right. I *really* needed to get laid. "I'm not going to play with you until after we've practiced and perfected a lineup."

His lips twitched. "Practice, huh? So, you're agreeing then?"

I took a deep breath, staring out at the stage rather than at him. I was doing this for my future. Seeing his stupid, arrogant smirk wouldn't help me in that endeavor. "Yes."

His arms uncurled, and he stepped forward so suddenly, I snapped my gaze to him, ready to throw hands if needed. The man was hot as sin, but I'd break his pretty nose if I needed to.

But he stopped a foot away from me, reaching into his jacket and removing a pen. Not breaking eye contact, he leaned closer, his chest pressing against my shoulder as he reached around me to snatch a napkin off the table.

His proximity sent an instant livewire through where we touched, making all the hair along my arm rise, like a sixth sense alerting me to danger. I immediately retreated, stepping out of his way and putting a healthy distance between us.

"You could've just asked me to grab one," I said, my voice wavering slightly as I fought the urge to touch my shoulder.

But he just stared down at the napkin, his fingers gripping his pen harder than necessary before he seemed to shake himself out of it. Loosening his grip, he jotted his number down and raised the napkin out between two long fingers.

I stretched my hand out to take it, but he yanked it back, keeping it just out of reach. "I want to make sure we're on the same page, Davis. If you take this, it means you're not only agreeing to perform together, but also to put your best effort into it. Every practice, every show."

I rolled my eyes, dropping my hand to place both on my hips. "Obviously. I take my job seriously, remember?"

"*And*," he drew out, "to not be a difficult, raging bitch if I try to help and point out things like when you're pitchy."

Pitchy? This motherfu—I inhaled again, filling my lungs and holding it before exhaling heavily toward the heavens, silently asking for grace. "Fine. As long as you agree to stop calling me that and to not be a fucking dick when I point out your lyrics are basic and cliché."

The mixture of insult and surprise on his face was enough of a high to keep me satisfied for the rest of the night. Flashing him a grin that promised chaos, I thrust my hand out between us, making him flinch back.

His lip curled as he looked down at my hand, but instead of setting the napkin in it, he grasped it, squeezing his number between our palms as the edges of his calluses ground into my skin.

So, I squeezed his right back, silently mouthing, "I hate you," and wishing with everything I was that I had long enough nails to dig into his skin when he winked at me in reply.

And when I got home that night, I put his number in my phone under *Satan*.

Chapter
⤳ 10 ⤝

ONE DAY WHEN I was in middle school, sixth grade to be exact, our P.E. teacher took us outside to run a mile on the track around the football field.

I hated P.E. in general. The games, the sweat, all of it. But I *abhorred* the idea of running a whole mile. Up until that point, I was pretty sure I'd never even run half a mile in my whole twelve years of life.

Middle school kids were fucking mean, and the fear of falling behind and having everyone wait on me, whispering and staring as I came in last, quickly hit the top of my list of fears. I dreaded it with every fiber of my being each day leading up to it.

So, naturally, as one does when they're an idiot child drowning in anxiety, I ran my mouth the entire walk there about how well I ran and how easy it would be.

We'd just arrived at the stadium, cutting through the side entrance the golf carts used to move supplies, and there'd been this chain going across the little driveway. Not fully blocking it, just hovering about three inches above the ground.

And while spouting my athletic prowess to every student around me, I'd hopped over that tiny, three-inch-high chain, only to catch my foot on it and fall face-first onto the gravel drive.

A week's worth of trying to convince myself it'd be fine and twenty minutes of bragging to my peers that I wouldn't struggle the entire way around the track, and I'd ruined it in two-point-five seconds. That's all it'd taken.

Having Adrian come over to my house to practice playing together felt a lot like that fucking chain. It'd been so easy to talk a big game the other night when I'd agreed to this, but now that I was minutes away from actually playing with him?

I was terrified of tripping over that godforsaken chain in front of him and ruining the perfectly crafted persona I'd let him see.

I'd stared at the clock every minute of the last half hour at work, white-knuckling my purse straps and keys, ready to bolt the second I was clocked out. Then I'd sprinted the entire way across the truck yard, heaving in gasps of air, even as I whipped my seatbelt across my lap and shot out of the parking lot faster than I ever had.

Because there was no way I was going to let him get to my house before me. And there was no way *in hell* I was going to invite him into it before I'd had a chance to run around, Adrianproofing it. Or at least the parts of it he'd see.

I'd barely locked my car before I'd burst into the house loud enough to terrify both dogs and began sprinting around like a crazy person, picking up pop cans that I'd left on the coffee table, organizing Jamie's game controllers onto his system, hiding the creepy bug-eyed stuffed animals Madison and I hid around the house to scare each other, and everything else I could see that needed to be done.

That man wasn't going to get a single piece of ammunition to use against me about my own home. It was going to look like no one even lived here by the time I was done with it.

I sat on the edge of the couch, staring at the door with my phone clasped in my hands. I'd already brought out my guitar, tablet, and anything else I might need and set them on the floor beside me, aware he was set to arrive any minute.

Yet, I somehow could not have felt further from prepared when a knock finally sounded against the front door. I tensed, my body locking down at those three loud raps. Rugpants, however, had no such problem and shot across the room like an apex predator, barking her little hotdog heart out.

Forcing myself to my feet, I ran after her, snatching her up around her middle and running her down the hallway while she wriggled in my arms, continuing to bark.

"Sorry, Rug, it'll only be for a little bit," I whispered, all but tossing her into Madison's room and shutting the door. Madison and Jamie were set to be home in less than an hour, so she'd be fine.

Two more knocks came, and I spun, darting back down the hall and avoiding tripping over Sadie by pure luck. I felt like I was about to suffocate. Whether that was because my heart and nerves were still residing in my throat or because I'd just run around like an idiot, who knew. But I needed to bottle that shit up and fast.

Pulling my hair over my shoulders, I took a deep breath and willed my breathing to even out. I was a strong, independent woman. It was Adrian who should be nervous about entering my home. Not me.

But when I twisted the lock and yanked the door open, I found myself second-guessing my conviction and freezing for a reason that had nothing to do with the winter wind that blasted inside.

Wearing his usual black jacket over a gray hoodie, combined with his fitted jeans and black guitar case resting against his thigh, Adrian stood on my porch, looking every bit the leading role of a rockstar wet dream.

I dragged my untrustworthy eyeballs up to his face, which only made it worse as they made direct contact with his, wicked humor sparking in their depths.

"I charge a fee, you know."

My face heated, and I gripped the door again, planning to slam it in his smug face, but he held his free hand out, not so much as flinching when it smacked against his palm with a loud *thunk*.

"Go away. I changed my mind," I snapped, pushing my body weight against it.

"I'm sorry," he said, pushing back and not looking sorry at all. "I'll behave, I promise. Please let go of the door so I can come in. It's fucking freezing out here."

I stared at him a few seconds longer, leaving him in cold limbo before I slid to the side and silently allowed him inside. The quickness with which he stepped over the threshold, as if worried I'd change my mind and lock him out, had me pressing my lips together to hold back a smile.

But it quickly fell into a frown when a blur of tan fur leaped past me with unrestrained enthusiasm.

"Jesus Christ," Adrian said, stumbling back as Sadie barreled into him like a wrecking ball, jumping up onto his thighs and begging for attention like she never got any. My frown turned into a glower. Of course, she'd instantly love him. I couldn't have gotten a nip or a deep-chested bark? Figured.

"You could've warned me you had a giant dog," he said, finding his footing again and trying to calm the beast who appeared to be attempting to climb into his skin.

Sadie was only half pit, but she had enough of it in her face to make the majority of people who met her still hesitate. Making them look at her like she was a danger to society, simply for just existing as she was.

So, I instinctively tensed at his comment, ready to defend her with the same spew I gave anyone who side-eyed her at dog parks.

Yes, she's half pit, but she's the sweetest dog you'll ever meet. She's more like a loaf of bread with legs than a dog.

But as I examined his expression for any hint of irritation or uncertainty, I found none. He just grunted and set his case on the floor so he could reach out and scratch behind her ears with both hands.

Chuckling to himself when her entire butt began to sway with her tail, he gifted her a dazzling smile that had my stomach clenching in a way I was going to promptly ignore.

"Come on, Sadie, give him room to breathe."

His eyes darted up to me and then behind me, toward the hall, where at least one animal had my back. "You have more than one?"

"Yeah, but the other one would happily chew your toes off, so I put her up when you got here," I said, pulling Sadie away by her collar and instructing her to go lay down. She didn't look happy about it, but she listened, jumping up onto the couch.

Picking his case back up, he toed off his shoes and examined the living room, a note of surprise filling his expression. "This is where you live?"

"No. The owners are on vacation, so I'm just squatting in it until they return. Why?"

He shot me an unimpressed look and walked toward the couch to lean his case against it and remove his jacket. "I don't know. I guess I just pictured you living somewhere different."

"Different, how?" If he said an institution, I was going to impale him with his guitar and hoist him over the roof like a victory flag.

"Somewhere significantly hotter."

I flipped him off, even though part of me wanted to laugh at the irony considering his contact name in my phone. It was nice to know we were at least on the same page about each other.

"I'm kidding, Davis. Put your horns away," he said, sitting on the far edge of the couch and gesturing around him. "It's nice. Do you live here alone? Besides the dogs, I mean."

I wasn't sure if he was asking because he wondered how I could afford a three-bedroom place by myself, or if he'd noticed Garrett's giant ass shoes on our shoe rack. With how annoyingly observant he seemed to be, probably both.

"No, I live here with my best friend, Madison, and her son, Jamie," I said, watching my traitorous dog throw herself at the man again like she had no self-respect at all. "Her boyfriend lives on the other side of the duplex."

A blonde eyebrow raised at that. "What about yours? Are they roommates too? Double dating, neighbor-style?"

The idea of Garrett allowing anyone who wasn't family, Madison, or Jamie, into his personal space was comical. "Why would it matter where he lived?"

He shrugged, giving Sadie the love and pats she was pathetically begging for. "It doesn't. I just wanted to make sure I wasn't about to have my ass beat when someone walked through that front door with the wrong idea."

"First, don't insult me by insinuating I would invite a man into my house alone without telling my boyfriend about it," I said, coming to stand in front of him, "and second, I don't have one, so the only person who will beat your ass is me."

His lips twitched. "Noted. Well, since we only have one

short hour to work, let's jump right in and get started, then."

I smirked at his jab, remembering how our last conversation had gone after I'd texted him my address.

Satan: I'll be there from 2 to 4.
Me: No, you won't.
Satan: Okay, 3 to 5, but I'll have to leave at 5 sharp.
Me: Can't.
Satan: Davis, we have to practice.
Me: I work until 3.
Satan: What? Where? You never mentioned another job.
Me: Wouldn't you like to know.
Satan: 4 to 5
Me: Fine.

Had I been difficult? Sure. But it wasn't for no reason. Making Adrian's life difficult had quickly become my favorite thing, and I saw no reason to stop doing something that brought me such joy.

"So, how would you prefer to do this?" he asked.

I slapped a hand to my chest, pitching my voice higher and fluttering my eyelashes. "You're giving *me* the reins? *Willingly?*"

He rolled his eyes and popped his case open, removing a manila folder and his guitar, the black face of it glossy and smudge-free. "You were already going to try to do so. No reason to fight nature."

I dropped to the floor on the other side of the couch where I'd previously left my own, less shiny but tried and true acoustic.

"Look at us already getting to know each other. Larry would be so proud."

He snorted but didn't reply, reaching his arms back to quickly finger comb his hair away from his face. Holding it all in one hand, he yanked a hair tie out from under his hoodie sleeve and twisted his hair into a quick messy bun.

It was honestly impressive considering it usually took me three tries to get mine up without it looking like I had seventeen children and hadn't slept in ten days.

I'd never thought a man with long hair would be my personal cup of tea, but the way Adrian pulled it off, I might just add that to my list of *yes, pleases* for my dating roster. Especially when I thought about how nice it would be to sink my fingers into and pull.

I mentally slapped myself. Then slapped myself again when my eyes lingered a second too long on his exposed neck and jawline. Nope. Latching onto the first thing I could, I pointed to the folder he'd pulled out.

"What's all that?"

"Music. Namely, my most requested covers."

I nodded, already figuring. I'd only asked to distract myself. Honestly, I appreciated that he'd taken the time to bring lyrics. I was a fast learner and could memorize any tune, but memorizing the words to hundreds of songs was an entirely different story.

I settled in and got comfortable, resting my back against the couch and popping open my glasses case. The nerves I'd felt about Adrian showing up were slowly disappearing as my excitement for the music increased.

Although I'd never admit it out loud, I couldn't wait to see what we could do together. Nothing made my heart sing the way creating amazing music did.

"You wear glasses?"

His question caught me off guard, and I glanced up to find Adrian now sitting in the center of the couch, much closer to me than he'd been a moment ago. I shifted, feeling weird with the way he was looking at me, like how I imagined I looked at baby sloths. "All right, get it over with."

"What?"

"I'm assuming you're pointing it out because you're trying to set up an opportunity for some witty comment about them. Let me guess, it highlights my round face and isn't the right look for a performer."

The last part wasn't something I believed myself, but I'd heard it enough from Larry and a few other performers back in Kansas that I no longer wore my glasses during shows. I just increased the text size on my tablet to whatever I needed.

"Well, come on, let's hear it so we can move on."

His face tensed, causing a slight pull between his brows. "That's not what I was thinking at all."

Not quite believing him, I narrowed my eyes behind the lenses and pursed my lips. "Fine. Yes, I wear glasses to read. Especially small typeface, paper things that old people print out," I added, nodding toward his folder.

"And before you ask, no, I don't like contact lenses. Just the thought of touching my eyes makes me want to vomit."

He continued looking at me for several more drawn-out heartbeats before clearing his throat. "I was just going to tell you that they looked nice, but thank you for all that additional information."

Balancing the folder on top of his guitar, he opened it and flipped through several pages, eyes darting from one to the other until he found whatever he was looking for. He pulled out several loose sheets and handed them to me.

"Let's start with this one. I get asked for it at every show, and we can easily make it into a duet."

"Wait, is all this just sheet music?" I asked, taking them and flipping through the pages. "I thought they were lyrics."

He pointed at the song he'd handed me. "I think it's best if we stick to popular covers for our first show, if not the first couple. Just to get a feel for how we play together and to hype up the audience."

I'd already planned on recommending the same, so I didn't bother mentioning that him picking the first song was the opposite of me taking the reins.

I read the song title on the top sheet and handed them back to him. "Okay, so, you want to start with this one? Incipientz sings the original, right?"

He nodded again, seeming pleased. "Do you already know it?"

"Nope. I mean, I've heard it; I just haven't played it. But I can figure it out."

He frowned and leaned over his guitar, holding the sheets back out to me. "Okay, then take these."

I didn't move to take them, shifting farther away to put more space between us. "Just play the song for me. I'd look it up, but my phone is in my room." Where I'd left it after the third text from Madison asking if he'd shown up yet.

Adrian made a sound in the back of his throat that was half grunt and half curse. "I printed these for *you*, Davis. I already know the song."

"I figured as much when you stated it was requested at most of your shows."

The hand holding the sheets fisted, crinkling them. "I thought we'd agreed you weren't going to be difficult when it came to practice?"

"I'm not being difficult."

"Yes, you—"

"Jesus Christ, I can't fucking read music, Waters," I snapped, sounding pissier than I'd meant to. But I felt annoyingly defensive. I hated admitting when I wasn't good at something. And in this case, I wasn't just not good at reading music, I couldn't do it, at all.

He froze, lips still parted, and stared, his brows raised clear up his forehead. I rubbed my temples, lowering my voice to be the calm, collected adult I knew I could be. "I'm a musician, not a technician, Waters. I play by ear, not by sight. So, again, play the original for me…please," I tacked on.

He still didn't look confident, but he silently pulled out his phone and thumbed through it for a minute before dropping it onto his lap and letting the song fill the room.

I listened to the entire thing through and then picked up

my guitar and pointed at his phone. "Start it over one more time."

He listened without comment for once, and I stared a hole into the carpet, letting the music fill my head until it was all I could think or hear or see. I played out a few chords, humming the melody as I went. "Can you start it right at the chorus again?"

He did, and I listened and worked for another minute before I smiled and sat up straighter. "Got it. You can turn it off."

"That's it? It's been like four minutes."

I rolled my eyes and snatched his phone off his thigh before he could react, pretending like I didn't notice how high my pinkie had grazed up his thigh. Pulling up the song lyrics, I laid it on the floor in front of me and played the entire song, adding my flair here and there as I went.

I had to hand it to him. Adrian was right. This was the perfect song to start with. Especially with how well I bet he could harmonize.

"That's amazing."

"Thanks," I said, scrolling back up to the top of the lyrics and hoping my face didn't give away the pleasure I felt from his words.

His fingertips brushed the side of my arm a second later, shooting lightning through my body. "I'm not fluffing your ego, Davis. I mean it. I've met musicians making six figures a year who can't do what you just did. Not that fast, at least."

I glanced up from my strings, expecting to see humor or a guarded look in his gaze, but I saw nothing but naked honesty.

And I wasn't sure what to do about it.

"Thank you."

An emotion I couldn't quite place crossed his eyes, and he opened his mouth to say more, but just then, the front door swung open, and a string of excited rambling strode through.

"I'm telling you, Mom, it was awesome. There was a—"

Jamie made it all of two feet into the house before he slammed to a halt, eyes zeroing in on Adrian. Madison entered just behind him, side-stepping his statue form with a hand on the back of his shoulders.

"Layla," she said, eyeing Adrian and then me as she set her purse on the bar, "there's a man in the house."

I bit back a laugh, my cheeks twitching with the effort. Leave it to her to remember I'd said the same thing when I'd first found Garrett in the house, and use my words against me. "*Man* isn't the word I'd choose, but yes."

Adrian's head slowly swiveled back to me, but I kept my eyes on Madison, counting sheep in my head to help me keep a straight face. She rolled her lips in and turned away from me, digging her phone out of her purse and slipping her coat off.

Jamie still hadn't moved, and for a second, I worried about what it might be like for him to have a strange man in the house. I mentally kicked myself for not thinking about it and was gearing up to stand when he suddenly crossed his arms and demanded, "Who are you?"

Adrian blinked, darting another look at me before focusing back on the stone-faced kid in front of him. "I'm Adrian. And you must be Jamie."

Jamie narrowed his eyes in a way that had my mind racing through every conversation Madison and I had ever had in his presence about Adrian. Jamie was always overhearing things we didn't exactly intend for him to, and if he repeated any of them now, I might actually perish on site.

But then his slitted eyes cut to me, and he asked, "Is he your boyfriend?"

I choked out a laugh, seeing Adrian's brows shoot up his forehead. "No, he's not my boyfriend."

"Then why are you sitting so close?"

"We aren't—" I began on instinct, but when I looked over to emphasize my point, I stopped short. While I'd been staring at the floor, learning the song, Adrian had inched even closer, like he'd been subconsciously pulled in by the music without even realizing it. He was sitting about as close to me as he could without his thigh touching my arm.

I cleared my throat and scooted away, seeing Adrian do the same on the couch. "We're just practicing some music, bud."

"*Mhm*," he murmured, still looking at me accusingly. Like I'd disrespected him by not telling him about Adrian. A chuckle fought to escape. I may not have had a boyfriend to kick his ass for me, but I did have a not-so-little-anymore boy who would.

Adrian sat forward and laid his guitar flat in his lap, an amused smirk on his face. "How old are you, Jamie?"

Jamie straightened, making himself as tall as possible before snapping back, "I'm basically nine. How old are *you*?"

"Thirty-two," Adrian said, barely containing his humor right as Madison came power walking from the kitchen, horror painted across her face.

Placing both hands on Jamie's shoulders, she lowered her head next to his and said, "Why don't we hang out in my room? It sounds like poor Rugpants could use some company, and Layla needs to get to work. We can even bring Sadie."

That finally took his attention away from Adrian, and he twisted his head to look at her, his face lighting up. "Can she get on the bed?"

I bit the inside of my cheeks, watching the internal battle on Madison's face as she fought the idea. The woman loved Sadie, but she didn't love how much she shed.

"All right, fine. Let's go."

Giving an exaggerated fist pump, Jamie called for Sadie, who'd been at the ready the second he'd entered the house. They raced down the hall, Madison bringing up the rear.

I didn't bother restraining my smile when I heard thumps and giggles immediately erupt from the room as soon as the door shut. I shook my head, twisting back to Adrian to continue where we'd left off. Adrian was only here for an hour before he had to leave, so we needed to get going if this was going to be a successful practice.

"All right, let's do this song together with no lyrics first and then…What's that look for?"

He rubbed his hand along his jaw, his fingers gliding over his facial hair as bewilderment lingered on his face. "When you said you lived here with your friend's son, I was picturing like a cute little toddler or something."

That didn't surprise me. Most people did. And I could hear

the question hidden in his statement. How the hell did innocent-looking, curly-haired Madison have a kid that old? There was no malice or judgment in his gaze, just open curiosity. Even so, it wasn't his business to know Madison's story, nor was it my place to give it without her permission.

"No, definitely not. If anything, he's more like a grouchy old man than a toddler these days."

His eyes lingered on me and then darted down the hall before he chuckled. "Yeah, I can see that. He seems like a good kid, though."

"He is."

He smiled and something passed between us with that one look, something that didn't feel at all like hate. The feeling had me throwing my guard back up, not trusting it even a little. As if sensing the change, his smile immediately fell, and he picked his guitar back up, nodding at my own.

"All right, Davis, you start, and I'll pick up."

"That didn't seem to go so bad," Madison said, bumping my shoulder with hers.

I snorted. Once Adrian and I had finally gotten started, the practice had gone decently well. We'd been able to focus and perfect several songs, most of which we'd both already known, and I felt pretty good about it. We weren't quite ready to play an entire show together at Jemmy's yet, but I had another one that weekend at the martini bar downtown and had agreed to let him come up and play a couple songs with me. It'd be our test run to judge the reaction.

Adrian hadn't spoken much after the conversation about Jamie besides a few comments about the music. And like he said, right at five, he'd been packed up and slipping out the door with a half-wave.

Now, an hour later, Madison and I were sprawled out on my bed in our pajamas, staring at the ceiling. Jamie was tucked into bed with Sadie, Rugpants was curled up for the night in Madison's room, and Garrett was currently in the shower, leaving us in perfect, blissful silence.

Garrett had, thankfully, gotten off work a little late and missed Adrian by a few minutes. As much as I would've loved to force Adrian through yet another awkward meeting, I hadn't been in the mood to see them go toe-to-toe.

Adrian didn't strike me as a pushover—hell, I'd say he was the opposite with how he pushed and poked at me—but if Jamie had been nosey and blunt, Garrett would've been ten times worse.

Not out of jealousy, but just to make sure Madison was safe and comfortable with a man she didn't know in the house. I turned toward her, reaching out to pull on one of her curls that was extra tight, like a perfect curly fry. "It was okay. It could've been worse, I guess."

She snorted. "The house is still standing, he's still alive, and you're still willing to work with him. I'd say that's more than just okay."

True. I'd actually been surprised it'd gone as well as it did, figuring he'd butt heads with me the entire time. But what I didn't tell her, and what I wasn't yet ready to accept myself yet, was that I couldn't wait to do it again.

My phone buzzed next to my head, and I slapped my head around to find it, bringing it up over my head to read the new text.

Satan: Do you have any black outfits?

I sat up and rolled to one side, resting on an elbow as I replied.

Me: Everyone has a black outfit.
Satan: Good. Wear it this weekend.

I snorted. Yeah, okay.

Me: Try again.
Satan: What part confused you?
Me: The part where your audacity drowned out your manners.
Satan: Davis.
Me: Waterfall.
Satan: It'll look good if we match. Wear black.

I didn't respond, flopping onto my back again and handing my phone to Madison to read.

He was right, of course. It would look good for us to match, even if he wasn't playing with me the entire time, but that didn't mean I had to appreciate his tone.

Madison handed the phone back to me. "Are you going to do it?"

I nodded. "Yep."

It just wasn't going to be in the way he envisioned.

Chapter 11

SHIT. I GLANCED at the clock for the third time, nodding my head to whatever video game Jamie was jabbering about beside me. Something about a blue fairy that followed his character around and asked annoying questions.

"Yeah, that must suck to have someone following you around talking all the time," I said, darting a look to the clock, yet again, as if the time might magically change in the two seconds since the last time I'd looked at it.

Shitty shit, shit. Of course, I was going to run late to the first show Adrian was coming to. Of fucking course, I was. Although, in full transparency, was it still considered running late if you made the choice yourself, *knowing* it'd make you late?

"Ugh, he's going to rip into me."

"What?"

I glanced over to the passenger seat to see a frowning face staring back at me.

"Nothing, bud. Hey, will you do me a favor and call your grandma?" I asked, digging my hand inside my purse and reaching over the console to hand my phone to him, keeping my eyes on the road. "Just let her know I can't come inside today and to make sure the front door is unlocked for you."

"But you always come inside with me," he said, taking it from my outstretched hand.

And cue guilt. "I know I do, but I couldn't fit both my equipment and you in my car so I have to go all the way back home before trying to make it to work on time. So, I can't today, I'm sorry."

There was a short pause as he unlocked my phone and dialed Beth, letting her know exactly what I'd told him. Then he hung up and handed it back to me. "I'm sorry I'm making you late."

I pulled into his grandparents' neighborhood, circling around the lake until I hit their cul-de-sac. "You're fine, bud, I wouldn't have offered to bring you if I couldn't do it." Except the fact that I'd done just that.

I'd heard Madison up at one o'clock the previous night, studying for some test she had to take by noon. She'd looked like the star of an apocalypse show when she'd trudged out of her room that morning, and I'd offered to take care of bringing Jamie to her mom's without taking the time to think about my own schedule.

In her defense, she'd tried to brush me off, but I knew

Garrett had gone in to work to fix some issue that had come up, and that she still needed to get her quiz taken before noon, so I'd stuck my ground. No one to blame but myself.

"Okay," he said.

I looked at him again, but he was already staring out his window, watching his grandparents' house pull into view. Unbuckling his seatbelt the second I'd shifted into park, he went to open his door, but I whipped my hand over and clicked the lock button before he could. His eyes snapped to mine.

I twisted toward him, ignoring the way it made my own seatbelt dig into my boobs. "I would rather spend a few minutes talking about blue fairies with you than spend those minutes at work."

He rolled his eyes, but I didn't miss the smile that fought against his pressed lips. "I know, Layla."

"All right, just making sure. Now get out, you're making me late."

The smile broke free, just like I knew it would, and he dashed out, slamming the door and sprinting all the way to the porch like the ground was made of lava.

I shook my head, putting my car in reverse. If I ever had kids of my own one day, they'd have to be pretty damn awesome to beat out that kid as my favorite.

It wasn't the first time I'd played at Meg's Mini Martini, the martini and cigar bar downtown, but it'd been several months, and I'd forgotten just how tiny the place truly was. The door opened immediately into the seating area, with two tables literally bordering the doorway, in an effort to fit as many tables as possible. Directly to the left of the tables was the bar, which could fit maybe ten people all at once if they stood sideways and held their breath.

However, it was cute and decently popular on Saturdays and Sundays when they had their lunch time Happy Hour and fresh, homemade dips. The walls were painted a bright red and were plastered with hundreds of customer photos and random gadgets that people had brought in or left throughout the years.

The owner, a tall, goddess of a woman in her early forties, paid well and always made sure to have a live show on the weekend, but damn, it was fucking small on the inside.

Meg's, as most people called it, was one of the top bars to visit during the summer because, although their inside was mini, their covered deck was three times the size. It certainly hadn't been my favorite place to play given the living mushroom of cigar smoke that always occupied it, but at least I'd had space when I played out there.

Whereas now, when there was still a mild bite to the air, they used the deck for smoking only and had me set up inside the bar, tucked in a back corner that felt a whole lot like being put in timeout than anything else.

It was just enough space for a backless stool, a mic stand, and one square foot of empty space behind me for my belongings, which was currently also housing a black guitar I knew all too well.

"You're late."

I didn't look up, having already sensed his approach before he'd opened his mouth. His disapproval was like a beacon pulsing behind me. He'd zeroed in on me the second I'd stepped into the bar, waiting on pins and needles to rip into me just like I knew he would.

"I know."

His arm grazed mine when he squeezed in beside me, his body warm against me even through my coat. He reached down to pull my guitar out of its case and began checking the tune of the strings while I searched for the cord to plug it into the speaker and adjusted the mic height.

He glanced at the clock on the wall, conveniently hanging above where we stood. "By the time you finish sound check, you'll be starting over ten minutes late."

"I said, I know."

"When we have our first show next weekend—"

I shot up from where I'd been leaned over the speaker and whipped around, the motion putting us almost chest to chest, his face even with mine.

A flare of satisfaction mixed with my irritation. One of my favorite things about wearing heels was the fact that it enabled very few people to have the power to stand over me. If Adrian wanted to try to talk down to me and mansplain what being late meant, he'd have to do it eye to eye.

He didn't move an inch. We were standing close enough that I could make out a handful of sporadic silver hairs hiding within his beard, but I forced my eyes up to his, making sure he could hear my whispered retort over the background music that was still blaring.

As angry as I was, I had a business image to uphold and couldn't risk anyone hearing me curse someone out at my job.

"I said, I fucking know, Waters. I didn't plan on being late, nor do I plan on being late to any of our shows, so back off. For all you know, I wrecked or got mugged on my way here. But thanks for the concern."

Unfazed, he only leaned in, hovering his mouth over my ear and his pointer finger in front of my face. "First, I saw you drive up in a perfectly functioning car, so I already knew that wasn't the case."

He held up another finger. "Second, I know for a fact you'd have walked in here with red cheeks and hate in your eyes if anyone was stupid enough to try to mug you."

He dropped his hand and closed the last inch of space between us, his chest pressing flush against mine. His breath teased the top of my ear, sending goosebumps shooting down my chilled skin. "And third, we're partners, Davis. That means everything you do is my concern now. So no, I'm not going to back off."

Something about the way he murmured the last part of his tirade made a fire kindle in my chest. It'd felt intimate. Like he hadn't just meant right now.

I blinked, realizing how inappropriate our position would look to anyone in the bar watching us and swallowed, dowsing the embers. I stepped back and quickly turned away to grab my tablet and set it up next to my mic, hoping the flush in my face was only obvious to me.

I could still feel his words in my ear and the warmth of his breath on my skin, my body practically coming alive and begging for more.

I couldn't deny that I found Adrian physically attractive. I'm not sure anyone could. But the last thing I needed was him *knowing* the kind of effect his body had on me with such little effort. It was embarrassing.

After an extended—very awkward—pause, he nudged my arm, pulling on my sleeve. "I'm going to go sit down. Give me your coat."

I glanced down behind my stool again, cringing at the small area behind it that was now full of guitar cases. It was like performing in a fancy linen closet. "No, it's fine. I'll just toss it…behind me with my keys and shit."

"Davis, you barely have room for your ass, let alone that ridiculously huge coat. Stop being stubborn. Just hand it to me, and I'll stick it with mine."

I raised a brow, eyeing him over my shoulder. "Are you insinuating I have a big ass, Waters?"

His gaze dropped to my hips, still hidden beneath my coat. "No, I'm stating it outright. You could make a dress out of a sleeping bag, and it'd still be noticeable. Now, stop fishing for compliments and give me your goddamn coat."

I narrowed my eyes, shoving my smile deep, deep down. Teenage me might have wilted under his blunt remarks, but adult me fucking preened. I *did* have a large backend. It was my best feature. And knowing that Adrian had noticed? Yeah, that felt pretty damn good.

"You're an ass man. Got it. Here," I said, unbuttoning my coat and slipping it off my shoulders before shoving it into his arms.

He gripped it in his hands and openly gaped at me, his eyes practically caressing me as they slowly made their way down my body and back up. His nostrils flared when he stopped to stare at my chest. To the words right in the center of it.

I'd worn all black, just like he'd demanded. Just like he, himself, was wearing. However, paired with my black strappy heels and my faded black mini skirt, was a snug t-shirt that read *The Layla Davis Band* on it, with my social media handles listed directly under.

It was a merchandise shirt I still had from Kansas when I'd first started booking gigs after high school. Back then, I'd had two friends who'd played base and piano for me, and we'd formed a very simple band together. It hadn't lasted long before they'd each broken away to focus on their full-time jobs after college.

I'd almost tossed the shirt a few times since it was snugger than I typically preferred, but seeing the look on Adrian's face? I'd never been happier to still have it.

Because now, when he came up to perform with me, he'd look like a no-name member of my own band, rather than two independent musicians collaborating.

Adrian's mouth snapped shut, and I had to bite down on the inside of both cheeks to keep from laughing as I swam in my unending pool of satisfaction.

"Why am I surprised?" he muttered, arching his neck back to stare at the ceiling.

Glancing down at my chest, I shrugged. "You really shouldn't be. I followed the directions I was given. Next time, be more specific."

"God, you're such a brat."

I just flashed a bright smile and spun around, feeling the heat of his gaze on me for several agonizingly long seconds before he mumbled something under his breath and walked off.

Although I wasn't sure where we were in our tally marks, I was pretty sure, however many it was, I was winning.

Finished setting up, I began my sound check, chatting with the crowd as I did. I had a strong voice that carried, so when I was inside small places like this, I always liked to double-check that I wasn't going to blow someone's eardrums out.

Getting the go-ahead from the crowd, I took my seat and unlocked my tablet, tapping my finger on the icon for the app all my lyrics were saved on. It'd been a gift from my stepdad a few years ago and was my most prized possession after my guitar.

Because although I could learn a tune by ear, I sure as hell couldn't memorize the words to every song I'd ever been asked to play. Not when the crowd tended to yell out random ones that differed each night.

Today, I was going to start off strong with a popular hit that should get most of the crowd involved. It was a bit of a high one, chord-wise, so I adjusted my capo where I needed it and looked back down at my tablet, only for my hand to freeze just above it.

The app had opened like it was supposed to, but instead of

my normal dashboard showing me the index of songs, it was completely empty. My stomach sank and my neck heated, knowing everyone was waiting on me.

I tapped around the screen, hoping maybe it was just taking a while to load for some reason, but still nothing happened.

Trying not to assume the worst, I closed out of the app and restarted it. Again, the dashboard loaded up empty.

My heart sped up, an icy trail shooting down my sternum. No, no, no. This was not happening. The lyrics to every song I'd ever played—which was literally hundreds—were all saved on that app.

Starting to panic and feeling the weighted silence of the audience waiting for me to start, I put on the calmest smile I could. "Sorry, everyone, today apparently isn't my day. Just some technical difficulty, give me one more second."

I restarted my entire tablet, praying that it was a random glitch that would sort itself out. But as soon as it came back on and I opened the app, I was greeted with the same glaringly empty dashboard.

All my songs were gone.

"What's wrong, Davis?"

I snapped my head up to see Adrian, who'd snuck back up to come stand on my right, with a frown marring his features.

"Nothing," I said, flicking my hand, "just some technical difficulty, like I said. I'm ready now." I smashed the power button on the cursed electronic harder than necessary and moved it out of my way.

No biggie. I knew more than enough songs to make it

through a show, especially if I mixed in a few originals as well. It'd be fine. Totally fine. No reason to fall apart over it.

"Are you sure—"

"For the last time, I'm fine. Go sit back down."

His frown deepened, his eyes straying to my dark tablet, but he listened, disappearing back into the crowd to whatever table he'd found.

I took a deep breath, filling my cheeks, and then let it all out, replacing my frustration with a perfect smile. I'd have a panic attack about being late and losing all my shit all in one day later. It wasn't the end of the world, and I sure as hell wasn't going to waste another second fretting about it when I could be kicking ass and earning tips instead.

I'd just make sure to scream extra loud into my pillow when I went to bed tonight.

Re-adjusting myself on the stool, I crossed one leg over the other and rested my guitar on my thigh, my first genuine smile of the day lighting up my face when I started the next song.

A mixture of soft and melodic with a perfect dose of feminine rage, it was one of my own and my favorite so far. I'd written it on a whim, not thinking too hard about it at the time, and it'd just come together in a way I couldn't have planned if I'd tried.

I studiously ignored Adrian's gaze as I announced it to the crowd, part of me a little nervous for him to hear it. Especially after my dig to him about his own lyrics. I wasn't worried about what he thought of my voice, I knew he liked it if he'd asked to play with me, but it was more of having him hear and judge something of my own creation.

But the further I got into the song, the more that feeling began to fade. I knew this song was good, knew it in the way it made me feel and the way it made the crowd hush around me, their own conversations less important than what came out of my mouth.

And when I finally allowed myself to look in his direction and saw his slack-jawed attention zeroed in on my hands, I felt nothing but adrenaline and excitement fill my veins over the idea of sharing it with him.

My audience might hear the melody of it, but Adrian would hear the heart of it, and despite all the acquaintances I'd had over the years, I'd never had that before.

And I liked it.

As if noticing the change in my demeanor, even as I sang, Adrian's eyes snapped up to mine, his body shifting forward ever so slightly as he watched me. And if I didn't know any better—which I definitely did—I'd say he might just enjoy having me stare at him while I performed.

I shot him a wink and his nostrils flared, his fingers straightening out to lie flat on the table, like he'd shove off at any moment and jump up on stage with me. The sight sent heat down my spine, lighting me up until I forgot about every bad thing that had happened so far that day.

"Hey, baby!"

I blinked, breaking eye contact with him as a loud, slurred comment brought me back to the present. Although I didn't deign to glance over toward the drunken shout, I had a good feeling by the sheer volume of the comment that it was directed at me. Because if not, it meant some guy was screaming his pickup line directly in some poor woman's face. And I'd like to hope even a drunk guy wouldn't be stupid enough to do that.

So I continued on, neither looking at him nor Adrian as I went straight into the chorus like I hadn't heard the comment at all. He wouldn't be the first drunk guy to holler at me mid-show, and sadly, he wouldn't be the last.

For every decent man in the world, there were a handful of trashy ones to ruin it for all of them. All I could do was hope this particular one had a slightly more sober friend to whack him upside the head and tell him to shut it.

But he apparently didn't.

"Why don't you come down here, and I'll show you a little bit of hot lovin'!" His voice rang out again, louder this time, and much more obnoxious as he twisted my lyrics into what I could only assume was either a gross pickup line or a sarcastic jab at my song.

I still didn't look in his direction, knowing that's what he wanted. Making eye contact would only encourage him, and that was the last thing *I* wanted. Men who catcalled women, especially while they were obviously working, were the epitome of the bottom of the barrel.

At this point, several patrons closer to me were twisting their necks to the side, trying to get a good look at the garbage man sitting at the bar. Their unimpressed lip curls told me all I needed to know.

"Why don't you hop off that stool and give us a little twirl, sweet thing?"

Jesus fuck, people could be the worst sometimes. This right here was why I needed Adrian to help me score better, higher-paying gigs. Not that Meg's was a shitty place, because it wasn't by any means. But I wanted out of the small-city bars that were always filled with men who were content to come in every night and hit on women while still expecting their wives to make them sandwiches at home.

That simply wasn't the scene that I wanted to have connected with my name.

Not that I wasn't thankful to Jemmy's and Meg's and every other bar like this for giving me a chance when I'd been a fresh nobody with zero local references. But I was tired of it. I was ready for more.

And I was also ready to show this drunken asshole, who was still talking, just how fucking *sweet* I could really be.

Nearing the end of my song, I finally dared a quick peek, hoping my hair would hide my eyes, and immediately knew which one was him. Backward hat, buttoned-down shirt only halfway done up, board shorts in the winter, and a beer bottle swaying side to side in the air like a lighter. Just what every lady hoped for.

Regret simmered hot in my stomach when he caught me looking.

"Eh, there she is! What are you drinking, baby? I'll get you whatever you want."

I took it back. The guy wasn't even the bottom of the barrel. He was the putrid sludge that was seeping *out* of the barrel and staining the ground.

Maybe I'd get lucky, and he'd fall backward off his stool. I glanced over again with high hopes only to see that all the stools at the bar had backs. Damn.

"Come on over here! I bet you'd sound even better with my—"

His voice suddenly cut off, a thump and a curse taking its place. I didn't pause my singing, but I did look back over at him, wondering if the universe had finally given me a crumb and he'd somehow fallen, despite the backed stool.

My fingers almost dropped my pick at the sight that was waiting for me instead. Because the man was definitely off his stool, but not because he'd fallen.

Only dedication, pride, and experience kept me from fumbling as I saw Adrian standing over him, fury painted all over his face, while his hand was around the back of the man's neck, practically bending him in half.

I let the last note of the song ring out as Adrian slowly leaned down to whisper something in the man's ear that had him lifting his hands in surrender. A glance at the floor confirmed both his beer bottle and hat were no longer in his possession.

A hesitant applause filled the sudden silence after I'd finished, everyone else's eyes watching the scene play out along with me as Adrian dragged the man by his neck across the small room and out the door like a misbehaving dog.

"All right, everyone, I think we'll take that as our cue for a break," I said, forcing a chuckle even while my gaze never left the door. Most of the audience nodded or smiled, a few even apologizing on the guy's behalf, but I raised my hand, brushing it off.

Sliding off my stool, I leaned my guitar against the wall behind me and winced at the pain already forming in my lower back. I reached back and pressed my fingers on either side of my spine, trying to massage the ache away while my eyes strayed back to the door.

What was he doing out there? I mean, I was all for putting an idiot in their place, but I also didn't know Adrian well enough to know what he was capable of when pissed.

Was he a "punch the guy until he's unconscious and stuff him in a portable toilet" kind of man, or a "lock him in a trunk and toss him in a river" kind of man?

I'd like to assume the first, but the intense fury in his eyes as he'd glared down at the man had me considering going outside and double-checking, just to be sure.

Deciding a murder happening at one of my shows wasn't in my best interest, business-wise, I turned my back to the door and crouched down to grab my phone and keys. That way I'd at least be able to call 911 and stab a man in the eye if I needed to join in on a tussle.

I straightened up, only for my ass to bump into someone standing directly behind me. I spun around, half expecting the drunken guy to have burst back in to take out his humiliation on me. The movement had me losing my footing in my heels, and

I tipped to the side only for a hand to curl around my elbow and steady me.

Blue eyes met mine. Their usual frozen temperature gone under the heat that still blazed through them. When the hell had he walked back in? My eyes darted down to his hand on me and then back up, something I didn't want to acknowledge swirling in my gut when I saw the reddened skin of his knuckles.

He immediately released me, and I licked my suddenly dry lips, trying to act unaffected even as the absence of his hand left a chill to my skin. I opened my mouth, preparing to take a note from Madison's book and make a comment about him going all caveman, but the words died on my tongue when he leaned in toward me.

He didn't say a word, he just stared me down and stretched his other arm out, setting a bottle of water in the cup holder of my mic stand. I waited for him to step back once he was done, but he didn't.

Swallowing, I tried to plaster a smirk to my face in the hopes of faking the bravado I didn't at all feel. "You know, Waters, if you keep doing shit like this, I'll think you actually like me."

He shrugged and tucked his hands in his pockets, the tiny twitch of his eyes the only indication that the action stung. "The asshole was annoying the fuck out of me. Enjoying a few drinks is fine, but I have no patience for people who can't control their impulses."

I quirked a brow and grabbed the bottle of water he'd brought, twisting the top open. "You mean you've never enjoyed losing control of an impulse? Not even a little bit?" I teased, taking a sip to hide the smile fighting my lips. "How very disappointing for you."

He still stood way too close to me, and although I knew I should step back, I didn't.

"On the contrary, I have very specific impulses, Davis," he said, his eyes dropping to my mouth. I subconsciously ran my tongue along my bottom lip, and his jaw ticced, something dark flickering across his gaze.

"However," he continued, his eyes finding mine again, "I can promise you, I exercise complete control over every single one. A firm chokehold, if you will."

I choked and looked away, nearly spurting my next sip out of my nose. Jesus Christ, was he talking about what I thought he was talking about? And why did the idea that he was, have my insides tightening up like a fucking coil?

Wiping my mouth and trying not to drown on dry land, I darted a sidelong look his way, and I could've sworn he had the barest hint of a smile teasing the corner of his mouth.

I shook my head and set the bottle down, twisting to grab my guitar from behind me. I needed to get started again. I usually took at least a fifteen-minute break to give my voice a rest, but I didn't want to take too long today since I'd been late to start.

"You game to come up after my next two songs?"

Finally taking a step back and adding some much-needed space between us, he nodded. But as I settled back onto my stool and situated my guitar, waiting for him to walk away, he hesitated.

"Davis."

"Waterfall."

That time I definitely saw a curl to his lips. "I don't *not* like you."

I smiled back, unable to resist answering the mischievous look he was giving me. "So, just a little bit of hate, then?"

He winked. "Just a little."

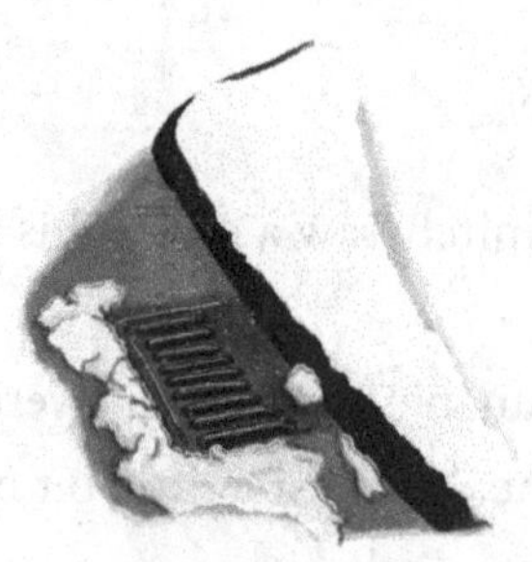

Chapter
→ 12 ←

I NEEDED A bigger car.

Hands on my hips, I took a deep breath—or as much of one as I could after lugging all my shit across the parking lot—and shoved my body against it again, attempting to cram my guitar case, mic stand, and rectangular speaker into my passenger seat with about as much grace as a newborn giraffe playing football.

Scratch that, I *really* needed a bigger car. Because there was absolutely zero chance of me fitting any new equipment into the toy car I was currently driving.

Not that I could afford a fancy sound system anytime soon, but the day I did, I'd need to actually be able to cart it around to shows. Not to mention a rolling cart, and maybe even a chair that was at least marginally comfortable.

I'd been sitting on the hard, small stool at Meg's for three straight hours, and my back and neck were screaming at me. Not that I'd ever be able to play with a cushy, armchair or anything, but having my own stool that I didn't hang off of while I played would be an extremely nice change.

Hell, even Adrian had looked uncomfortable on his, and he'd only come up for two songs.

The show had been a success. More than I'd anticipated. I'd lost count of the number of people who'd approached us during the break directly after his last song with me to ask where we'd be playing together next. It was kind of amazing, even with the smug *I told you so* face Adrian kept shooting me over everyone's heads.

I sighed, rolling my shoulders back and shutting the door. I rested my forehead against the cool metal, hoping it'd force my blood to move a little faster and wake me up. It wasn't even dark out, and I swore I could hear my bed screaming out my name from across town.

The second I'd ended my show, Adrian had appeared back at my side, like the silent giant he was proving to be, saying he wanted me to stay and talk business for a bit. Probably to pinpoint a dress code, I thought, chuckling.

But his request had gone in one ear and out the other, and I'd made haste out of Meg's the second he'd slipped off to the bathroom.

If I'd learned anything in my life so far, it was that no matter what your career path was, business and exhaustion didn't mix well.

Making sure I hadn't missed anything, I made my way around my car toward the driver's side. The weather was significantly warmer today than it'd been most of the year so far, but I still shuffled carefully, aware of the small bits of snow stubbornly clinging to the concrete. But apparently, my feet didn't get the memo.

The second the spike of my heel hit the edge of the concrete, my ankle twisted, forcing my knee to give out and sending me flying backward onto the curb.

My hands slammed down first to catch the majority of my body weight, but the left side of my ass took the rest of the fall, tearing the skin of my thigh that was visible just beneath the hem of my coat.

I hissed, pressing a stinging hand against the burning flesh of my leg. What the actual hell was my life today? First my tablet losing all my songs, then the asshole inside, and now this? And all that after being freaking late in the first place.

I slowly pushed my body up to sit on the curb of death, breathing heavily while I tried, and failed, to keep my shit together. Bringing both hands up, I stared at my scratched-up palms and cursed, the word sounding even more vulgar in the otherwise silent parking lot.

I considered myself a pretty tough bitch, but even I had a limit on how many shitty things I could handle in a row, and today was finally pushing me over it.

My eyes burned, and I sniffed, looking up at the sky and blinking rapidly to control my tears. The last thing I needed to add to this day was a puffy face and raccoon eyes. But it was no use. The mess of the day, mixed with my torn skin, sliced through the last layer of my shield, and hot tears began to drip down my cheeks.

I cursed again, but it turned into more of a hiccup as I wiped them away angrily. I fucking hated crying and avoided it at all costs, jumping straight to anger anytime there was even a chance at getting upset over something trivial like this.

And because I'd spent so many years keeping a tight leash on my emotions, Madison and my mother were the only two people in my life who had ever seen me cry as an adult. And I could count the number of times on one hand.

Strong women bottled that shit up and waited until they were alone in the privacy of their rooms to have a meltdown.

At least, that's what I told myself.

But this time, instead of locking it away deep in the pit of my stomach to work through later, it was like the angrier I got, the faster the tears leaked out. Until the only thing I was succeeding at was smearing my makeup. I felt like I was balancing on a tightrope, flailing side-to-side, seconds from tipping over and falling into the abyss completely.

What the fuck was wrong with me?

Steps sounded behind me, and I steadily ignored them, staring at a crack in the pavement and pretending like I wasn't sitting on the curb with a damp ass, crying over a tablet, a drunken jerk, and a fall that was my own fault.

But rather than pass me and continue to his or her vehicle like a polite person would, the intruder stopped a few paces away from me. I glanced up, ready to tell whoever it was to get lost, but immediately snapped my lips together and looked away, instead.

The universe, it seemed, really fucking despised me.

"You doing all right there, Davis?"

"Peachy keen," I said, finding a random pebble to be

exceptionally interesting.

Adrian shifted his weight, his gaze searing into the side of my face. "I didn't actually think I'd find you out here. With how fast you bailed on me, I figured you'd already be home and in sweatpants by now."

I knew his comment and flippant tone were purposefully crafted to get a rise out of me, but I no longer had the energy necessary to poke back. I was putting too much of it into not letting another tear trek down my face while he could see me.

At my continued silence, he untucked his hands from his pockets and tipped his head, trying to get a better look at my face. "You okay?" he asked, his voice almost hesitant, like he didn't know what to do with this version of me.

I dared a peek at him to see he was staring at my palms. I immediately flipped them over and carefully rested them over my knees.

"Just go home, Waters. I'm too tired to fight with you."

Silence. I looked back down, assuming he'd listen for once and drop it.

But of course, he didn't. Because the next thing I knew, his body was lowering down to sit next to mine, his arms resting over his bent knees.

I cleared my throat and shifted away from him, adding a few extra inches between us. "I mean it. I'm not in the mood to bicker."

"Who says we're bickering?" he asked, staring out at the steady line of traffic on the far side of the parking lot.

I shot him a narrowed side-eye even though he couldn't see it. Why on earth was he sitting out here on this slush-covered curb when he could be having a drink inside the warm bar with someone? I hadn't failed to notice all the appreciative looks he'd been getting from the group of single women sitting near the door.

Releasing an irritated huff, I shook my head and then winced, feeling my neck muscles pull from the act. I wrapped my hand around the back of my neck and squeezed, slowly massaging the pad of my thumb into the aching muscle.

"Since we're not bickering," he said after a long minute of silence, stretching one leg out and swinging his face my way, "tell me something, Davis. Why do you only take weekend gigs?"

When I didn't immediately reply, he went on. "There are a ton of places looking for more weekday performers, and I know for a fact Bosenet has to be up your ass about them. So why aren't you snagging them up?"

"I can't take weekday gigs," I said, continuing to dig my fingers into the back of my neck even while his question had all my muscles tensing.

"But why?" He pushed, tipping one long leg to the side to nudge my knee with his. "Because of your day job?"

I nudged his leg back, less gently than he'd done to me, and prepared to tell him it wasn't any of his damn business. Because it wasn't. We'd made it clear from the beginning that we didn't know each other. Just because he didn't *not* like me, didn't suddenly make us friends.

But when I twisted to look at him, I found myself telling him the truth instead. Or at least, part of it. "Yes. That and other reasons."

His eyes were latched onto the hand I still held at my neck, a deep furrow appearing in his brow. "Why can't you take the shows instead of that job? I'm assuming you're not making good money there since you agreed to work with me despite your poorly backed reservations."

I gave him an unimpressed look, dropping my hand from my neck so he'd stop staring at it. "I'm not available to work in the evenings."

"Why?"

"Because I'm not," I snapped, feeling defensive. Just because we played together and he maybe beat the shit out of a guy for me, didn't mean I was obligated to tell him my whole life story. Especially when I knew, for a fact, he wouldn't agree with my reason.

"Here," he said, twisting toward me so that one of his legs rested on the concrete between us. He reached both hands out toward me, his face its usually controlled mask like he was completely unaffected by my testy attitude.

I flinched back, unsure why the hell he'd need to be touching me. "Here, what? What are you doing?"

His hands dropped onto his thigh, and he looked up at the sky like he was asking the heavens for patience. Then he lifted one hand again and gestured to my head. "Your neck is bothering you."

"Yeah, so? You know the kind of shitty chairs we're given," I said, making air quotes around chairs. "There's no way to not have our necks and backs killing us. All part of the job."

"I know," he said, exhaling heavily, like I was some random, errant child, refusing to listen to reason. "Which is why I know how to help."

I shook my head. Yeah, nope. No way was I letting my literal rival get his hands on my neck behind a bar where I'd made him play next to me while I wore my band shirt. That was a *True Crime* episode just waiting to happen.

I waited for him to snap at me only to be shocked speechless when he burst out laughing, a deep, rumbling sound that was so at odds with the softer, melodic version of his singing. "Jesus, Davis, I'm not trying to strangle you. I already told you I don't hate you."

I bit the inside of my cheeks, my throat feeling thick. But I forced the words past my lips, still trying to edge away from him even though the thought of someone working the knots out of my neck sounded near orgasmic.

"I don't need help."

"Liar." He sighed when I shot daggers his way. "Look, I'm not asking you to get rid of the moat you have around your damn fortress. Just lower the drawbridge for five minutes and let me help you. The last thing I need is a broken partner."

I blinked at him. And then blinked again. Waiting him out to see when the other shoe would drop. When his face didn't so much as twitch into a hint of a smirk, I found myself slowly turning my back to him.

Long fingers dipped into the collar of my coat and pulled it away from my neck, sliding it to the edge of my shoulders to bare my neck to him. Then he gently tipped my head forward and wrapped one hand around the back of my neck, and his other hand over my left shoulder to keep me in place.

Adrian Waters was touching me. Not just touching me, but *massaging* me. In a parking lot.

And I was letting him.

A second later, his fingers found exactly where they needed to be and pushed in hard. And no amount of pride or bad bitch energy could've prevented the absolutely indecent groan that my lips betrayed me with.

His fingers froze for a split second, but then continued, digging into the exact spot that was killing me without me having to tell him. Because I didn't have to. Not when he likely experienced it himself.

"So, are you going to tell me why you were crying?"

I tensed, and he immediately clicked his tongue at me, pushing down on my shoulder until I relaxed them again. "I wasn't crying."

"Of course not." A pause, one that I knew occurred only because he was smirking behind me. "So, are you going to tell me why you were sitting on the curb, not crying then?"

I huffed. "Maybe I'm just angry at the world," I said, knowing he wouldn't let that answer slide. But although it wasn't the full truth, it also wasn't a lie. I was pretty freaking peeved at it.

His fingers moved up into my hair, rubbing deep circles just behind my ears, and I had to bite down on my tongue to keep from moaning again.

"Okay."

Yeah, that's what I—wait, what? *Okay?* My mouth opened and closed, fumbling for words. "Just okay? You caught me weeping over a bad day, and that's all you're going to say?"

"What was I supposed to say?"

"I don't know," I said, throwing my hands up. "Tell me to

get over it? That if I'm unhappy, I should probably just smile more, or some other stupid shit men like to say?"

His hands paused but didn't retreat. "Smile more for who? You don't owe me or the world anything. Least of all, a goddamn smile. You want to glare and sit here hating the world? Fucking glare."

I twisted my neck just enough to look at him over my shoulder, our noses almost touching. I hadn't noticed how close he'd leaned into me, but now that I had, I realized just how much of his warmth I could feel seeping into my back.

"You don't think it makes me a raging bitch?" I asked, nearly choking on my own saliva at the way his eyes narrowed at my reuse of his own words.

"Oh, it definitely makes you look like a raging bitch," he said, the corner of his lip twitching. "But it suits you." He raised the hand that'd been on my neck and flicked me in the nose.

In retaliation, I reached back and pinched his thigh, earning me a sharp hiss that had a genuine smile spread across my face. Adrian might drive me nuts, but at least I could always count on him to be honest with me about whatever he was thinking, even if I didn't want him to be.

His eyes dropped to my mouth and his throat bobbed, the hand on my shoulder sliding in toward my neck. "You know, Davis, we don't—"

"Layla!"

We both spun around at my name, and Adrian shifted out of the way just in time for a head of voluminous, dark brown curls to streak past him. Two brown arms wrapped around my neck as a full bosom squished into the side of my face, nearly suffocating me when she squeezed.

"Hey, Tarah," I said, my words muffled against cleavage as I awkwardly patted the woman on the back, who was currently wrapped around me koala-style.

I had no idea how much of Adrian's and my conversation she'd overheard, but I could imagine what we had to have looked like from a passerby coming across us. I automatically shifted away from him the second my head was freed from her grasp.

"I just heard what happened," Tarah said, straightening back up and roving her brown eyes all over me for battle wounds. "I'm so sorry that asshole was allowed to go on for so long. Our bartender is new and flustered, and I was in the bathroom trying to explain to a customer why she couldn't sleep on the floor, and—"

I stood as well and reached out to gently squeeze her arm. Coming in at only five foot two on her tallest day and the longtime girlfriend of the owner, Meg, Tarah was a literal walking ray of sunshine. I'd literally never met a soul sweeter than she was. Although, Jamie came in at a close second.

"It's all right, Tarah."

She sputtered, vocalizing her disagreement and placing her hands on her hips like she was about to scold me like one of her and Meg's adorable, yet rambunctious, kids.

I chuckled and raised my hands between us in surrender. "I promise. It's not the first time some idiot's embarrassed themself at one of my shows, nor will it be the last." I shrugged. It sucked, but it was the truth. There would always be pathetic people in the world.

"It'll be the last."

Tarah's gaze whipped over my shoulder at the man now standing behind me, and her eyes widened as if just now realizing who, exactly, had been sitting on the curb with me.

Her eyes flicked between us, her lips forming an "oh" shape that had me immediately taking yet another large step away.

I knew exactly what that look meant, and Adrian and I had absolutely not been doing anything that warranted it in our direction. Although, even as I thought it, the memory of Adrian's warmth and fingers on my body had at least a small, minuscule part of me wishing that we had been.

I rubbed my hands up and down my arms, dashing away the thought, and pointedly rolled my eyes at the man in question. "You can't possibly promise that, Waters. There will always be a stupid drunk man in a bar."

He huffed, a wicked smirk appearing on his lips. "Maybe so, but I can guarantee it'll be the last time *he* does it."

Chapter
13

WHEN MADISON TOLD me that I'd have the day to myself today, I'd whooped and fist pumped the air, pretending to shoo her out the door even faster. And I hadn't been exaggerating my excitement. She'd be at work for the next six hours, and apparently Garrett was taking Jamie and Rugpants to visit his brother and sister-in-law for the day.

I was a little jealous about that one, since I absolutely adored his sister-in-law, Sarah, but still. A day alone to strut around in my underwear, drink pop without a child trying to barter with me to see if he could have one, and do whatever the hell I wanted? Yes, please. I'll take two.

Especially considering it was my last free Sunday for the foreseeable future.

Madison and I had finally worked it out with Ken for me to

take her Sunday payroll shift so that, although she'd still be working seven days a week, she'd no longer be working any doubles. Granted, that meant that I'd now be working a Sunday double instead, but as I explained to her the twenty times we argued about it, it wouldn't necessarily be *every* Sunday.

My shows were never set in stone, as I learned quite painfully with Jemmy's, so there'd be some Sundays that I didn't have to work both jobs. It'd be rare, but still a possibility.

And plus, like I'd told her in what felt like a ten-minute-long persuasive presentation, my gigs were only ever three to four hours long, whereas her night shift was always over eight. She was the default parent to a kid. I wasn't. She was a full-time student. I wasn't.

It just made sense regardless of her disagreement.

But ten minutes after everyone had left, and I stood in the center of our living room with nothing but silence surrounding me, I had no idea why it'd sounded so enticing. The silence felt weighted, like I'd been left behind rather than being gifted privacy.

I wasn't sure what was suddenly causing my weird mood, but I was determined to get myself out of it. I tried taking a bath, turning on a movie, reading a book, and taking a morning nap to pass the time. But even blaring music from my phone didn't overpower the loud ass silence that greeted me at every step throughout the house.

Maybe because, with everyone's absence, my mother's words had begun to creep back into my mind, circling around and seeking a place to burrow in and stay.

That someday soon, Madison and Jamie were going to move into a new house with Garrett and start their own family. One that didn't include me. And when they did, all that would be left in their wake was this.

Silence.

I threw myself down on the couch, patting the spot next to me for Sadie to jump up and snuggle. Maybe I'd flick through the online dating app on my phone. I'd installed it a few weeks ago after Madison had teased me about it, but I hadn't actually opened it up since.

I unlocked my phone and stared at the tiny icon, willing myself to click on it. To find someone. To have a life outside of my music and my dog.

But clicking on it would mean dating. And dating would mean men. And men would mean suffering through ten or more "nopes" before landing on one that *seemed* like a "yes," but only because the first ten had set the bar so damn low his "meh" ass was able to step right over it.

And then, even if I said yes to the "maybe," the chance of him ghosting me the moment he realized I wasn't a quiet, demure partner was high. Society didn't like loud women, and I'd never been the type to lower my voice for anyone.

"Ugh." I groaned, tossing it into my lap and sprawling my head back on the cushion. "It's official, I'm going to die alone."

Adrian's face flashed across my mind. Unlike my previous relationships, he'd never once batted an eye or acted like I was too much. In fact, he seemed to almost like it, pushing me on purpose to get a rise out of me.

I thought back to last night, when it'd felt like the world was chipping away at me, one daggered shard at a time, and he'd come outside and somehow put me back together again. By pissing me off and soothing me all at once.

Sadie bumped my hand with her nose, and I lifted my head to smile down at her, booping her on the nose. "You feel restless, too, huh?" She laid her head on my lap, gazing up at me with big puppy dog eyes.

I chuckled at her silent begging and picked my phone up again to check the current weather. It wasn't spring by any means, but it wasn't freezing either. It was warmer than yesterday had been at least.

"All right, girl. You want to take a trip to the park?" There was one close by where we lived that I'd started going to before winter had hit, to let my vocals free in a way I couldn't do at home.

She didn't waste a second, immediately leaping off the couch and huffing a low bark at me, as if to say, "Is that a rhetorical question? Let's go, bitch."

I gripped the slobbery Frisbee again, scrunching my nose as I fought to wrestle it from my dog's mouth.

"Sadie," I whined, leaning down over my legs until we were nose to nose. "I'm never going to get this song finished if you keep shoving this in my lap and dripping spit onto my papers."

Her butt wagged harder in answer. I shook my head, sitting

up and tossing the disc back across the open field, watching her take off like a bullet, chasing after it again.

I loved how open this park was, and the fact that not only was it clean and pet friendly, but it was huge and open, with both a kid play area to one side, and a two-mile-long path that wrapped around the entire thing and weaved in and out of the trees.

A few people jogged or walked by while I sat, sending me the closed-mouth tip of the lips that was universal of all human beings. But otherwise, we had the majority of the area completely to ourselves. Several yards away, Sadie snatched up the toy Frisbee and shook it around, looking like a fluffy, lovable, lunatic as she growled at herself.

I chuckled and raised my guitar back up, looking down at the notepad of lyrics I had jotted down on the bench next to me. The tune had started to come to me on the trip over, lyrics trickling in steadily as I drove. I'd nearly pulled over onto the side of the road to jot them down, terrified of forgetting them.

I closed my eyes and picked my way through what I had so far. *"Baby, I despise you, but you hate me too. When you suffocate me, I suffocate you..."*

I stopped, keeping my eyes closed, and frowned. Something was missing from the music aspect, but for the life of me, I couldn't quite put my finger on what. I started again, speeding it up to see if that would help me pinpoint what it needed.

"But then I hear your heartbeat in rhythm with mine. And just like that, you bring me back to life."

"It needs an electric guitar."

My eyes snapped open, and I twisted around sharply, almost dropping my guitar and falling clean off the bench. Adrian stood on the walking path a few paces behind me, hair up in a bun, hands on his hips, and his chest visibly rising and falling as he stared at me.

"Jesus Christ," I muttered, one hand over my heart while my other white-knuckled my guitar's neck like a lifeline. "You scared the shit out of me."

He tipped his head, a ghost of a smile gracing his lips. I dropped my eyes from his face, taking in the rest of him. He wasn't sporting the usual dark jeans and black jacket I always saw him in, but a pair of gray sweatpants that left little to the imagination and a fitted, white undershirt that did nothing to hide the definition of his chest and upper arms.

Holy shit.

My eyes widened and shot back up, attempting—but failing miserably—to wipe the image of Adrian's pecs from my brain. I rubbed my free palm down my thigh, feeling suddenly too hot in my own skin as I studiously stared at his face like my life depended on it.

A blur shot past the bench, and he grunted, stumbling back a step when Sadie barreled into him. He righted himself, huffing a quiet laugh as she continued to shove her toy into his crotch, all but demanding his love and attention.

Succeeding at getting the Frisbee from her, he looked at me and held it up, silently asking if it was okay for him to throw it. I nodded, unable to get my mouth to work just yet. He tossed it significantly farther than I could and watched her take off after it before crouching down and tightening the laces of one of his shoes.

"What are you doing here?" I finally asked, unable to keep the wary tone from my voice.

The last time I'd seen Adrian, he'd had his hands on me and his mouth dangerously close to my ear. I'd felt his warmth at my back and his focus on my body. And I might've been able to brush it all off as a single, stress-induced event…if that had been all that happened.

It wasn't the memory of his hands working my muscles and pulling noises from my throat that plagued me, but of how hard I'd orgasmed in the privacy of my room later that same night when I'd imagined the feel of his hands everywhere else.

Although I could thank my battery-operated friend for being the one to technically push me over the edge, it'd been the thought of Adrian that'd put me there to begin with. And that admittance alone made me want to crawl into a hole and die.

Not because I necessarily regretted it—it'd been the best orgasm I'd had in forever—but because I had no fucking idea how to act around him now. He may not know I'd given my libido the reins for the night, but I did.

A line had been crossed, and I wasn't sure how to get back over it to where we'd been before. Or if I even wanted to. And that made every wall I had snap up around me, determined to keep him out.

At my question, he straightened back up, causing my eyes to drop to his chest again against my will. His sweaty, sculpted, stupidly fucking perfect chest that was not even remotely hidden beneath his damp shirt.

He gestured to his body, making it even harder to pull my gaze away. "I feel like answering that question would be an insult to your observation skills."

That snapped them back up, and I narrowed them at his smug face, flipping him off over my guitar. I mean, he was right. It was a stupid question, but still. He didn't have to point it out to my face.

Would I have done the same to him? Yes. But that was also beside the point.

He sighed at my overly welcoming presence and fidgeted with the earbuds hanging around his neck, looking back out over the field. "I come here almost every day, Davis. I have been for weeks."

I followed his gaze to Sadie, who'd finally abandoned her game of fetch to roll all over something in the grass. He went running every day? Even during the winter? Good Lord. No wonder he was such an asshole. The man was probably frozen solid all the time.

But it was the last part of his answer that stuck with me. How long had he been in town before he'd run into Larry? If he'd been here for several weeks prior to when I'd met him, he couldn't have come for work.

So then why did he move here? What did Adrian Waters do outside of his shows? Because I refused to believe that the only life he had outside of work was running laps around a park.

He raised a blonde brow at me, and I belatedly realized I'd said at least part of my thoughts out loud. "I feel like the better question is, what are *you* doing here?"

I huffed. "Now who isn't using their observation skills."

Ignoring my jab, he stepped closer, tapping his phone—which was tucked into an arm carrier—and removed his earbuds from his neck to stuff into a pocket.

"Your song," he started, nodding toward my notebook, "I was saying it needs an electric guitar."

My heartbeat picked up, my mind already hearing what an electric guitar would sound like behind this. Maybe even some drums. God, what I'd give to have access to a recording studio and the ability to create my songs exactly the way I wanted to. But shit like that was only available to those with money or connections. And I had neither.

"Yeah, well, not all of us can afford to buy all the instruments we want. So, acoustic will have to do," I said, a bitterness seeping into my words. Whether he meant to or not, his suggestion had me on edge. Did he not like it? And why did I care?

He took another step, until he was only a foot or two away, towering over me. "I could do it. I don't use mine all that often anymore, but I have one."

He picked up my notebook, avoiding me when I tried to snatch it first. He perused my lyrics, his face betraying nothing. "I also think it'd benefit from drawing out the last word of the chorus."

I didn't move, not liking the way he was stepping into my business and taking over my song like he knew it better than I did. Even as my fingers itched to try out his suggestion.

He tossed my notebook back down, nodding to himself, and reached toward me, motioning to my guitar.

"Here, I'll show you what I mean."

I lurched back, yanking it out of his reach and smacking my spine on the unforgiving metal of the bench. "Touch my guitar, and I swear I'll jam it into your balls, Waters."

He scoffed, placing his hands back on his hips and rolling his eyes to the sky. "Jesus, help me. I know how to handle a guitar, Davis. I'm not going to drop it."

"I'm aware."

"So?"

I raised my brows. Someone had his arrogance pants on today. "*So*, just because you know how to use one doesn't mean I trust you with mine. And besides," I snapped, "I don't need you telling me how to play my own songs."

His features changed at that, hardening into something sharp and guarded. "I'm not trying to tell you how to do anything, I was just offering advice. You know, like how we agreed to?"

Angry for reasons I didn't quite understand, I shot up straight, darting out a hand to stop my guitar from sliding off my lap. I didn't know why I suddenly felt like lashing out at him. All I knew was that I'd started getting a weird tightening in my chest the second he came into view, and I wanted it to go away.

I wanted to feel in control again, and being around Adrian was starting to make me feel like I no longer had any left at all.

"Correction, we agreed to accept advice from each other when it came to our shows, but since this song is one of my own and has nothing to do with you, I'm under no obligation to listen."

Something flashed across his eyes before he blinked it away, and if I didn't know any better, I'd have thought it was hurt. But that couldn't have been right, because in order for my words to hurt him, Adrian would have to care what I thought about him.

Shaking his head, he took several steps back toward the path. "Unbelievable."

"What? The truth, or the fact that I pointed it out?"

He made an irritated noise in his throat and ran a hand over his head, brushing back the errant strands. "Do you even know how to let anyone in, or are you simply content to be your only source of company for the rest of your life?"

He shook his head again, and that feeling in my chest worsened. "I don't know when you got it into your head that I'm out to get you, but I'm not."

"Oh, I don't know," I said, putting a finger to my chin and pretending to think, "was it when you ignored me to my face and accused me of trying to sleep with you?"

He flinched, but I kept going, flicking the same finger up in the air. "Oh, no, I got it. Maybe when you took money from my pocket without even having the backbone to talk to me first?"

I dropped my hand and smacked it on the body of my guitar, the echo ringing out like a curse. "Or maybe when you and my agent practically blackmailed me with losing even more income unless I agreed to play with you? Take your pick, Waters."

His nostrils flared, and for a moment, I thought he might actually yell back at me. But he didn't. "You know, for someone who doesn't know everything, you sure enjoy acting like you do."

I faltered for a moment. That was the second time he'd hinted that there'd been something going on that first night we met. Something that had set off all the other events.

But I was too worked up to listen. I didn't want him to have a solid reason for everything that had happened between us because then I'd have to rethink what I thought I knew about him. And admit that maybe I was wrong.

Crossing my arms over my chest, I said, "I know enough."

He sucked on his front teeth and nodded, looking away from me. But I didn't fail to catch the look of disappointment on his face as he did.

"Yeah, all right, Davis," he said, walking the rest of the way onto the path and taking his earbuds back out. "See you around." And then he was gone.

I watched him jog off, half expecting him to glance back over his shoulder at me. But he didn't. And he didn't come back around again either.

Later that evening, when I was curled up on my bed, staring blankly at my lyrics and playing the encounter out in my head over and over again, two things were abundantly clear to me.

The first was that my song did sound better with the drawn-out chorus. And the second was that I couldn't wipe the disappointed look on his face out of my head.

And that maybe, just maybe, he might not deserve my hatred.

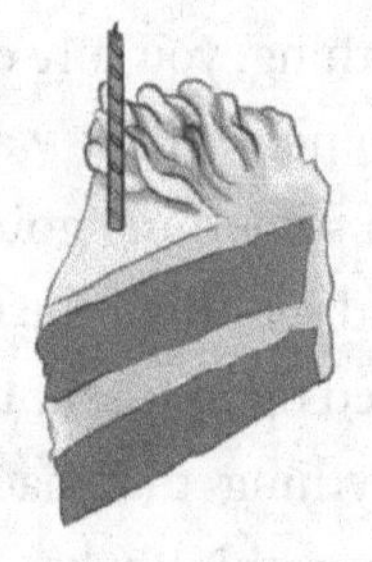

Chapter
14

I STARED AT the plastic, golden crown nestled in navy tissue paper and then up at my friend, who was wearing an outrageously large grin.

"Is there any specific reason you're giving me a bachelorette crown?" I asked, trying not to embed the plastic into my hands from how hard I was gripping it.

There's no way Garrett already asked her to marry him, and if he did, no way she'd have been able to hide her giddiness from me a single day, let alone several, while she'd gone shopping for a crown.

If possible, her smile widened. "It's not a bachelorette crown, you weirdo. It's a birthday crown!" she said, giving me something like jazz fingers and laughing.

I glanced back down at it, relief filling my entire chest cavity at her answer. Thank God. As much as I knew a marriage was coming eventually, I couldn't imagine either of them being ready to take that step *this* soon. Which was fine by me because I wasn't even remotely close to being ready to find a new place yet.

Grabbing the crown by the little combs at the end, I lifted it from its bed of tissue, eyeing Madison over the gaudy top. "My deepest apologies. Is there a reason you've handed me a *birthday* crown?"

Her smile dropped into a mock glare, and she reached out and swiped the crown from my grasp, balancing it on top of my head. "I may not always remember what day of the week it is from lack of sleep, but I know when my best friend's birthday is, woman."

"Are you sure? I'm pretty sure you can't even remember your own name these days," I said, dodging her responding slap and laughing. Then I laughed harder when she had no verbal argument against it.

She circled around the bar, into the kitchen, and grabbed an apple from the counter. "Thank you, Madison, I'm so glad to have a friend like you, Madison," she singsonged, overexaggerating my voice.

I plopped onto the stool across from her, stealing the apple from her hand the second she'd finished washing it. She glared at me, but knowing Jamie was close enough to hear her curse, she made do with flipping me off and grabbing another.

"Anyway," she said, coming back to lean against the bar next to me, "since I have no intention of staying out late on a Monday when your actual birthday is, I made plans for us tonight."

I narrowed my eyes, trying to chew quickly without biting a chunk out of my cheek in the process. "Tonight? But I thought you said you and Garrett were having a movie marathon tonight."

"Yep, I know," she said, popping the 'p' and grinning evilly at me. "I lied. Honestly, you should've seen it coming. Must be an age thing. Brain stops working as well once you get to a certain age."

I gave her a deadpanned look which only earned me an unattractive snort as she cackled. "If that's true, what does it say about *you?*"

"Why do you think I can't remember my name anymore?" she said, taking a giant bite of her own apple and shoving away from the bar. Stepping over Rugpants, who was aimlessly following her in the hopes she'd drop her food, Madison headed toward the hallway, talking over her shoulder.

"Go get ready and make it quick. I'm going to drop off Jamie at my parents', and then I'll swing by to pick you up to meet everyone."

Wait, what?

"Who's everyone?" Now that she mentioned it, I realized Garrett hadn't come over to see her yet like he usually did before he went home to shower. But even he was only one person.

She just moseyed into Jamie's room, singing, "You'll see," in a way that had me more nervous than anything.

"Nope, not happening."

She gaped at me; Jeep keys held aloft over her purse. "What do you mean? You always pick Jemmy's."

I fidgeted, ashamed to tell her that I was technically supposed to be *playing* at Jemmy's tonight with Adrian, up until I'd canceled on him a few days ago.

I did it out of pure selfishness to avoid the inevitable embarrassment I'd feel at seeing him again after my snappy attitude at the park. I rarely regretted my harsh tongue, but there was something about the look he'd given me before he'd run off that had me simmering with regret.

Not that canceling helped at all, since I'd felt just as much embarrassment afterward when I thought of all the lectures I'd given him about taking gigs away from me.

Ugh. I put my face in my hands, hating myself just a little, and my godawful pride a lot.

"Layla?"

"Because Adrian's performing here tonight," I muttered into my palms, sliding them down to cup my chin and stare out the windshield to the parking lot. I didn't even know what kind of car Adrian drove. I hadn't even thought about glancing outside my house to see the day he'd come over for practice.

For some reason I pictured him as a motorcycle type of man. Or maybe a Mini Cooper. I huffed a laugh at the image of him tucking his long-ass legs into one like a praying mantis in a nutshell.

Madison dropped her keys inside her purse and pulled out her phone, all the while looking at me like I'd lost one too many marbles. "Okay, so Adrian's playing tonight. And…"

"And he kind of hates me now," I finished for her, knowing she wouldn't understand why. I'd opted not to tell her about the park, nor of the singular "k" Adrian had sent in reply to my cancelation text.

Because let's face it, everyone knew that "k" was the texting equivalence to when a woman said she was "fine." Adrian was, in fact, not fine with me canceling.

The last thing I needed was Adrian seeing me strut my ass into the bar after that. Rule number one when playing hooky was to make sure you didn't get caught playing said hooky. If he could recognize me in a ballcap, squeezed between drunk people, there was no way I'd be able to hide from him looking like a fucking snack in my silver, sequin dress.

Madison twisted in her seat, fully facing me and cocking an eyebrow in a *what the hell haven't you told me* way. "I thought you two were getting along and working together now?"

I cringed. Getting along might have been a stretch, but whatever we'd been, I doubted we were still there now. "We had a fight." I paused and sighed. "That's not true. I ran into him at the park and I was kind of…"

"Kind of what?" she asked, her eyes wide and brows high, like she was nervous of whatever I was about to say. As if she thought he'd caught me running around butt-ass naked or something.

"A bitch."

"Oh."

I narrowed my eyes. She'd said "oh" like I'd just told her I'd been kind of sitting, or breathing, or something else normal. Like being bitchy was just part of who I was.

She continued staring at me, her eyes asking, "Have you met you?" I shrugged. Touché.

"Let's just go somewhere else, Mads."

She glanced over my shoulder, out the window, worrying her bottom lip. "I would, but…"

Banging against my window had me nearly peeing myself, and I twisted sharply, ready to verbally destroy someone for whacking their door against Madison's Jeep. But instead of a car door, or random stranger, I saw none other than Garrett's sister-in-law, Sarah, waving her hands.

I looked back at Madison, to see her still biting the shit out of her lip, and caved. There was no part of me that wanted to see Adrian tonight, but it was my own damn fault. Both for being a bitch to him, and for not telling my best friend about it. A friend who had gone out of her way to try to plan a surprise for my birthday.

Was I dreading the evening with every fiber of my being? Absolutely. But I had no one to blame but myself. Consequences of my own actions and all that.

I sighed and picked up my purse, yanking on the handle to open my door and step out. Sarah backed out of the way, her smile looking near painful as she pulled me into a hug the moment I shut the door.

"Happy birthday! I made Harry and Garrett save our table

so I could watch for you guys. Hey, Madison!" She pulled Madison into a similar tight hug and then beamed at us, leading the way toward the door.

"When Madison told me this place serves dollar drinks on Fridays, I was already down, but just wait until you see the hunk of a man on stage tonight. *Oof.*" She fanned her face, "I'd pay five dollars a drink just to look at that eye candy all evening."

Madison screeched to a stop at the doorway, snagging me by the arm and looking seconds from crying. "I'm sorry, Layla, I didn't know it'd be a problem. We don't have to go in. It's your birthday. I can go tell everyone we're going somewhere else."

I smiled at her, thankful to have a friend who loved me as much as she did. "It's fine, Mads. I'll live. I'll just ignore him, I'm quite good at it." Lie. I wasn't sure I'd ever been able to ignore Adrian Waters.

Sarah frowned, pulling open the door and letting Madison and me in first. "Who are we avoiding?"

Madison flashed her ID at the check-in, and I nodded at Tony, pointedly not looking toward the stage as Sarah led us past him and through the bar. "The eye candy."

I knew the second his gaze landed on me. I swore every hair along my entire body stood on end as his eyes tracked me all the way to the table. But still, I didn't look over at him. Even when his voice and music practically begged me to. I held firm.

I straightened my spine and adjusted the golden crown atop my head. I wasn't here for him, nor to perform. I was here for my birthday, and I was going to enjoy it.

Garrett and Harry both stood as we approached, the first

giving me a half smile and wishing me a happy birthday, while the latter stuck with a quiet nod. I smiled back and took a seat, cringing internally when the act made the deep cut of my dress bare my entire thigh toward the stage.

A line of seven pink shots, each with a puff of whipped cream on top, took up the center of the table, and I eyed them curiously, wondering who the extra shots were for. Because if they expected me to take three shots right off the bat with no food, tonight was about to go south real quick.

I circled my hand in the air over them, crossing my legs and trying in vain to cover a little more of my leg. "So, what's all this? A drinking game of some kind?"

I aimed my question at Sarah, knowing she'd be the one behind all things alcohol related. Neither Madison nor Garrett were very big drinkers.

"Not yet," she said, sliding a shot glass in front of each chair, including the two empty ones. "First, a birthday shot. Fran— whom I've decided I'm leaving Harry for—said it was cake flavored."

I grabbed the shot she pushed in front of me and took a sniff. It smelled more like vodka than anything else, but Fran knew their way around a bar and had yet to steer me wrong.

"Who are the other two shots for?" I asked, my mind flipping through the people I knew like a very short, sad stack of cards. There was no way Madison would've invited Ken, and her parents currently had Jamie. So, who did that leave?

"Are you cheating on me?"

The yelled accusation carried over Adrian's music, and I

turned, shot glass still in hand, expecting to see some marital spat occurring in the center of the bar. And although there was a ridiculously attractive man stomping through the bar with a heavy glare on his face, he was beelining for our table.

He looked extremely familiar, but I couldn't quite place where I knew him from. Another musician I'd seen in passing at a party, maybe?

He had clean-shaven, sharp features and jet-black hair that was slicked back, nearly matching the black jacket he had dangling from one fist. Tattoos covered every inch of his arms down to his wrists, and his green eyes were bright and zeroed in on none other than Madison.

Reaching our table, he pointed at her shot glass and sucked on his front teeth so that they made a loud hissing sound. "And out in public too. Who knew you had it in you, Curly."

Slowly setting my own glass back on the table, I uncrossed my legs, ready to jump up between them, if necessary. Madison, however, didn't seem fazed in the least by his accusation.

She tossed her curls over her shoulder and fluttered her eyelashes. "I take my pleasure where I can find it." Then she ran her tongue over the dollop of whipped cream and tipped her glass back, downing her shot. Her eyelashes continued to flutter, now more to blink back tears from the burn than flirting.

I glanced at Garrett, worried we were about to have a dead body on the floor, but he hadn't moved from his place beside her. Except to place his hand very, *very* high up on her thigh as he watched her lick a smear of whipped cream from her lip.

O-kay then.

The newcomer slapped a hand to his chest, feigning hurt rather than anger now. "I'll remember that the next time you want a drink after work." Madison only winked at him and laughed. And then those green eyes popped over to me. "I hear a happy birthday is in order, Blue."

I pressed my lips together and gave him several exaggerated blinks. The man was hot, but I wasn't much of a fan of nicknames from random men in bars. "Should I know you?" I finally asked, drumming my fingers across the tabletop in a way that reminded me of Adrian, who was currently singing a slow ballad. I was tempted to look up on stage, but somehow refrained.

The stranger's mouth transformed into a sensual smirk at my comment, but before he could say what I could only assume would be a pickup line or a dirty joke of some kind, a delicate, pale hand shot out from behind him and wrapped around his mouth.

A gorgeous woman stepped around him, her form-fitted maroon dress accentuating her curves and bright pink hair and showing off deep cleavage I was instantly jealous over. Her blue eyes, several shades darker than Adrian's, danced.

"Don't worry, he can't remember your name either. This is Nate," she said, patting his mouth. "He works with Madison. I'm Marissa. His girlfriend when he's behaving. Madison said it was your birthday and invited us to celebrate with you, if that's okay."

That's where I recognized him from. He was the bartender at the restaurant Madison worked at. Him gesturing to her drink suddenly made way more sense. I vaguely remembered seeing him in passing while visiting Madison during her night shifts once or twice, but not enough to have recognized him on sight.

I smiled, immediately deciding I liked them. "Thanks, Marissa. Sarah here has shots lined up if you guys are down."

She nodded vigorously, but then her eyes went wide, and she yanked her hand from Nate's mouth, wiping it down his arm. "Did you seriously just lick me?"

He raised a brow, smirking down at her while he pulled her body flush against his side. "Don't act like you don't love it when I lick you."

Jesus, was everyone here having sex but me? It was *my* birthday goddamnit, why was I the spare wheel? If anyone should be getting laid tonight, it was me. The bitter thought had me tearing my eyes off all the couples eye-fucking around me and landing on Adrian for the first time since the park.

Like always, he was dressed in black, his guitar almost blending into him if it weren't for the sheen of the overhead lights reflecting off of it. His hair was down and unruly, like he'd spent almost as much time running his hands through it as he'd been singing.

His cheeks were flushed, and his fingers danced up and down his guitar, but the usual content smile he wore while he played was missing. I re-crossed my legs and turned fully toward him, studying his face to try to make out more of his expression.

Why did he look so emotionless? He didn't look happy, or sad, or even angry. He just looked…there. Like he was simply going through the motions, waiting for the hours to pass. It bothered me more than it should have, and I squinted harder, convinced I had to be imagining it.

Like he had a sixth sense to my attention, he suddenly turned and locked eyes with me. As if I'd been shouting my thoughts about him across the bar. I lurched back, almost knocking my chair over if it hadn't been for the hand Nate wrapped around the back of it.

"Just how many of those shots have you had there, Blue?"

Chapter
→ 15 ←

"LET'S PLAY A game or something," I burst out, desperate for a distraction. Anything to keep Madison's keen attention off my face and to hopefully make Adrian think he'd just imagined me blatantly staring at him.

Sarah knocked back what had to be her third shot by how big her mannerisms were and how flushed her face was. "Ooo, like what?"

Hell, I didn't know. I was about to suggest Quarters since it was the first game to pop into my head, but stopped just before I could as a better suggestion came to mind. I grinned wickedly and nudged Madison's foot with my own below the table. "We could always play Never Have I Ever."

I felt, more than saw in the dim bar lighting, her blush ten shades of red next to me. "Hard pass."

Nate's eyes darted back and forth between us, and then at Sarah and Harry who were chuckling on the other side of the table. "Why do I feel like I'm missing an inside joke to something."

Controlling her giggles, Sarah waved her hand, teetering slightly. "No inside joke. Layla's just teasing Madison about the time she and my brother-in-law both admitted to having butt sex in front of everyone."

Madison choked, and Nate whipped his head toward her, eyebrows disappearing into his hairline. "Like…okay, wait…I have questions. Several of them."

Madison's blush intensified, and she mumbled something I could barely hear over Adrian's singing, but it sounded a lot like needing another drink. And then she was twisting out of Garrett's arms, head down, and practically running for the bar.

Nate's face lit up, and he threw back his shot like it was water. He placed a firm kiss on Marissa's lips and then made his own way toward the bar as well, shouting after Madison. "Curly! Wait, did he do it to you, or did you do it to him? I have recommendations! Stop walking so fast."

I stood next to Garrett, who was watching them and shaking his head. It was nice to see he'd finally relaxed a little when it came to seeing Madison interact with other men. The gentle giant was terrifyingly protective.

Thankful for the distraction and trying not to let my smidgen of jealousy get the best of me, I pursed my lips and pretended to consider him.

"You know, one of these days, I'm going to convince her to

spill the answer to that question."

He just pushed off the table and stood, knocking his fist against the wood, and winking at me before turning to trail after the love of his life. "Who says it's not both."

We ended up playing Quarters, after all. Shockingly, a loud ass bar was difficult to converse and play any real games in. However, the dollar drinks were working their magic, and an hour in, everyone seemed to be having a good time. Silent, broody company included.

I picked up a coin and bounced it, using more focus than necessary. But I could feel Madison's attention from where she sat, knowing even through my smile, she could sense something was off.

It wasn't that I was having a bad time; I wasn't. Even with the company on stage staring daggers at my back most of the night. I'd half expected him to approach our table during his first break, and when he hadn't, my mood had soured against my will. Not even a free drink from Fran had perked it back up.

And that only soured my mood even more. I'd never let a man get to me before. Ever. And I'd certainly never felt guilt over being testy with one. But for whatever stupid reason, I couldn't stop my mind from wandering to Adrian and wondering what he was thinking right now. If he'd even continue playing with me now that I'd blown him off and rubbed it in his face.

I picked up another quarter, angling it to bounce just right against the table when I heard it.

My hand froze midair, the quarter clenched between my thumb and middle finger hard enough to whiten my fingertips, and my eyes turned into giant saucers in my face. Shock burned a path straight through me, lighting every inch of me on fire. No way. No, he didn't.

Slowly, like my body no longer knew how to operate correctly, I twisted in my seat, pushing my glass of vodka and lime away and setting the quarter on the table next to it.

"What's wrong, Layla?"

I tuned Madison out, my eyes, my ears, my entire being focused with laser-like precision on the man strumming out a song on stage.

A familiar song.

My song.

He didn't sing. He couldn't. Not without making up his own lyrics since mine hadn't been done when he'd swiped up my notebook to read them. He was just humming along to the tune, his voice as smooth as silk, and staring right at me as he played my song on a fucking electric guitar. Exactly as he'd told me I should do, at the park.

How long had that taken him to learn it? Adrian didn't learn songs by ear with ease the way I did. I knew he could, but he preferred, and excelled, more at reading music. Which meant that he had to have been humming it on repeat in his head and have practiced it. *A lot.*

My body warmed, and it had nothing to do with the large

amount of alcohol I'd consumed in the last hour or so.

To anyone else, it would just appear like he was warming back up after his last break, testing his voice and strings. Only he and I knew what he was doing, the challenge he'd laid at my feet, like a secret tensing between us, teetering us both on the edge.

You wanna push me off a tightrope, but you'll fall too…

The lyrics flickered through my mind, keeping pace with the notes he was still playing. My fingers ached to whip out my phone and jot them down before I lost them to the void of the alcohol haze, but I couldn't pull my gaze away from him.

Adrian had both hands pressed to my back, hovering me at the cusp, daring me to react. To flip him off and stomp out again like I'd done before. But I didn't.

All I could do was sit there frozen and listen because he'd been right. The arrogant asshole had been completely right, and now that I'd heard it, I knew I had to have it just like that. And not with just any random electric guitar bit. I wanted *exactly* what he was doing.

I wanted to punch him for making me need him for yet another reason. And by the smirk on his face as he finally faded out and started up his next song, he knew it. And for a reason I wasn't ready to look at yet, when I turned back toward the table, my own smirk graced my lips.

I spent the remainder of Adrian's performance being

extremely invested in the company around me. Anything to keep my wandering eyes from betraying me again.

Luckily, it wasn't that hard. Nate and Sarah immediately hit it off, bantering back and forth until most of us were in tears from laughing, and their significant others had to replace their drinks with water. Now we were all starting to shift and stretch from sitting at a table for hours, getting ready to call it a night.

One by one, everyone started to make their way toward Fran to pay their tabs, and I stood as well, stretching my arms above my head.

"Sit back down, Layla. I got your drinks."

I gave Madison a look I hoped she'd read as *shut the fuck up*, and lowered my arms. "I can buy my drinks, Mads."

If Sarah or Marissa had offered, I'd probably have taken them up on it and been thankful. But there was no way I was going to make the single mother of the group buy my alcohol. Especially since I'd drank more than just the dollar drink options.

She glowered at me. "Garrett already paid for his and my drinks, so it's fine. Besides, I didn't get you any other gifts. So, let me at least buy your birthday drinks."

"You could always pay me in sexual favors," I said, snorting when Nate whipped his head toward us as he and Marissa arrived back to the table from paying their tab. The intrigued look he wore earned him a smack upside the back of his head.

"Mads, I love you dearly. But please let me pay for my own tab."

Her face tightened, and I geared up for an argument, but

Marissa piped up before Madison could say anything. "Actually, your friend already paid for your tab, Layla."

She flashed me a wide grin. "I told him we weren't staying much longer, but I invited him to join us until we leave."

My friend? "Who are you talking about? Garrett and Harry?" I asked, looking around the bar for them to inquire if they'd done it. It'd be a little weird, but I wouldn't put it past either of them if they thought it'd make their women happy.

Marissa shook her head and pointed a long, manicured nail past my shoulder, toward the stage, and a rock dropped in the pit of my stomach. Oh God, she meant—

Her smile fell, a mixture of distress and horror filling her eyes as she lowered her voice and whispered, "Shit, is he a total jackass or a stalker or something?" At the same time a new voice behind me said, "Happy Birthday, Davis."

My entire body tensed, and I slowly turned, giving myself the fastest pep talk I'd ever received in my life. I was not going to let him talk shit to me in front of my friends. Not when they'd all gone out of their way to be here for me.

Fight or no fight, I had a right to go out with my friends to celebrate my birthday without Adrian calling me out for it in front of them. Especially Madison.

In the time it took me to turn all the way around, a handful of strangers had offered hellos and compliments to him for his show. I swallowed down a bite of bitter disappointment. If I'd have played with him, those compliments would have been to the both of us.

God, my emotions were a total fucking wreck.

Adrian dipped his head and acknowledged each person as they passed, but his eyes never left me. He tucked his hands in his pockets and tipped his head down toward me, his hair still just as unruly as it'd been on stage.

I itched to run my fingers through it and smooth it away from his face. Fuck. No, I didn't. *What the hell, Layla?* I hadn't seen him in almost two weeks, and somehow I'd forgotten just how magnetic he was up close.

I held my glass in a death grip, begging my body to find any other person in this bar attractive to help my libido forget about this goddamn man.

Finally finding my voice, after a way too long stare down, I nodded. "Thanks."

With me seated, he towered over me. His eyes trailed down my shimmering, mid-thigh dress, pausing on the large slit, and then continued up past my head to land on the golden crown I'd forgotten I was wearing.

"I didn't know you were into playing dress up."

I swallowed the lump in my throat, aware that we were drawing the attention of every member of my group, including the men who'd returned from paying. "I thought we'd already addressed the fact that you don't know anything about me, so that tracks," I said, tipping my head back to finish the last bit of vodka left in my glass.

I hadn't wanted it, and didn't need it, but I *did* need something to do with my hands.

"I know more than you think," he said, eyes focused on my mouth.

I darted my tongue out to lick the dribble of alcohol that leaked out, and I swore his eyes heated for a moment before he blinked it away. Yep, I definitely didn't need any more because I was clearly seeing shit.

"You had a good lineup tonight," I said, needing to change the subject. The competitive side of me wanted to find a flaw to point out to get him back for the shit he'd pulled with my song, but no one in my group would understand why.

I'd just look like I was being a bitch for no reason, and I was getting kind of tired of always being seen as one. It was exhausting.

"Thank you," he said, still not looking away from me. It felt like he was memorizing every inch of my face. Like he'd somehow forgotten what I'd looked like in the days we hadn't seen one another.

"I originally had an even better lineup with another musician, but had to change it last minute when she canceled. So, I'm glad my performance passed your approval."

I stiffened at the underhanded remark. "I didn't say anything about your performance passing my approval. I merely said your song lineup was well chosen," I said, already failing at my newfound *don't be a bitch* attempt. It was like I had no control around him. He brought the feistiness right out of me.

A thick, weighted silence fell, and it felt like every eye in the bar was on us, even though it was only the eyes of approximately six, overly nosy people.

Nate was the first one to break it. He leaned toward Marissa and whispered, loudly enough for us to hear, "This is why you shouldn't go poking around trying to matchmake people."

She huffed at him, her cheeks stained a nice shade of pink as she toyed with the glass of water in front of her. "I assumed they were friends because they both kept staring at each other."

She snapped her lips together when she saw us both now staring at *her*.

"We are friends," Adrian said, at the same time I said, "We're mild acquaintances, at best."

If anything, Marissa's face went from pink to maroon, and I honestly felt sorry for the poor woman. She'd just been trying to find me a hot guy to chat with. And honestly, if she'd have picked any other guy in the bar, I might've kissed her.

Adrian smiled at her, one softer than any he'd ever given me. "Ignore Davis. She's just cranky because it was brought to her attention that I was right about one of her songs, and her pride is still in mourning."

Marissa popped her lips, eyes darting back and forth between us. "Okay," she drew out, not sounding at all convinced, "you know what, I think we're just going to take off and pretend like the last five minutes never happened."

A choked laugh slipped out of me at her blunt comment, but she wasn't joking. With a quick elbow jab at Nate, she thanked Madison for the invitation, waved at the rest of us, and dragged her boyfriend to the door.

Madison cleared her throat and shifted away from Garrett to hold a hand out toward the irritating man still standing over me. "So, you must be Adrian." He nodded, taking her proffered hand and giving it a firm shake.

"We didn't really get to officially meet at the house. I'm Madison, and this is Garrett." Adrian nodded as she continued around the table, introducing the others who remained.

Sarah, who'd of course been ogling him from the moment she'd arrived, immediately jumped in and began asking questions about him and how we knew each other. I didn't answer. Because I'd have either had to explain the entire, messy way we'd met, or lie. And I didn't want to do either.

But Adrian, it seemed, had no such problem with slipping an easy lie through his teeth. "We met through our agent, who paired us up to work together. We were supposed to play tonight, and now I guess I understand why she canceled," he added, eyeing my crown again.

"That's my fault," Madison chimed in, an apology written all over her alcohol-flushed face, whether at me not playing with him, or at bringing me here to begin with, I didn't know. "I didn't ask her if she had to work, I just kind of made birthday plans."

I frowned, not sure why everyone seemed to be covering for me, trying their best to make me seem nicer than I actually was. It was weird.

Adrian's lips tipped up. "It's no problem. Layla's the best performer in this area, so I'm honestly just lucky to have her partner with me at all."

Wait, come again? My mouth fell open, unsure if I'd heard that correctly or if I was drunker than I thought. Had he just complimented me? On purpose? Of his own accord? Who was this man, and what had he done with the real Adrian?

He continued chatting with Sarah and Harry about the popular covers he'd done, and Madison leaned toward me, whispering in my ear. "I thought you said he hated you?"

Getting my bearings, I swallowed, pulling the two sides of my dress together, and crossing my legs so I'd stop flashing Adrian the entirety of my thigh.

"Maybe not hate, but he certainly isn't a fan of me. This is just an act for the public." One he was annoyingly good at, because if I didn't know any better, by the way he was going on, I'd think he actually liked me.

She looked skeptical. "I don't know, Layla, he seems genuine." She hiccupped and then shrugged, like I should just give him a chance and hope for the best.

But he'd burned me once before, and I wasn't the kind of person to step back into the same flame. "Yeah, well, so did Satan when he convinced Eve to eat the apple," I whispered back.

She frowned at him and then at me, and I sighed. "I'm just saying, everyone has multiple sides to them, and I don't know enough about his to know whether I can trust him."

"Do you want to trust him?"

Yes. No. "I don't know."

She nodded, contemplative. "Yeah, I know what you mean." She leaned her head on my shoulder, her breath reeking of alcohol. "Do you want to go home?"

"I thought you'd never ask."

She stepped away to talk to Garrett, and I slipped my wrist through the strap of my clutch and slid off my chair. The mixture of several drinks combined with my heels had me misjudging the placement of my feet, and I swayed slightly, teetering back before a large hand wrapped around my bicep and steadied me.

I closed my eyes, enjoying the warmth of the hold, before realizing who it belonged to. I snapped my eyes open to see Adrian looking down at me, worry lines in his face, and his other arm outstretched, like he was ready to catch me if needed.

I stared at his full lips, my body subconsciously leaning into him, before I wrestled the control back into my limbs and stepped back. His nostrils flared and his jaw did that weird tic thing it sometimes did when he looked at me, but he dropped his arm.

"Are you all right?"

"I'm not going to pass out or vomit on your shoes, if that's what you mean," I snapped, embarrassed, not only that I'd lost my balance in front of him, but that he'd seen the way his touch affected me.

He sighed and ran a hand through his hair. "I wasn't implying anything, Davis. I was checking to make sure you were okay. Will Madison be driving you home?"

I nodded, unsure what to do with this version of him. Why was he being nice to me? I'd been an ass and then blown him off to get tipsy. I'd be furious if I were in his place. "Why aren't you pissed off at me?" I blurted.

He blinked at me, his eyes roving all over my face like he was searching for an answer. "I was."

Okay, now we were getting somewhere. "But you aren't anymore. Why?" I demanded, grabbing onto the back of the closest chair to keep myself from swaying. Okay, maybe I was more than a little tipsy.

He ran his hand through his hair again, something I was beginning to realize he did when he was exasperated or stressed out. "I was pissed because I thought you'd bailed on me just to get back at me for whatever *you* were pissed at *me* about."

He lowered his hand, and it almost seemed to twitch toward me before he tucked both hands back into his pockets. "Yes, I wanted to play with you tonight because we'd agreed on it, but you're allowed to enjoy your birthday, Davis. You should've just told me that's why you were canceling so I didn't spend the last few days thinking you bailed on me."

My stomach sank at his words, my fuzzy brain fighting with itself on whether I should admit the truth or not. That I hadn't canceled because of either of the reasons he thought, but because I hadn't been able to find the fucking ovaries to face him.

In the end, I opted for honesty. Because Adrian and I may have both had a bad habit of being asshats to each other, but we were at least honest. Even if it sucked.

"I didn't cancel because of my birthday," I said, tucking my hair behind my ear and staring hard at his chest. Why did he have to be nice to me all of a sudden and make me feel even worse?

"Okay," he said, his blue eyes pinned on my face, "so why did you cancel on me then?" He stepped closer to me and raised his hand again, as if he might reach out and pull me into his chest.

I swallowed, realizing that I wanted him to. My eyes

dropped to his lips, wondering if they'd be as soft as they looked, or as hard as his eyes. "Because—"

"Layla!"

I jolted back, holding on to the chair for dear life to keep from falling and cracking my skull. Sarah grabbed my arm, laughing her ass off. "You won't believe what your roommate just—oh, sorry. Did I interrupt?"

I shook my head, clearing my thoughts. I'd been thinking about kissing Adrian. *Adrian.* God, I needed a huge glass of water, some meds, a vibrator, and a long-ass night of sleep.

"No," I said, plastering a fake smile on my face and shuffling back from both of them. "Adrian was just saying goodbye. Which is good, because if Madison is tipsy enough to be doing dumb shit, then we should definitely be heading home."

A loud grunt from Garrett to our left backed up my comment and had me insanely curious as to what Madison could have possibly just done or said.

I looked back up at Adrian, expecting to see disappointment painted across his face, but he only stared and stared at me. His eyes boring into me.

And it wasn't until after he'd nodded goodbye to everyone and slipped away toward the stage for his gear that I realized I'd called him by his first name.

Fuck, I was tits deep in trouble.

Chapter
→ 16 ←

REGRET FELT A whole lot like knives stabbing into the backs of my eyelids. It was wrong how poisonous a delicious drink could feel like only a few hours after consuming them. I wasn't one to often have hangovers, but that was because I typically stuck to one liquor all night. Combining several, it seemed, did not please my body at all.

"Kill me. Please."

Madison barely twitched from where she was curled up on the bed next to me. "That would involve getting up to find a weapon, so no," she grumbled.

I slapped my hand around until I found her face and prodded her cheek with my fingers. "You don't even have to get up, just lay your pillow over my face. Please. As a birthday gift to me. I won't ask for anything else."

She grunted and finally rolled over, glowering at me with one eye, while the lashes on her other appeared to be stuck together from the mascara she hadn't washed off.

By the time Garrett—who'd only had the one shot hours before we'd left—had driven us home, Madison and I had become more ragdoll than human, our bodies limp against the Jeep windows.

Both of us had barely dragged our butts into the bathroom to pee before Garrett had gently ushered us into her room and left water and meds on her nightstand. And by the slight noises I could hear coming from the kitchen, he was now currently making breakfast.

Bless that fucking man.

Manually prying her lids apart, Madison huffed a breath that made me instantly want to shrivel up and die inside. "I already got you a gift, so I'm off the hook." She slid her pillow out from under her head and shoved it at me. "Smother yourself."

"You didn't even buy my drinks. Ad—Waters did."

She raised a brow, suddenly looking more awake than she had a second ago. "Well, then I guess it's a good thing I lied about not getting you anything so that you'd let me buy your drinks." She gestured lazily over me. "There's actually something hidden in my nightstand drawer for you."

"Liars burn in the fiery depths of hell, you know," I said, tossing her pillow back at her and flopping onto my back.

"At least I'll have *Satan* to keep me company."

I gave her the finger, knowing full well she was referring to

Adrian. Her throaty chuckle confirmed it.

"Anyway," she said, finally hoisting herself to lean back against the wall and snatch the water and meds off the other nightstand, "if you opt not to kill yourself, it's right inside the drawer."

I stared at her for another second, considering waiting her out to see if I could make her get up first, but my parched mouth was unbearably thirsty. "Ugh. Fine. But only because I was already getting up for the water anyway."

The wench huffed a laugh and began massaging her temples as I downed my own meds and opened the drawer. Nestled inside was a folded square of the same tissue paper the crown had been in. A crown I no longer had any idea where I'd placed.

I sat back in bed and pushed up into a sitting position next to her, tearing open the tissue. And then proceeded to laugh hard enough to make my already aching head pound.

"Oh my God, these are fantastic," I said, squinting an eye shut against the pain beating a drum in my forehead, and lifting a set of necklaces out of the tissue. They were two halves of a heart, clicking together to read "best friends."

I unhooked them from the cardboard back and handed her one of them, while holding the other in my open palm. "This is the most worthless gift I've ever received, and I shall cherish it above all others."

We were both still laughing like smelly, wrinkled lunatics when Garrett knocked on the door. "If you two aren't still drunk in there, I made eggs and toast."

A loud, unladylike noise came from me, but I honestly

wasn't sure if it was my moan, my stomach, or a mix of both. "Oh my God, Mads, I might steal him. A man who cooks holds the key to my heart."

"I didn't know Adrian cooked?"

Like a doll straight from a horror flick, I turned to stare at my best friend, who was suddenly extremely interested in her cuticles.

"Don't make me throw this necklace in your face, wench."

She rolled her eyes and hefted herself off the bed, cringing when she remembered she was still in her crumpled shirt and underwear from the night before. She wandered around the bed and picked up her bra and jeans, trying, and failing, to look innocent.

"It was just a question."

"Bullshit."

"So, you don't know then."

I stood as well, grabbing the first pair of leggings I could find on the ground and shaking it around to release at least a few pieces of dog hair before dragging them on.

"Did you meet the same man I did? I'd bet my left tit he's a good cook. The man is stubborn as shit and super fucking fit. Not to mention single. No way is he surviving off ramen and Twinkies."

She shrugged, opening the door and allowing the mouthwatering smell of food to fill the room. Thank God hangovers didn't make me nauseous.

"Maybe he buys pre-made meals."

I blew a loud raspberry and followed her down the hall,

readying myself for Sadie when she jumped up to greet me. "Not on a musician's salary, he's not."

Garrett thankfully interrupted our conversation to wrap his arms around Madison and plant a soft kiss to her lips. They murmured quietly to each other, him apparently not caring about her alcohol-infused morning breath. I blew out a breath into my palm and sniffed. Jesus. I wasn't one to talk.

Squeezing past them, I grabbed a plate and loaded food onto it, thanking Garrett as I settled myself at the bar. "Is there, by chance, coffee?" I asked, talking around an absurdly large bite of eggs.

Garrett nodded and turned to grab a few mugs as Madison took the pot and began filling them. "In all seriousness, Layla. He didn't seem all that upset to see you. He actually seemed a whole lot nicer than you'd painted him out to be."

She raised her hands, warding off the hexes I was silently aiming her way. "Don't throw the necklace at my face. I'm just saying, maybe he's not as bad as you think he is. Maybe just give him a chance."

I took another huge forkful of eggs and washed it down with coffee that immediately scalded my tongue. She was lucky I'd left the necklace on the bed.

"I put out an olive branch the night I met him, and he lit it on fire and whacked me in the face with it. Burn me once, shame on you. Burn me twice?"

She sat down at the bar next to me, cradling her own mug and making room for the plate Garrett slid to her. "Did you ever figure out why he came to town?

I shook my head. "No, and I don't care anymore." Lie. My nosey ass wanted to know so bad. My money was on a nasty breakup. That'd explain the sudden move and the unhappiness I sometimes glimpsed on his face. Plus, the attitude and untrusting look he'd given me that first night.

And suddenly, I wanted to know who this no-named woman was, who'd pushed him to the point of moving, more than I wanted to eat my damn breakfast. Ugh.

"Anyway," I said, feeling both Madison's and Garrett's eyes on me, as well as the dogs that were waiting to see if I would drop any food, "what I do know is that Waters puts his work above everything else. He cared more about jumping in the pool and snagging gigs than he did about the people that might affect."

Because what if it hadn't been someone like *me* he'd kicked out of Jemmy's?

"What if I'd been a country singer he couldn't have paired up with? Would he have backed down, or would he have kept the gigs and told me I was shit out of luck?"

I twisted my mug around, watching a bead of coffee drip down the side and land on the bar. "That kind of mentality is great for climbing the ladder, but not so great for trust outside of work."

Adrian's words to me from last night niggled at the back of my head, telling me that he couldn't only care about climbing the ladder and booking gigs if he'd been so understanding about me bailing on our show. I pushed them down with a vigorous bite of buttered toast.

Madison leaned up over the bar to reach for the liquid creamer, adding more until her beverage looked more like milk than coffee. "Outside of work, huh? I didn't realize we were seeing Mr. Waters outside of work already." She waggled her eyebrows.

I scoffed, hoping the combination of my headache and dry throat would help make my dismissal convincing. I hadn't technically ever seen him outside of practice and work discussions. Not on purpose, at least.

"Don't even go there. I'll admit, he's hot, and his arrogant personality probably means he's got a big dick," I said, earning me a raised-brow side-eye from Garrett. "But no. He's not my type."

I swallowed down more inferno coffee, attempting to wash away the chalky feeling those words left in my mouth. The truth was, I wasn't *his* type. I found myself again, wondering about the woman who'd likely broken his heart and pushed him here, toward me.

And then a memory of something Adrian had said at the holiday party flickered in my mind, one I'd shut out because I hadn't cared at the time. Hadn't wanted to be anywhere near him.

"You know, besides Larry Bosenet, you're the only person I know here."

I sat up straighter, ignoring Madison's questioning grunt over her mouthful of food. I was too busy reorganizing the thoughts in my head, trying to make sense of them past the drum beat.

I was bitchy, and feisty, and testy, and every other similar term people had come up with. I'd been called them my entire life. And it didn't bother me. They were all true. It was my go-to personality trait.

Because I'd rather be seen as a bitch than as weak or soft. A newborn kitten was far less likely to survive this harsh-ass world than a pissed-off porcupine.

Yet, here I was, judging Adrian for the exact same behavior. He'd been dumped and had to move to a new town where he knew no one and had to start his career all over again. Just like me.

Sure, our reasons for moving couldn't be more different, and sure, the venues here knew his name, whereas I'd had to start from scratch, but still. Maybe Adrian and I weren't all that different.

And as much as I loathed to admit it, I owed him a few apologies at this point.

I glanced at the oven clock to see it was close to the time I'd gone to the park the day I'd run into Adrian. If I hurried, and chugged a whole lot more water, I could maybe run into him again.

"When are you picking up Jamie?" I asked, shoveling the last few bites of breakfast into my mouth.

Madison glanced at the clock as well and winced. "As soon as I'm done eating. I should've picked him up already, I didn't anticipate sleeping in so long."

Garrett reached out and squeezed her hand. "I talked to your dad this morning to go pick him up, and they were putting together some new train set, so he's fine, Maddie."

Perfect. Was I about to use a kid as a middleman to make it less awkward if I did succeed at running into Adrian? Absolutely, I was. But it wouldn't be the worst thing I'd ever done.

"I'll pick him up," I said, pushing off the stool and walking over to deposit my dishes into the sink. "I'm going to head to the park to get some practice in since it's supposed to be decent out today." *Please let it be decent out so it's not obvious how* not *planned out my plans are.* "He can tag along with me so you two can shower. I'll just have to take your Jeep so we can all fit."

"Are you sure? It'll be hard to practice if he talks your ear off."

Garrett chuckled at her comment, and I couldn't help but join him. Madison wasn't wrong, it was extremely hard to focus when that kid began lecturing about dragons or video games. But since I didn't actually care about practicing, I wasn't worried about it.

"Yeah, I'm sure. I don't mind. He can run around with Sadie for me, so that I don't have to exercise with a headache." Win-win.

She worried her lip, and I already knew what was going through her head before she even opened her mouth.

"Mads, it's fine. He'll talk my ear off for a few minutes on the ride over, I'll attempt to understand whatever he's telling me, and then I'll send them off with a nice big stick. They'll have a blast."

"All right," she said, her face not matching her words at all.

"I just feel bad about you watching him when you're trying to work."

She followed me down the hall back toward her room, watching me while I dug around the blankets looking for my phone. "Plus, you're taking my shift tomorrow. You need you time."

Finding it on the floor next to the dress I'd worn last night, I picked both up and slipped from her room to mine, squeezing her arm on my way.

"I took my own shift, not yours. You don't work there anymore. Delegate, woman."

"I told you I'm not the only one who thinks you need to do that more," Garrett said, coming to stand against the doorway of Madison's room, his arms crossed with one ankle propped over the other.

I dug around my dresser drawer, looking for a pair of clean socks. Laundry would be my villain origin story. "Listen to your boyfriend. I got our kid. You do whatever it is you two do when no one is home."

He waggled his eyebrows at her in a way that was so unlike him, I couldn't help but cackle. I may live alone for the rest of my life, but at least I knew she'd be loved for the rest of hers by a man who was the best sugar daddy she'd ever find.

Chapter
➳ 17 ❧

IN THE END, although I did bring my guitar, I left the case unopened on the ground by my feet, opting instead to devote more focus on Jamie. I'd felt like I hadn't been able to do as much with him lately, and since I'd be missing out on Sundays now, that wasn't likely to change anytime soon.

Beth had given him a brand-new animal book, this one about ocean creatures, and we'd spent the drive talking all manner of fun shark facts. I now knew that sharks didn't technically have bones, and their skin felt like sandpaper. Or something like that.

He was now running across the field as fast as his legs could take him, attempting to race Sadie to the other side. Sadie, bless her heart, stuck right by him, letting him think he stood a chance. I, on the other hand, was sitting on a park bench, holding a notebook in my lap that I was pretending to write in, while not paying attention to it at all.

We'd been there at least twenty minutes by then, and I was starting to think that today was one of the days Adrian didn't frequent the park to run, when his form finally came into view.

I instantly knew it was him. Not because he was wearing a neon sign or because he was singing at the top of his lungs or anything, but because I was staring down the path like a serial killer. That, and I was beginning to think I could recognize his body anywhere, but I'd rather blame it on the serial killer stare.

The second I realized he was, indeed, coming over, I dropped my face to my notebook, drawing little swirls in the margins until his steps grew louder.

I looked up as he began to slow, and the sight of him sent heat barreling straight down to my core. His hair was tied back with wild strands framing his face, his clothing stuck to him just like last time, but it was his eyes that did it. They were on fire, and they were pinned to me.

"Waters."

"Davis."

"I was starting to wonder if you were running today. Thought maybe you'd exaggerated a bit when you said you came every day," I said, allowing my eyes to peruse his muscles for one very quick second. Only a blind person would think this man lied about daily exercise.

He wasn't as filled out as Garrett, but damn, this man was toned.

He blinked at me, pulling the earbuds from his ears and

tapping on his phone. For a second, I thought he wouldn't say anything, his jaw working back and forth. But then he shot his eyes up at me. "You were waiting for me?"

I swallowed. Okay, maybe I should've worded that a little better to not make me look like a stalker. No use denying it now though, I'd already dug the damn hole.

I pushed up off the bench, not wanting him to be standing over me for this. Just because I was admitting to being wrong, didn't mean I'd suddenly lost my dignity.

"I was," I said, nodding and smoothing my hands down my leggings. "I wanted to…apologize," I said, muttering out the last word as fast as possible.

I felt, more than saw, him straighten his spine, like I'd startled the shit out of him. His mouth opened and then shut. I rushed on, feeling my face warm from the way he was staring at me.

"Not about the show last night, but about the last time we were here. I may have…" I looked at the ground, shuffling my feet, "overreacted a little about my song."

He made a noise that sounded an awful lot like a swallowed laugh birthing a choked grunt. "I'm sorry, I didn't quite catch that. You may have what?"

I lifted my head up to glare half-heartedly at him, only to find that his attention was most definitely not on my face. His eyes darted up from where they'd strayed to my ass—which was all the more pronounced in my tight leggings—and something sharp and intense flickered across them before he blinked it away.

"I charge a fee, you know," I said, throwing his same words back at him that he'd said to me at the duplex. But on the inside, my chest fucking hummed. It was nice to know he wasn't as unaffected by me as I originally thought. It felt good to have him look at me that way. Really good.

If I'd expected Adrian to flush with embarrassment at getting caught, or shrug it off like it hadn't happened, I couldn't have been more wrong. He let his eyes trail down my body again, and his lips curled into a wicked smirk that had the heat already building in my core, licking all the way up my spine.

God, I bet this man was good in bed. Those long, talented fingers, calloused just enough for a little extra friction, those full lips, and those goddamn muscles that could probably keep him pumping and moving for—

"Sadie, no!" yelled a voice behind him.

I'd never been more relieved to see my dog jump all over Adrian than I was in that moment. Because what the hell had my mind just been doing? I sat back onto the bench, crossing my legs tighter than necessary, and gave Jamie a smile I dearly hoped wasn't strained.

"I'm so sorry," Jamie rushed out, "I don't know why—oh. It's you," he said, his worried expression falling off his face when he recognized who Sadie was snuggling up to.

I bit the inside of my cheeks to keep from laughing at the unworried look the kid was aiming at him. But Adrian didn't appear to take any offense to Jamie not caring about Sadie knocking *him* over.

He smiled at him. "Hey, Jamie, how are you?"

Jamie's eyes darted back and forth between us, his chest still moving at a rapid speed from his sprints across the field with Sadie.

"I'm fine. What are you doing here?" he asked, but unlike the first time they'd met, his question had more curiosity than sass. Being out in the open, rather than in the enclosed space of his home, was probably less stressful for him.

Adrian walked over to take a seat on the bench next to me, an appropriate distance away. And I definitely didn't watch, nor did I notice the way his sweats pulled at his thighs and crotch as he got settled.

"I live close by and was just going for a run before I saw you guys. I hope I'm not intruding."

My instinct was to tell him he was, just to see that smirk grace his face, but I refrained, allowing Jamie the courtesy of answering. If he truly didn't want Adrian here, I'd ask him to leave, although I had a feeling the man wouldn't have to be asked.

Jamie considered him for a moment, but then shook his head. "No, it's okay. We're just hanging out so my mom can have a rest day," he said, coming to sit between us while Sadie plopped down on his feet, tongue hanging out of her mouth.

Adrian tipped his head down toward him, resting an ankle over a knee. "I bet she appreciates that a lot."

Jamie toed at the ground and shrugged, and my heart squeezed a bit. There was once a time when his feet couldn't reach the ground, and he'd swing them back and forth while he ate apple slices next to Madison. It seemed like forever ago now.

"She deserves it. She works really hard."

Adrian's responding smile was kind, but there was an edge to it, one I only caught because I was paying such close attention. "Most mothers do."

Most. What did that mean? It was true that not all mothers were good mothers, but the word seemed more loaded than that, and I immediately wanted to ask him more. But as if sensing my attention, Adrian shifted back, resting his arm along the back of the bench.

"Do you play any instruments, Jamie?" he asked, changing the subject and nodding toward the guitar case at my feet.

Jamie followed his gaze and shook his head. "No, they're too expensive, and I prefer playing soccer. But I think if I ever did, I'd choose piano. I like the clicking noises Layla's keyboard makes."

Adrian's head whipped up to look at me over Jamie's head. "You play piano too? Is there anything you don't play?"

I flashed him a saccharine smile. "You'll find I'm good at playing all kinds of things, Waters. I'm quite skilled with my hands."

His throat bobbed, but then he shifted and looked away from me to speak to Jamie. "Yeah, I like the sound they make, too. But unlike this talented woman," he said, waving his hand in my direction, "I can only play string instruments."

He said it so naturally, like complimenting me was no different than saying the grass was green or the sky blue. And I blinked at him, wondering how and when we'd gotten to where we were. Him complimenting me like he actually liked me, and me apologizing as if I cared what he thought about me.

What the hell was happening?

I shook myself out of it, I'd figure it out later. When I was at home. Alone. And under a fluffy comforter.

I focused back in on what Jamie was saying to him. He'd somehow moved on from instruments to video games. Everyone on the planet gasped with shock.

"Yeah, Garrett and I are pretty good," he was saying. "You could join us next time if you think you stand a chance, but I won't go easy on you just because you're Layla's boyfriend."

My eyes widened, and I was about to jump in and explain that we were absolutely *not* dating, when Adrian spoke first, saying the last thing on earth I expected.

"I might take you up on that, Jamie," he said, not correcting the kid's assumption. His blue eyes met mine. "I do always love a challenge."

He continued to stare at me, his insinuation hovering heavily in the air between us. I suddenly felt too hot in my own skin, let alone these tight clothes, and I squirmed, readjusting my position on the bench.

His eyes danced as I shifted, and when I narrowed mine, he had the audacity to wink. And although I flipped him off over Jamie's head, I still felt that fucking wink all the way down to my toes.

"You two seem really close," Adrian said, once Jamie had

finally finished his verbal thesis on the quality of old game storylines versus new game storylines and had run off with Sadie again.

Adrian had listened to every word out of Jamie's mouth, even though it was obvious by his neutral nods and vague comments, that he didn't have a whole lot of personal experience in the gaming world. Not the way Garrett did, at least. But then Jamie had moved on to chat about his soccer team, and Adrian's face had lit up. Apparently, he'd been a soccer kid, too, growing up. I'd never heard the man speak so many sentences in the same conversation before.

I smiled, watching Jamie attempt to throw a stick across the field, only to stomp after it and glare when his throw only landed it a few feet away. "Yeah, we are," I said, answering Adrian's question.

At some point, he'd shifted closer to me in the short amount of time Jamie had run off and was now more in the center of the bench than the far side he'd originally sat on. I eyed the distance from under my lashes, but I didn't move away, content to simply sit there with him without hating his guts. It was nice. More than nice.

"He's known you most of his life I'm assuming?"

I nodded. "I was literally in the hospital room when he was born, so his entire life to be exact."

That had him looking away from Jamie, toward me, a question in his eyes. I could tell he assumed Garrett likely wasn't Jamie's father, but he wasn't a hundred percent certain of it. I didn't fault him for his curiosity.

Having your best friend hold your hand during birth instead of the father wasn't exactly the norm. Then again, neither was having a baby at seventeen.

I twisted the friendship pendant back and forth along the chain, thinking back on everything that had happened over the last nine years. I smiled. "Jamie is the bonus kid I never asked for, but was lucky enough to get anyway."

He hummed deep in his throat. "Have you all always lived in that duplex? Since Jamie was born, I mean."

"Nope. Jamie was born in Kansas. It's where we're all from, actually. Well, apart from Garrett, he's the odd one out and is from California."

His brow furrowed, and he angled his body toward me even more until the knee of his bent leg was inches from rubbing against my thigh. "You're not from around here?"

I shook my head. "I haven't even lived here a year yet."

He blinked at me, surprise lighting up his features.

"What?" I asked, unsure why he was looking at me that way. I had no accent, not even a slight one like many here did, and used words like "pop" and shuddered at the term "pocketbook."

"Why do you look so surprised?"

He looked away, shrugging and rubbing a hand along the back of his neck, almost self-consciously. "I don't know, I just expected you to have been here longer."

I grinned, not sure what to do with this version of him, but absolutely loving his awkwardness. "Oh my God, Waters, are you blushing? Why are you embarrassed?"

He cleared his throat and gave me a glare that held no heat.

"I'm not blushing."

"You are."

Flinging his hand out, he blurted, "I didn't realize you were so new to town when I accepted the Jemmy's gig that Larry offered me. I thought you'd been around and wouldn't have any issues."

My mouth fell open. That's why he'd taken my show without feeling guilty? Because he thought I was some hot shot who could land whatever gig I wanted? "Why would you think that? Didn't Larry tell you anything about me?"

He shook his head. "I didn't ask him. I didn't trust what he'd say," he added, glancing up at me like he was afraid of how I'd take that.

When I said nothing, he continued, answering the other part of my question. "I thought that because everyone speaks so highly of you. The bar owners and venues around here fucking love you, Davis."

"Except for Jemmy," I added, chuckling.

He joined me, crossing those last few inches to nudge my thigh with his knee. I tensed at the connection, and my heart began to beat just a little bit harder when he didn't move it away. He dipped his chin in agreement. "In your defense, I don't think he's a fan of anyone who isn't Fran."

"Agreed."

We both smiled, and I was the first one to break the moment, looking back out over the field where Jamie was now kicking some kind of pinecone around like a soccer ball. Attempting to show off and *look cool* for Adrian, no doubt.

There was a short silence as we sat there, barely touching, but it was surprisingly comfortable. Like we'd finally found the last elephant in the room and collectively kicked him the fuck out.

I don't know why it mattered that Adrian wouldn't have taken my spot had he known I was new, because doing so to any musician was still shitty, but it did.

He nudged me again. "So, tell me, Davis, why did you move here of all places?"

"Why did *you?*" I asked, instead. A lock of hair shot across my face, and Adrian's hand seemed to twitch at the same time I reached out and tucked it back behind my ear. I raised a brow, waiting for his answer.

"Come on, Waters. We're bound to hate each other again tomorrow, so you might as well tell me while I won't talk shit to your face."

He gave me a deadpanned look that had me snorting. "Was it about a woman?"

He stared at me for a long moment, considering me, as if he wanted to trust me but wasn't quite sure if he could. Hell, *I* wasn't even sure if he could. If there was anyone who didn't trust my ass lately, it was me.

"Yes," he finally said, speaking slowly. "I suppose you could say that."

I wasn't sure why, since I'd expected it, but his answer caused a harsh squeeze in my chest. Although, it could have also been the acid reflux from all the alcohol the night before. I much preferred that excuse.

Pasting a smile I didn't quite feel on my face, I shifted on the bench, pretending to be checking my shoes as an excuse to put an inch back between us. "I knew it."

His gaze dropped to that inch of space, a muscle feathering in his jaw. He opened his mouth to say something, maybe explain what had happened, but I spoke first, not wanting to hear about his ex.

"I moved here for Madison. She needed me, and I had nothing holding me in Kansas." I shrugged. "And now here we are."

I avoided his eyes, not wanting him to see any more of me than I was allowing him to see. But I could feel his gaze on the side of my face.

"You didn't have family or music there?" he asked, and I could hear the frown in his voice. He'd seen my Layla Davis band t-shirt. He knew I'd obviously been singing since before I'd moved.

"I did."

He waited for me to say more about my history, but I didn't. I was done sharing about myself.

"Madison was alone for a long time. Even when she wasn't, she was," I said as Jamie ran back toward us, looking like he was about to keel over any second. Adrian's brow furrowed, and I sighed, pushing off my thighs to stand.

I glanced down at him, fighting back the desire to smooth those furrowed lines from between his eyes. "She needed me more."

It was the truth. The only one he, or anyone else, needed to know. She'd needed me. She *still* needed me. Moving hadn't even been a question. Shitty day job and all, I'd do it all over again.

Jamie came huffing up, yet again saving me from continuing a conversation I didn't want to have. Especially with the way Adrian was watching me. Like I was an onion he was suddenly very determined to peel every single layer off of.

"Can we go home? I'm starving."

"Do you know how to cook?"

He put his hands on his hips, ignoring the nose jabs Sadie was giving him as she attempted to coerce him into running again. "I know how to open a snack."

I grabbed the water bottle I'd stuffed in my purse and let a stream run out for my lump of a dog. She eagerly ditched him to lap at it. "All right, sassy pants, it was only a question."

He narrowed his eyes, darting a quick look at Adrian. "I'm not sassy, I'm hangry."

Adrian chuckled and stood, giving me a loaded look that said, *you have your work cut out for you with that one*. I could only suck in my cheeks and nod in agreement.

He worked his ear buds back in his ears but didn't touch his phone to turn his music back on yet. I wanted to know what it was he listened to when he went on runs. What music pumped through him and gave him the motivation to come out here every day and work out.

But since I had no intention of walking over there and pulling one out of his ear to stuff in mine, I'd have to find out another day.

Adrian raised a hand to fist pump Jamie. "Enjoy the rest of the day, Jamie."

He shot his own, much smaller, fist out, smacking Adrian's and yanking it back to wiggle his fingers like an explosion. "You can call me J-man if you want. That's what my—what Garrett calls me."

Adrian smiled and mimicked his finger motions. "Sounds good, J-man." He flicked his gaze up to my shocked one, Jamie's words rendering me completely speechless. There was so much to unpack in that statement.

"You up for playing at a private gig with me next Saturday night?"

I had no idea what gig he was talking about, but I didn't have a show Saturday, and I certainly owed him. Swallowing back my reaction to Jamie's comment, I forced my vocal cords to work. "Yeah, I'll be there. Just text me the details."

He nodded, a secret smile teasing his lips, and then turned away from us to continue on the jog I'd interrupted. I looked at Jamie, who'd taken over water bottle duty and was giggling at Sadie as she flicked water in his face.

Adrian might not have understood the significance of Jamie giving him permission to use Garrett's nickname for him, but I did. And I was convinced of two things. That Adrian Waters was apparently a goddamn snake charmer with my entire little family, and that I didn't hate it.

Not one bit.

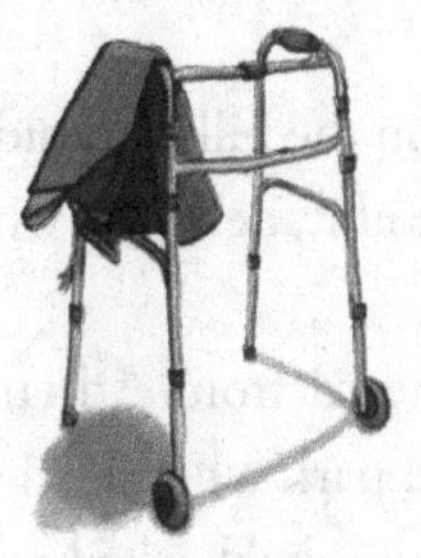

Chapter
18

I WATCHED MY fan circle above my head. A slow, steady pace that was almost hypnotic. It really needed to be dusted.

When I was young, I used to focus on one blade at a time, watching it go around and around without blinking to see if I could keep my eye on it. After a while, it would almost seem to slow down, as if I was controlling the fan with some weird, telekinetic ability.

I did it again now, trying to distract myself from the thoughts running through my head. From the urge to reach out and text someone that I absolutely should not be texting outside of work.

I sighed and pulled my comforter higher until only my head poked out, the cool fabric soothing against my naked skin. Sadie grumbled at the shuffling of the blanket and shot me a disapproving look before readjusting herself at the end of the bed.

My phone rested on the pillow beside me, and I twisted my head to the side to stare at it, debating whether or not I'd despise myself if I grabbed it.

I hadn't seen or heard from Adrian in a week. Not since about an hour after the park when he'd shot over the time and address for the private gig he'd asked me about. Which wasn't necessarily weird. It wasn't like we were friends who texted or anything.

But for some reason, I'd expected him to reach out during the week to schedule a practice, or at least discuss songs, before tonight's show.

Unlike the three-hour one we were supposed to do together at Jemmy's, tonight was a five-hour show at someone's private residence. The couple had apparently approached him after the last show, offering him a pretty sum to come to their house while they entertained friends. Although, *house* was putting it mildly.

I wasn't sure why Adrian had asked me to join. It might've simply been because they would've asked us both if I hadn't canceled, but I had a sneaking feeling it was more because he didn't want to go alone. Private gigs could be super awkward sometimes.

Reaching out, I grabbed my phone and pushed up a little higher in bed, keeping the blanket high enough not to expose my very bare chest. I wasn't a fan of sleeping with clothes on.

What would I even say if I texted him? I knew part of the reason I was so tempted to text him was because I was bored out of my mind, but I had also finally accepted that the other part was because I liked his wit and sarcasm. I liked his blunt humor and pointed glares.

I could always just invite him over to practice, I supposed. Then it would still be work-related, we'd get some practice in that couldn't ever hurt, and I'd have something to help pass the time until tonight.

Win-win all around.

Within a few quick taps, I had my phone unlocked and *Satan's* text thread pulled up. Although, I no longer believed him to be the ruler of hell, I had no intention of changing his contact. Seeing it brought me a simple and pure kind of joy. And I could guarantee he had me in his phone as something just as bad.

I decided to skip the hello. That seemed too personal, and even getting along as we were, I sure as hell wasn't going *that* far out on my fucking limb. I still wasn't sure I trusted him not to come at it with a chainsaw the moment I turned my back.

Me: I thought of a song we should play tonight if you're free to come practice.
Satan: I'm busy this afternoon or I would.

Ugh, of course he was. I had to hand it to the man, he was dedicated as hell to anything he deemed worthy of his time. Luckily for my eyeballs, his body was high on that list.

Me: You can work out tomorrow, Waters. I promise your abs will still be there if you miss a day.
Satan: You've been looking at my abs?
Me: Yep. Wasn't impressed. Six packs are overrated.
Satan: What about a solid four?

The cackle I let out was positively witch-like. I nervously glanced around my room, as if Madison or some random person was hiding in a corner, waiting to point out the stupid smile I had on my face. But my only companion was still snoring down at my feet.

Given I'd only seen a hint of his chest through his damp shirt and couldn't refute or confirm, I decided not to comment on that, and sent an eyerolling emoji instead.

Satan: I'm not working out, but I do have plans I can't change.
Me: Wow, color me surprised. You have something you care about more than your precious music?
Satan: I actually have two things.

I immediately wanted to know what they were. Oh, did I want to know. I typed out half a text to demand he admit what they were, but then stopped and deleted it. Not because I was nervous of his answer or anything, but because nosiness wasn't attractive on anyone.

It definitely had nothing to do with the realization he might spout his ex's name as one of those two things. Nope.

Me: You're deflecting.
Satan: Yes.
Me: Waters.
Satan: I have another show.

The second his text came through, I hissed and smashed my

thumb on the call icon. He answered on the second ring. His deep sigh mixed with shuffling in the background was his only hello.

"And this is why I was deflecting."

I sat up, letting the comforter fall to my waist. Since I was alone, I didn't bother covering back up, but I did pluck it up enough to tuck it under my boobs. There was something about the way it felt to have my boobs stuck to my stomach that made me want to crawl out of my skin.

"Where are you playing?"

A door shut in the background. "Nowhere you've played before."

"Are you sure?"

"Positive."

My heart picked up. I figured he was saying that because he knew what I was going to ask and wanted to dissuade me from the conversation, but all it did was intrigue me even more.

This was exactly why I'd started working with him in the first place. To get my foot in the door with new venues that he could land me better than Larry.

And if Adrian had taken this one on when he already had a long-ass show tonight, it had to be either high paying or good exposure. It was the latter I was hoping for.

"How about I come play with you?" He started to speak, but I kept going, talking over whatever he was about to say. "I'm not trying to take your cut. I won't even take a penny. Scout's honor."

Sure, I could use the money, but I truly didn't care about it this time.

"Please, Adrian? I have nothing else to do."

He sighed. "I have to be there in twenty minutes. Are you even ready? There's no way all that makeup and iron work takes less than that."

I snorted. "Iron work? What am I, a fucking blacksmith?"

"Your hair, Davis. You knew what I meant."

I chuckled. "I wear makeup because I like it, not because I need it. And my hair will be fine." It wasn't curled or dolled up by any means, but I'd make it work. The best thing about having blue hair, was it made almost every style look fancy.

He sighed again, this one heavy enough I could picture him hunched over a table with his thumb and forefinger pinching the bridge of his nose. "What are you wearing?"

I glanced down at my boobs. "At the moment? Nothing."

The responding pause was so silent, it was almost loud. A pin could've dropped on Garrett's side of the duplex, and I would have been able to hear it.

"You called me…naked?"

Great, when he put it that way, I sounded like a total creep. "No, you ass, I hadn't planned on calling. I was sleeping naked."

Something clattered wherever he was, and I swore I heard him growl, murmuring something under his breath I couldn't quite catch. What in the world was he doing?

"You good there, Waters?"

More muttering, and then he finally put the phone back to his face and said, "Put some clothes on. If you're here on time, you can play. If you're late, you're out of luck."

I held back my squeal. Barely. "Send me the address."

He grunted and hung up, not bothering with a goodbye. I tossed my phone on the mattress and rolled off the bed, grabbing things from the floor to try to make some magic happen with an outfit. My phone dinged behind me, and I smiled.

This could be the door I'd been waiting for. I just needed to make sure they liked me enough to open it all the way for me. Which meant I needed to both sound and look really damn good. I may not have time for a full face and a head of luscious curls, but all that wasn't necessary.

Not if I made a statement another way.

Belting out the chorus to a song on the radio, I flicked my blinker and turned into the designated parking lot, nearly bouncing in my seat. I couldn't put my finger on why I was in such a good mood, but I was ridiculously excited about this gig, and not just because of the opportunity it could pose for my career.

I loved performing at new places and meeting new people. As much as I wasn't normally a people-person, one of my favorite parts of the job was seeing the look on new faces when they heard me for the first time and enjoyed it.

It was like chicken noodle soup poured directly over my dry, crusty soul.

It also helped that Adrian was easy to work with. We just sounded good together. A fact I'd finally admitted to myself.

Turning off the ignition and removing my seatbelt, it took me a second to actually take in my surroundings. I'd seen the large building in front of me from the main road, but I'd pulled in, assuming wherever I was going was tucked behind it or something.

I leaned to the side until my face was pressed to the window, trying to see around the side of the building. But all I saw was a cute little yard of trees. What in the world?

Maybe I'd gone to the wrong place. I grabbed my phone and double-checked the address Adrian had sent me to what I'd typed in. It was the same.

I looked up again, squinting at the building in front of me.

Young Souls Assisted Living

Great. Adrian was never going to stop giving me shit for being late to a gig I'd assured him I'd be able to make it to on time. Maybe if he told me what else was around it, like a popular restaurant or something, I could still figure it out.

Swiping away the Maps app, I pulled up our message thread again and shot off a text.

Me: What other things are around this place? My GPS took me to the wrong parking lot.
Satan: No, it didn't.

Oh perfect, now he was going to mansplain to me how to use my eyeballs. Just what I'd hoped for.

Me: How helpful.
Satan: I can see you. How's that for helpful?

I snapped my head up, twisting left then right like a

reincarnated owl trying to see him. No motorcycle or Mini Cooper in sight. Although, there was a very nice truck parked to the far right, under an overhanging tree. Why had I still not asked him what kind of damn car he drove?

Trying not to lose my shit at the chance this man, whom I'd begun to trust against my will, had just taken my hopes and crushed them, I shot off another text.

Me: Are you fucking with me right now?
Satan: Get your ass inside, Davis.

I dropped my phone in my lap and narrowed my eyes at the large double doors. If this man was playing a joke on me, I was going to end him. Or at least put a triple dose of laxatives in his drink before his next show.

Grumbling, I shoved open my door and stomped to my passenger side to get my shit, or at least stomped as well as I could in three-inch heels. The thought made me freeze with my guitar halfway out of the car, and I slowly looked down at myself.

Or more specifically, at the statement outfit I'd put together when I'd assumed I was headed to a bar or restaurant of some kind. At the short, faux-leather skirt and off-the-shoulder, iridescent blouse I had on beneath my jacket. Combine that with my glittery heels and the blue space buns on my head, some pearls were sure to be clutched when I walked in.

Awesome.

Lugging my guitar and stand in through the double doors, I immediately second-guessed my choice to listen to Adrian when every single head in a packed lobby swiveled my way.

I plastered a small, confident smile on my face, mentally urging myself not to tuck tail and run. All I'd wind up doing is tripping and falling and showing my bare ass to everyone here, successfully traumatizing them for life.

I was about to head to the front desk area and ask if they'd by chance seen a hot asshole wandering around, when I spotted said asshole tucked into a corner. He had his hair tied back at his neck, was wearing jeans and a simple t-shirt, and was leaned over his guitar to shuffle some cords near his feet. His stand and speaker were already set up, and there was a chair right next to him, waiting for me.

We really were playing here. Well, all right then.

As if sensing me the moment I got close, his head came up, and his eyes immediately locked onto me. They dipped down, taking in the clothing visible through my unbuttoned jacket, and a singular eyebrow cocked.

"Interesting choice of clothing, Davis."

Hiding my hand behind my guitar case so no one else could see it, I flipped him off. What I wanted to do was sling a few curse words his way, but I couldn't exactly do that with our current audience.

"That tends to happen when my partner fails to mention where we're playing at."

"First of all, *we* weren't playing anywhere. I volunteered to play here, and you invited yourself. Secondly, you look fine. I'm just giving you shit. Now hurry up, they've been patiently waiting."

I glanced behind me to see nothing but excited smiles as a few watched me walk up, while a few others chatted among themselves. No one seemed surprised at a live show. And since I doubted they had many interested musicians donating their Saturdays, it meant Adrian was likely a regular.

"Do you play here often?" I asked, removing my jacket and folding it on the ground behind my chair. What I wanted to ask was if he'd been coming since before he'd even moved, because it sure seemed that way with the familiar way everyone was looking at him.

He watched me take a seat beside him, not even trying to hide his smirk as I awkwardly removed my guitar from my case, attempting not to flash everyone a straight hallway view of my crotch.

"Yes."

When he said nothing else, I nodded and sucked in my cheeks. I was going to ask so many questions when we were done with this.

I crossed my legs and got comfortable, testing my strings and adjusting a few. "In my defense," I whispered, leaning slightly toward him, "Young Souls sounds like a bar."

His answering chuckle slid down my spine, drawing an answering one from my own lips. It felt strange to get along, but I found I didn't hate it. At least, not as much as I'd have thought.

Looking out at our audience, a huge smile lit up his face, making my heart do a weird flip in my chest.

"All right, you rowdy youngins, what would you like to hear?" His voice was light and chipper, nothing like the usual one he used with me, or the bored, clipped one he used with Larry. He sounded younger, more carefree.

A cacophony of options were hollered out until he picked

one, giving me a side-eye to silently ask if I knew it. I nodded.

He smiled again, this time at me, and I suddenly wished I had a bottle of water. Seeing Adrian Waters happy was like looking at the fucking sun, beautiful and painful all at once. The man was stunning.

He gave me a quick introduction, and then we were playing. Song after song, taking recommendations, sneaking in a few of our own, and trying not to burst out laughing when some of the more energetic members started dancing.

It was the most fun I'd ever had at a show.

Or maybe it was the man I was sitting beside who made it so amazing.

Chapter
19

WHEN WE WRAPPED up our final song and set our guitars back in their cases amid a chorus of disappointed voices, I was half-expecting my cheeks to melt from my face. My poor facial muscles weren't used to smiling so much in a two-hour window.

Not everyone stayed for the entire thing, some taking off after the first hour while other new people appeared sporadically as we played, but they were by far the most devoted audience I'd ever had.

"Thank you," I murmured, peeking up at Adrian as I slid my guitar case away from my feet and stood, "for letting me tag along. This was fun."

He looked up at me from where he knelt on the ground, a rolled-up cord in his hand. The position put him almost eye level with my hips, and even though it hadn't been intentional, it still sent painfully graphic images racing through my mind. My face flushed, and I shuffled back, wincing at the scrape of my chair across the floor when I bumped into it.

His nostrils flared and the muscles of his jaw seemed to tense, and for a second, I feared I'd said my thoughts out loud. But he slowly nodded his head. "Thanks for staying."

I blinked; my embarrassment forgotten at that. "You thought I'd leave just because it wasn't a venue?"

He placed the cord on top of his speaker and stood, running his hands down his sides. "I wasn't sure. Not because of last time," he added, raising his hands, "but because I know you came hoping to make some connections."

I flinched. I couldn't help it. He had every right to believe so given my record, but it still hurt a little to hear.

"But if it's any consolation, I'm glad I was wrong."

Unsure what to say to that, I mumbled something about thanking the women at the front desk who had brought us waters and helped set today up, and walked off.

Adrian's and my relationship might've been the most confusing one I'd ever had. We certainly weren't friends, nor did we hang out or trust one another. But it seemed neither of us could fight the desire to *want* to do those things.

I released a heavy breath and made my way across the lobby, needing something, anything, to get my mind off the man behind me whom I'd just had the best time with. I'd made it about halfway across when I felt a hand land on my forearm.

I stopped, expecting Adrian to be on the other side of that hand, only to find a short, round woman looking up at me instead. She had soft brown eyes, deep wrinkles in almost every valley of her face, and her hair was an adorable, permed pixie cut that didn't at all match the mischievous grin she was giving me.

"You have the voice of an angel," she said, relaxing her grip enough to pat my arm.

I smiled down at her. Yep, my cheeks were definitely about to stop working here soon. "Thank you, I'm glad you—"

"But your body is as far from angelic as could be," she continued, giggling to herself and stopping me mid-sentence. I blinked, aware that my mouth was hanging open, but I honestly had no idea what to say to that.

Was she complimenting or admonishing me? The ornery gleam in her eyes made me think the first, but even if she was, what did you say to that? Thanks?

"And with all this spicy hair too," she added, rising onto her toes to pat one of my buns.

I about choked. Never in all the time my hair had been blue, had someone ever called it *spicy*.

"It's no wonder that boy can't keep his eyes off you."

Wait, what? Now who were we talking about? The devil? I huffed a laugh despite myself, thinking of Adrian's contact name. She winked at me, and I was almost positive she and I were having two very different thoughts.

"Don't be scaring her off, Ms. Waters. Then we'll never convince her to come back and play again."

The small woman removed her hand from my arm to smack Adrian in the chest as he approached, and I had a feeling she'd have chosen his head if she could've reached it. "Ms. Waters? What do I look like to you, the lunch lady?"

Emotion flashed across Adrian's features, so sharp and severe that it took my breath away. He swallowed and blinked rapidly for a moment before he found his voice again. "Sorry, Nan."

The woman—Nan, apparently—just cackled, a raspy wheezing sound that shook her entire body. "Besides, I was just teasing her. She looks too tough to be scared off by the likes of me. Lighten up, boy."

I glanced between them. I was definitely missing something. Adrian sighed; exasperation evident in every shift of his hand as he rubbed it across the back of his neck. I bit my lip. Flustered Adrian was ridiculously cute.

"Davis, this is my grandmother, Doris. Nan, this is Davis."

My eyes widened. His grandmother lived here? Well damn, that made him playing here make a whole lot more sense. Not that it wasn't amazing that he did it no matter the reason, every resident here deserved it in every way. But with how focused he was with his career, it made more sense as to why he'd use a day for a free gig.

"It's nice to meet you, Doris. You can call me Layla."

Doris reached out and smacked him again, this time hard enough to make him huff out a breath and rub the center of his chest. "If her name is Layla, then use it. I didn't raise you to be disrespectful."

"I'd actually prefer he stuck to Davis if it means you'll keep whacking him in the chest. Honestly, he could use a few more." I grinned.

She *tsk*ed, narrowing her eyes on her grandson. "When I was a girl, they used to say boys were mean to the girls they liked. What would you say to that, *Mr. Waters?* Does it still hold true?"

I snorted loud enough to draw the attention of a few

residents standing closest to us. Oh, I liked Doris a lot. And it sure explained where Adrian got his sense of humor from.

His blue eyes shot up from her to me, and my next laugh died in my throat. I couldn't grasp what it was in his expression that made my own chest squeeze like Doris had smacked me, too, but something about the way he was looking at me made my entire body hum.

Instead of answering her question, he wrapped an arm around her shoulders and pulled her in for a tight hug. "Is that why you're always so mean to me? Because you like me so much?"

"I'm just keeping you on your toes."

"That you are." He leaned down to press a quick kiss to her cheek. "I just watched them bring out some ice cream for you all. Why don't you go find a seat at one of the tables, and I'll come join you once I've helped *Layla* carry her stuff out."

She patted his chest, softly this time. "Don't you worry about me, Adrian. It's about time you found yourself a good woman. If she's as sweet as her voice, she's a keeper."

May the Lord have mercy on my soul, I deserved a medal for not cackling like a hyena. If I had to be as sweet as my voice to be a keeper, I might as well climb into the nearest dumpster and make a home.

Stepping out from his hug, Doris came up and laid a hand on my shoulder, whispering loud enough to make sure Adrian could still hear her. "Don't be afraid to teach this one a thing or two. Men never get it right the first time."

"No, they really don't," I said, giving Adrian a saccharine smile over her head. I considered telling her I wasn't dating her grandson, but Adrian hadn't corrected her either—much like he hadn't with Jamie at the park—so I bit my tongue and let her believe whatever truth about us made her happy.

She winked at me and then sauntered off, hollering out to another woman that she better not eat all the ice cream.

We watched her go, me still cracking up, and Adrian just shaking his head, his expression equally appalled and adoring at the same time. He nudged me with the side of his arm. "Go ahead and say whatever it is you're dying to say. You look constipated trying to hold it in."

"I think I'm in love with your grandma."

He glared over at me, but there was no heat in it, and his lips twitched just enough to ruin it. "Remind me to never leave you two alone in a room together."

My heart did that weird flip thing again, like the dumb organ was doing acrobatics in there. He'd said it so naturally, like it was only expected that I'd see her again.

"You don't have to help me," I said, as we made our way back to our equipment. "I carried my stuff in just fine. I can carry it out."

"Have you lost your mind?" he asked, rubbing at his chest. "She'll come at me with some poor soul's cane next if she even thinks I'm not out there helping you."

I concurred, and that's how I found myself, yet again, sitting outside on a curb with a man I kind of, semi, partially liked.

Adrian was the first one to sit. After he'd carried my guitar out like I was utterly incapable, and stuffed it in my car, he'd made it about a foot before all but collapsing to the curb.

He rested his elbows on both knees, his hands cupping the back of his neck as he stared at the pavement beneath his feet. He looked completely depleted. And all I could remember was the way he'd sat with me on a curb just like this, minus the ice, when I'd felt like the world was against me.

Guess it was my turn.

Slipping my jacket off my arms, I tied it around my waist, letting the body of it cover the front of my legs and crotch. Then I dropped down next to him, close enough I could've bumped his leg with mine if I wanted to.

He tipped his head toward me, and I gave him a straight, closed-mouth grin, already staring at him. He huffed a laugh and looked away again.

"I'm assuming you have qu—"

"Waters, I have so many fucking questions, it's not even funny," I interrupted, turning my body so that I was fully facing him, one leg resting on the curb between us. My skirt bunched up over my thighs uncomfortably, and I knew I'd have indentions if I sat like that too long, but he had all the tea, and I was fucking parched.

Because I was seriously beginning to think I didn't know this man at all.

He grunted, and I decided to take that as my go-ahead. Adrian was blunt as hell. If he didn't want to answer a question, I had no doubt he'd happily tell me to go fuck myself.

I looked out at the Young Souls Assisted Living Facility sign, sensing he didn't want me staring at him. That was another thing we had in common. "I did not expect this at all."

He darted an amused look at my jacket-covered crotch and raised a brow. "I thought we'd already agreed that your outfit confirmed that."

I curled my lips and stuck my tongue out. "That's not what I meant."

He sighed and stretched out his legs, letting his arms fall limp in his lap. "I know."

"How often do you come here to play?" I asked, focusing my attention on a single leaf blowing across the parking lot to keep me from analyzing his face.

"As often as I can."

"Wow."

His head lifted, stealing my attention. His guarded expression told me more than his lips did, and it made my stomach sink. "I'm not making fun of you, Waters. I mean it. That's awesome." I glanced behind us toward the doors, imagining what Doris was likely saying to all her friends about us, and smiled.

"How long has your grandmother been here?"

He didn't answer at first, and I thought I'd somehow crossed a line already. It was becoming a habit. It was like I no longer saw the lines anymore when it came to him.

But then he rolled his neck and looked up at the sky. "Less than a year, but it feels like longer."

Understanding his need for a distraction, I turned my head away and began counting ants as they made their way across the sidewalk, aware of every movement he made next to me. "Is there a reason she's in here? She seems…"

"Ornery?"

I chuckled. "I was going to say healthy, but yes, that too. Definitely that."

A small smile pulled at his lips in reply to mine, but it quickly dropped. His brows fell low over his eyes, and I had the sudden urge to smooth the tense expression away.

"My grandmother has dementia," he started, staring at his hands. "I saw the beginning signs years ago but ignored them. It was small things, like forgetting where she'd put something only a few minutes before, getting confused at the grocery store, or telling me the same story several times in a week."

"I didn't—" he sighed, shaking his head. "I didn't want to admit it. To her. To myself. But then last year, she left to go run a quick errand, and she never came home."

"Oh my God, was she okay?" I asked, feeling two-inches tall for bringing it up. I would never have guessed she was suffering something as significant as that. She'd seemed so sharp and clearheaded. Then again, I had no experience with dementia or anything like it.

He nodded but didn't look up. "Yeah, she'd just gotten lost. She couldn't remember where she was or where she lived, and I was over an hour away in Raleigh and couldn't help her."

He scoffed angrily. "The only reason I even knew she was in trouble was because a good Samaritan convinced her to let them see her phone, and they called her most recently used contact."

I reached out and laid my hand over his without even thinking about it. His head snapped up to look at me. "I'm so sorry, Adrian. Was there no one else to help her? Your parents or an aunt or uncle?"

He shook his head, staring at my hand on his. His hand twitched, and for a moment I thought he'd twist it around and lace our fingers, but he didn't.

"There isn't anyone else. My grandfather died before I was even born, and my mother was their only child."

And Adrian was an only child too. I remembered him mentioning it during our practice when I'd made a snarky comment about only family being capable of liking him. "Is your mother…"

"Dead?"

I winced, not wanting to voice it out loud. It'd been rude as fuck to ask in the first place, but for some reason I couldn't fathom, I wanted in this man's head. To see what had sculpted him and made him the way he was. The scorned, blunt, broody ass man who could also be fucking hilarious, and who rubbed my shoulders and hugged his grandmother in public.

"No, my mother's not dead. Not literally. At least, not that I know of. She and my dad got mixed up with drugs when I was still pretty young. Five, maybe? They disappeared soon after and Nan got stuck raising me ever since."

He didn't specify exactly what had happened with his parents, but the details didn't really matter. I understood enough. His parents had chosen what meant more to them, and it hadn't been him.

"I wouldn't say Doris was stuck doing it. With her husband and only child gone, she might have needed you just as much as you needed her."

He made a frustrated noise in his throat, like I wasn't

getting the point. "She gave up her entire life for me, Davis. All her wants, her dreams of traveling to every state, she gave up all of it for me." He said "me" like he was an unwanted lump of coal at the end of a stocking.

"And now that I'm old enough to take care of myself and she could've had her freedom, she's stuck here." He threw his free hand back, gesturing behind us angrily, and I didn't fail to see the way his jaw moved beneath his beard, or the way his eyes shimmered just slightly. "She put herself last, and all I have to offer her in thanks are a few songs every weekend."

Without overthinking it, I did the first thing that came to mind, and I scooted closer, curling my hand around to the underside of his and lacing our fingers together.

It might not have been as soothing as rubbing his shoulders the way he'd done for me, but I hoped he'd understand my intention.

"She loves you, Adrian. Anyone with eyes can see that in the tender way she slaps you." He cut his eyes at me, but I gave his hand a squeeze. "I doubt she sees it as giving up anything. She gained something by taking you in. You can't tell me that woman didn't know what she was doing."

He didn't reply. He just sat there, tightening his fingers around mine and staring at them like he could find the answer to life in the way our skin rested against each other.

"She doesn't always."

I frowned. "Always what?"

"Look at me like that." He raised his head, and the sorrow in his eyes was enough to make my heart feel like it was being gutted with a dull knife. "She doesn't always remember me anymore."

Oh God. He'd called her Ms. Waters when he'd walked up to us, not because he was teasing her, but because he hadn't been expecting her to remember him. That's why he'd looked so taken aback when she'd answered him.

"It's why I moved away from Raleigh," he continued, "and why I started playing here every weekend. I always hope she'll recognize me, but even when she doesn't, I can at least make her smile with her favorite songs. She still remembers a lot of them."

I stared and stared at him, our park conversation replaying on repeat in my mind. When he'd asked me why I'd moved, and I'd avoided answering, asking him instead because I thought his reason would be so much different than mine.

Was it about a woman?

Yes, I suppose you could say that.

But it was closer than I ever could have thought. He'd moved here, not because of some shitty ex, although I guess he could technically still have one, but because he'd wanted to help someone he loved, in whatever way he could.

If my heart expanded any further, it'd take up my entire ribcage and shove my lungs up out of my throat.

I sat there silent, unsure what to say. What could you say to someone you'd been completely wrong about? More than that, what could you say to make them feel better about a situation that was never going to get better?

He began drawing gentle circles over my skin with his thumb, and I swore I felt the motion reverberate throughout my entire body.

"When did she start to…"

"Forget me? Around the time I moved here."

Jesus.

His thumb trailed higher, curling around to caress the inside of my wrist. Goosebumps erupted up my arm, but I didn't move a muscle. I wasn't even sure he knew he was doing it.

He cleared his throat. "You know the night we met? The one where I was—"

"Paddling your douche canoe down Jackass River?" I finished for him on instinct, unable to completely swallow down my chuckle when he ever so slowly met my eyes and blinked at me.

"Yes," he said, lips twitching. "That one."

I bit my bottom lip, trying not to burst out laughing at the expression on his face. "Just wanted to make sure we were discussing the same night. Continue."

He shook his head, his own quiet laugh escaping. I soaked it up. "Anyway, that was the first time it'd happened to that extent. She'd already started to lose some memories of me and often called me by my dad's name, but that day was the first time she had absolutely no idea who I was.

"I wasn't prepared for it to happen so soon, and I didn't know then how to handle it. I'd selfishly tried to get her to remember me, and she became agitated and upset."

He paused, his frustration crumbling apart to reveal the broken sliver of his heart. He cleared his throat, his voice sounding like he'd suddenly started chewing gravel. "She'd ended up crying, and I was advised to leave."

"I'm so sorry, Adrian." My heart broke for him, for her, for every family like them.

His eyes flashed up to me, emotion, and something else, churning in their depths. "It's not your fault things like dementia exist."

"Not that. I mean, I am sorry about Doris, but I mostly meant I'm sorry I asked in the first place. I was being nosey because I thought you'd say you had community service for some stupid transgression or something." I flailed my free hand around, not knowing what I was saying, just that I was rambling like an idiot.

"Davis."

"I didn't think—"

"*Layla*," he said more pointedly, yanking on my hand until my arm stretched across his lap and my shoulder smacked into his chest. I looked up in surprise from where I was pretzeled out next to him, thanking God, I'd tied my jacket over my skirt.

He smirked down at me, his eyes flickering to my pursed lips. "Shut up."

I smacked at him and pulled away, resituating myself next to him and swallowing down the flare of desire that single look had stirred. "I was trying to be nice, you asshole."

He nudged my shoulder, and if I didn't know better, I'd have thought he was looking for any way to keep touching me. "You? Nice? I don't believe it."

I chuckled. "Yeah, it tasted pretty bitter on my tongue, to be honest." We shared a smile and then both looked back out at the parking lot, letting each other swim in our own thoughts.

After several minutes of comfortable silence, Adrian heaved out a breath and stood, holding a hand out to me.

I considered ignoring it and standing on my own in an effort to redraw even the faintest line between us, but my body had other plans, and I reached out and accepted his hand.

Once I'd readjusted my skirt and untied my jacket to slip it back on, Adrian pulled out his phone and tapped the screen, checking the time. "We play the private gig in a couple of hours."

I yanked my own phone out and checked it, as if I thought my clock would read differently than his. I hadn't realized I'd been here so long. "Yeah, I guess we do."

His lips curled up in the corners, and he tipped his head toward the large black truck I'd spotted earlier. "Come have lunch with me."

His invitation hovered between us, heavier than any other question he'd ever asked me. Because it wasn't just an invitation to lunch. Not when I could sense the tension building between us and feel the way his eyes seared through me like he saw all of me. Even the nastiest, bitchiest parts. And he still wanted to hang out with me.

It was an invitation for *more*.

I shifted from one foot to the other and tucked my phone back in my pocket, looking anywhere but at him. "I can't. I need to get back home and feed Sadie and make sure Madison doesn't need help with Jamie before she goes into work tonight."

"Doesn't she have a boyfriend for that?"

Although he hadn't meant it to, his words stung. Reminding me, yet again, that my happy little bubble wouldn't last forever.

"I can't," I repeated, my excuse sounding like a flimsy lie even to my ears.

He nodded and stepped back, tucking his hands into his

pockets and bidding me farewell in a stilted way that almost had me blurting out that I'd changed my mind.

But I didn't. I watched him walk back toward the building with my lips smashed firmly together. The truth had nothing to do with Madison. The truth, the bitter painful one I kept trying to ignore, was that I couldn't go to lunch and hang out with Adrian like we were friends.

I couldn't be his friend, period.

Not because I hated him anymore, but because after today, I knew friendship would never be enough. I'd want his lips against mine, his hands on my skin, his sarcastic humor pissing me off, and his wicked smirks when he succeeded. I'd want all of it.

And that absolutely terrified me.

Chapter
20

"LAYLA IS A strong-ass, independent woman who can do whatever the hell she sets her mind to."

Deep breath.

"Layla is a strong-ass, independent-as-shit woman who can do whatever the hell she sets her fucking mind to."

I repeated the mantra out loud at least five times, adding more curses each time in an attempt to pump myself up.

This would be no different than the show I'd literally just done a few hours ago at Young Souls. Minus the old, skating-rink-style carpet and fold-out chairs, and add a mansion and way more animal statues than any sane person needed.

Yep, I could totally do this. I could easily sit next to a man I was pretty sure I might be in serious *like* with and play a multi-hour show without letting him find out. After turning down an offer for a casual, friendly lunch directly to his face.

Fuck, this was going to be weird.

Come on, Layla, you smile at total strangers every day and pretend to love whatever conversations they bring up. You once had a woman talk to you about the difference between bulldogs and French bulldogs for twenty minutes without letting her know you wanted to die. You can do this.

Releasing the chokehold grip I had on my steering wheel, I plucked my phone from between my thighs and sighed in relief that Adrian had finally texted me back. I'd seen his truck the moment I'd pulled up and hoped he'd still be in it, but the cab had been empty. Not that I'd actually expected him to wait for me.

Me: Am I supposed to knock? Because I'm going to tell you now, if I have to knock, I'd rather stay in my car.
Satan: Only a sadist would make you knock. Walk around back.

I smiled at his reply despite myself, hope kindling that I hadn't put our partnership on a fast track to awkward town.

Exiting my car, I hauled my guitar out for the second time that day and walked down the perfect, bleached-white driveway. My stomach growled the entire way there.

I'd been such a mental case after everything Adrian had told me this afternoon, I'd completely forgotten to eat lunch, and the irony of that wasn't lost on me.

However, I had at least replaced my outfit for a much more appropriate one. This one consisted of chunkier heels, straight black jeans, and a low-cut blouse that was just flowy enough to hide the way the button of my jeans was going to implant itself into my stomach when I sat. Yet another reason why my zip-up skirts were superior.

Hearing the sound of laughter and chatter grow stronger as I approached the house, I walked around the corner to see a large, double-door gate propped open in their ridiculously tall privacy fence. A flower arch emphasizing its existence.

And I knew, before I'd even fully crossed under the arch, that I'd find distressed wood, painted Mason jars, and white tablecloths on the other side. I wasn't disappointed.

Leave it to HGTV to convince a woman who had animal statues lining her driveway and a waterfall pool in her backyard that burlap ribbons and lace were fancy.

There were at least fifty people scattered around the left side of the yard, closest to the house. Tables were set up like they were celebrating a wedding, and there were enough bottles of wine, loud giggling, and teetering women, to have me convinced there wasn't a single sober person here.

A few heads turned my way as I walked farther into the yard, no doubt taking in my scuffed guitar case and blue hair, but I pretended to be too interested in the waterfall to notice.

Making it my life's mission to avoid any and all eye contact, I circled around the pool, searching for Adrian. I had no idea where he'd be, but I'd start with as far away from the loud, drunk people as possible, and work my way back up.

I nearly broke my neck a few seconds later when he stepped out from around a tree, and I slammed into him. He grunted and rocked back, placing both hands on my arms to keep me from tackling him to the ground.

I shifted awkwardly, still gripping my guitar case, but my

focus was zeroed in on the fingertips pressing into my skin. All I could imagine was how they'd feel pressing into the crease where my hips met my thigh, or wrapped around my love handles, angling me where he wanted.

"No need to be embarrassed, Davis. I sometimes run into people standing in plain sight too. Happens to the best of us."

Glaring at him to cover up the fact that I was, indeed, blushing, but not for the reasons he thought, I moved back. "You stepped in front of me."

He smirked. "That's a weird apology for stomping on my toes, but I accept."

I looked to his feet and then back up, not enjoying how well he looked with his suit jacket hanging open and the sleeves rolled up to his elbows. I was about to stomp on his feet again, with the heel of my shoe this time, just to punish him for looking so damn good.

"You nearly flattened my chest with your four pack, Waters. I think your feet will live," I said. That wasn't necessarily true given my heels put us at the same height, but still.

His eyes dropped to my chest, and by the way his jaw tightened, I wondered if he could tell I wasn't wearing a bra. It hadn't been my intent to draw attention to it—the only reason I wasn't wearing one was because I couldn't find my sole strapless bra—but that didn't change the fact that Adrian was definitely staring at my boobs.

He ran a hand through his loose hair, shoving it roughly away from his face, and flung his hand out, gesturing to the corner of bushes behind him.

"Come on, we only have about ten minutes before she wants

us to start, and I can almost guarantee half of that time will be stolen by Andrea once she sees you're here."

I took all of two steps and then stopped again, blinking at where he was pointing to. At the small clearing no larger than an elevator, in the center of a group of bushes and potted plants.

"This is where they want us to play?" I asked, my eyes wide as I lifted my case toward the chairs.

He stared at it right along with me. "Yep."

"On plastic yard chairs."

"Yep."

"In the shrubbery," I said, my voice pitching slightly with my growing irritation. These people were rich. Like, stupid rich. Enough to pay out the ass for us to come play last minute at their party. Yet they'd stuck us in a corner of fucking mismatched plants like we were a gaudy speaker they were hoping to hide out of sight.

He nodded.

I slowly turned my head to look at him, trying to figure out why he was so calm about it. Shit like this was outright disrespectful. We weren't part of their damn décor.

There was nothing worse than being hired by people who treated musicians and artists like *they* were doing *us* a favor rather than the other way around. Entitlement at its best.

"Where the hell do they think we'll be putting our guitars?" I asked, white-knuckling my case handle to prevent myself from spewing a lot worse. Because the chairs they'd picked reminded me of the ones Madison and I had on our porch. Thin ones with armrests that would very much be in the way.

He met my eyes and shrugged, another smirk pulling at his

lips. "Come on, Davis. Where's your sense of adventure."

My chest swelled at the sight of that smirk. I hadn't realized I'd been so nervous he wouldn't give that to me again. "Lost somewhere in the tropical forest we're about to sit in I'd wager."

His soft, answering laugh stuck with me the entire time I set up, humming through my body more than the strings I was plucking to tune.

Loud, rhythmic clicking sounded behind me five minutes later as I was readjusting myself to sit sideways in the chair. Adrian, doing the same, lifted his head to look over my shoulder, and his face immediately smoothed out to the stone-like expression he used with Larry.

That told me all I needed to know about who was approaching. The woman who'd hired us—well, him—Andrea. I twisted around to see a stunning woman in a white button-down dress making her way toward us.

If her gorgeous skyscraper heels hadn't already announced her impending arrival, the perfume jamming itself up my nostrils when she came within a few feet, certainly did.

I hid my reflexive gag in a cough, fighting to keep my face neutral even while my eyes watered from the effort not to inhale. I could only hope that her husband was the main bread winner while she worked part time in a bath and beauty store, or else she and I were going to have to have a woman-to-woman talk about wearing more than one scent.

A muffled choking sound came from beside me, and I

glanced back to see Adrian fighting for his life to maintain his flat expression. It just ended up making him look constipated. I cackled, forgetting not to inhale as the heels finally came to a halt just before me.

Adrian's eyes sparked as they met mine, and I had to adjust my attention to the woman standing over me to prevent myself from laughing.

Ignoring the horrendous cacophony emanating from her skin, the woman, Andrea, was flawless. Her skin was a little too orange-toned to be natural, but her body was a perfect hourglass beneath her form-fitted dress, and her soft, chestnut hair flowed around her shoulders in perfect waves.

I stretched my hand out over my guitar. "It's nice to meet you. You must be Andrea."

"That I am," she said, taking my hand in a loose, dry shake before turning her attention to Adrian and fluttering her eyelashes, her hazel eyes already glassy. "Hello again, Adrian," she cooed.

"Good evening, Mrs. Bowler," he said, enunciating the *Mrs.* in a way that told me Andrea Bowler had acted very un-Mrs.-like when he'd first arrived.

And although I couldn't blame her, a thread of satisfaction weeded its way through me that he clearly hadn't appreciated, or reciprocated, whatever flirting she'd attempted.

I flashed her a wide-toothed smile. "Adrian and I were just finishing up getting situated." I shifted in my plastic chair, making sure my guitar knocked against the armrest. "Did you need anything before we start?"

She raised the hand not holding her champagne and patted

her flushed cheeks as she swayed slightly. "No, no. Don't mind me. I just wanted to say hello and get some fresh air." She raised her flute at Adrian. "Thanks again for squeezing me into your tight schedule."

I snorted, unable to rein it in that time. The provocativeness with which she said the words *squeezing* and *tight* were downright disgraceful to the act of flirting everywhere.

She cut an irritated look my way, smoothing out her already wrinkle-free dress. "Anyway, I'll let you two get started."

She teetered back a step, hiccupping behind her glass and winking at Adrian. "You know where to find me if you need anything."

He nodded, and we watched her walk off, already waving at someone else across the yard like she was a reincarnated windmill.

"Wow."

Adrian huffed. "She sells perfumes in some social media group she's in. They were on the deck when I arrived, spritzing themselves to try each one."

Well, that would certainly account for the smell. Between all that perfume and the alcohol, they probably couldn't even detect the scents anymore.

I must've said that thought out loud because Adrian grunted. "That would explain why she'd practically shoved her chest in my face, asking me to tell her which one smelled better."

Realizing I'd left my capo in my case, I pushed up, leaning my guitar against my fancy chair, and rolled my eyes at him. "Yeah, I'm sure that's the reason she wanted to shove your face in her cleavage."

He shot me an unimpressed look from beneath his lashes, and I wiggled my eyebrows as I stepped to the side and squatted down to open my case. I'd just clasped the edge when I realized I could hear my phone vibrating in my purse next to it.

I always left my phone in my purse for a reason. I didn't like answering calls or looking at texts when I was at a show. It felt unprofessional. But I decided to reach in and lift it up to glance at the screen just in case it was Madison. She was at work and knew I was as well, so she'd only be calling if it was an emergency.

The name that stared back at me on the screen made me glad I did as my heart dropped to my feet.

"What's wrong, Davis?"

I held up a finger to Adrian, letting him know I'd be right back, and walked around our Bush City of a stage area, to find some privacy to answer, just in case I burst into tears or vomited.

"Hey, Momma Number Two," I answered, plugging my free ear and craning to hear her over the hyena-like laughter echoing throughout the yard. "Sorry, I'm at work. Ignore the background noise."

Please don't say Madison was in a car wreck, or robbed, or that the house caught on fire. Oh God, what if it was Aaron? It wouldn't be the first time Madison's piece-of-shit ex had shown up, uninvited.

My mind was taking off one-hundred miles a minute before Madison's mother, Beth, had even uttered more than "Hello," to me.

"I'm so sorry to bother you, Layla. I tried calling Madison first because I knew you were playing tonight, but she won't answer her phone."

A huge sigh heaved out of me that it wasn't about Madison. I slapped a hand to my chest, seeing Adrian's outline appear in my peripheral as he slowly made his way toward me.

"Yeah, she's started leaving her phone in her purse because one of the other waitresses had theirs swiped from their apron while delivering food to a table. Is everything okay?"

Then another thought hit me. One even worse. "Is Jamie okay?"

There was a pause, one that lasted ten years and then some. "Beth, tell me he's okay."

"Yes, he's just—yes, he's okay. Madison dropped him and the dogs off on her way to work tonight."

I nodded, wondering why she needed to call me while I was working to tell me that. It wasn't uncommon for either of us to take the dogs to her parents' house to have some freedom in their yard.

Beth and John had a large, fenced-in backyard that was perfect for them to stretch their legs and play, while ours was barely enough space for them to do their business in.

"Are you needing me to come pick them up or something?" I asked. Adrian, finally reaching where I'd tucked myself away at, crossed his arms, slowly shaking his head at me. "Don't even think about it," he mouthed.

I turned away from him, staring at the perfectly cut grass and wishing my hair was down to help block out Adrian's disapproving face.

"No, you don't have to leave work," Beth answered, "I just wanted to make sure one of you knew that Sadie got hurt. She was out back and got bit by a copperhead."

My head snapped up, a cold sense of fear filling my chest. "Oh my God. Is she okay?"

"I don't know, I'm sorry. We immediately brought her to the emergency vet to be checked. That big one right off Ridge Road. They took her back a few minutes ago, but I stayed in the lobby because I have Jamie with me." She lowered her voice. "He refused to stay home."

Sadie had been taken back with a bunch of people she didn't know, in pain, and probably terrified. "I'm heading that way. Can you stay until I get there?"

As soon as Beth agreed, I hung up and shoved my phone in my back pocket, trying to stay calm. A bite from a snake didn't necessarily mean anything fatal, she was just being checked over. I pressed my hands to my face and breathed in deep. She'd be fine.

I spun back around and nearly face-planted into the glowering man now standing way too close to me. Disappointment oozed from every inch of his expression and posture, and as much as I hated it, Adrian's feelings weren't my priority.

Shouldering past him, I jogged back to my chair to snatch my guitar and jogged back, shoving it into its case harder than it deserved. I'd apologize to it later.

"Davis."

I ignored him. All I could think about was the tiny puppy Sadie had been when I got her, small enough to fit in my hands with her floppy ears and cute pink nose. She wasn't just a dog I bought to leash to a pole outside day-in and day-out to scare away potential robbers.

She was like a child to me. One who laid with me when I was sad, cuddled Jamie when he was scared, and put herself in the corner when she was in trouble. She meant everything to me.

As much as I loved snakes, in general, I didn't know a whole lot of details about specific ones. What I did know was that copperheads were venomous. It was *how* venomous that was the vital question. And not knowing the answer was enough to get my ass moving.

"Davis."

"I'm sorry, Waters. You'll have to play without me. I have to leave."

He growled, and the frustrated sound skated down my spine. "Are you fucking kidding me? You're bailing on me *again?* Why, because your friend needs you to pick up her kid? Do you ever plan on following through on a show, or are your words as pretty and pointless as your makeup?"

I flinched, but I didn't snap back at him. He was lashing out because he was mad, and I understood it. I did. But that didn't mean I needed to explain anything to him right this minute. He may not have wanted to play alone here, but it's not like he *couldn't.* He'd been the only one Andrea had asked for, anyway.

"I get that she's your friend, but it's not your job to help her raise her own kid. Especially when you keep rearranging your own plans to do so. You don't always have to put your life on hold for her."

Eyes burning, I whipped around and pointed a finger an inch from his face. "You have no idea what the hell you're talking about, so I suggest you pay attention to social cues before opening your mouth. That boy is just as much mine as hers, and if you have no experience with that kind of friendship, I truly feel sorry for you."

I attempted to storm away, but his hand shot out, grasping my arm just above my elbow. "Hey, I'm sorry. I say stupid shit when I'm pissed. I didn't mean it like that."

Yeah, I knew how that went. Story of my life.

He sighed, his face softening ever so slightly as he leaned closer to me. "But we have a show. One you agreed to. I know we're our own bosses, but the people who hired us are expecting us to play. Not me. *Us.* You can't ditch out seconds before we're supposed to start."

"Yes, I can," I said, yanking my arm out of his grasp. "It's an emergency, and I need to go."

His eyes ran down me and back up, as if needing to double-check that the emergency didn't have anything to do with me. His entire body tensed. "What kind of emergency?"

"None of your business. I'll text you tomorrow."

I didn't give him another chance to reply before I was ripping off my heels and running out of the backyard.

Chapter
21

SMASHING MY FRONT door open, I sprinted into the duplex, straight back to my room where I had a small folder filled with important documents. Including all of Sadie's vet records.

I wasn't sure if they needed them, but I didn't want to risk showing up without them and having to come all the way back. I knew nothing about vet care or the do's and don'ts of treating venom.

I'd just found what I was looking for and was making my way back down the hall when my phone went off again. I had it out and glued to my ear before the first ring ended.

"Hey, Beth, I'm on my way. I had to swing by the house for her records. Is she okay?"

She cleared her throat, speaking quietly in a way that had me guessing Jamie was close by, and she was attempting to be discreet. "They still haven't told me much, but someone did come out and ask what measures I was willing to pay for to save her life in the worst-case scenario. They gave me a sheet listing all the possible procedures and their costs."

I sucked in a breath, a sharp burning sensation prickling behind my eyes. The cost of the vet hadn't even crossed my mind yet. Fuck. I could barely afford Sadie's regular checkups, let alone whatever they thought she might need.

"Is it bad?"

She made a croaking noise that did nothing to make me feel better. "Not all the possibilities are. I wasn't sure what you wanted me to say. You know we'd cover the cost upfront if you needed it, Layla."

"I know, Momma Two. I appreciate you so much, but don't worry about it. I'll be there soon and will look it over and tell them myself."

"All right, dear."

Sniffing, I said a quick goodbye and dropped my arm. I sniffed again, my face feeling uncomfortably warm. Don't cry, Layla. No problem in the world ever got fixed with tears. Get your shit together. Get your shi—

Wham, wham, wham.

I yelped, dropping my phone from where I'd been trying to tuck it back into my butt pocket. Who the hell would be here? Garrett? He had a key, but maybe he forgot it. I thought about not answering it, I wasn't in the mood to talk to anyone. But then I remembered my car is clearly out front, and he'd know I was ignoring him.

Irritated, I didn't even bother peeking out of the window before I yanked the door open. A blast of chilly evening air hit me, and I was going to use that as the reason why my entire body turned into a statue in the doorway. I blinked, and then blinked again, unsure if what I was seeing was real.

"Waters? What are you doing here?" And who the hell was playing at Andrea's?

"You ran out of a show, Davis. You spouted shit about an emergency and then *left* without saying anything else."

"So?"

He crossed his arms, glaring at me. "So, I came to check on you, you infuriating woman."

"Why do you fucking care? You'd have made even more money with me gone," I spat, blinking rapidly to keep my tears contained.

He didn't deserve my nastiness, but I was pissed that my dog was hurt, pissed that I lost out on money when this vet bill was sure to cost a fortune, pissed that I was about to cry, and pissed that Adrian would see it if I did.

But he didn't balk from my anger. He did the opposite, taking a large step into the house toward me and lowering his arms to his sides. "Tell me what's wrong."

"No. I need to go." I moved to sidestep him, but he mirrored me, blocking my path.

"Tell me what's wrong."

"No. Move."

"Davis."

"Move out of my way," I yelled, tears finally streaking down my cheeks. "My dog got bit by a fucking snake and was rushed to the vet, and I don't know if she's dying or not, and she's all alone."

I shoved at his chest, more and more tears raining down as I lost control over the emotions I kept restrained so tightly to my chest. Adrian stumbled back a step but quickly righted himself, his face unmoving.

"I don't care if you think a dog isn't a real emergency. I don't care if you think business comes first or that I'm being irresponsible." I heaved in a breath, ready to knee him in the balls if he said anything bad about Sadie.

"Davis."

"I don't care what you think of me or my self-made family. I don't care—"

"Would you shut the fuck up and come here already?"

I snapped my mouth shut, blinking up at him a second before his hands wrapped around my biceps, and he pulled me in. The second my face pressed into his neck, he released his grip only to wrap his arms around my body and hold me close.

His lips brushed dangerously close to my ear, his breath causing goosebumps to erupt over every inch of my skin. "It doesn't matter what I think, Layla. *You* care, and that's enough."

A choked sound burst from my throat. I didn't know what to do or say, so I said nothing, breathing in his warmth and familiar smell.

One of his hands came up to cup the back of my head while the other traced soft lines up and down my spine. "But for what it's worth. I do care."

We stood there like that for another minute until I had my breathing and tears under control. My heart, however, was a completely other matter. The stupid organ was beating like my lifelong celebrity crush had just professed his undying love for me.

Traitorous fucker.

Chuckling awkwardly, I pushed back, putting some space between us and sniffing. "Guess you're going to use this against me for a while, huh?"

I looked up in time to catch something that looked an awful lot like regret flicker in his gaze. But then he shook his head and sighed. "Come on. I'll drive you to the vet."

Come again? Was the world ending? "No. You're supposed to be at Andrea's. I can drive myself."

He ignored me, snatching my phone up off the floor and walking toward the door. "I'll drive." He repeated. "You'll want to be able to sit in the back with Sadie if she's able to come home. Besides, I got someone to cover our gig. Now, let's go."

I blinked at him like a deer in headlights. "Who did you get to cover?"

"Get your ass in the truck, and I'll tell you."

The first thing I saw when we entered the lobby was Jamie's body curled up in a chair. His skin was red and splotchy and his face so puffy I wasn't sure how he could possibly see. The sight tore something inside of me. He looked so small and lost as he raised his head.

His chest heaved with huge gulping hiccups as he spotted me, and he shot out of his chair, startling Beth, who'd been looking at a magazine next to him. He sprinted across the lobby, slamming into my chest with a force that would've knocked me over if it wasn't for the hand Adrian placed on my back to steady me.

"Layla, I'm sorry, I'm so sorry. It's my fault. She's going to die, and it's all my fault. Please don't hate me, I'm sorry."

"Shh," I said, extricating his vise-like grip from around my waist to squat down in front of him. I took his face in both my hands, making sure he looked me directly in the eyes. "This is not your fault. Do you hear me?"

Beth stepped up to our sides, arms crossed over her middle. "That's what I've been trying to tell him."

I didn't respond, my focus on the boy shattering to pieces in front of me. "I could never in a million years hate you, Jamie Hartland. Ever. I love you. Sadie loves you. This is not your fault."

His face crumpled as he broke down into soul-crushing sobs that made me have to bite down hard on the inside of my cheeks to keep from breaking down right alongside him.

"I'm so sorry, LayLay," he whispered.

Hearing the nickname he used to call me but hadn't used in years was almost too much to bear. My shoulders stiffened, and I swallowed hard, trying to keep it together. I'd already had my cry at the duplex. I needed to keep my shit together because I refused to cry a second time in front of Adrian.

"I'm going to check in with someone and see how she's doing. Why don't you go home with your grandma and give Rugpants a few extra cuddles. She's going to need company tonight."

He hiccupped again, leaning back to wipe his shirt sleeve across his nose. "I don't want to leave. I need to tell Sadie I love her."

Fuck.

"I will tell her for you, and then you can tell her yourself when she comes home, okay?"

Beth stepped closer, placing a hand on the back of his head and drawing him into her side. "We've been here awhile, and it's late. Why don't you go to the bathroom real quick, and then we'll go home and make some hot chocolate?"

He sniffled, but nodded, making his way toward the bathroom in the corner, staring at his feet the entire way.

We all watched him go until he disappeared through the door. I felt the heat of Adrian's body standing just behind me, and I leaned into it, knowing that I needed to put some space between us, but unable to do so in that moment.

Beth turned back toward me, her face appearing ten years older and tired. "This is better than he was before. He cried so hard on the way here, I worried he was going to vomit."

God, that poor kid. I opened my mouth to say something, but the words died when Adrian suddenly ran his hand down my arm and walked past me, aiming for the bathrooms.

"Waters! Where are you going?"

He barely twisted his head, calling over his shoulder, "I'll be right back," and disappeared into the bathroom after Jamie.

I was torn between following him and making sure he was behaving himself, and staying to talk to Beth. But something flickered to life in my chest, telling me I could trust him. Adrian had held me while I cried and drove me all the way here. He wasn't going to be an asshole to a crying kid. He probably just needed to go to the bathroom too.

"So, tell me exactly what happened."

"It happened so fast, Layla. I was up on the deck, reading a book while Jamie ran around with the dogs. He was kicking his soccer ball back and forth across the yard and yelling like he was a sports announcer," she said, a flash of amusement darting across her face at her grandson.

"He moved closer to those bushes we have on the side of the yard, and I wasn't paying any attention." She swallowed, shaking her head, and I knew, like Madison, she was going to overthink today for a long time.

"Suddenly Sadie just went crazy. She crashed into Jamie and sent him sprawling to the ground, and then started barking and growling at the bush. I immediately started screaming at Jamie to back away and ran down the stairs toward her.

"She'd somehow seen or smelled the copperhead hiding there and pushed him out of the way just in time. She had it pinned to the ground with her right paw. I watched it rear back and bite her, God, at least three times."

I sucked in a breath. It'd bit her more than once? How venomous were copperheads? Shit.

Beth placed a hand on my arm. "She didn't hesitate or back

up even when it kept biting," she said, giving my arm a squeeze. "John came running out at all the commotion and killed it. He helped me load her in the truck but stayed back to make sure there were no more."

I nodded. Madison's dad would rip those bushes out with his bare hands if he thought, for even a moment, there was a chance for more snakes to show up.

"Thank you for bringing her in, Beth."

I turned and had just taken two steps toward the front desk when the bathroom door opened again, and Jamie and Adrian walked out together. Jamie's face was still puffy, but he looked far more put together than he had been when he'd entered.

His hairline was damp, like he'd splashed water on his face, and he was taking steady, deep breaths. I glanced up at Adrian in time to see him mutter, "Good job," as he patted Jamie's back.

Then he stuffed his hands in his pockets and met my eyes, raising a brow as if to ask, *What?* I just shook my head. I'd circle back around to what he did later. Right now, I needed to check on my dog.

Giving Jamie one last hug and promising to call him in the morning, I walked to the young girl at the front desk who'd been watching us the entire time.

My chin raised, and steel wrapped firmly around my spine where it belonged, I asked her for an update. She had nothing to say other than when they'd taken Sadie back and that the vet would speak to me as soon as she had the chance.

So, accompanied by the one person I never thought would be there with me, I sat in the lobby of the vet and stared at the wall.

Chapter
→ 22 ←

"YOU WERE SUPPOSED to turn there."

"No, I wasn't."

"*Yes*, you were."

"*No*, I wasn't."

"Waters."

"Davis."

When the vet had finally called me back to talk to me, Adrian had been right on my heels. I hadn't asked, and he hadn't offered. He'd just done it.

And when I'd seen Sadie laying there with her shaved and swollen leg, I found myself subconsciously reaching back for his hand, gripping it and readying my heart for the worst.

And when the vet had given me a small smile and told me Sadie was stable and going to be fine, I almost—almost—

collapsed against him.

Staring at him now, I couldn't fathom how I'd gotten to that point. Because now all I wanted to do was grab the back of his head and smack his pretty face into his steering wheel.

The veterinarian, Nikki, had gone on to say that since most copperheads hibernate in the winter, it had likely sensed danger and attacked as a warning. Because of this, it hadn't released any venom into its bite. All that had entered Sadie's system was residual venom that had already been on its fangs.

Basically, she'd gotten really fucking lucky.

Nikki warned that her leg would turn a purplish-black and look significantly worse than it was as it healed, but that Sadie should make a full recovery and could go home the next day as long as nothing happened overnight.

So now, here I was, with a stress headache, sitting in Adrian's car on my way back home. Or at least, that's where we were supposed to be going.

I bit back a growl when he continued going the wrong way. Damn men and their inability to take directions. "This is not the right way, you stubborn ass. I know where I live."

"So do I," he said, not bothering to look at me, and certainly not bothering to do a U-turn. "But since we're going to my place, where you live is irrelevant."

Ex-fucking-cuse me? I pressed my thumb and forefinger into the corners of my eyes, praying to God and every holy ghost that I didn't strangle him while driving. "I'm not in the mood to go at it right now. Please, just take me home."

He darted a glance my way, a devilish smirk on his lips. "I

didn't say anything about going at it, Davis. I think we're both far too tired for that tonight."

For the first time in my life, I was utterly speechless. Adrian Waters did *not* just make a dirty joke to me. Slowly leaning toward his side, I reached out and pinched his arm, hard. He hissed, rearing away from me as much as he could while keeping us on the road.

"What the hell was that for?"

I pulled back and made a show of pinching myself next, though not nearly as hard. "I'm trying to figure out if we're asleep. Or somehow traveled to an alternate dimension."

He rolled his eyes, staring back at the road ahead. Then he hit his blinker and turned onto a long gravel drive that disappeared behind a line of sparse, brown willow trees.

For a split second, I thought he was finally going to reverse and back track, but as he continued going, and a large, white Victorian house appeared, I realized I was wrong.

My eyes widened, taking in the breathtaking home, and then I whipped my head toward him, wincing when it made my head throb. "Seriously?"

He sighed, putting his truck in park and plopping the back of his head against his headrest. "Look, I'm exhausted. It's been a long night, and you live across town. I don't feel like driving all the way there and back tonight."

"Fine," I said, pulling out my phone and mentally logging that tidbit away. I'd definitely assumed he lived near me. "You could've just left me at the vet then. I'll order a ride."

His hand thrust out, snatching the phone from my grip and

clicking it off before I even had the app opened. "What is your problem? I don't mind getting a ride," I said, even though just the thought of putting another charge on my card after that vet bill made me instantly nauseated.

"Jesus, Davis, I'm not going to accost you. I'm tired. You're tired. And this way, you're two minutes away if something happens. I have a spare room and two couches. Take your pick."

I glared at him, hoping he'd catch on fire. But it was the second thing he'd said that made me pause before spewing an insult his way about accosting me.

He wasn't wrong. This was right down the road from Sadie. I bit my lip, hating that I suddenly very much wanted to stay. My heart said yes, but my pride was a prickly bitch who hated giving in.

Turning his truck off, Adrian grabbed his keys and phone— still also holding mine—and shoved his door open. "Stop thinking so hard, you'll give yourself wrinkles."

I flipped him off, but he only chuckled and slammed the door in my face. I was still grumbling, arms crossed over my chest like a child throwing a tantrum when he appeared at my side, opening my door and all but pulling me out.

"I can walk myself. This is close enough to kidnapping as it is, so you should probably keep your hands to yourself," I snapped. My anger felt good. Not as good as his arms had felt wrapped around my body, or his hand clasped in mine. But still good.

"Why am I suddenly tempted to toss your ass over my shoulder and fireman carry you inside?"

If looks could kill, Adrian would've been a white outline on the graveled drive. "I'll walk inside the Chop Shop myself, thank you."

The Chop Shop in question was not what I'd expected at all. And not just because it was an old-style Victorian home, whereas Adrian was as modern as they came, but because the second I stepped inside, I felt every inch of stress melt from my shoulders.

The smell hit me first, that comforting, recognizable smell that all grandparents' homes had. Like if I walked into the living room, I'd find relaxed, spring couches and a glass dish of strawberry-shaped candies on the coffee table next to a dusty magazine with the Golden Girls on it.

As much as it surprised me, I wasn't sure why it did. Adrian had told me he'd moved to town for Doris, so it only made sense he'd also be taking care of her home. The same home he'd once lived in as a boy when she'd taken him in.

I stole a peek at him over my shoulder, wondering what he must've been like as a child, running through this house. When he turned and caught my eye, I looked away, busying myself with taking in my immediate surroundings.

The entryway walls were covered from ceiling to floorboards with a cream wallpaper with tiny green flowers. The wood flooring was a gorgeous cherry hue, and a gold coat rack was tucked in the corner just beside the door.

Slipping my coat off, I carefully draped it over a hook and walked through the first wide arch to the right, officially intrigued.

I couldn't help the smile that broke across my face when I made my way around the dining room table, complete with pink upholstered chairs, and entered the kitchen.

It was like a replica of my own grandmother's, and probably many others. The floor was a yellowed tile with diamonds in the center of each square, the walls a pale pink that matched the dining chairs, and the cabinets a bleach white with huge knobs.

My smile fell and sadness washed over me as I took another step in, staring at the lacy curtain hanging over the sink window. I hadn't seen my grandma or anyone else in my family in months, and sometimes I missed them so much, it physically hurt.

"Your room is that way if you're not too stubborn to use a real bed, but you should probably eat something first."

I tore my eyes away from the curtains to see Adrian leaning over the kitchen island with his arms splayed out in a way that highlighted every curve and dip of his biceps.

I swallowed, suddenly parched. "I'm not hungry, but I could use a glass of water."

He narrowed his eyes, his tongue poking the inside of his cheek. "You haven't eaten in hours."

"I'm aware." What I wasn't aware of was that he kept a check on my eating habits. Then again, my stomach had been our only source of music during both drives we'd taken together.

"You need to eat something."

Something about his insistence caused a weird fluttering sensation in my chest. I subconsciously raised a hand and rubbed at it, noting the way his eyes darted down to watch my fingers press between my breasts.

Something settled between us, something dangerous and heavy. Something I was too emotionally depleted to contemplate tonight. Or ever. "Can I please just go to bed, Adrian?"

His eyes flared, probably at me using the word 'please', and he shoved off the counter and nodded before wordlessly leading me out of the kitchen.

I may have been too emotionally depleted to consider the weird thing growing between us, but not so much that I didn't enjoy the view of his ass in his dark jeans as he walked down the hall.

The room was no bigger than my own room at the duplex, minus the mountains of clothes and dog hair. The bed had a thin cream-colored quilt, topped with a soft lilac crocheted blanket folded at the end. There was one side table with a lamp, a wooden bench at the foot of the bed, and a velvet green armchair by the window. Simple, but homey all the same.

"It's not much, but it'll do." He rubbed at the back of his neck and grimaced. "I'm not sure when the sheets were last washed though, so I'd recommend just laying over the top and using the throw blanket."

Wandering in and dropping my butt unceremoniously onto the mattress, I leaned forward and rested my elbows on my knees, pressing my thumbs into my temples. "It's fine. Thank you."

He hesitated at the doorway. "Headache?"

I nodded absently wishing he'd leave while simultaneously not wanting to be alone. "Yeah. Crying like an idiot will do that to you."

I waited for him to agree, or make a smartass remark of some kind, but he didn't say anything. He just twisted around and walked back out. It stung, but I didn't blame him. I wouldn't want to be around me any longer either. It was late, and my emotions were more of a mess than when it was shark week.

But a minute later, just as I was about to fall backward and nurse both my headache and wounded pride, he returned, holding a glass of water and two white pills. "Here. I also found an extra toothbrush for you and set it in the bathroom across the hall."

My lip curled just at the sight of those two white pills, and I leaned away from his outstretched hands like they might jump out at me. There weren't a whole lot of things I hated, but taking pills was one of them.

He looked almost angry at whatever he saw in my expression, and he shoved them in my face. "I don't know when you decided to believe I'm some kind of monster who preys on upset women, but I'm not trying to drug you, Davis. It's acetaminophen."

I rolled my lips in and bit down, feeling embarrassed for the hundredth time tonight. At this rate, I might as well give up, huddle under the blankets like Rugpants, and wave a white flag at my life. "I can't take them."

"Yes, you can. You have a headache. I have the remedy. It's common sense. Or are you bailing on that too?"

I shot a glare up at him, wanting to dump the water over his head. "I mean, I literally can't take them, you asshole. I can't swallow pills."

He lowered his hands and tipped his head to the side, analyzing my face like he was trying to detect if I was lying. "Your gag reflex is that sensitive?"

I shook my head and blurted without thinking, the comfort of the house lulling me into a sense of ease it shouldn't have. "I don't even have a gag reflex. I can swallow just about anything else."

The silence that settled in was thick and heavy as he stared at me. His face betrayed nothing, but I swore the blue in his eyes darkened ever so slightly.

Feeling my entire face flush beet red, I continued on like I hadn't just told Adrian Waters my sexual capabilities.

"It's stupid, I know," I rambled. "I swallow larger bites of food than those pills every day, but I just can't do it. I don't like how they feel going down my throat."

I smashed my lips together, scrubbing my hands down my face and groaning. "Ugh, just go away before I dig this hole any deeper."

There was a beat of silence and then a laugh burst from his lips, loud and carefree. My head shot up at the sound, shock lancing through my chest. In all the weeks we'd argued and played, I'd never once heard him give more than a quick chuckle or a soft, quiet laugh.

His laughter was deep and raspy, so different from the smooth, melodic sound of his singing. And as it tapered off, and he cocked an eyebrow at me and grinned, I immediately wanted to hear it again.

I wasn't sure what to think about that desire, but we were

going to blame it on the night I'd had. Looking away again and hoping he wasn't able to read the thoughts on my face, I distracted myself with a loose thread on the crocheted blanket.

Seeing it reminded me that I still needed to call Madison. She'd texted me after finally calling her mom back, and I'd shot her a reply but hadn't had it in me to call.

But she'd definitely panic if she went home tonight and I wasn't there, so I'd have to let her know where I was, eventually. I could already hear the shrieked *"What?"* she was bound to scream into the phone when she realized I wasn't being sarcastic.

The silence continued on awkwardly until I finally dared to look back up and see Adrian still staring at me, the same small grin on his face.

I slapped my hands on my thighs. "Is there something you need from me besides trying to force me to swallow something?"

His grin only deepened. "That's a dangerous question."

"Ugh." I flopped back and stared at the ceiling, willing myself to fall asleep. But the sound of glass clicking against wood, and then the dip of the mattress had me shoving up to my elbows, narrowing my eyes at him.

"You're never going to let this go, are you?"

"What? You staying here?" He shifted, pulling his phone out of his back pocket and setting it next to him. The movement caused the outside of his thigh to press against the bottom of my foot, but he didn't seem to notice or care. And for some unknown, idiotic reason, I didn't either.

"Me ditching out. Me staying here. Seeing me ugly cry. Just…everything," I said, waving my hand.

He frowned. "What makes you think you ugly cried? Did you have snot pouring from your nose I didn't see?"

I kicked him, unable to completely rein in my quiet laugh. "No. But there's not a single person in the world who looks good crying. And of all people to see my swollen, red face, it had to be you."

He looked at the wall, tiny creases appearing between his eyes as he seemed to contemplate my words. "I'm not sure that's true."

I scoffed. "Okay, all-knowing Waters, I'll bite. Why isn't that true?"

Dipping his head my way, he raised one brow, staring at me with icy eyes that suddenly felt too hot. "You say I walked in and saw you swollen. I say I walked in and saw your tears making the blue in your eyes pop against your dark lashes. You say I saw you red-faced. I say I saw a flush across your cheeks that highlighted your freckles."

He leaned his torso closer, way closer than was necessary for a casual conversation. "You say I saw you embarrass yourself. I say I saw a woman unabashedly show how much she cares about those around her." He shook his head. "There's nothing ugly about that."

With each word out of his mouth, the tingle around my spine grew until I could feel it coursing down my arms and into my fingertips. No one had ever said something like that to me before. Sure, I'd had sweet boyfriends—Rick had been the definition of one—but it had always been a corny sweet. Not this naked, bare truth laid out between us.

I didn't know what to do about it. So, I did the only thing I could think of. Which was to do absolutely nothing. I cleared my throat and looked away, well aware that the flush, as he so elegantly called it, was back across my face.

"Well, I think I should probably get to bed."

He nodded and pushed to stand, handing me the folded blanket from the edge of the bed. I silently took it, wishing I could throw it over my face and hide. This man confused the fuck out of me.

Slipping his hands in his pockets, he rocked back on his heels, and I could feel him still staring at me. So, I busied myself with laying out the blanket and tucking my phone under the pillow.

"You were right, you know?"

I paused, shooting a quick glance up at him. "What?"

"You were right."

I swallowed, unsure where this was going. "About what?"

And for the first time ever, Adrian Waters looked at me like he saw me. Not the bitch version of me. Not the musician me. Just *me*.

"I don't have experience with the kind of friendship you and Madison have. I've only ever had Nan. I've never..." he cleared his throat. "I've never been good at making friends."

I rolled my eyes, huffing a laugh to cover the way my heart beat rapidly in my ribcage. Like it wanted to leap out and give him a hug. "With your glowing personality, I can't imagine why."

But he didn't laugh or banter back at me. He just kept

looking at me with that intense, unflinching stare. "I've never had a friend like you before."

My heart flipped. "Who says I'm your friend now?"

Something flashed across his eyes as they dipped to my mouth and back up. "I do."

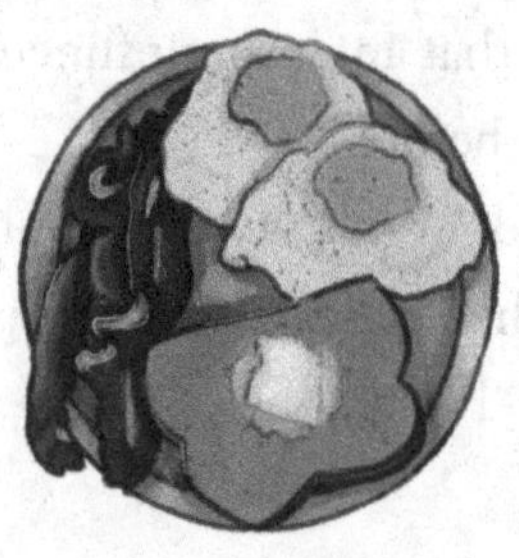

Chapter
➤ 23 ⬿

BURROWING MY FACE deeper into my pillow, I sighed, content to lay in bed and not move for at least another hour. Or two. Maybe three.

I hated mornings. I really did. The heaviness that sat behind my eyes, the weariness in my limbs as I trudged out of my room, all of it. What I didn't hate, however, was a pillow that felt like a cloud, the hint of bacon in the air, and the sound of a perfect voice humming my song.

And it was only the holy trinity of those three things that got my eyes flying open and my body shooting up out of bed with my heart in my throat.

I blinked, trying to clear the fog over my vision, and didn't recognize my surroundings at first. And even after the events of the previous night stabbed into my memory, my heart stayed right where it was, blocking my ability to swallow or even breathe.

I'd stayed the night at Adrian's house. Or his grandmother's house, I guess. Or maybe it was officially his now? I rubbed my eyes and groaned, why the hell did that matter?

Snatching my phone from beneath my pillow, I glanced at the time. Five o'clock in the morning. Gross.

I looked at the window then, wondering if it was locked and if it'd be possible for me to climb out of it without making a sound. The room was on the main floor, and I could easily book a ride before Adrian even knew I was awake.

Gripping my phone tightly in my fist, I chewed my lip, debating it. I was tempted, like *really* tempted. And I might have done just that, and hauled my clammy, miserable ass out of the window, if it hadn't been for the man still humming my song from somewhere in the kitchen.

The man who'd held me as I cried, and who'd given Jamie a pep talk in the bathroom about how brave he'd been. It was that last thought that had me sliding out from beneath the warm blanket and begrudgingly walking out of the room, unable to disappear without saying something.

That…and the smell of bacon.

Shuffling into the kitchen barefoot, since I only had my heels from the night prior and didn't want to announce my arrival Andrea-style, I wrapped my arms around my torso and shivered, squinting as the light scorched my retinas.

The humming came to an abrupt stop. "I wondered when you'd finally find the courage to wander out. Should've known bacon would do the trick."

I glared, or at least, I think I did. I was too busy finding my jaw from the floor and putting it back where it belonged to know. My hip knocked into the edge of the kitchen island, and I hissed out a breath, not taking my eyes off the sight before me.

Of Adrian standing in a pink and white kitchen, cooking breakfast, in nothing but a pair of loosely fitting gray sweatpants. His hair was tossed up in a messy bun that left pieces hanging sporadically around his face and neck, and his usually trimmed beard was a little longer and scruffier.

"Don't get growly with me. I've only had one cup of coffee and am not yet up to par," he said without turning around, misinterpreting my hiss of pain to be in reaction to his comment. "I only meant that bacon would wake anyone up."

The lean, yet defined muscles in his back and arms twitched and shifted as he moved between the counter and stove, flipping bacon slices onto a plate and tossing more raw slices into the pan.

"What if I was a vegetarian?" I asked, desperately trying to distract myself as I leaned over the counter and attempted not to drool all over it. From the delicious bacon smell. Yeah. That was the reason.

"You're not."

"But what if I was?"

He slowly turned from where he stood before the stove, his eyes caressing up my body at the same time mine took in his. Holy fucking shit. The man had said he only had a four pack as if that meant he was lacking in some form, but there was nothing lacking about Adrian Waters.

I'd never cared much about bodies. Rick had been shorter than me and on the rounder side, and I sure wasn't going to win a body builder competition with my soft stomach and wide hips.

But there was no *not* noticing the way Adrian's chest flexed under my gaze, or the happy trail that disappeared into the front of his sweats like a neon arrow showing me the way.

"That'd be a shame."

I flicked my gaze back up to his eyes, wondering if my own were as dark as his. "What would?" I asked, suddenly having no idea what we were talking about. The words came out huskier than usual, like my voice was just begging to betray my thoughts.

He tipped his head and perused my body again, his knuckles whitening over the counter. "It'd be a shame if you didn't like meat."

His statement felt like a challenge, like he was baiting me, waiting to see what I'd do. It wasn't the first time he'd done so, but this felt different from our usual banter. More intimate.

Because right now, what I wanted was to answer his challenge and show him what I'd rather be doing than eating bacon and eggs. I wanted to dip my fingers beneath his sweats and see just how dark his blue eyes could get when they filled with lust.

I wanted him in every way. The man whom I'd sworn to hate forever and ditch the moment I could. And not just for a quick fuck against the kitchen island.

I wanted to run my lips across his pecs, bite at his nipples, and trace the dip of his hips with my tongue. I wanted to straddle this man and slide down onto him slowly, rolling my hips and taking what I needed.

And when he looked at me the way he currently was, I wanted to do it every morning for the rest of my life. That alone was my clear sign that I needed to leave.

I'd crossed yet another invisible line last night, one that was dangerously close to the last and final one, and I needed to redraw the boundary before I tripped over it and face-planted in a world of hurt.

"I appreciate the offer of breakfast, but I'm actually going to head out."

He blinked at me, surprise lighting his face, and maybe even a hint of hurt. But I threw that thought out. That was stupid. Adrian didn't get hurt, and certainly not from something as ridiculous as me not staying for breakfast.

His brows lowered, and I raised my hand, already knowing the argument he was about to give me about needing to eat. "I have to be at work in a few hours, Waters. You don't have to take me home. I'll order a ride, it's fine. I'm just going to go grab my stuff and then I'll be out of your hair."

Spinning on my heels before he could respond, I practically power walked back into the bedroom. The second I was out of sight, I pressed the heel of my palms into my eyes, trying in vain to scrub the sight of a half-naked Adrian from my mind. But it might as well have been etched in fucking marble.

I groaned and dropped my arms, looking around for my phone and shoes. Thirty seconds later, I was stomping back into the kitchen.

"Have you seen my shoes? I left them right by the door last night."

He didn't turn around this time as he scraped a spatula across a second pan to flip some fried eggs. "Mm. Possibly."

That was a yes, then. Hands on my hips, I widened my stance. If he was going to be difficult, then two could play that game. "Well did you *possibly* move them somewhere else? Because I can't find them."

Nothing. Not even a grunt of acknowledgment.

"Seriously, Waters? You snuck into the room while I was fucking sleeping and took my shoes?"

He slid the eggs onto the plates next to the bacon and then reached over and pushed two slices of bread into the toaster. "I can guarantee to you, if I ever found myself sneaking into the room of a naked, sleeping woman, it wouldn't be to steal her shoes."

I wasn't going to touch that statement with a ten-foot pole, let alone inform him that I had slept completely clothed last night.

"I took them while you were brushing your teeth."

I threw out my hands, imagining wrapping them around his neck. "What the hell for?"

He sighed, turning off the gas flames and setting the pans to the unlit back burners. "Because I knew you'd do this."

"Do what? Try to go home and shower? Get to work on time? Check in with my best friend who's texted me no less than ten times this morning? Take your pick."

Finally turning around, he leaned his ass against the counter next to the stove and crossed one ankle over the other. His hands gripped the granite top on both sides of him, making his arm muscles dance as he stared hard at me. "Run away."

"Excuse me?"

"Yes, excuse you. Excuse you that you're too chicken shit to sit and eat with me. It doesn't have to be weird, and you have the time. It's just breakfast. It's okay for us to get along for fifteen minutes."

I crossed my arms and cocked a hip, pursing my lips. "That seems excessive."

"Ten minutes."

I shook my head. Even nine minutes was too long to be in the same room with this man when he was topless and making me food. Pissed off as I was about my beautiful shoes, I still wanted to climb him like a fucking tree, even now.

No, I needed to go home, fill in Madison, comfort Jamie, shower, and apparently rub out a quick orgasm. But mostly, shower. I didn't even want to know what I looked like after falling into bed without so much as face lotion or a brush.

I patted my hair down, realizing Adrian was still staring at me, and I had no idea what I looked like standing next to his God-like physique. Perfect.

"I need to go," I repeated. I didn't wait for him to say anything else before disappearing back down the hall. I'd rather get in a car barefoot than beg him for my heels. He could keep them as a memento or wear them around the house, himself. Whatever floated his boat.

Double-checking I had no calls from the vet, I tucked my phone into my pocket and quickly made the bed. I wasn't a complete asshole. I'd just finished folding the crocheted blanket and was laying it at the foot of the bed when I heard his footsteps approach the door.

I studiously ignored him and could practically hear the way he ground his teeth together. "Let me feed you. You haven't eaten in almost twenty-four hours, and we both know you'll end up spending the morning taking care of someone else rather than yourself."

The verbal reminder of my unintentional fast had my stomach clenching and twisting painfully. "That's not true."

"Yes, it is."

"I'll grab something on my way to work."

He muttered a curse, his voice a low growl that skirted up my spine and had me unable to resist turning around.

Adrian was standing in the doorway of the room, arms stretched out to hold the frame in a way that was absolutely indecent. It implanted an image in my head of the way he might look as he held himself above me, hands braced on the headboard as he rocked in and out.

I swallowed.

You are not in like with this man, Layla. It doesn't matter that he loves his grandma and isn't the selfish bastard you'd painted him to be. It doesn't matter that he ditched out on a show to be there for you. You do not *want to fuck his brains out and snuggle your cheek against his perfect pecs afterward.*

You don't. You don't. You don't.

But I was starting to realize I was the biggest liar of them all. And knowing that fucking scared me more than anything else. Because no matter how much my feelings for Adrian had changed, that didn't mean that his had.

Him being a decent human being and helping me out didn't mean he wanted to date and defile me. I needed to remember that.

Bottling that painful fact up and shoving it down deep in my belly to hate myself over later, I beelined for the door, incorrectly assuming he'd step out of the way for me. But he didn't. He just tightened his grip on the doorframe and stared at me.

"Five minutes. Give me five damn minutes, Davis."

God, with how wound up I was, I probably didn't even need two, and I'd be falling right off the edge. But that definitely wasn't what he meant.

My shoulders sagged, and I heaved out a heavy breath, trying not to look too much into the way his face softened into a look of relief.

"Fine, you win. But I want extra bacon."

"Deal," he said, shoving off and sauntering out of the room.

I watched his ass shift in his sweats the entire way and didn't let myself feel shame for it. I deserved the few seconds of eye candy because I was officially in uncharted waters, and I had no idea where I was or where I'd put the fucking oar.

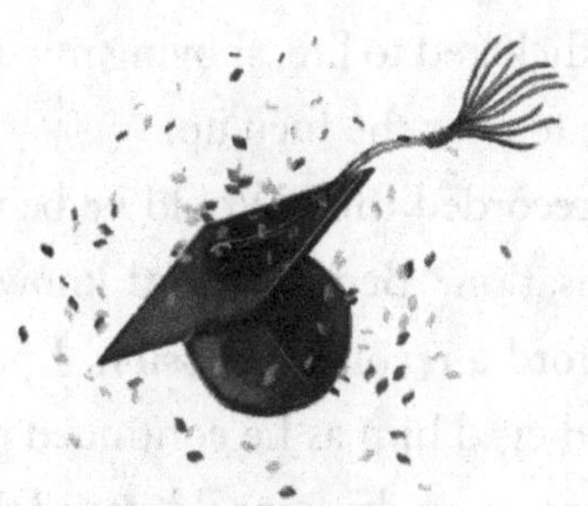

Chapter
→ 24 ←

BLUE EYES STARED at me. "Guitar solo."

I stared back, narrowing mine through my glasses. "You want an electric guitar solo…in *this* song."

Adrian nodded, chewing quickly through a mouthful of food. "Just trust me. Something along the lines of this. Sing that last part again real quick, and I'll pick it up."

I pursed my lips but listened. "*You're so hot and cold and uncontrolled, I can't get enough. I hate the way I feel more than a little bit of love.*"

He hummed as I sang and picked up his guitar from where he'd rested it over his legs before sinking his hand into the bowl of popcorn. The second the last note left my lips, he picked right up from where I ended, flying into a fast-paced solo piece I never would've thought to put in the song myself.

Excitement flickered to life, shoving my stubbornness to the side and telling it to shut the fuck up.

What if we recorded this? Would he be willing to do that? Without compensation? Because Lord knows, it'd take all my savings just to afford a recording session. I pushed the thought down for now and eyed him as he continued playing.

It'd been over two weeks since I'd stayed the night with him. Two weeks and I hadn't wanted to murder him even once. In that time, we'd met up twice for practice and had played at Jemmy's both Fridays. The first one had been such a success that the following Friday, Jemmy's had been forced to close the doors to keep from going over the allowed-occupancy capacity.

In just those two days, I'd made enough money to cover Sadie's vet bill and have some left over to tuck away for a rainy day.

Glancing at the sleeping ball of fur on the couch, I smiled. The vet hadn't exaggerated how horrendous her leg would look as it healed. Twice I'd almost taken her back, convinced her entire leg was about to fall off, and had only refrained after Adrian had aggressively talked me down.

He'd even swung by a few times outside of practice to check on her and bring her toys and treats.

I may, or may not, have had to grip onto the couch to prevent myself from launching off of it to hug him each time. Who would've known the asshole I met in the bar was a fucking cinnamon roll for dogs and grandmas.

The man in question wrapped up the song and looked at me expectantly, like he was waiting for me to break out into applause or bow at his musical genius. "What do you think?"

I pursed my lips and pretended to ponder it even though I was one-hundred percent in love with it. "I think, it's very convenient…for one of us…that you think *my* song needs an electric guitar solo that only *you* can provide."

His lips tipped up in that way that had my toes curling, and he set his guitar back in his lap, reaching for another handful of popcorn. "It's not my fault you didn't have the intuition and ear to know it needed me."

"The day my intuition tells me I need you, Waters, is the day I throw it in the trash." Too bad that hadn't worked out for me so far.

Faster than I could blink, he flung up his hand and threw his handful of popcorn at me. I flinched as several pieces bounced off my forehead and cheeks.

I glanced down at the kernels now decorating my lap and arched a brow high at him. "Did you seriously just throw food at my face?"

"No," he said, a wicked gleam to his eyes, "I was actually aiming down your shirt."

Something hummed in my chest when his eyes dipped to the inch of cleavage visible above my simple, scoop-neck shirt. Every time we'd seen each other since *that* morning, it'd been like this. A tentative friendship that was patched and taped together to hold back the *something more* that kept battering at the door.

And, like always, I didn't know how to respond to it. I didn't know if I should add more tape and take another step back, or tear it all off with my teeth and fling the doors open. I couldn't get a good enough read on him to know.

He flirted and said things that made me think he was interested in more, but I had no history to go on with him. For all I knew, he flirted like this with all his female friends. Or would, if he had any.

So, I did what I'd done every other time, and I ignored it completely. "I'm going to remember that when this song makes me famous and you come crawling to me to help you land connections."

His jaw worked back and forth for a minute as he eyed me, and then he ran his hand over his head and huffed a laugh that seemed a little forced. "You'd have to quit your day job and actually focus on pushing your music for that to ever happen."

"Party pooper," I said, arching my back and rolling out my neck. He was right, of course, but a woman could still have dreams. Even if they were ones that might only ever be that.

He watched me stretch, his hands shifting and fisting in his lap. "Seriously though, where *do* you work, Davis? Am I allowed to know yet?"

I groaned and closed my eyes, digging my fingers into the back of my neck. Constantly sitting on stools and the floor was going to make me permanently hunched before I was even forty.

"I work at a shipping company. I do timesheets and schedule stuff for the truck drivers to deliver the goods and whatnot. It's all very interesting."

There was a pause. "That's not, at all, what I was expecting. I figured you taught guitar lessons on the side or something.

Why the hell do you work at a trucking company?"

I opened my eyes and pushed my glasses higher up my nose from where they'd fallen, my head still tilted to the side. "Food. Rent. Clothes. The list goes on, Waters."

His entire body seemed to go still, his eyes moving all over my face, like he was putting pieces of a puzzle together that'd been a jumbled mess before. I frowned, what in the world was that look for?

He rotated his jaw and gently moved his guitar to the floor next to him, side-eyeing me with a serious look. "There are a ton of restaurants and bars in this town actively seeking live music. I can almost guarantee you'd make more money at them."

"Oh, I absolutely would," I agreed before I could stop myself.

"Then why the hell are you slinging timesheets when you clearly hate it? Music is your life, and your originals," he added, pointing to my page of lyrics, "are fucking phenomenal. Focus on that."

I waved him off, swallowing down the bitter taste on my tongue. I did want to focus on it. I wanted to play at every venue in this town until everyone knew my name. Not because I truly wanted to be famous, but because I loved my music and wanted to share it with people who would love it just as much as I did.

And although I didn't say any of that, Adrian could see it. Hell, the man had been able to read me like a book from the moment we met.

"Quit your job. It's a waste of your time and energy, and you know it. Call Larry and tell him you're available, and he'll have you fully booked by the time your two-week notice is up."

"It's not that easy," I snapped, leaning over my guitar, and keeping my voice low so Madison wouldn't hear from her bedroom. I didn't want Adrian to point all of this out. I didn't want to know how easy it would be to have everything I wanted.

He scoffed, practically glaring at me. "Yes, it fucking is. You'd have no lull in your paycheck, be playing music almost every day, and be able to share this," he said, grabbing my notebook and shaking it, "with everyone."

I snatched it out of his hand, tossing it back to the floor. "I don't need to share it with everyone. It's just a song. I write them all the time and sing them on the weekends."

That was partly true. I did sing my originals at my weekend shows, but this had been the first song I'd written since the one I'd done for Madison. And the first one that felt like *me*.

I was proud of it. Really proud. And I knew if we recorded it with the electric guitar and drums Adrian kept mentioning, that others would love it too.

"That's bull—"

A door clicked open from the back end of the house, and I shot daggers at Adrian, silently demanding he drop the conversation. Soft steps came next, and then Madison appeared at the mouth of the hall.

Keeping her face forward, she studiously ignored us as she headed for the bar to grab her purse. God, I loved that woman.

Although there was no reason to pretend we didn't exist when she lived here, too, I appreciated that she was trying to give us privacy. It wasn't really possible in a smaller place like this, but it was the thought that counted.

I tipped my head down, watching her slip on her shoes over the rim of my glasses. "Are you heading out to pick up Jamie from your parents'?"

Beth had picked him up from school today so they could have dinner together. Or at least, that's what they'd told Madison. What she didn't know, was they'd actually picked him up so they could go shopping for a graduation present for her.

I assumed they'd be bringing him home, especially when Madison had a huge test to take tonight, but I highly doubted she'd be leaving the house for any other reason.

She twisted just enough to look at me over her shoulder. Her eyes darted quickly between Adrian and me, likely counting the inches between us. Or lack thereof. Then she nodded once.

I frowned, noting the circles under her eyes. She hadn't been sleeping well, the stress of her finals getting to her. Years of working her ass off, and she was utterly terrified of ruining her GPA when she was so close to the finish line.

"They can't bring him home for you?"

She grabbed one of Garrett's hoodies from the closet and shrugged it on. "I'm sure they would, but I offered to go get him. No reason to make them get out again when they already picked him up from school."

She said it nonchalantly, but I could also tell by her mannerisms that she didn't want to get stuck chatting with her parents when she could be studying or taking a short break, instead.

"Want me to go get him?" I asked, taking my glasses off and

setting them on the coffee table. "I don't mind—"

"Don't even think about it, Davis. We only have tonight to nail this song before our next show, and right now you and I both know we've yet to get it to your liking."

"It's fine, I'll figure that last part out later," I said, even as my heart screamed the opposite, my fingers itching to keep going.

And as if sensing that, he hooked a thumb toward the hallway and scoffed. "When you have a kid asleep just on the other side of that wall?"

He was right, of course, but it wasn't a big deal, and I definitely didn't want to have the conversation in front of Madison. She struggled delegating as it was. I'd just squeeze more practice in later.

"It's just a song, Waters," I said, flicking my hand toward my lyrics and adamantly not looking at him, even as the words tasted bitter on my tongue. "Seriously, go rest for twenty minutes, Mads. I'll do it. You look like a racoon."

I slid my guitar off my lap onto the floor and folded my legs beneath me, getting ready to push up onto my feet when a hand snaked out and wrapped around my wrist, stopping me.

"No, it's not," he said, irritation coating his voice, "and you know it."

I yanked my hand to no avail, his expression telling me he wasn't going to let go until I sat back down. "Let go."

"No."

"Waters, I swear, if you don't—"

He gripped me tighter, pulling my face toward his, his

words hitting me harder than if he'd slapped me. "It is not *just a song*, Layla."

I stared at him, feeling like my chest was on fire even while his icy blue eyes froze me in place. My name on his lips hit me like a fucking high note at the end of a ballad, the kind that changes the mood of an entire piece and makes goosebumps erupt down your arms in response.

How long had I waited for someone to say something like that to me? To understand, on the same level as I did, what my music meant to me? That it wasn't just words on paper or notes on strings, but my heart and soul that I was laying out raw and naked for the world to hear.

That it was everything to me.

My eyes subconsciously flicked down to his lips, pressed thin with determination, and then back up. My lungs suddenly felt tight, and I wasn't sure what to do with my body or my face with the way he was looking at me.

He leaned in closer, his hand still wrapped around my wrist. "If you want to quit your job, *this* is the way to do it. With *this* song."

I licked my lips, and his eyes flared, pinning to the movement. He began to raise his other hand, like he might wrap it around my shoulder or something, and I tensed under the anticipation, unsure of whether I wanted him to or not.

But then four soft words filled the silence, pausing his movement and breaking the spell. "What does he mean?"

Chapter
25

MY HEAD WHIPPED toward Madison, heart in my throat, to see her squeezing the keys in her hand, her brow furrowed. "Layla. What does he mean?"

Shooting a death glare at Adrian, who reluctantly released my wrist, I stood, straightening my shirt and trying to even my voice out to sound steadier than I felt. Especially when I could still feel the residual warmth of his hand on my arm.

"Nothing, Mads. He's just being a typical man and trying to tell me what to do. Ignore him. That's what I do."

I felt, more than heard, him stand and step up behind me, his anger slithering over me. "Yep, just like everything else. You're a pro at ignoring things, aren't you, Davis? You're perfectly content to ignore everything you want and continue working your dead-end job rather than take the weekday shows that would make you happy."

I bit the insides of my cheeks, cursing up a storm in my head when I heard Madison's sharp inhale.

"You told me there weren't any decent weekday shows," she said, confusion making the words come out slow.

"There aren't. At least none that work for the schedule I need," I said, trying to hedge around the conversation while also not completely lying to my best friend's face.

Adrian grunted and shifted behind me, and I shot my elbow back, blindly aiming for his gut to stop him from moving around me. But I wasn't fast enough.

He stepped next to me, looking down at me with fury in his eyes. I glared back. The asshole had no right to be angry at me. This had nothing to do with him. If anything, I had a right to be mad at him for saying something in front of Madison that I'd told him in private.

Soft, hesitant words speared across the room, cracking my heart right down the center. "Because they don't work for your schedule…or because they don't work for *mine*?"

I closed my eyes, hearing the panic in Madison's voice, the guilt and the doubt, and wishing I could lie and make her feel better. "It's not important, Mads."

It was apparently the wrong thing to say. Adrian growled, causing my eyes to snap back open and land on him. "Stop doing that."

"Stop doing what? Being honest?"

"Stop acting like everything you want doesn't matter. Stop being a stubborn ass and ignoring what's right in front of your face."

A pit grew in my stomach, and I swallowed, no longer sure

if we were still talking about my job and shows. Movement caught my eye as Madison moved to the door, blinking rapidly, and grabbing the doorknob. "I need to go get Jamie," was all she said, and then she was gone, closing the door softly behind her.

I whirled on Adrian, practically spitting my next words. "What the fuck was that, Waters? You had no right to do that. None. She's never going to let this go."

He didn't so much as flinch, crossing his arms and meeting my anger head-to-head. "And she shouldn't. We're your friends, and that means stopping you from walking all over yourself."

"Really? Because all I feel is the fucking bus you just threw me under," I yelled, throwing my hands out between us. "Now she's going to hate herself, thinking she stole my choice from me when it was never her decision."

I placed my hands on the sides of my face, trying to rein in the tears that were beginning to threaten. This was going to kill her, and nothing I said was going to fix it.

"Goddamnit, Davis, stop putting her feelings first. It's not your job to take care of her."

Closing the already-small space between us, I jabbed a fingernail hard into his sternum, causing him to hiss and bare his teeth at me. "Yes, it is. You have no idea what she's been through, so your opinion of her, or our friendship, is irrelevant."

He widened his stance but didn't back up, even as his eyes softened. He closed the last inch between us until we were chest to chest, and I swore I could feel his warmth radiating through me.

"You're right, I don't know."

"Exactly."

His fingers brushed against my own at my side. "But when did someone else's trauma mean that the rest of us matter less? She could've been through hell—"

"She *was*," I snapped, practically snarling the last word as I tried to shove past him, but he gripped my upper arm and pinned me in place, forcing me to face him.

"And I'm sorry for that. Truly. But that doesn't make you any less important than she is. And if she's a real friend, which it sounds like she is, she'll agree with me."

I met his eyes, refusing to answer, but my silence was answer enough. He was right. He knew it, and I knew it. But the truth didn't change anything. I didn't know how to be different. If I was being honest with myself, I didn't even know what I wanted at all anymore.

His free hand wrapped around my other arm until I was caged in, his smell surrounding me as he lowered his head and waited for me to meet his determined gaze.

"Stop putting yourself last."

Overwhelmed with everything, I tried to back away, to free myself from the conversation and his suffocating presence. It was infuriating how much he saw and understood about my thoughts and feelings without me granting him the right to that information. Sometimes it felt like he saw more than even I did.

And I hated it.

So, I shoved harder, lashing out at him. "This is what people do for the ones they care about. Something I wouldn't expect a selfish prick like you to ever understand."

He held on, refusing to let me go. "Not when it's at the expense of yourself."

A tear slipped past my control, leaving a hot trail down my face. "What could you possibly know about what I do?"

His eyes latched onto the single wet streak, and he raised a hand, swiping the pad of his thumb across my cheek. "I know you give everything you have to the people around you, while you've convinced yourself you're content with the scraps left at the bottom."

I sniffed and looked away, wishing he'd do the same. I couldn't think with him so close. I couldn't remember why I was supposed to hate him for this. I couldn't do anything but fall apart.

He leaned closer. "What do you want?"

"To take care of the people I love."

"That's not what I asked. What do *you* want, Davis? Just tell me what you want, and I'll let it go. That's it. Just one sentence, and I'll leave."

"*I don't know!*" I screamed, every muscle in my body deflating until I wondered if it was possible to meld into the floor beneath me. "She's my best friend."

"I know she is, but I also know she's a grown-ass woman who has plenty of people who love her." His hands twitched around my shoulders, his thumbs slowly moving up and down.

"Just because the bottom of the wick gets lit eventually, doesn't take away from the fact that it's also drowning in the melted wax of another's flame."

My nose curled against my will, and I shot an unimpressed look at him. "What are you, a fucking poet now?" But there was no bite to my voice.

His hands left my shoulders, and for a second I thought I'd

finally pushed him too far, but they were immediately back on me. One hand dropped to my waist to hook around my hip while the other shot into my hair and fisted a handful at my nape.

I couldn't help the small sound that slipped past my lips at the sharp sting on my scalp.

He cursed under his breath but didn't release my hair. Instead, he pulled down just hard enough that my head was forced to tip back. "You're such a fucking pain in my ass, woman."

Then he slammed his lips to mine.

And just like his eyes, there was nothing soft or sweet about Adrian's kiss. His grip on my hair was unyielding, his lips firm and demanding, like his entire survival depended on this kiss. This moment. Like he might die without it.

I stood frozen in his arms, surprise keeping me planted in place for several seconds, my brain unsure if it was hallucinating or not. Because holy shit. Adrian was kissing me. Adrian Waters was kissing me *hard*.

When another second passed that I didn't move, he growled into my lips and stepped into me, forcing me to back up until my spine knocked into the wall beside the slider door.

His mouth never left mine the entire time, even as his hands did, planting on the wall on either side of my face and blocking me in on all sides. I couldn't move, couldn't breathe, couldn't fucking think past the warmth of his body on mine.

His hard chest pressed flush against my soft one, his heart singing in a chaotic rhythm with my own, just as the tip of his tongue flicked across the seam of my lips. And I broke.

I shot my hands up from my sides and sank them straight

into his hair like I'd been dying to do since the night we'd met. It was just as soft as I'd imagined it'd be, and it only made me crazier, wanting to touch more, taste more. Have more.

Taking a fistful like he'd done to me, I yanked hard on his roots, wanting to cause him just enough pain that he'd know he wasn't in charge here. He was kissing me because I allowed it, and because I fucking wanted him to. Not the other way around.

Slanting my mouth, I opened for his tongue to dive in and dance with my own. I felt like I was burning up from the inside out, needing to pull more air into my lungs, yet not willing to break away in order to do so.

I grazed my teeth against his bottom lip, pulling it into my mouth and he groaned, dropping one hand back to my waist. He slid it back until he was gripping my ass and rolled his hips into me. Again and again.

I lifted a leg and wrapped it around his waist to give him better access. He took the hint and ground into me harder, rolling into me in a perfect, steady rhythm. I sighed against his lips, feeling myself tighten for someone, who wasn't myself, for the first time in months.

He suddenly pulled away from me, and my eyes flew open in surprise, only for him to drop his mouth to my shoulder. He worked his way along my skin, kissing and nipping all the way up to my neck until he reached my ear.

"Layla," he murmured, sending wave after wave of goosebumps and fireworks all across my body.

I arched my neck back, resting my head against the wall, and shuddered. "Adrian."

My chest was heaving in and out, and I could only hope he

didn't catch the waver in my voice. But he said nothing. He just captured my lips again, sweeping his tongue in and taking everything I had to give.

He adjusted his weight against me until his thigh pressed between my legs, and I unabashedly ground into it, desperate for any amount of friction to ease the coiling heat in my center. I could feel the straining bulge in his jeans as I rolled into him, and it just made me move faster, straddling him so that my thigh rubbed against his erection even as I chased my climax.

I was going to orgasm all over Adrian's leg in the middle of my living room, and although I knew it would kill me later to give him that satisfaction, God, I just didn't give a shit right now.

I moved faster, working myself closer and closer until I could see stars behind my eyelids. And just as I tipped toward the edge, firm fingers slid over the front of my pants and pressed against my clit, sending me flying over, headfirst.

I moaned into his mouth, possibly cursing and praising him all at the same time, as my body shuddered and fell apart beneath his touch. As my mind turned to mush and every single line between us disintegrated into ash.

He hummed in pleasure, even though he was still hard as a rock against my leg, and he kissed me softly. Once. Twice.

Then he pulled back, and we both stared at each other, our chests heaving and his fingers still resting against my clit and cupping my ass. I wanted him to circle those fingers, but more than anything, I wanted to move my own down to him. To palm the impressive length I could feel, and make him see the same stars I had.

His mouth opened, and I readied myself for him to say it'd

all been a mistake, when the front door suddenly slammed open like a tornado had come to visit, scaring the shit out of both of us.

Garrett stood in the doorway, wearing nothing but a thin pair of basketball shorts while his hair was soaked and water dripped from his body. His breathing was erratic and his eyes wide as they darted around the room and landed on us.

I shoved away from Adrian like he was a demon come to kidnap me, my face a mini-inferno as I came down from my orgasm and stared at my best friend's boyfriend.

His gaze moved back and forth between us, and then stopped on me, his hazel eyes narrowing as he took in my reddened face and expression, his own hardening to stone.

"Everything okay, Layla?"

"Yep," I squeaked, nodding more vigorously than was probably believable. I was so screwed. There was no way Garrett was going to keep this a secret from Madison. Adrian said nothing at my right, but I could see his own chest still moving a little too rapidly in my peripheral.

Garrett took another step in, the door still wide open, his jaw working back and forth as he considered my words and mannerisms. "Are you sure? I heard yelling when I stepped out of the shower, and saw several missed calls from Madison, and I thought—" He shook his head, his hands fisting at his sides.

Madison. He'd thought the yelling had been from her. Something flickered across his face, and I suddenly felt a surge of guilt for Adrian's and my fight. It'd probably terrified Garrett, especially since the last time he'd heard shouting from over here, it *had* been Madison, and she hadn't been okay.

"I'm sorry, Garrett," I said, smoothing my hands down my sides and crossing the living room to pick up Adrian's guitar. "Everything's fine. We just got in an argument. One I started."

Garrett's eyes flicked down toward Adrian's legs so fast, I barely caught the movement before they came back up, his face returning to solid stone. Jesus Christ, he'd noticed Adrian's fucking boner. Of course, he had. Adrian wasn't even trying to hide it. I was so fucked when Madison got home.

Clearing my throat, I moved toward Adrian's case and tucked his guitar in, making sure it nestled in carefully before latching it and picking it up.

Garrett hadn't moved a muscle, his jaw ticcing. "Do you want me to stay?"

I held out the case in Adrian's direction, pointedly not making eye contact. I could still feel his teeth grazing my lip, his tongue swiping into my mouth, and hear the deep moans vibrating up his throat as his hands molded my ass.

I shook my head, mentally screaming at the thoughts to leave. "No, it's okay. Adrian was just leaving," I said, my voice failing to come out as strong as I'd wanted it to. I nudged the case toward him again, demanding he take the hint.

And to my relief, he didn't argue. He just reached one long arm out and wrapped his hand around the handle, his fingers brushing mine for only a moment before I released it like a hot potato.

Adrian gave me one more long look, one I didn't meet, and then turned away and headed for the door. "Have a good night, Davis."

Davis. I suddenly hated my last name, the syllables feeling

like two hits to the gut. I dared a look, watching his shoulders and arms flex and move as he leaned down to slip his feet into his shoes. My traitorous heart hoping he'd glance one last time over his shoulder so I could gauge what was going through his head, but he didn't.

He just slipped passed Garrett, who'd moved to the side just enough to let him through, and walked out of my house without another word.

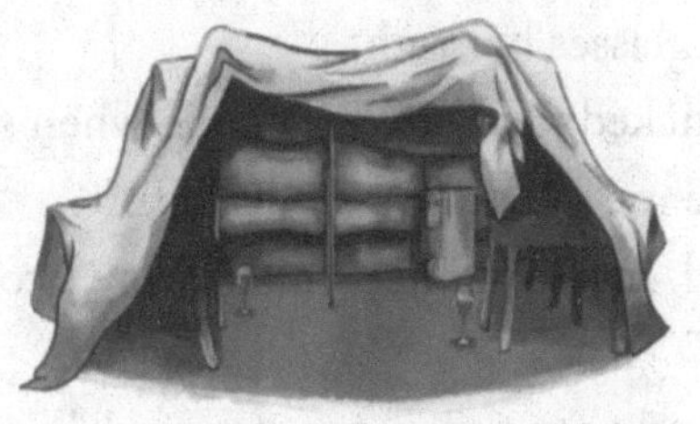

Chapter
26

THERE WAS A blanket fort taking up the entire living room. Not a small one like what we used to make for Jamie when we'd have our movie nights, but a huge one that used more blankets and chairs than we even owned.

I paused in front of the door, keys still in hand, phone in the other, and listened for the sound of Jamie whispering or the dogs' tails thumping. But I didn't hear anything.

Looking the tent over again, I noticed at least two blankets I didn't recognize, confirming that Madison had not only built it, but had gone over to Garrett's and retrieved his own kitchen chairs and blankets.

I crouched down and tipped my head to the side, staring in through what was clearly the entrance. Madison sat right smack in the middle of the tent, wearing a pair of sweats, one of Garrett's oversized hoodies, and her typical hideous socks. A bag of marshmallows accompanied her left side, and a box of wine and two empty glasses her right.

Her eyes flicked up from her phone when she saw me peek in, and she gave me a tentative smile. "Hi."

"Hi," I said, matching her smile. "May I come in, or is this a private party?"

"Only if you know the secret password."

Without batting an eye, I said, "Cookie dough ice cream."

She nodded seriously, waving her hand out in a grand gesture to silently invite me inside. I snorted at her antics and plopped all my shit onto the floor.

"Where is everyone?" I asked, reaching down to unfasten my heels. The house was suspiciously quiet considering we had a motor-mouth kid and two dogs.

She tilted her head in the direction of Garrett's side of the duplex and tossed an oversized marshmallow into her mouth, talking around it. "Garrett took them all to his place to watch a movie." She chuckled. "And before you ask, Sadie is fine. He carried her out the door like a giant infant even though I assured him she could walk."

I lowered to my hands and knees and crawled in, accepting the wine glass she handed me once I'd gotten settled. I tipped it back and took a drink, admiring the cozy abode my friend had created. However, cute as it was, I wasn't stupid enough to believe she'd just randomly decided to find her inner child on a Wednesday after we'd both worked all day.

"All right, Mads, spill. What's all this for?" I asked, even though I already knew the exact words that were about to come out of her mouth. *We need to talk.*

She sat up a little straighter, like she was steeling her spine. "We need to talk."

And there it was. I nodded, taking another sip of wine and dreading every second of the approaching conversation. I'd known from the second she left the house to pick up Jamie that it was coming, but that didn't mean I'd ever be ready for it.

I'd holed myself up in my room last night after Adrian and Garrett had left and hidden like a complete coward. I hadn't even come out to greet Jamie or to secretly ask him how his shopping went.

Every time footsteps passed by my door, I'd tensed, assuming it was Madison coming to drag me out by my hair and demand we talk, but she hadn't. Like the amazing friend she was, she'd given me my space to work everything out in my head without the pressure of her questions or opinions.

I didn't do well with emotions and big feelings, even with her. I never had. It was easy to listen to her thoughts and feelings and give advice, but having the tables turned always made me uncomfortable. Like the entire universe was staring at me while I whined about my life problems.

"And I figured," she continued, grabbing the bag of marshmallows and tossing it into my lap, "that you'd be more comfortable doing so if we also got tipsy and played fuzzy bunny while we did it."

I snapped my head up from the bag, a choked laugh slipping past my lips while my brows jumped clear off my forehead. "You're going to get tipsy on a work night?"

"Yep."

"Who are you and what did you do with Madison?"

In answer, she just held her glass under the wine box's spout and topped it off. "I take my friendship necklace very seriously, Layla Davis."

I chuckled, grabbing a handful of marshmallows from the bag and tossing it back to her. God, I loved this woman. "All right, wench, you win. We'll talk."

I said it assuming there'd be an awkward silence for a minute before she tentatively began, but she'd been ready and waiting. She didn't waste a single second before pulling out a proverbial knife and slicing it right across my jugular.

"Why did you lie to me about the weekday gigs? I just don't understand why you lied about that of all things. We tell each other everything."

"I mean, not *everything*," I hedged, trying to joke it off in a way that was more instinctual than anything else. At least her first question hadn't been about the kiss, which is what I'd assumed she was going to ask first. I mentally crossed my fingers that maybe Garrett hadn't told her that particular story yet.

She narrowed her eyes, not letting my answer slide even an inch. "Really? Because I happen to remember you telling me in painful detail which tongue motions you like—"

"Okay, okay!" I laughed, holding my hands up in surrender as best I could with them full of alcohol and sweets. "I get it."

She didn't laugh, putting her mom face on and looking at me pointedly. The woman would wait me out for as long as she had to.

I sighed and dropped my gaze to the marshmallows in my hand. Why was telling her how I felt so hard? If I could hold my own against Adrian, I could have an honest conversation with my best friend.

I popped a white morsel in my mouth and tucked it into my cheek long enough to say, "Fuzzy bunny," and then stretched my legs out, chewing as I worked through my thoughts.

"I feel like…" I paused, hesitating. I didn't hesitate with Madison. That wasn't how our friendship had ever worked. But this, I knew, would hurt both of us, and the thought of breaking her heart made me want to puke.

Taking a deep breath, and trying to calm the nausea coiling in my stomach, I tried again, unable to meet her eyes. "I was there when you found out you were pregnant, and when you found out you were having a boy."

I smiled, remembering the way Beth had taken us shopping afterward to pick out some baby clothes to celebrate, even though the idea of Madison being pregnant had to have still been a struggle for her mother.

"I was there when he was born and there for his first birthday and first steps."

There was a beat of silence, and I knew she was watching me, giving me the time I needed to continue without pushing me. I took another breath. "And sometimes, because of that, I feel like I have to be there for you two anytime you need me. No matter what." I didn't look at her. I couldn't. Not when I knew the guilt my words would make her feel.

"Until Garrett, I've been the only father figure he's ever known," I added, trying to slip some humor in to cover the sting of my admission.

She reached out and placed her hand over mine, squeezing gently. "You weren't the one to get me pregnant, Layla."

I nodded. I knew that.

"You're my best friend," she continued, "and I love you. But it's not your job to take care of us."

I shook my head. She was right, but she was also wrong. "I moved here to help you. You didn't ask. I offered."

"Demanded was more like it," she said, chuckling into her glass and following it up with two marshmallows. "Fuzzy bunny."

But I didn't return her smile. I vividly remembered the day I'd agreed to move here. The phone call that had solidified my decision when she'd called me in tears because she felt like she was failing Jamie by working so many jobs just to pay the bills.

I hadn't thought twice after that call. I'd just settled what I'd needed in Kansas and booked a moving truck.

"Exactly. And what kind of friend would I be to promise you that help only to bail on it the second something I preferred to do came up?"

"Quitting a job you hate isn't bailing on me, Layla. Even if you didn't take the shows, and you just quit, it still wouldn't be bailing on me. Yes, affording rent and doing everything on my own was hard, but I made it work. Just like I could make it work again if I had to."

I shook my head. "Just because you can doesn't mean you should have to. If I take those gigs, I'd make more money, but I'd never be home in the evenings to help with dinner, or dishes, or read to Jamie."

She looked at me over the rim of her glass, one eyebrow shooting up. "Garrett does more dishes than the two of us combined, and you know Jamie's been reading to himself lately, so try again."

She was right. I knew she was. But if I wasn't here to help her anymore, then what was the point in staying in North Carolina away from all of my family? I shoved three marshmallows into my mouth, stretching my cheeks out to mumble, "Fuzzy bunny."

"Do you even want to live here? Truly?" she asked, reading me in the way she always could.

I took a large drink of wine, letting the dry bite swish around my mouth because I didn't know the answer to that question. Because I now had people I loved in both states. Adrian's face flashed in my mind, and the memory of how my heart had beat in time with his as he'd kissed me.

"I don't know," I finally said, setting my empty glass on top of the box of wine and laying across the carpet. I stared at the yarn tufts in the quilt above us, fully content to not move again the rest of the night.

Madison set her glass next to mine and laid out beside me, silently staring up at our blanket ceiling as well. "Would taking on more shows make you happy?"

"I'd almost never see you and Jamie."

"Would it make you happy, Layla? Not me. Not Jamie. *You.*"

Since my throat felt like it was going to close for a reason unrelated to the wine and spongy confection, I made do with nodding.

"What else would make you happy? Because I'll make it happen whatever it is," she said, leaning her head against my shoulder.

Performing every day. Writing music and having someone who understood me listen and give advice. Living close to my best friend and seeing her and her son get their happily ever after. Seeing my mother and other family members more than once a year. Having Adrian Waters love me back in the same overwhelming, angry, chaotic mess of a way I suddenly realized I loved him.

But I didn't say any of that. I just held those thoughts close to my chest as if I could make them happen by pushing them deep enough into my heart.

"A steak dinner, Broadway musical, and the souls of my enemies would be a good start."

She nudged my side with her elbow. "Are you sure about that? Because from what I heard, your *enemy* is quite the kisser."

I elbowed her back and heaved out a breath dramatically. "Your boyfriend is a gossip whore," I muttered, feeling her arm shake against me as she laughed.

I knew he'd only said something to her to make sure that he did *not*, in fact, need to hunt Adrian down and punch his lights out. Still, I was absolutely going to slog him in the arm the next time I saw him.

Unless Jamie was watching. And in that case, I'd make do with a well-timed wet willy.

"So...?"

I huffed, trying to keep my voice as neutral as possible so she wouldn't sense the depth of my attachment to the memory. "Of course, he's a good kisser. There's no greater passion than hatred. You said it yourself; the hate sex would probably be spectacular if we didn't kill each other during it."

The words tasted awful, like I was insulting Adrian by insinuating I still hated him. But by the knowing look Madison shot me as she leaned up onto one arm, she didn't believe me for one fucking second anyway.

"I know you won't believe me, because I've been in your shoes while you said the same to me," she said, her face serious, "but I've seen the way Adrian looks at you, Layla."

"And what way is that? Like he's wondering where to shove the knife?"

"Like you're *his*."

I scoffed, internally telling my heart, which had kickstarted like an engine, to calm the fuck down because Madison was clearly delusional. The man might want in my pants because of some hate-induced lust that had been kindling from the get-go, but that didn't mean he wanted to be more than friends. Right?

Friends partnered up to help make connections for each other. They rubbed each other's shoulders when they were in pain and beat up drunk men who were being assholes. Friends ditched their plans and made time for you when you needed them most and weren't afraid to show their soft sides. They made breakfast and paid attention to know when you weren't taking care of yourself.

Adrian Waters was just my friend. A good friend, I'd come to realize. But still just that. A friend.

But friends didn't look at you with so much heat you thought you'd combust on the spot, and they certainly didn't run their thumbs up and down your skin, or murmur in your ear. And they definitely didn't throw you against the wall and rock against you, moaning your name until you came all over their leg.

I wasn't sure how much of that I'd voiced out loud, but it had to have been quite a bit because Madison eyed me like I'd suddenly forgotten what two plus two was.

"Layla, no man who looks at you the way he does, and isn't afraid to go head-to-head with your wrath if it means taking care of you, just wants to be friends."

Groaning like a petulant child, I smacked my hands to my face and pressed my fingertips against my eyelids. "God, I don't know what the fuck I'm doing, Mads."

"None of us do. But what I do know is that Jamie and I will always be here. Whether you live in North Carolina or Kansas, whether you're sleeping in a blonde man's house across town or in a room right next to mine, we're not going anywhere."

She smiled and climbed over me, grabbing my keys from outside the tent and tossing them onto my stomach. "So, for once, forget about us, and go get something *you* want."

"What if I just want to go buy ice cream and cry into it while I lick my wounds?"

She just grabbed a handful of marshmallows and started pushing them into her mouth. "Then I'd say he'd probably be a whole lot better at licking you." She smirked. "Fuzzy bunny."

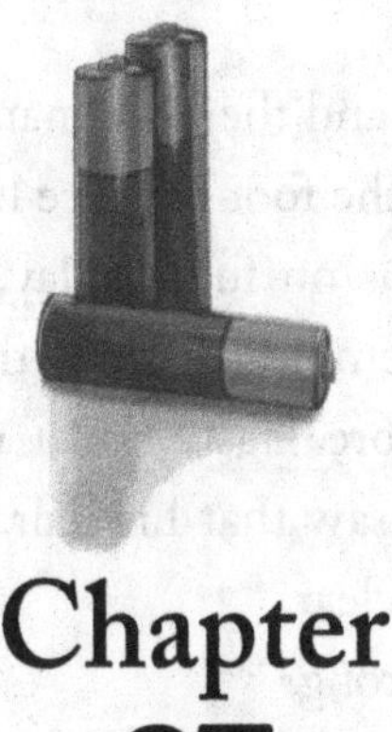

Chapter
~ 27 ~

THE ICE CREAM dripped down my hand, pooling between each finger before continuing on its path. I was going to blame it on the fact that the boy working the window had filled them to the brim, and not because I'd tripped up the porch stairs and almost dropped one.

Lifting the dripping cup, I considered licking the smear of vanilla off the side, but who knew how many hands had touched the outside of it. Instead, I just shot it a glare, like it was the ice cream's fault I was a nervous, jumbled mess, and used the toe of my sneaker to knock on the door.

Only a few seconds passed before I heard the quick staccato of footsteps across the wood floor as they approached the door. The sound almost sent me bolting down the stairs. Only the knowledge that I'd rather face Adrian head-on than sprawled on the ground with ice cream coating my shirt, kept my feet planted.

The lock twisted, and then the man I was in love with was staring at me through the foot of space he'd opened between us.

His bare chest was on full display, a pair of loose sweats hanging off his hips, reminding me of the morning he'd woken up early to cook me breakfast. For a moment, I worried I'd woken him up until I saw that his hair was still tied back in a neat bun, and his eyes clear.

"Davis? What's wrong?"

His eyes dropped to the Styrofoam cups of ice cream I was holding, and I shifted awkwardly, unsure if I should just shove one at him, or ask if he wanted one, or just tuck tail and pretend this never happened.

But then my eyes trailed down his torso again, pausing on the slight 'V' that disappeared into his sweats, and my resolve cemented. Coming here wasn't for Madison or Jamie, or even for Adrian. It was for me, and I wasn't going to back out.

When I said nothing, Adrian opened the door all the way and walked out, his eyes flickering to the darkness behind me like he was checking to make sure I wasn't seeking asylum after being chased by someone.

The instinctual action was surprisingly heartwarming, and it gave my kernel of hope a little nudge.

"What are you doing here?"

I took a step forward until we were less than a foot apart and I could see the goosebumps trailing his skin from the night air. I held out one of the cups, praying to every deity in every religion that I hadn't read all the signs wrong and wasn't about to make a fool of myself.

"I brought ice cream."

He stared down at it, and then back up at me, raising his hand to take the proffered dessert. "I can see that. Am I allowed to know why?"

I took a deep breath. This was it. "Because I'm making a choice for me. Something that I want."

His eyes found mine again, and his hand tightened around the cup until it made a slight popping sound beneath his fingers. "And what is it that you want, Davis?"

"You. This. Whatever this thing is between us."

He didn't move, not even a shift of his chest to indicate he was breathing. And then, slowly, as if he was tasting each word, he repeated, "Whatever this thing is between us."

I nodded, shivering and realizing how ridiculous I looked bringing ice cream in the middle of the night while we were both standing out here, cold. "Can I come in?"

He continued staring at me, and I started to wonder if I'd somehow broken him. "You brought me ice cream…so we could figure out this *thing* between us."

"Jesus Christ, Waters, are you drunk? I brought it as an ice breaker because I didn't know what the hell to do with my hands," I said, shaking my cup like it proved my point. "I'm here because I haven't been able to stop thinking about how hard you made me orgasm in my goddamn living room."

His nostrils flared, and he reached out and wrapped his hand around mine. "You do realize that after saying that," he paused, prying the cup from my fingers, "I'm going to throw these straight in the fucking garbage and drag you to my room."

Thank God. I nodded again, anticipation and nerves making

my stomach feel too coiled up to voice a response, let alone stand in a kitchen and eat.

"Good," he growled. "Then get your ass in the house."

I listened to his order, not because his sex eyes were turning my lady business into a swimming pool and making me feel like I was going into heat, but because it was a little nippy outside. That was all.

The entryway looked different than it had the last time I'd been here, but I couldn't quite put my finger on why. I glanced around, admiring the cherrywood floor I'd loved the first time and the potted plant that was tucked into the corner where the golden coat rack used to be. Wait.

"You got a plant." I looked around again, focusing harder this time, and my mouth fell open. "And the wallpaper is gone." Sure enough, instead of the cream, flowery wallpaper, the walls were painted a light slate gray.

Adrian's voice rumbled behind me. "I didn't do anything. But yes, I hired someone to come remove it. I figured it was about time."

I walked farther in, peeking my head around the corner to see the kitchen was still the same for now. "So, this house is yours now? You're not just…house sitting?"

I knew Doris was never going to be able to come home, a fact that broke my heart and made me want to visit her every day, but I didn't know how these things worked.

"Yes, it belongs to me. And no, this isn't the time I want to talk about it."

A tug on my clothing snagged my attention from my surroundings, and I looked down to see Adrian's fingers fisting the bottom of my shirt, right above my belly button. The cups were nowhere in sight. He tugged again. "Take this off."

I looked at his hand and back up, arching a brow. Oh, I liked this version of Adrian *a lot*. Hiding my smile, I said, "I'd much rather have a tour of all the changes you've been making. Any new furniture—"

"Let's set some things straight," he interrupted, yanking on my shirt until I was forced to follow like a string puppet.

Wearing sneakers rather than heels, he was a few inches taller than me, and he glared down with a look I was fairly certain was about to set me on fire.

"The only furniture you're going to see for the next few hours is my fucking bed, Davis. There's a time and place for house tours and witty sarcasm."

Fluttering my lashes, I said, "And this isn't it?"

He tightened his fist, punctuating each word. "Take this off."

I stared up at him and sucked on my teeth, torn between listening to my lady boner and following his demand, or telling him to fuck off because I thrived on being a stubborn brat. In the end, I opted for a little of both.

"Do it yourself."

Adrian's eyes sparked with my challenge, and he didn't waste a second before his hands were at the hem of my shirt. His thumbs brushed against my skin so quickly, I thought I'd imagined it, and then he was peeling the garment up my body. Not once releasing me from the fire in his stare.

It wasn't until he'd pulled my shirt over my face, blocking our connection, that I finally felt like I could inhale. But the breath didn't make it far before getting lodged in my throat when his face reappeared just over my own.

"Better."

I ran my hands down my lacy black bra and over my bare stomach like I was smoothing out a dress. "You didn't like my outfit?"

His lips smashed to mine before the last word had even left them. And every witty remark left my head with each stroke of his tongue against mine. We were nothing but tongues and teeth and touch as I roved my hands over his chest, and he steered us to his room. How we made it up the stairs without breaking our necks was a mystery.

It was clear from the second we entered his room that it'd been the first place he'd changed. It was also clear that Adrian Waters had zero experience with the color wheel.

Gray curtains were pulled over the large window, apart from a small crescent moon pane above it, and a simple gray comforter stretched over the king-size bed on the left. The room was annoyingly clean. Even his music set up—his acoustic, electric, and general gear—tucked in the far-left corner was organized.

I smiled to myself. He was going to shit a brick when he saw the mountains of dirty laundry in mine. But that thought had my smile dropping. I was getting ahead of myself. I needed to focus on *this* moment. The here and now. Just in case.

Fingers caressed down my spine, and I turned, trading the view of the monotone room for the gorgeous sight of the half-naked man looking at me under hooded eyes.

I trailed my gaze down, to the erection visible even beneath his loose sweats, and my mouth watered. I reached down to grasp him, desperate to run my palm along his generous length and reinforce in my head how much he wanted me.

But he snatched my hand away before I could, and I couldn't stop the small pout that graced my lips. So close. "Are we doing this or not, Adrian?"

Because I was going to have to rub one out, or three, in the car before I left if we weren't.

His eyes fluttered shut for a split second when his name left my lips, and then he opened them, a low hum in his throat. "How long have you wanted me?"

Oh, I don't know. Since the moment I met you? Since the time I still hated you and wanted to push you in front of a herd of bulls, yet somehow still wanted you to bend me over the nearest surface first?

"I don't know, how long have I been here?"

His eyes flared with a wicked gleam that had anticipation swirling through every nerve ending in my body. He gripped the back of my head and yanked me closer until my chest was flush against his.

His other hand trailed up my spine to the clasp of my bra, undoing it on the second try. "I won't ask you again, Davis. How long have you wanted me?"

I wasn't usually a fan of bossy men in the bedroom. I found it annoying at best, libido crushing at worst. Especially when my orgasms only came to be if I very vocally gave orders, given most men turned into inflatable waving arm tube men when it came to locating a woman's clit.

But there was something about the way his voice deepened and turned to gravel that made me want him to tell me what to do. Just a little. I ran the tip of my tongue over my bottom lip, watching his eyes track the movement. "Why does it matter?"

"Because I want to know how many times you've had to squeeze these fucking thighs together, pretending your pussy wasn't wet at the thought of me ramming my tongue inside of it."

Wet? Fucking drenched was more like it.

Flustered and more turned on than I'd ever been in my entire life, I couldn't come up with a single damn comeback. He smirked at my silence, his grip tightening until the strands at the nape of my neck screamed.

I glared at him. "How about you tell me how many times you've fucked yourself in the shower, wishing your hand was me."

He didn't bat an eye. "Almost every day since I met you."

The image of Adrian in the shower, one hand on his dick while the other held his weight against the wall, working himself in fast strokes, was going to be imprinted in my mind for the rest of eternity.

"Liar."

He released my hair to grip my bra straps and slide them down my arms, his eyes latching onto my painfully taut nipples as it dropped to the floor. "I have no reason to lie to you, Layla. I'm not afraid to hurt your feelings."

Wasn't that the damn truth.

He walked me back until my legs hit the edge of his bed. I imagined he'd toss me back and immediately rip my pants off or at least cup my breasts, but he just guided me to sit, using his knees to nudge my legs apart.

"But I'll admit," he said, kneeling on the floor between my

legs, "all the times I wished to see these feet over my shoulders, I definitely imagined them ending in heels." He ran his hands down my thighs and along my calves, gently kneading the muscles as he went.

"Every time you stomped up to me with your burning gray eyes and skyscraper heels, I had to flood my mind with Larry Bosenet's face and recite lyrics in my head to keep from ruining my goddamn pants."

I groaned, his fingers feeling like magic as they pressed into my skin and worked muscles I hadn't even known were sore. "That," I said, taking a steadying breath, "would've been a sight to see. I'm almost sad I didn't wear any."

Releasing my legs, he slowly crawled back up my body to dip his fingers into the waistband of my leggings. "Consider it an official request for next time."

My heart flew out of my chest, and I had to sink both hands into my ribcage and force it back down, demanding it stay there. Many a person had their heart broken by words spoken in the heat of the moment, and I would *not* be one of those. And two seconds later confirmed exactly why.

"I can practically see the thoughts swirling behind those eyes, Layla. Stop overthinking. It's just sex."

I stilled, his words banging around my head like a wrecking ball, destroying everything I'd let myself hope for. Taking his pretty words and proving I'd been right, and that's all they were. Pretty words. This wasn't *more* for Adrian. It was sex. It was a night to get this attraction out of our systems so we could move on.

It's just sex.

When several moments passed, and I hadn't moved, he lifted a hand and traced the side of my face, a furrow in his brow. "If you want to stop, we can stop right now. I will never try to force you to do anything you don't want to do. Just tell me what you want. If you want me to go fuck off, I will."

God, could he? Because I wasn't sure if I could ever walk away from this, even with my heart in literal pieces across his mattress like a crime scene. *It's just sex.*

"What I want, is for you to shut your mouth and take my fucking pants off."

His posture immediately relaxed, and his answering smirk was pure sin. "You got it, baby."

But instead of immediately peeling them off, he leaned down over me and pulled one of my nipples into his mouth. My back bowed from the unexpected sensation, pleasure shooting down my spine to pool between my legs.

He alternated between my breasts, flicking his tongue and pulling each nipple between his teeth again and again until I was a thriving mess. I groaned when he gave one a particularly aggressive pull, and grabbed his hair, ripping the hair-tie from it in my effort to pull him off of me.

"Pants," I heaved. "Now."

His dark chuckle vibrated against my overly sensitive tip, and I fisted his now loose hair and pulled, all but shoving him lower. But he listened and moved down to my waist, leaving hot, searing kisses along the soft planes of my stomach as he went.

"Condom?"

I nodded even though he couldn't see me. "I'm not on the pill," I breathed, my focus zeroed in on the teeth scraping over my hip, the hair caressing my sensitive skin, and his acknowledgment vibrating against me.

I'd been meaning to get back on the pill ever since I'd moved. I'd seen first-hand what could happen with an accidental pregnancy, so I was pro-birth control all the way. But pills meant doctor's appointments, and appointments took time. That was something I didn't have a whole lot of these days.

When he'd successfully peeled my pants and underwear from my legs and tossed them God only knew where, he sat back on his heels and unabashedly took me in. I mentally thanked the universe for giving me the motivation to shave all my bits during my last shower.

Adrian took his time admiring me, his eyes sliding from one thigh to the other and everything in between while his other gripped himself over his sweats.

Giving himself an almost angry stroke, he grimaced. "Fucking hell, you're going to kill me."

I watched his hand move, itching to replace it with my own. With my mouth. "Feeling that inadequate to the job, are you?"

"Baby, if you aren't a limp mess by the time we've finished, I haven't done my job."

Landing a stinging smack to the side of my ass, he shoved up off the bed and walked around it toward the lone nightstand and opened the drawer. He rifled through it and then slammed it shut with his leg, ripping open the small square package with his teeth.

Then he met my eyes and dropped his sweatpants to the floor, his right hand going straight to his dick and stroking himself in hard, rough movements while he stared at my naked body sprawled across his bed.

"God, you're so fucking stunning."

I licked my lips, torn between wanting him to climb over me and slam home until I felt that impressive length hit my fucking tonsils, and wanting to shove him down and climb *him*.

Moving my hand down my body, I parted my fingers and slid them down myself, baring me to him. He twitched toward me, like he was struggling to restrain himself, and it made me feel fucking powerful.

"Unless you've got a battery-operated friend hiding in that drawer with your latex goodies, Adrian, I highly doubt *limp* is going to be the case." I'd had decent sex in my life, but I couldn't say I'd ever been a limp mess afterward.

Finished rolling the condom on, he walked back over to me and stopped between my legs, reaching for my hand. I pouted when he pulled it from my clit, only for the sound to cut off when he placed my fingers in his mouth and sucked. If his comforter hadn't already been wet beneath me, it sure as hell was now.

Kissing each fingertip, he placed them over my nipple and tipped his head, silently demanding I continue touching myself. "I'm surprised you don't have one stashed away in that giant purse you carry around."

I worked my nipple, the tip painfully hard under his gaze, and nearly combusted on the spot when his hands slipped between my legs. He hummed deep in his throat, spreading me open with one hand while his thumb circled my clit in a hard, steady rhythm that had my back arching and my free hand clawing the bed.

I groaned, my eyes fluttering closed. "Oh, I keep at least two on me at all times, but sadly, they're dead," I said, unsure of what I was even saying as he pressed closer, and a thick finger slowly eased inside me.

"You often find yourself in need of two?" he asked, voice more gravel than anything as he thrust that damn finger in and out. Then a second joined it, and I felt myself climbing that hill, scrabbling for it with both hands as he picked up speed.

"*Mhm*," I murmured, half speaking, half moaning it. "You don't happen to have…spare batteries in your pocket…do you?" My words were breathy and low. Hell, I didn't even know what we were talking about anymore. I couldn't think past those rough fingers slamming into me again and again while his thumb never stopped its steady circles.

"No, although now I'm tempted to leave you here and go buy some." Suddenly both of his hands disappeared, and my eyes flew open in shock, my orgasm so close to the surface I wanted to scream.

"What the hell?" I said, glaring at him with all the blue-balled vehemence I possessed.

"Baby, if I can't feel you come on my bare cock, I'm sure as hell not going to waste it on my fucking fingers." And then he descended on me, skipping all sense of teasing, and swiped the flat of his tongue through me.

I was going straight to hell for whatever came out of my mouth in response.

He worked my entire center in slow leisurely strokes, like he wanted to savor the taste of me and implant it into his memory to relive again and again. And then, just when I thought I might have to speak up and urge him to go faster, he shifted his weight and his mouth met my clit. And oh God, did he know what to do with that.

He circled it with his tongue, adding pressure with each flick until I wasn't just at the edge, but smashing through it and shattering it into a million pieces.

He groaned in satisfaction, sliding both hands under my ass and yanking me up to his face, lapping at me through every last shudder of my orgasm.

When he finally lifted his head, I was already clawing at him, grabbing at his arms and yanking him up. "I want you inside me."

His eyes darkened until they no longer even looked blue, and he continued up my body until he hovered above me, his waist tucked between my legs so that his dick pressed firmly against where I needed it. "Say please."

I scoffed. "The orgasm was good, but it wasn't that good."

His responding laugh made my heart swell painfully. But it was the kiss he pressed to my lips, the one that tasted like a combination of him and me, that made me realize I would never feel like this with anyone else.

And that made me feel more vulnerable than I'd ever wanted to be over someone. I didn't want him to have that control, not when I knew this didn't mean the same to him as it did to me. I needed to get it back.

Placing my hands on his chest, I broke our kiss, shoving him off as hard as I could. He reared back, more from the shock of it than my actual strength, but I was already pushing him back on the bed and straddling him before he fully processed what I was doing.

I wanted this man inside of me, but I was going to do it my way. Because staying in control of this night and this moment was all I had left.

His hands wrapped around my hips the second I got settled, his tip pressing at my entrance. His eyes seared into me as he stroked his calloused fingers over the dips of my stomach, down along the crease where my hips met my thighs, and back around to my ass, cupping as much as he could.

"God, this ass." He squeezed hard, and I was sure I'd have ten tiny bruises the next morning. "Always teasing me with this fucking thing."

I reached down and finally wrapped my hand around him, giving him a firm squeeze that had his face tightening in a mixture of pleasure and pain. And then I pressed his tip into my entrance and lowered down an inch.

"Oh yeah? How so?"

He groaned, bucking his hips up enough to push another inch into me. "The day you showed up wearing your band shirt and that goddamn skirt that hugged your ass so tight, I wanted to bend you over the nearest table and spank the shit out of you."

My entire body clenched at that, and I was officially done with foreplay. Laying my hands flat on his chest, I sank the rest of the way down until his entire length was impaled inside me, my already-soaking-wet center accepting him with readied glee.

"Fuck, Layla."

His hands tightened, his nails digging into my skin as he gazed at me, thrusting his hips up sharply. His breathing escalated and his eyes were dark blue pools.

I rolled my hips, taking him deeper, and the desperate

sound he made slithered through my body. My veins.

"You're definitely going to kill me," he repeated, cupping my breasts and pinching my nipples while meeting me thrust for thrust.

I smirked, moving faster and leaning down farther so his pubic bone rubbed up against my clit just right. My hair curtained down around us. "If you come too early and deprive me of my orgasm, Adrian, I *will* kill you."

His eyes flashing was my only warning. One second, I was rolling my clit against his body, feeling myself climb higher all over again, and the next I was slamming onto my back, his dick never leaving my body as he held his weight above me and slammed forward. Hard.

"I meant that it was going to kill me to let you take control, baby, not that I couldn't fucking keep up." He picked up his pace, punishing me, and I tipped my head back and let him.

This wasn't supposed to happen. There was a reason I was supposed to be in control. But God, he felt so fucking good, I couldn't remember why anymore. His right hand dropped to my clit, splaying over my skin as his thumb began working me in tight circles.

"You want to come again, Layla?"

I nodded, not trusting how desperate my voice would sound in that moment.

He flicked my clit in reprimand, and I snapped my eyes open, glaring up at him even as it teetered me on the edge of my climax.

Leaning down over my face, he continued ramming into me, his lips hovering just over my own. "I want to make you come again and again, each one stronger than the last, until you're begging me to stop."

"Prove it."

He smirked down at me, his fingers continuing to circle my clit with the exact speed I needed and turning the heat simmering in my center to a full-on inferno inside me. I arched my back, begging my body to give up the second release he was urging—hell, demanding—of it.

He kept his thrusts deep and steady, rocking his hips up and hitting that goddamn spot until I was half moaning his name and half weeping for mercy.

"Oh God, I can't," I said, unsure if I was whispering it or yelling it, only knowing I was overwhelmed and over-sensitized, feeling Adrian everywhere and never wanting it to end.

"Oh yes, you fucking can," he growled, shoving into me as deep as my body would allow him. "Give it to me." And then he rolled his hips right as he pinched my clit, and I exploded.

My entire soul turned into a live wire, and for a moment, I swore my vision went black. I shoved my face into his shoulder, biting down to muffle my cries and digging my nails into his back.

His answering groan was deep and ragged, like the sound of me breaking beneath him and not immediately joining me was pure agony. But he stayed just like that, rocking deep into me and circling that swollen bundle of nerves until the last wave of my orgasm washed over me. Leaving me completely and utterly *limp*.

I waited for him to smirk and make some off-hand remark about being right, but when I met his blue eyes, there was nothing but intensity and something I couldn't name staring back at me.

He dropped down onto his elbows so that his chest pressed flush with mine, and then he was stealing my mouth into a searing kiss and bucking into me like a man unhinged, chasing his own climax.

The sounds he made against my lips made me feel like I could take over the entire world, if only he'd keep making them.

I tightened my legs around him and dug my heels into his ass, urging him to go faster and take more, all while crying out his name and silently begging him to leave a mark. To claim me. Want me. See me as more than just sex.

And just when I thought he might truly fuck my soul right out of my body, he cursed into my lips and slammed to the hilt, emptying himself inside of me.

He stayed just like that, his lips pressed to mine, his dick shoved as deep as he could possibly go, until the last tremor swept through him. And then he dropped his forehead to mine, his chest heaving and his breathing erratic.

"Am I dead?" he asked, breaking the tense silence that had settled between us as our breathing and hearts began to return to normal.

I snorted, and then winced when my chuckles caused him to slip out of me. Fuck, I was going to be so sore tomorrow. And I didn't regret a single second of it.

His eyes dropped to my mouth, and he smiled. Not a smirk, but a full, wide smile, and then he kissed my lips so softly, that I almost blurted out that I loved him. That I hated his guts for it, but that I was stupidly in love with him anyway.

But then the moment slipped away, and he was pushing away from me and wandering into the attached bathroom to dispose of the condom, asking me if I wanted a drink of water like it was just another day.

Like it was just sex.

I'd just finished double-checking that my alarm was set for work when Adrian returned to the bedroom, picking up his sweatpants from the floor and slipping them back over himself. I tensed, suddenly wondering if I should go.

I'd assumed since it was so late, and he'd been so against driving me across town at night last time, that I'd be staying, but seeing him get dressed, now I wasn't so sure.

Keeping my mask in place, the one I'd recrafted from scratch in the time he'd taken to clean himself up, I raised a brow as he slipped back into bed.

"You didn't have to put pants on, you know," I said, closing my eyes and pretending to yawn. Even though it was honestly only half-pretend. I was fucking exhausted. "I wasn't going to defile you in your sleep."

"No, you wouldn't have, because if I had your soft ass tucked against my cock all night, I'd never fall asleep to begin with."

That had my eyes flying back open, heat flickering back to life like Adrian had a goddamn circuit breaker to my sex drive.

"No," he said, *tsk*ing and shaking his finger at me. He gestured for me to roll over. "If you're set on leaving and going to work in the morning, you need to go to sleep."

There was something about the way he said it, the assured, almost cocky tone, like me staying wasn't even a question, that tapped at my shield, seeking entrance. But I ignored it.

Just because he didn't want me driving across town at night, didn't mean he necessarily wanted me to stay for any other reason.

"I'm not that old, Adrian. I can survive off a few hours of sleep," I said, running my fingertips down his chest and between the ab muscles that tensed beneath my touch. If this was the only night that I was going to let myself have him, I was going to enjoy every single second of it.

But he snatched my hand, halting it just as it reached his waistband. He tucked it on the pillow next to my face, his expression pained. "Go to sleep, baby."

I wasn't going to let that nickname get to me. It was post-sex happiness. That was all. "I bet one more round would knock me right out."

He growled, the sound deep and ragged, like he was barely holding on to his resolve. "If you go to sleep like a good girl, I'll fuck you as hard as you want in the morning."

My eyes widened, and I lifted my head off the pillow, resting it on my upturned palm so I could look down at him. This man had officially lost his mind. "You did not just call me a good girl."

"Technically I didn't, since you're still awake and yet to be one."

I reached out and gently pinched his nipple, earning me a satisfying glare and a sharp curse. "Not even when I admitted to enjoying two at once?"

His eyes heated until they were two dark pools in his face. "Especially not then. Go to sleep."

Seeing the stone look of determination in his expression, I flopped back to the pillow, ceding defeat. I really was exhausted, not that I'd admit it to him.

Grumbling, I rolled over, letting a chuckling Adrian tuck me into his body so that my ass pressed right up against his very hard dick. I wiggled back and forth, pretending to adjust my position, and soaked up his hiss.

"Fine. You win. I'm going to sleep. But I expect you to make me breakfast before I leave for work."

His arms tensed around me, his fingers digging in for just a second before they relaxed again. He buried his nose in my hair and sighed before murmuring, "As long as you feed *me* before we get up."

Fuck. I was never going to recover.

Chapter
28

SEX AND LOVE weren't the same thing. I knew that better than anyone. Casual, no-strings-attached sex had been my jam for years. Even when I was dating Rick, I hadn't been attached. He'd been a convenient distraction when I'd lost the desire to go out and woo other guys, but that was all.

It hadn't been fair to him, but I'd preferred it that way. It kept things from getting messy and prevented hearts from being shattered. Granted, it was usually someone *else's* heart I was trying to protect rather than my own, but apparently, it was finally my turn.

Stretching my arm across the mattress, I grabbed my phone and shut off my alarm, not wanting it to wake Adrian. It wasn't set to go off for another ten minutes, and if all went according to plan, I'd be up and out before then.

Although I'd passed out with his body wrapped around my

own, we'd shifted apart sometime in the night, both of us subconsciously seeking cooler parts of the sheets in our sleep. I was glad for it now, because I doubted it'd have been possible to wiggle out of his arms naked if he'd still been wrapped around me like a backpack.

Slowly twisting my neck, I peered over my shoulder to see him still quietly passed out behind me, his lips parted and expression relaxed, making him look softer. His hair was a mess and his beard a little extra scruffy, but if anything, he looked more beautiful to me than any other time I'd seen him.

Burning tears stung my eyes, and I blinked rapidly, refusing to let them escape. I was *not* going to break apart in Adrian's bed. I was going to be the mature, independent woman I was and do it once I made it to my car.

I repeated it over and over as I slid, inch by inch, across the mattress toward the edge. But no matter how fast, or how angry, I shouted it in my head, I couldn't keep my heart from feeling like it was being chipped away with each inch I put between us.

I couldn't stop the tears or the hurt that felt like it was stabbing into me and twisting. No matter how hard I tried to lock it away in the iron box I kept all my emotions and wants in, I couldn't.

I couldn't put on my face and act like this didn't feel like I was ripping my heart out of my chest and abandoning it on Adrian Waters's bed.

People saw what I wanted them to see. The bitch personality, the stone face, and the tough act that made everyone, but Madison and Jamie, believe I had no real emotions apart from hostility and dark humor. But all of it was a lie. Even when I acted like I didn't care and felt nothing. I did. I felt every bit of it completely.

No one understood just how exhausting it was to keep every weak, fragile emotion locked tightly away twenty-four seven. Pretending like I didn't actually have a heart *to* break. And right now, I couldn't even find the box, let alone the key.

I couldn't lock it away. I couldn't do anything other than feel it. Feel the humiliation of falling in love with someone who didn't love me back. Feel the agony of knowing I'd found my matching piece only to realize that although we fit together, we weren't the same color.

Adrian had made it very clear last night, that it was just sex. Just a night to get it out of our systems so we could move on, and I needed to respect that and get over it.

Easing my feet down to the floor, I stood, darting my eyes around for my clothes. God, I'd been in such a lust-filled haze, I couldn't even remember *when* he'd ripped them off, let alone where they'd landed.

But I was pretty sure my shirt, for sure, was somewhere in the entryway of the house. Fuck.

"I thought we had an agreement, Layla."

I jumped, his gravelly, sleep-heavy voice startling me. I wanted to turn and hide my naked body from view, but I couldn't. Not without him seeing my tear-streaked face. So, I ignored him, chewing my lip and wondering if I should grab his shirt that I could see crumpled on the floor, or make a run for it. I still hadn't caught sight of my leggings.

"You want to tell me what's wrong, and why I woke up to see you halfway across the room when you should be grinding against my face?"

I cleared my throat, even as his words sank in exactly where he'd intended them to and lit me on fire. "Although I appreciate the offer, Waters," I said, focusing on the space his last name put back between us, "I'm going to head out. No need to drag this morning out and make us both uncomfortable."

There was a pause. One long enough that I'd have thought he'd fallen back asleep if it wasn't for the two laser points on my bare skin where I could feel his eyes staring at me.

"And what," he said carefully, "changed so suddenly overnight that has made you uncomfortable, *Davis*?" His words were low and calm, but the way he said my name sounded like a curse.

I shrugged; still very aware I was standing naked in a dimly lit room. "Nothing, I'm just trying to find my clothes so I can go home and shower before work."

"Come here."

My body twitched, my subconscious eager to listen and climb back into bed with him. To go one more round and prolong this as long as I could. But I refused to do that to myself.

"Don't make this weird, Waters," I said, finally deciding on his shirt and taking a step toward it. "We had sex. It was good. But we need to put some boundaries back up," I said, hoping he didn't catch the waver in my voice.

"Turn around and tell me why."

I huffed a laugh that sounded about how I felt. My entire body was shaking at that point, as I desperately tried not to burst into loud, gulping tears. "Because I'm trying to save our friendship, partnership, whatever-ship this is."

"Bullshit. Tell me the truth." I could hear shuffling, and I knew if I turned, I'd see him sitting upright, spine straight, and his bare chest on full display.

I laughed again, this one sounding unhinged while I snatched his shirt off the floor and yanked it on over my head. Given we were almost the same height, it didn't come close to covering my ass, but it made me feel like there was at least some form of shield around me. Even if that shield smelled like Adrian.

"Trust me, you don't want the truth."

"I'll decide for myself what I want. Now stop being a fucking coward and tell me why you're running out of my bed, upset. Did I do something last night? If I did, I'm sorry—"

"Because I'm an idiot!" I yelled, unable to handle the doubt in his voice that he'd done something that had made me uncomfortable when the only person I had to blame for it was myself.

I whipped around, and he lurched back, his frustrated expression going slack when he saw my tear-streaked face. I knew I needed to stop while I was ahead, but I couldn't. The box wasn't just open, it'd fucking exploded, and there was no putting any of it back inside.

"Because somehow, along the way of hating your fucking guts, I stupidly decided to want something more with you," I cried, twisting my head back and forth. I needed to find my shoes in the next two seconds, or I was running out of here barefoot.

But in less than one, Adrian was out of the bed and standing between me and the door, his chest heaving in and out like the three feet from the bed had been a mile. "Jesus Christ, Layla."

I pressed my hands to my face, willing myself to stop crying. "Forget I said anything. Please. Just—"

"About time you fucking caught up."

I snapped my face up, my hands falling limp at my sides. What the hell did that mean? But I shook my head. It didn't matter.

I didn't have time for his games or his sarcasm. I needed to get the hell out before I broke apart into a million pieces. I needed more ice cream, my dog, a bottle of wine, and possibly a cigarette. I'd never smoked before, but I felt like this was the kind of situation that made people start.

"Please move, Adrian. I'll see you Friday at Jemmy's." I swore to myself, I would. No matter how much it crushed me. I wouldn't bail on him, and I wouldn't throw my career down the drain over feelings that I'd already known were one-sided.

"I want to hear you say it."

I glared at him, no sign of my shoes in sight. I'd accuse him of hiding them, but I had a very small memory of losing them before we'd ever even made it to the room. I'd just snag them on my way out. "Please. Move."

"That's not what I want to hear, and you know it."

I shoved against his chest, hating how familiar the feel of it was beneath my hands. "What do you want to hear, Adrian? That I love you? That I know this was just sex for you, but it wasn't for me? That I thought I could settle for that, but I can't? That I know you'll never look at me the same after this?"

Realizing I wouldn't be able to get past him until he was ready to move, I dropped my arms, slicing my eyes to a spot on the floor. Broken. "Does knowing all that make you feel better?"

"Do you remember the holiday party? The ridiculous pink one?"

I frowned. I just poured my heart out, and he was talking about the holiday party from weeks ago? Ouch. I made a sound of acknowledgment but didn't raise my head.

"I lied to you that night. Sitting next to me hadn't been by chance. Hell, if it had, we should've gone out to buy lottery tickets."

A small grin pulled at my lips because I'd thought the same thing when I'd first seen his name beside mine. I tipped my head enough to steal a peek at him and see him running his hand through his bedhead, a nervousness to the movement I hadn't been expecting.

"I'd called the coordinator and asked to be placed next to you, Layla."

That had me fully looking at him now, my mouth parting. What? And then I remembered how he'd accused *me* of doing that exact thing, and I narrowed my eyes. Or at least as much as I could with how puffy they now were.

His hand sank into his hair again, and he laughed uncomfortably. "I know that sounds creepy, but I'd just wanted the chance to talk to you and apologize. But you'd immediately gone on the defense, and it was so fucking sexy and enticing, I couldn't help but play along. And once I did, there was no going back."

He released a heavy breath, and I stood there dumbfounded, just staring and staring at him. His words were clear and blunt, just like every conversation with him had always been, but somehow, they still didn't compute. Because that would mean he'd been interested since almost the first time we'd met.

"You said you had no desire to work with me. You called me a bitch. You hated me," I said, stumbling through the words as I tried to make sense of what he was saying.

"Because that's what you wanted me to say, Layla. I let you string me along and played this hating game with you because it was better than nothing. Because I thought I could change your mind."

He sighed and took a step toward me, slowly, like I was a frightened deer he was afraid to scare off. "But you were so focused on cutting yourself off and worrying about everyone else, that you couldn't see it. Even now you're determined not to."

I faltered, blinking up at him. "See what?"

His fingers brushed down my arms until they cupped my elbows, pulling me an inch closer. "That I am foolishly and undeniably in love with you."

My breath caught in my throat. I couldn't breathe, I couldn't move. I couldn't do anything but stare into the damn blue eyes holding me captive. He pulled harder, closing another inch of space. "Fuck, Layla. I've wanted you since the moment I first laid eyes on you."

A half snort, half laugh bubbled up my throat. I was officially losing my mind. There was no way Adrian Waters just admitted he was in love with me.

"Liar," I whispered, wanting him to pull me closer, yet push me away all at the same time. "You hated me. I hated you. It was a mutual relationship of hatred."

He closed another inch. "Baby, I hated you because you wanted me to, and I'll continue to hate you now if that's what you want. Or have you still not gotten it through your head that I'd do anything you fucking asked of me and more?"

I let the warmth of his hands seep into my skin, and closed my eyes, desperately wanting this moment to be real. For his words to be real. But I was too scared to trust it. Not when I'd finally put my heart out for someone for the first time, and he had the power to utterly destroy it.

"You said it was just sex."

"Yeah, after you said you just wanted to figure out this *thing* between us."

"You don't know anything about me," I said, throwing the words out between us like a brick wall. They'd protected me the first time I'd said them to him, and I could only hope they'd do it again. But this time, it was because I wanted him to prove me wrong and knock it down.

One hand lifted from my arm to sink into my hair and carefully pull the strands through his fingers. "Your favorite color is blue."

I huffed. "Anyone could guess that."

His eyes dropped to mine and held them, his fingers sliding around my scalp until he was cupping the back of my head. "You think your best feature is your ass, but really it's these fucking eyes."

I swallowed. "That's not what you were saying last night."

He pretended like I hadn't spoken. "You hate mornings and would rather skip breakfast completely than wake up the extra few minutes it would take to eat it."

I blinked and attempted to pull back. "Everyone hates mornings."

His hands tightened to steel rods around me, his eyes never once looking away from mine. "Your idea of a perfect date wouldn't be to dress up and go out like you make everyone believe, but to lie naked in bed eating junk food and watching shitty movies."

I didn't have a snappy comeback to that one. He'd nailed my perfect date so thoroughly, I second-guessed if we'd actually gone on one. "How did you—"

"You love rats and snakes but are terrified of spiders, and your biggest fear is that you'll never be good enough."

Okay, well that took a turn. I narrowed my eyes, but he just leaned in and brushed his lips over one eyelid and then the other, the hand at my head tightening around my roots.

"You give and you give without expecting anything in return, and you lash out at anyone who tries to do the same because you don't know how to let someone take care of you."

I sucked in a breath and fisted my hands in his shirt, not even sure when I'd lifted them to his body. "And you're apparently a complete and total stalker."

"No, I just pay attention to the things I care about."

I stepped closer, the tips of my breasts brushing his chest. My heart pounded a steady rhythm, and I wondered if his was doing the same. "I thought there were only two things in the world you cared about more than your music?"

He didn't answer. He didn't so much as blink. He just lowered the remaining hand on my arm to my hip, and I knew.

All those weeks ago, and he'd been laying out hints for me

like damn breadcrumbs, waiting for me to see them. And I'd just been fumbling all over them with my hands over my eyes.

"You told me I was a raging bitch and a pain in your ass."

"And not a single breath of that statement was a lie."

A laugh burst out of me, ragged and carefree, and his smile fell as his eyes dipped to my mouth. "Your passion drew me in, Layla, but it was your heart that made me unable to walk away."

"Shows what you know, my heart is solid steel. No feelings there," I said, patting my chest and chuckling when he pointedly wiped away the remaining wet spots on my cheeks.

"Woman, you set aside your life plans to help raise a kid you had no part in creating. No steel heart would do that." Something flickered in his eyes, and I knew he was thinking about how Doris had done the same for him. He may not have been in Jamie's exact shoes, but he understood.

He focused back on me, his fingers dipping under my shirt—well, *his* shirt—and causing goosebumps to erupt across my body. "You may have a spine of steel, but your heart is pure pudding."

And then he drew his lips to mine, kissing me so thoroughly I swore my soul left my chest and nestled into his. His hands gripped my body like he couldn't bear the thought of ever letting go. His tongue danced with mine and his teeth pulled at my lip, each action a claiming and a demand.

I wasn't sure how long we stood there, consuming every part of each other, when I suddenly broke away, my eyes wide. *Oh, shit.* I twisted in his arms, searching for wherever I'd tossed my phone in my mini-crisis. "Shit, I need to get to work."

"Call in sick."

I sputtered. "What? I can't call in sick."

He ground against me, eliciting a noise from me that I didn't even know I could make, and moved his hands higher until his knuckles brushed the underside of my breasts. "Yes, you can. You plan on quitting. It doesn't matter. Call in sick."

I shot him a glare about the quitting remark, but I didn't say no. Because of course I didn't want to go to work minutes after hearing Adrian Waters tell me he loved me. Fuck. No. I wanted to ride him until my calves cramped.

He leaned to the side and ran his lips down my neck, leaving soft bites along the way. I shuddered, immediately wanting that mouth around my already-peaked nipples. Sucking in a sharp breath, I asked, "Will you call me a good girl again if I do?"

"Are you going to be one?" he asked, at the same time his right hand lowered to slide between my legs. He groaned when he felt just how wet his kiss and hands and words had made me, and he pinched my left nipple right as his fingers found their goal.

"No," I breathed. I was many things, but a good girl wasn't one of them.

His answering smile as he circled my clit was positively wicked. "God, this fucking mouth," he murmured, and then he stole my lips in another soul-altering kiss, his lips moving over mine again and again. Softly. Tenderly.

Like we had all the time in the world.

Chapter 29

THERE WERE A lot of things in life that brought me joy, but there were three that topped that list. The first was the sound of Adrian's naked body slapping against mine. The second was people-watching with Jamie while we ate freshly baked, cinnamon apple muffins at We Mean Beans-ness coffee shop. And the third was witnessing my best friend drunk.

"Where's your big caveman courage?"

Garrett grunted, flicking Madison in the nose and then immediately leaning down to kiss it when she pouted and scrunched it up. "Courage, huh?"

"Yes," she said, trying to keep her face serious even as she hiccupped. "Taking a chance and doing something even if you think you won't like it. It might suck, but it might not, so you do it anyway and see what happens."

I snorted into my glass. "I wouldn't recommend putting that

in a speech or on a billboard anywhere since the same could be said of stupidity."

Madison wadded up the napkin next to her drink and threw it at me, missing completely. "You're not helping."

"What are we helping with?"

I twisted in my seat, which happened to be my boyfriend's lap, to spy Sarah and Harry approaching our table. Taking another sip of the delectable honey whiskey Adrian had convinced me to try, I flicked my hand toward the happy couple across from us. "Mads here is trying to convince your brother-in-law to go up with her and sing karaoke."

Sarah blinked at me, shocked into silence for possibly the first time in her life. And it was Harry who slowly asked, "*Madison* wants to sing karaoke…in public?"

Nate snickered from my right, lifting his face from where he'd been trailing kisses up the column of Marissa's throat. "Curly here has already had several drinks," he said as way of explanation.

Marissa smacked his thigh and shushed him. "Leave her alone. The woman is school free, kid free, and work free for an entire weekend, she's allowed to get trashed and embarrass herself."

Sarah whooped behind me and swapped her current drink to her left hand to reach across the table with her right and steal the full shot sitting in front of Nate. She downed it before he even realized what was happening. "I'm down, let's go!"

When Madison jumped up to follow her, Garrett practically melted in his seat in relief. Adrian chuckled, and I shuddered when his breath tickled the shell of my ear.

The women, including Marissa, disappeared, and it wasn't long before they each downed another shot and went on stage to sing the most off-key, glorious rendition of a popular 90's song to ever exist.

Halfway through, Madison was already stumbling, and Sarah was full-on dancing while somehow successfully holding her drink above her head. Harry just chuckled to himself, smiling when he caught my eye. It never failed to baffle me when I saw them together. His quiet, down-to-Earth personality and her wild, flamboyant self.

"What?" he asked, tipping his head in my direction.

I smiled back, setting my glass on the table and dropping my hand to glide up Adrian's thigh. "One of these days, you'll have to tell me how you two," I made a circling gesture with my hand, "came to be. Because I have no idea how you keep up with her unique brand of crazy."

He winked at me and turned back to watch his wife, a small, almost arrogant, smile on his face. "I keep up with her in the ways that matter."

I rolled my lips in and gave an exaggerated nod, opting to take another burning drink of whiskey rather than respond to that. Beside Harry, his brother grinned down into his beer, and Nate choked out a comment that had Adrian's chest rumbling with laughter.

Adrian leaned in close, his beard scratching the side of my neck while his fingers traced circles on my leg, his calluses snagging the fabric. "If she and he don't work out…" he murmured, nodding his head toward Sarah, who was now trying to convince a wide-eyed Madison to do a body shot.

I twisted in his lap, shooting him a mock glare while Garrett stood in my peripheral, charging across the bar to go save his very drunk girlfriend. "I'd be very careful what you say, *dearest*. I called dibs on her months ago. Get in line."

His head tipped back, the raspy laugh I loved so much bursting out before he recovered, firmly cupping my face. "You never cease to surprise me, Davis."

I worked my jaw back and forth in his hold, feeling everyone's eyes on us and really fucking liking it. I hoped every woman and man in the entire bar knew this man was all mine.

"Are you ever going to stop calling me that?"

He smirked, tipping my head back and leaning down so that our noses were only a hairsbreadth apart. "And what would you recommend I call you, instead?"

I closed the distance, flicking the tip of my tongue over his bottom lip. "Oh, I don't know. A well-timed 'good girl' never hurt."

A soft groan climbed up the back of his throat, and he swallowed, sliding his other arm around my waist and gripping the side of my ass.

"I think I'd much prefer 'mine'."

My body heated, and I squeezed my thighs together, knowing I still had to make it at least another hour before I could make an excuse to leave and slide my hand down his jeans while he drove us home. To the beautiful Victorian home he'd slowly been moving me into over the last three months, one item at a time.

Neither of us had the money to replace the furniture or do any serious renovations, but we were making it ours, slowly but surely.

I pretended to ponder it. "I feel like that'll just confuse everyone around you when you yell it across the bar to get my attention."

"Baby?"

"Yeah?"

"Shut the fuck up and kiss me."

I did. Again and again, not caring at all where we were or who was watching.

Adrian and I would never be the sweet, loving couple that Madison and Garrett were, nor did we have the years of silent pining that Harry and Sarah had, but we were perfect all the same.

Some days I hated his guts, like when he'd finally convinced me to quit my job, and I'd panicked for a solid week. Some days he wanted to strangle me in my sleep because I was a raging bitch during shark week.

Other days I couldn't breathe over how much I loved him, and he'd browse through engagement rings on his phone when he didn't think I was looking.

We had a hate-love relationship that was more chaos than anything, but I wouldn't have it any other way. He was mine, and I was his, and that was all that mattered.

You're gonna be the death of me, but baby I can finally see that this kind of love ain't no mistake…It's just a little bit of hate.

Epilogue

FIVE LITTLE BLUE dots stared back at me from my neighbor's spot at the table. I glared at her card and then dropped my eyes to my own. To my sorry, fourth-in-a-row, losing Bingo card. Minus the Bingo.

"I want a different card. This one sucks," I mumbled under my breath, poking at the edge of it with my finger. Maybe I could swap hers and mine out before she was back without her noticing.

"Don't be a sore loser," a voice whispered to my left, thick from the effort of not laughing. I only grumbled in answer, and a large hand curled above my knee and squeezed.

I turned my glare on my boyfriend, who wasn't even trying to hide his smirk. "I'm not being a sore loser. Nan's just cheating," I whispered back. "She has to be. She's kicking my ass."

He chuckled, losing his valiant battle with holding it back, and trailed his hand up higher. "That's not exactly hard to do, baby. Have you seen your ass recently?"

I shot my hand out, and he reared back, barely avoiding the pinch I'd aimed at the soft spot of his arm. I *wasn't* a sore loser. I just hated losing. Especially a million times in a row from an adorable grandma who was impossible to be mad at. It was completely different.

The hand on my thigh tightened, and Adrian leaned in close, his breath coasting over the shell of my ear and sending goosebumps all the way down my arm. "If you can't behave, Davis, I'll have to—"

"Oh, leave the poor girl alone. The size of her derriere has nothing to do with it. I'd still kick her ass even if it was tiny."

We both whipped around to look at Doris—the adorable, cheating grandma in question—who'd finally returned from collecting whatever prize the non-losers got. In her case, a few skeins of yarn.

Adrian leaned back, his eyes comically large as he choked out a surprised, "Ms. Waters."

"What?" she snapped, reclaiming her seat. "Just because I'm old doesn't mean I'm blind. And don't you dare tell me not to curse, young man. Being old means I can speak however I want to. I've earned it," she added, organizing her stuff on the table, already ready to go another round.

"Yes, ma'am," he said, dropping his still-wide eyes on me, his expression partially hidden behind his hair as he mouthed,

"This is your fault."

The sound I made as I attempted to keep a straight face made me sound eerily similar to a dying hog. Doris might be dragging my competitive side out by the collar, but she'd quickly become one of my favorite people in the world. She said what she wanted and did what she wanted, and the more time I spent with her, the more I could see exactly how Adrian had turned out the way he had.

Adrian's lips pressed together, and he shook his head, eyeing both of us one last time before turning his attention back to his own card.

We'd been coming to see her together every weekend for a year now, both to perform and just to visit, and she never failed to make each trip memorable. Even if not always for happy reasons. Some days she recognized Adrian, and on those days, I swore my heart would burst from the strength of joy in his smile. But more often than not, she didn't.

And even after a year, as we sat here playing Bingo next to her as nothing more than friendly visitors, I knew it was still hard on him. But he was doing as well as anyone could in this kind of situation, and I was proud of him.

Adrian had simply put his entire focus, and that arrogant determination he'd used on me, into his music, his bedroom capabilities, and the house. And I wasn't complaining a single bit. Well, except for his focus on renovating the house. That one I could have done without.

If I had to sweat and suffer through one more DIY project, I'd either lose my mind, or he'd lose his head. Whichever came first.

However, with each bicker-filled project we completed, the house Doris had given him when she'd moved to Young Souls was beginning to look more like us with each month that passed.

We'd both agreed to keep the kitchen the same, as a memento to her, but the rest was coming together to feel like *our* home. And not only because living there gifted me the joy of seeing a half-naked Adrian cooking me breakfast every morning.

But that was a huge bonus.

My phone silently lit up on the table between us, and I glanced over, expecting it to be Madison reminding me for the twentieth time about her bridal dress appointment tomorrow.

Although she and I no longer saw each other as much now that we weren't living together, we still talked most days, which had recently turned to every day since her engagement to Garrett.

My heart swelled in my chest at the memory of her telling me. The pride in her eyes, the undying love in Garrett's, and the pure fucking elation in Jamie's. It seemed silly now that I'd ever been so worried about this inevitable future.

But instead of seeing my best friend's name pop across the screen, I saw a random number. I didn't know the caller, but I did recognize the area code. Raleigh. I let it go to voicemail, my lips curling when Adrian saw it and winked. Whatever venue it was, they'd leave a message. Just like every other one he and I had received over the last few weeks.

Business had been steadily increasing for the both of us over the last year, but even more so over the last three months. And although I had no proof that it was because we'd cut ties with Larry three months ago and had begun making our own calls and choices, my gut was saying that was exactly why. Call it intuition.

It turned out, most of the venues weren't all that happy when they learned how big of a cut Larry took from his musicians' pay. They cared a whole lot more about keeping Adrian and me on their line-ups and paying us fairly than they did about the convenience of Larry's services.

They'd rather have to handle a few more steps themselves to reach out and book us, than not have us at all. And that was more than okay with us.

Adrian and I didn't have the perfect meet-cute story, and we didn't blossom from a beautiful friendship like Madison and Garrett had. We weren't quite ready for marriage yet, nor would we ever go all Hallmark and form a band and name our firstborn child after it or anything, but I was pretty sure neither of us had ever been happier.

Sure, I didn't completely abhor the idea of having a little girl one day with icy blue eyes who'd love with her whole heart and vocally demand respect, but I'd be happy even if that particular adventure never made it onto our game board.

For now, Adrian and I kept ourselves busy with other things. We still played together every Friday, but every other day we played apart, building our own brands and names and supporting each other individually, every step of the way.

I still missed my family, some days so much it physically hurt, but I'd finally accepted the shitty reality that I couldn't have everything I wanted in life. I knew Adrian would move back with me in a heartbeat if I truly wanted to, but I'd never ask him to leave Doris. Even if she cheated at Bingo.

The truth was that no matter where I lived, I'd have to give someone up. And as much as I hated it and wanted to rage against the world for it, I'd be okay.

My music and my career were here, and the more I played and got booked in the surrounding cities, the more I was financially capable of traveling to see my family more than once a year.

Over the summer, Adrian had actually flown back with me to officially meet my mother and stepfather, and months later, it was still one of my favorite memories of all time. Especially the wide-eyed stare he'd given me across my parents' house when he'd realized my mother wasn't a sweet, demure woman, but exactly like me.

He hadn't stood a chance.

But he didn't run. No matter how much my mother teased and poked at him, and no matter how bitchy I was for a solid week after the trip when I couldn't handle how much I missed them. He didn't balk. He just brought me ice cream and cuddled me in bed while we watched a second-rate sci-fi film, and then rewarded me with two mind-blowing orgasms.

"If you stare at your card any harder, Davis, it'll go up in flames and you'll never win."

My eyes shot up from where I'd been zoning out, and instead narrowed on the man I was idiotically determined to marry one day. "Want to bet? If this catches fire, everyone will run out, and I'll have a perfect opening to grab all the prizes for myself."

He blinked at me and then released a low chuckle, combing his hair back out of his face. "Good Lord, woman. Only you would think about stealing Bingo prizes from an assisted living facility."

A throat cleared on my other side. "If you take the heavier stuff there on the left, girlie, I'll snatch the stuff on the right."

Adrian leaned forward until he could see past me to Doris, an incredulous look on his face. "And how do you plan on running out of here with an armload of stolen items, Ms. Waters?"

She didn't bother looking up as she said, "I don't."

He nodded, a *yeah, that's what I thought* look on his face, and sat back to grab his water bottle, only to choke on his next drink when she continued.

"You're going to carry me and all the stolen items out of here."

There was a beat of silence, and then Adrian was wiping the back of his hand across his chin, and hovering his mouth over my ear. "Davis."

"Yes?" I whispered back, fluttering my eyelashes.

"I think you've officially corrupted my grandmother."

"Seems like it," I agreed, twisting my head just enough to give him a shit-eating grin. "What are you going to do about it? Spank me and tell me to be good?"

He smirked and reached into his pocket to pull out his phone, locking eyes with me the entire time. Holding it up to his mouth, he alerted the phone's virtual assistant and said, "Add batteries to my 'to-buy' list."

I gaped at him, a mixture of shock and something much headier swirling in my chest, as it confirmed his request. And then he quietly tucked it back into his pocket and slid his hand high over my thigh. "I think I have a few ideas."

Oh my God.

Yep. I was going to marry this man. Not tomorrow or the next day. But maybe the day after that. We'd see.

It'd depend on how much of a good boy he was tonight.

Chapter
⇾ 2½ ⇽

Adrian

I STARED AT a spot on the far wall of the bar, eyes unfocused as I knocked back the last of my beer, chasing an alcohol-infused calm I knew wouldn't come.

Nan didn't remember me.

She'd smiled so big when I'd first shown up, that I'd thought nothing of leaning in and giving her a hug. She'd smelled like she always did, like lemon cleaner and the strawberry lotion she put on her hands. She'd smelled like home.

But when I'd pulled back, her smile had faltered and she'd blinked at me, brow furrowed and eyes darting side to side like she'd just entered a room and couldn't remember why.

Whether she'd recognized me at first, or whether she'd just been smiling at a stranger because she was just that wonderful, I had no idea. And I swore I could hear the crack that canyoned my heart and echoed off each of my ribs.

I swallowed hard, remembering how I'd immediately made the entire situation worse by trying to remind her of who I was. The more confused she got, the more I'd tried, desperate to help her remember so I could comfort her. And when she'd burst into tears, I'd felt my cracked heart shrivel and die, leaving only a black smudge in its place.

I'd never hated myself more.

The nurses had been nicer to me than I'd deserved and had taken me to the side, explaining what I should do the next time it happened. To just go with the flow of whatever truth Nan believed and let her lead the conversations. It'd crushed me.

There'd already been days where she'd thought I was my dad at first, or it took her a few seconds and several long blinks to remember, but I hadn't expected it to escalate so quickly.

How many good days did we have left before she never remembered me at all? Hell, maybe we were already there.

I wasn't sure what I'd do if that was the case. When she didn't know who I was, or who she was.

She was all I had.

Grimacing at the dark thought, I forced myself to take a deep breath and pin my mind to the present. To what I *could* control.

I tipped my head to the bartender, Fran, a petite, dark-haired individual I was pretty sure was older than they appeared. They nodded, understanding my silent request in the way all good bartenders could, and immediately returned with another beer, sliding it across to me.

Fran's lack of small talk was appreciated. That was the best thing about sitting at a bar. Bartenders had a knack for reading people and could usually tell which patrons wanted to chat and which ones did not. I fit the latter category.

Too bad fucking Bosenet hadn't gotten the memo. The obnoxious man was lucky I was desperate to settle in town and put more cash under my belt for Nan, or else I'd have told him to fuck off after the first five minutes of talking with him.

The only reason that man was good at his job was because venues agreed to book through him just to get him to shut up. I was sure of it.

A soft whoosh of air brushed past me, and the faint smell of lavender teased my senses, preceding the outline of a woman a mere second later, stepping up to the bar beside me. Her smell was intoxicating, and even without laying an eye on her, she had a presence about her that made it impossible not to be aware of her.

An acquaintance of mine back in Raleigh had whistled and waggled his eyebrows like an idiot when I'd announced I was moving, going on and on about how gorgeous and freaky the women were in the smaller towns.

I couldn't have cared less. Not when my mind was a fucking mess as it was. I didn't have the space to fit in wooing a random woman at a bar. So, I didn't bother glancing over, blocking her smell from my senses.

She ordered a drink—straight vodka with limes—and turned toward me. With only my peripheral to go off of, I couldn't be sure she was staring at me, but I swore I could feel the heat of her gaze as it settled on me. The same heat I'd felt earlier that'd crawled up the back of my neck and sent shivers down my spine.

"Hey, it's Adrian, right?"

Damn. Definitely looking at me. I bit down on my tongue. The last thing I needed was to deal with a fan tonight. I wasn't in the mood, not after the shit with Nan. I'd just end up being a complete dick. I couldn't help it. I had no control over my tongue when my emotions were a wreck. Hell, I barely had control over it when I *wasn't* upset.

The few friends I'd had over the course of my life always said it was my curse. To blurt out whatever came to my mind, no matter how fucked up it was. And I knew it would happen tonight of all nights.

So, I did the only other thing I could do. I ignored her.

She leaned in a little closer and repeated herself, raising her voice above the crowd. There was something about her voice that had me almost turning toward her, like a siren song crafted specifically for me. It was smooth yet somehow raspy at the same time.

Ignore her. Don't be a dick. Scratch that, don't be more of a dick than ignoring her already makes you.

"I'm Layla. I saw you earlier when you were talking with Larry Bosenet. Do you work with him?"

Wait, what? She knew Larry? I barely held in my scoff. I wouldn't put it past him to send a woman to try to seduce me into taking a few of the weekday gigs he'd been pushing my way. He wanted me to travel back to Raleigh, not even trying to hide the fact that he wanted to use me to get his foot in the door there. It wasn't going to happen. Not anytime soon, at least.

I was here for now. With Nan. Whether she knew it or not.

I cleared my throat, uncomfortable under her steady gaze, and accepted that I couldn't keep blatantly ignoring her existence forever. Maybe if I just kept it short, she'd be off sooner than later. So, I answered, "No."

The tension was practically pulsating from her. One look at her face would quickly tell me whether it was secondhand embarrassment at being shut down, or whether it was anger at being shut down so pointedly. But I didn't dare steal a glance to see.

"All right, I can take a hint," she said. Thank God. But then, to my dismay, she continued, "But if you feel up to it later, I'll buy you a drink. I'll be here until nine."

She sounded so hopeful that it made me grind my teeth together and sigh heavily. I wasn't in the mood for this. It's why I'd met Bosenet at this random bar to begin with. I was barely holding it together, and I just needed her to leave me alone to drink and simmer in my misery.

"Look," I said, feeling the words scrape up my throat like jagged shards, and knowing I might very well get slapped for them. "I don't sleep with fans." I raised my glass, taking a sip to cover my cringe.

Then I glanced down, seeing her white-knuckling her phone. "Nor do I particularly like pictures."

That was it. It was official. I was an asshole. I felt, more than saw, her entire demeanor change, and she rose to her full height, which I'd guess was a solid six-foot tall in her heels.

"My name is Layla Davis, and I'm not a fan," she said, proceeding to rip me a new one about how I treated my fans. Her points, although not accurate overall, were definitely true in the moment. However, all I took away from her lecture was her name.

I knew that name. And I knew that voice.

There was a reason my name had sounded so sexy when she'd said it. Because her voice *was* that fucking sexy. I'd never met Layla, but Bosenet had played her music for me during our last meeting when he'd tried convincing me to pair up with her.

I'd immediately fallen in love, even though I'd ultimately refused his proposal. It didn't matter how good she sounded when I had no desire to learn how to work with another musician. It wasn't as easy as walking up on a stage and nodding at one another.

You had to trust that they'd have your back and show up. Trust that they'd give it their best and not fuck you over last minute. And I hadn't dared trust anyone that way since I was a boy. No one except for Nan. Not when I'd learned the hard way that even the people who swore to love you could stab you in the back.

But even with that understanding, I couldn't ignore the overwhelming urge to put a face to that voice. I finally turned my head, unsure what I'd find, and nearly choked on my tongue. Holy fucking shit.

She was gorgeous. Beyond it.

Wearing jeans that clung to her curves and showcased thick

thighs I immediately imagined clamped around my waist, and an ass that would meld and ripple beneath my hand as I smacked it, she was fucking sex incarnate. Her top was loose around her stomach but showed the perfect hint of cleavage that had me dying on the inside.

And then there was her face. Her freckled cheeks, red lipstick, and smokey eyeshadow over a pair of blue-gray eyes. A pair of very *angry*, blue-gray eyes.

And that wasn't even mentioning the bright ass blue hair that hung in thick curls about her shoulders. The perfect length to wrap around my fist and pull tight as I—fuck. No. What the hell was I thinking? Absolutely not.

This woman had trouble written across her entire forehead. It might as well have been tattooed there, and I needed to focus. I couldn't be distracted. Not when Nan needed me, and I needed to work, and she was competition.

I cleared my throat, deciding to hammer the last nail in so I'd have no chance of changing my mind. Because her furious eyes and cocked hip confirmed she was nothing but trouble. And I didn't have the time, or the emotional fucks to give to trouble.

"Well, fan or not," I said, looking her directly in the eyes and hoping I didn't catch on fire, "whatever it is you're hoping to gain from me, I'm afraid you'll leave here empty-handed and disappointed."

She slammed her glass down on the bar, causing Fran to glance our way, but Layla didn't seem to notice. She was too busy trying to light me on fire.

"I don't need anything from you, Waters," she snapped, her

tongue wrapping around my last name in a way I immediately wanted to hear again. "I think I've learned enough tonight already."

She knocked her hand once against the bar, and then she spun away from me, the motion causing another wave of her delicious perfume to curl around me before leaving me in a silence that suddenly didn't feel all that relaxing.

Minutes later, I could feel her gaze searing into me even from the other side of the room. Part of me—the unstressed, carefree part—wanted to mess with her and see how she responded. Wanted to see those eyes flash again and feel that fierce attitude lash out.

But I didn't turn around. I'd been a fucking dick and deserved her vitriol. She'd either been doing her job and networking or was just being friendly to another musician. Either way, she hadn't deserved the way I'd spoken to her.

I finished my drink and waved Fran over to close my tab. This was why I had no business dating or even speaking to a woman. All I'd do was hurt them.

Pushing back from the bar, I made my way out the door, intent on leaving and continuing my drinking in private. Preferably with music blaring and no pants on. But I only made it as far as pulling out my key and standing at my truck door, shivering, when something stopped me.

I turned and stared back at the bar. She'd said she was about to go up, and I'd technically shown up tonight hoping for a drink and good music to drown out the voices in my head.

Nothing said I couldn't give a quick listen before I left. Just to get an idea. As long as I was stealthy.

I wavered another moment before shoving my keys back in my pocket and cursing, slipping back inside. I kept my head lowered and disappeared into the crowd, feeling ridiculous the entire time.

Since when did I hide from a woman I didn't even know? *Since you met a fucking terrifying goddess, that's when.*

I'd just plastered my back to the far wall when the first notes of her guitar hit. And when her voice broke the air, my head snapped up, stealth forgotten, and my throat went dry.

Bosenet's cheap phone recording had been absolutely nothing compared to this. Layla's fingertips danced across the strings while she sang an original, unique take on a well-known song. She'd altered it in a way I never would've thought of, changing it from hard rock to a slow, sensual ballad that had me locking eyes on her throat, imagining what else it could do.

It shouldn't have pleased me how phenomenal she was, shouldn't have made my blood race at the way her red lips parted, and my heart skip a beat when I saw she favored the same guitar I did.

I shouldn't have come back inside at all. But there was no turning back now. Not when I knew I'd be hearing her siren song even in my sleep tonight.

Not knowing where Larry Bosenet was, or if he was even still around, I pulled my phone out of my back pocket and shot him a text.

Me: I'm in.

Bosenet: Perfect! I'll talk to her this week but can't make any promises.

Me: Get her on board, or I'll find an agent who can.

My phone rang a second later. I pressed it to my ear, not bothering with pleasantries. "It's not negotiable, Larry."

He sputtered, mashing words together that only caused the frown on my face to deepen. "I'll do my best, Adrian, but Layla does what she wants. You'll understand once you've met her."

Oh, I understood. And turns out, I really fucking liked it. "Get her on board."

Shuffling came from the other side, and then the click of a door, like he was stepping away from wherever he was to speak to me. Good.

"I'll do everything I can. But you speaking to her might help as well."

I huffed a laugh. I highly doubted that.

He continued, having no idea I'd already met the walking inferno. "She'll be at that party coming up. The holiday one I told you about earlier?"

That caught my attention, and I sat up straighter, turning up the volume and plugging my other ear to make sure I was hearing him right. "Layla Davis will be at the Valentine's party downtown?"

"Yep. She won't want to, but she'll be there. Guarantee it."

Excitement simmered in my chest. I hadn't been planning to go, but now I wouldn't miss it. "Who's in charge of the event?"

Bosenet paused, whether from my question or my demanding tone, I didn't know. Nor did I particularly care. "What?"

"The event, Larry. Who's in charge of it?" More specifically, who would be in charge of the seating chart.

He rattled off a woman's name, but I interrupted him, knowing I wouldn't remember it. "Text her name and number to me." And then I hung up on him, resting the back of my head against the wall, and giving her my full attention again.

I watched her as she wrapped up her next song, and when her lips spread into a wide, exuberant smile that lit up her entire face, I was done for.

I wanted this fiery temptress of a woman. I didn't care how it happened, or what I'd have to do to convince her of it. I wanted her voice, her gaze, and her lips. I wanted her to serenade me and to hear what music our voices could make—in and out of the bedroom—together. Feel the heat of her anger and passion on my skin.

I just wanted Layla fucking Davis. And I had a feeling that want might just kill me.

Also in the Learning to Love Series

Interconnected Standalone + Extended Epilogue

Madison gave her heart to a boy at the age of sixteen, but all she got in return was a broken heart and a swollen belly.

Alone with a baby and desperate for the love she hadn't found, she turned to a man who sealed his claim of devotion with a diamond ring.

He promised her a family. A life. A future. But his lies had only been a cover for the personal hell he introduced her to daily.

Now, at twenty-five, Madison has long since stopped believing in love. Balancing single parenthood, three jobs, and online courses, she doesn't have the time anyway.

So when the broody neighbor living in the other side of her duplex leaves a rude note on her door, she's not interested.

Not in his dark hair, not in his physique, and definitely not in the dimples she's only seen a hint of. She's one hundred percent, absolutely, not interested. Not even a little.

Acknowledgements

As always, I could not have created this without my amazing editor, who continues to work with me even when I still confuse 'past' and 'passed' after five manuscripts. Thank you, Elaine, for dealing with my chaos and late deadlines.

I also must thank my beta readers, who have been with me throughout my entire author journey and have read every one of my unedited messes. You all give each story more life and depth with the way you consider the plot and characters in detail.

Then, of course, I suppose I need to thank my husband who suffers through my whining when my characters don't do what I want, or when I'm tired and don't feel like writing. I'm pleasantly surprised you're still married to me. You're a trooper.

But mostly, this entire book, down to every letter, is not only dedicated to, but all in thanks to, my best friend of over two decades. She has seen me through every phase of my life, the good and the bad, and has stuck by me every step of the way. Even when I didn't deserve it.

She held my hand when I gave birth at seventeen when the biological father wasn't there for me. It wasn't even a question. I needed her, and she went. She sat with me for fourteen hours and held my hand during my entire labor. Yes, I was young, but so was she. And I cannot imagine the pressure she had to have felt to be the strong one for me at such a young age.

She moved halfway across the country at the drop of a hat and lived with me and my son after I had an ugly divorce. She worked two jobs, six days a week to help me pay rent. And although she eventually moved back home and was able to start up and succeed in her music career, I will never forget that she gave up that time for me.

Woman, you are blunt, sarcastic, bitchy, and stubborn to a fault, but I wouldn't ask for you to be any other way.

Thank you for being there for me when I felt alone. Thank you for being the best first father figure my son could have ever had, and thank you for always telling me to my face when I'm being an idiot.

Come on over when you read this, I have wine and snacks.

About the Author

Lilian T. James was born and raised in a small town in Kansas until she finished high school. Enrolling at a University on the east coast, she moved there with her son and obtained degrees in Criminal Justice, Social Work, Psychology, and Sociology. After graduating, she met her husband and moved to the west coast for a few years before settling back in Kansas in 2022. She has three kids, one miniature dachshund, and has been an avid fantasy and romance reader her entire life. Lilian was finally able to publish her first novel, Untainted, at thirty-years-old and has no plans of stopping.